Duties of the Heart

SHERRILL BURNS

Contents

Mestopholes's Gift

Mestopholes lay tied to a post by a collar around his neck. He pulled his legs slowly to his chest. He had lost all track of time, lying there in the dark. Sandywinds swept across the grounds, sending shivers across his body that caused him to convulse every few seconds. The pit of his stomach felt hollow and churned with an empty heat. The dirt stuck to his blood-caked skin like tiny needles that stung when he moved. His back was on fire, but he shivered when the wind blew. He closed his eyes and tried to sleep; soon the night would be over and his mother would make him well again.

He should have heeded her warnings. One man could not change the Lavitians. He had been foolish to try. He thought over the day's events wishing he could go back and change them. The pain and humiliation were not worth it, and when he was healed, he would still be made to serve them. It wasn't fair at all and now he understood. His mother had been right.

He pulled his extremities as close to his body as he could get them, groaning from the pain that small movement caused, and drifted into a fitful sleep, his mind replaying the day over and over again.

"Mother, why must we serve the Chancellor?" He had asked her this question before, but usually, she would steer away from the answer by

changing the subject. Today he was determined to know. He was fifteen years old. It was time she started treating him like a man.

His mother, Clara, the villa's cook, added the potatoes to the pot and put the lid on the top.

"Because we are Veagans," she responded nonchalantly. "Our people have served the Lavitians for centuries."

But why? I don't understand. They are rich because we mine their gold. They are fed because we prepare their meals. They are clean because we prepare their baths. Why? Why must we serve them?" Mestopholes asked, confused. He sat down at the large table, watching his mother move about the room, preparing the dinner for the household. He had seen her perform this dance a million times over the years.

"We were brought into this land to serve them. We live in their homes. They provide the clothes on our backs and the food in our stomachs," she said, sitting down next to him at the table.

Mestopholes was a smart, inquisitive boy. She had become accustomed to him starting off a conversation with the words why or how. The Lavitians were not known for their tolerance, and she didn't want her son stepping out of place in front of their masters.

"We are made to live in their homes. We could find our own home and serve ourselves, Mother," he said, not understanding why he had to be a slave just because he was born a certain race. The only difference he could see between the two races was that Veagans had black hair and Lavitians' hair color ranged from golden to brown.

"Stop it! You are not thinking. Where could we go that they would not know us? Only priests have bald heads. The punishment is fifty lashes if you are caught on the streets without an escort," she said, looking around to make sure their conversation was private. She lowered her voice and grabbed her son's face, squeezing his jaw. She pulled him closer. "We are slaves and that's just the way it is. Do you want to be flogged?"

Mestopholes shook his head from side to side as best he could against her grip, his large brown eyes wide with shock.

"No. Then you had better get these crazy ideas out of your head before somebody hears you," she said, letting him go. "Now, off to the

sitting room with you. You will serve Mistress Rena and her guests. She has asked for you."

Mestopholes gave her an irritated sigh and left the room.

When he reached the sitting room, he took his place against the wall. Rena saw him enter. She sat up from the pillow she was lying on. Her sun-kissed golden hair shined brilliantly against the crimson red pillow. She arched her back and smiled, causing her eyes to flash with light. They were a little darker than her hair, with just a hint of green. Her skin was a bronze, almost metallic looking color from sitting in the sun all day.

Mestopholes tried to focus on a fixture on the wall. Perhaps she would choose someone else if he paid her no attention. There was a time when he would rush to do her bidding, but something had changed in her. She had become arrogant and abusive. She slowly tipped her goblet over, pouring the wine onto the floor.

"Mestopholes! I have spilled my wine. Come, clean it up," Lady Rena said, lying back down across the plush pillows next to her father's pool. Her friends giggled as they waited for the slave to obey her orders. She was the daughter of Chancellor Agelar Ling of Lavitia, and she was bored. Besides, there was nothing better than to have a man obey your every command.

Mestopholes was tired of being her pawn, a jester she kept to amuse herself. He would clean up the wine, and she would just pour some more in another spot, having him crawl around on all fours like some animal. Perhaps one of her new friends had convinced her that it was wrong to be his friend, just because his hair was a few shades darker than hers. It made no sense at all.

"Boy! Did you hear me?" she asked. Mestopholes turned and looked at her with pleading eyes. She smiled as he moved forward to obey her. With each step he took, he could see her smile grow into an evil grin. Suddenly, he stopped.

"No, I will not. Clean it yourself," he said, lowering his head. Something inside told him that he should obey her, but his feet would not move.

"What did you say to me?" she asked, rising from the floor to stand before him. Her maids rushed to her side to adjust her gown.

"I said no—" he started. She slapped him hard across the face. And to think she had decided to take him to her bed after she was married. He was tall and slender with square shoulders. His dark hair curled carelessly, like that of a new born. Rena thought he definitely had the potential of becoming an excellent consort after he grew out of this awkward stage and she had taught him a few things, of course, but now he had embarrassed her in front of her friends. She would not stand for it.

"I said clean up that wine," she said furiously. "Now, you insolent dog, or I will have you flogged!"

"No!" he said firmly, lifting his head to meet her gaze. His deep brown eyes flashed with defiance. Rena's grew wide with fury.

"Guards, this boy has refused to serve me! I want him stripped and flogged. Ten lashes. No…we had better make it twenty," she said, looking him over to see his reaction to her sentence.

He stood tall and proud, looking directly into her eyes. Abruptly, he was dragged away to the courtyard. Rena followed with her friends. When they reached the family platform, she rang the large golden gong suspended between two white pillars three times. It boomed through the courtyard; the long bongs vibrated off the wall and swept across the property.

All the slaves in the household knew what that meant. Someone was being punished. They were called to bear witness so as to not make the same mistake, which did not happen often; the Lavitians were cruel and ruthless when it came to the smallest infractions. They immediately stopped their work and headed to the courtyard.

Clara heard the gong, and her mind immediately went to her son and the conversation they had before he left. She prayed it was not her son as she turned off the fire under her pots and headed to the courtyard. He was so small and brittle compared to the guards that would handle him. Any punishment would surely kill her baby. She bent and swept the front end of her skirt back between her legs. She pulled a pin from her hair and secured the end of it to the top of her waistband, then raced to the courtyard as fast as her feet would carry her.

When she reached the court-yard, she ran quickly up the four short stone steps. It was shaped as an arena stretching out to form a complete circle in the middle of the property. There were four arched entrances all made of a white stone that lead up onto a covered platform. The floors and the outer walls here were made with course gray bricks. Benches and tall pillars circled the wall at intervals. A short white banister made of the same stone as the archways wrapped around the inner portion.

While the rest of the property was covered with lush grass and beautiful flower gardens, the arena floor was covered with hard, pale, yellow dirt. There was a dais at the north end with chairs for the family and their important guests. Two burly guards held Mestopholes by his upper arms in the middle of the arena just below the dais where Lady Rena stood with three other Lavitian girls around her age.

Clara had entered through the southern archway. She dashed across the field and was almost halfway across when she was overcome by two guards. They grabbed her by her arms and held her as she struggled against their hold.

When everyone was assembled, Rena stepped forward and projected her voice across the grounds.

"Today his lazy boy has refused to perform his duties openly and in front of my honored guests, no less. He has embarrassed me as well as my father. Such an offense could mean death, but I will show him mercy and spare his life. Twenty lashes!" She announced loudly then nodded to the guards that held Mestopholes.

They used short knives to cut his white linens to shreds, nicking him across his legs, arms, and chest as they carelessly tore the garments away. The guard picked up the collar and strapped it around his neck. His arms were tied at the wrist while his legs were tied at the ankles. The guard used a long bamboo cane to strike Mestopholes across his bare back. With each swing, Mestopholes cried out in pain as he pulled against his restraints. Blood sprayed across the ground as the bamboo ripped into his flesh.

"We don't need them. They need us. Why can't we be free… free to serve ourselves," he cried loudly as tears slid down his face. He winced and cried out in agony as the bamboo struck across his left side, cracking one of his ribs. After twenty lashes, the guards holding the chains dropped

them and he fell helplessly to the ground. Clara was then released. She fell to the ground but got up quickly to continue her pursuit but was stopped at once by Rena's piercing voice.

"Don't touch him," she said. And as much as it pained Clara, she immediately stopped in her tracks. Instead, she crumbled to the ground inches away from her son and cried. "Leave him there chained like the naughty dog he is until dawn. And maybe the next time he is given an order, he will obey it. Now disperse and return to your duties, immediately."

Two women came and ushered Clara back to the kitchens. They sat her down at the table. She couldn't let her son lie out on the cold ground and bleed to death. She stood and went to the door and leaned against the frame, but what could she do?

"We must do something," she said after a while. "Perhaps speak to the Chancellor. Surely, he will know that Mestopholes needs to be medicated. He is so small and fragile. He will bleed to death out there all alone."

"Clara, the best thing to do now is to make sure the evening meal is finished on time. Let us pray for the Great Creator to aid your boy. It is out of our hands—unless you want to be chained out there next to him," Eliza explained. Clara had been her friend for a long time and she didn't want to see her punished. Leasil nodded in agreement.

"Very well," she said. The three got down on their knees and put their palms together. They bowed low, touching their noses to the floor. "Oh, Great Creator, hear our prayer. Please help my son. He is brave, but he is foolish. Please see him through this night. Cover him with your warmth so that the night's cold air does not strip him of his strength. Fill his belly with your glory so hunger does not creep in as the hour grows late. Take away his pain and grant him the wisdom to be humble in the presence of our masters from this day forth."

"That was an earnest prayer. The Great Creator will surely take care of him. Let us finish with the meal. The guests must be served on time," Leasil said.

The shadows crept up the stones walls, laying their dark silhouettes over the grounds. Mestopholes had folded himself into a fetal position. He laid there next to the pole with only his loincloth to protect him from the chilly night's air. He opened his eyes and looked into the shadows. He thought someone had called his name, but he could see nothing.

"Mestopholes," a commanding voice called.

"Who is there?" he asked in a hushed voice, struggling to get up, looking around the shadows of the courtyard. He was sure now that his rib was broken because it hurt when he talked.

"Mestopholes," the voice called, "it is I, Creator of all things. Do not be afraid." The voice said. Suddenly, the wisp of wind changed to form a tall, broad-shouldered man before the boy in the court-yard. He wore a long flowing white robe with the hood pulled low over his head, shielding his face from view. A bright white light surrounded his form, causing him to glow. "I have decided to bless you this day with a special gift."

The boy put his hands together and bowed to the image before him, "Why do you favor me, most merciful Father? I am nothing but a slave."

You are a slave, but your heart is free. You are the first of the Veagan, in two hundred years, to rebel against the ill treatment of your people. You were severely punished, but your spirit was not broken. You continued to speak out against the cruel treatment of your people despite your torture. And for your courage, I bless you.

"This gift that I give you should not be taken lightly. It will require skill as well as imagination, for I will allow you to set the rules, but remember, once you have set them, they cannot be changed unless I see fit to change them. I will not free you from your bonds this day because your people will need the fight it takes to achieve freedom to make them strong enough to survive in this land.

"I have decided to bless you, Mestopholes of the house of Delong, with all the power contained in my pointer finger," he said, moving closer. He didn't take steps; though, he seemed to float across the ground to where Mestopholes crouched. "Rise, my child." Mestopholes moved slowly, struggling to get to his feet.

"This will put the power of the Gods in the palm of your hands. You will pass it to your sons and your sons' sons. It will be based on the forces of nature, for it was with my pointer finger that I created the world and everything in it. You must always remember to respect the natural balance of my world. Your powers will be fueled by the winds and governed by the pure of heart. Use it well," he said, laid his hand on the top of the boy's head as he faded away into the night. White twinkling stars passed around Mestopholes from his head to his toes. A tingling sensation ran through his veins as he stood up from the ground, his pains gone.

The power of the Gods, in my hands. He spotted the empty water bags that were hung up to be filled in the morning. He looked around the courtyard to be sure he was alone. Then he waved his hands over the bags. A warm, wet sensation crept through his veins as they were instantly filled with water.

And it came to pass that his descendants would come to be known among the Veagans as Pheolatians. As centuries passed, the story of the Great Creator's gift to Mestopholes and his descendants spread through the land as a mere folktale, the details changing at the whim of the teller. But for some, the stories were very real.

Part One

CHAPTER 1

The New King

The effect of the Great Creator's blessing to Mestopholes begins many years later in the royal bedchamber of Lavitia's ruler, King Hector Covax. The prince and sole heir to his throne stood at his father's bedside, holding his hand. The healer stood up straight again after examining King Hector and shook his head. He was tall, with skin the color of a pale winter day. His thinning yellow hair fell onto his shoulders.

"I cannot be sure. I've never seen such an illness, but I believe Your Majesty has been poisoned," he said.

The prince looked up at the man with big blue pleading eyes. His face was round and angelic with youth. His tanned complexion and golden-brown hair were identical to his father's, but where Hector's eyes were a dark brown, his son's took on the color of the clearest blue sky like his mother's. "If you know what is making him ill, why can't you give him some sort of herb that will save him?"

"I'm sorry.... if I had gotten here sooner, perhaps I could have done something, but the poison has already spread through his body. I would say he digested it through the wine during evening meal. His throat has been severely burned. His heart has already begun to slow down, and besides, I have no idea of knowing what poison was used. It will not be long, sire," the healer said.

The prince squeezed his father's hand. He had never seen his father look so weak and pale. Just this morning, Marsalis remembered looking up at him as he explained the journey he was sending him on. He was a big man, even for a Lavitian, which he continuously explained was the result of pure lineage and the highest royal breeding.

"My son, I will give you my final orders. You have only seen twelve years of life, but you are strong. The slaves that served me last night will be put to death. I know one of them is responsible for this. They've probably used their magic to poison me. Never trust them, my son; the hearts of slaves are weak and treacherous. They have destroyed me, but what they didn't know is that I will reign forever through you. Make me proud. Now send for your mother so I may kiss her goodbye," Hector said, struggling for breath. He coughed several times before pushing back against the pillow.

"I promise I will be a strong king, Father," the boy said. Laven Vyner, the king's nephew, crossed his arms and glared at the prince.

"You must be more than strong. You must be ruthless. You are young, so they will think you weak. Make them fear the name Covax," the king said. "Each time you open your mouth, make them pray that they are still in your favor."

"Yes, Father," the boy replied solemnly.

A slave arrived moments later and explained that the queen was also very ill. The prince sent the healer to her and was told moments later that it was too late, and his mother had died. Hector coughed several times and struggled to sit up in the bed.

"Lie back, Father, try to relax," the prince said with tears sliding down his cheeks.

"Are you a child or a man? Wipe away those tears. Kings do not cry," he coughed, pointing his long bony finger at his son. "They would have killed you as well if your escort had not been delayed."

"Father, reserve your strength. Perhaps the healer is wrong. You are strong. You can live if you fight," he said trying not to cry. If his father died, he would be alone in a castle full of slaves that hated him and wanted his bloodline destroyed. His father had taught him never to be afraid, for fear was a sign of weakness. Suddenly, his father's hand went limp. The young prince placed it gently across his chest then stood up straight. He stood before the bed, thinking of what to do. Laven, the only family he had left, patted him on the back. He was few years older than him, but he was a fragile boy, who cared little for politics. He was more concerned with riches so he could buy new fabrics for fancy robes. And besides, kings didn't ask for help.

Laven left the room and headed outside to the postern. He gave the guards a bag of silver so they would leave their post. Moments later, a hooded rider approached.

"My Lord, or should I say my king, surely the deed is done by now. When can I expect payment?" the hooded rider asked, coming up the walk.

"You expect payment for giving Marsalis the throne?" Laven exclaimed, disgusted by the idea.

"What do you mean? Silver flower poison is the deadliest poison in all Lavitia, and there is no cure. The boy could not have survived," the man explained. He had used that poison several times, and one thing was guaranteed: death.

"Some assassin you are! Prince Marsalis wasn't even here for evening meal. Now he will be king. He will be worse than Hector ever was."

"I can still kill him. Men still have to eat."

"Hector has already alerted the boy. He will never be taken in such a way. I fear it is too late. You should leave. I will summon you if I need your services again," Laven said, turning to leave.

"Wait! What about my payment? It was not my fault the prince was away."

"The agreement was that you would receive your own villa, a noble title, and an annual payment after I was proclaimed king. How can I pay you these things now?" Laven said, shrugging his shoulders.

"Well, I think some compensation is in order. I have gotten rid of most of the royal family. Perhaps a hundred gold pieces."

"I will give you nothing. I am not king. That was the agreement." Laven said crossing his arms.

"Two hundred gold pieces or Marsalis gets a message explaining that his dear cousin was responsible for his parents' murder and I will have mysteriously disappeared."

"You would not dare, Marsalis would find you wherever you decided to bury your head. I will not die alone," Laven said.

"Are you willing to risk it?" he asked, moving closer to the boy.

"Fine, I will pay you, but you must swear to never return," Laven exclaimed, regretting ever dealing with such a man as Cain Sisemour.

Marsalis stood next to his father's dead body, trying to think of what to do. He was lonely and confused. He had to be strong. *You have to be more than strong. You must be ruthless.* His father's words floated back through his head.

"Guards, have every slave in the palace brought before me in the main hall," he said, storming from the room with all the force a twelveyear-old could muster. He marched directly to the hall and sat on his father's throne. The slaves were brought in and assembled before him.

"Tonight, my father, your king, and my mother, your queen, were poisoned by one of you. Now they have both died. Guards, lock the doors! And so will all of you. Kill them!" he yelled as he stood up again to emphasize his anger. The guards moved forward to follow his orders. The slaves started screaming and yelling, trying to escape the hall as they were cut down by long Kwan Do spares, oblong-shaped knives that curve into razor-sharp points attached to the end of long wooden poles.

"Please, You're Highness! I have served your family loyally since I was a child. Please, sire, have mercy on my son. He is only three years old," a mother pleaded at the new king's feet. Her black hair was swept back from her face. Marsalis looked down into her eyes. They were blue like his mother's. She held her son securely to her chest.

"Children grow up. He will die as well. If you have served my family loyally then serve my parents as they take their places next to the Gods," he said sternly, then looked away as the guard stabbed her through the back into her heart, killing both her and the child instantly.

Screams and people pounding at the doors trying to escape were the only sounds he could hear as he retreated into his own head, trying to block out that rusty, metallic, salty smell of blood. The guards killed everyone; the men, the women, and the children. A dark red pool of blood spread across the palace floor. The new king sat back on the throne with an emotionless look on his face.

"Now go into my kingdom and bring me true Lavitians that will serve as servants in my palace. They will be paid a fair wage and will reside here at all times. And know this: as Lavitia's new king, my word is law; to disobey me will bring you and those closest to you death."

Marsalis Covax's first act as king spread through the country. As the years passed, the young king that sat upon Lavitia's throne grew in power, as did his reputation as a blood thirsty tyrant that despised the Veagan race. He hated everything about them and allowed his people to treat them in any manner they wished.

Now at the age of seventeen he assembled his army.

"It is time to rid the land completely of this particular race of slaves," he declared out of nowhere. His advisors turned and stared at him. Marsalis sat slumped on his throne his mind plagued with thoughts as he spoke to no one in particular. "The use of any unnatural powers will now be considered illegal and punishable by death. I want one thousand soldiers gathered and broken down into groups of ten. Find them and destroy them," he said as he rose from his seat.

"But Your Highness, they have been blessed by the Great Creator's own hand…" an advisor said, shocked by the suggestion.

"Damn the Great Creator! I want them dead," he said, rushing the man who had spoken. He was the same height as Marsalis, but he shrunk three inches as the king grabbed him by the collar and nearly picked him up from the floor. His body was that of a child's, compared to the king's chiseled physic. Marsalis's wide-eyed glare washed over the other advisors as he threw the man to the floor.

He even despised the Great Creator because he had shown them favor. His bloodline had ruled this land for three hundred years, and he took it as an insult that the Great Creator would favor a lowly slave over his much superior race.

"Your commands will be carried out, my lord, I will see to it," Lord Kail said, coming to stand beside their sovereign to calm his rage.

Marsalis looked at him, his fury melting away, "See to it. You are now the royal high counselor. Do not fail me." Kail bowed as the king stormed off.

His soldiers flooded the kingdom, killing the Pheolatians that were well known for their powers. Homes were destroyed. Children were left without parents. Their precious possessions were stolen and sent back to the capital. His soldiers would enter small villages and demand that all Pheolatians step forward. If no one confessed, they would randomly choose men and women to put to the sword.

The soldiers would accuse them of witchcraft or harboring the Pheolatians. They used terrible torture to make them confess to the crimes they accused them of, and whether they were innocent or guilty after enough suffering, everyone would confess and was then delivered into the peaceful awaiting arms of death. Men were placed in iron spiked cages or pressed with heavy sheets of granite until they gave up some information or were crushed to death. To avoid the king's wrath, the Veagans fled the cities and the soldiers, taking refuge in the forests. After years of persecution and ill treatment, the Veagans grew tired of Marsalis, and soon a rebellion began in the lands near the sea, led by a man named Alosis Shakur.

As word spread, their forces grew stronger. Men hid their families and left to join Alosis in his fight against Marsalis. They killed the Lavitians who ruled over them and pushed those Veagans who were faithful to Marsalis back across the mountain range, which would serve as their first line of defense. They fortified their border with soldiers and claimed the lands for themselves. The province known as Theslia would now be an independent country, and they declared the leader of their rebellion king.

The land was rich with gold and fertile for planting. Marsalis's advisors referred to the lands set nestled in the southeastern corner of

Lavitia, tucked in by the sea, as the treasure box of the country. The sea was full of fish, and merchants made good money selling jewelry made of shells and fine clothes. There were mountains and valleys, rivers and untouched forests.

Marsalis spent his days planning attacks and thinking of new ways to get past their frontline of defense. But despite his efforts, he was unable to penetrate the land because of the vast range of mountains that separated the two countries; he could never get a large enough force across at one time to make any real impact on the army that protected their border. Some believed the mountain range had also been enchanted.

He decided to seek the advice of his most trusted advisor, Shalyndria. She had the ability to see into the future. He brought her before his court and had her seated next to him. She was very petite in stature with a strikingly delicate type of beauty. Her face was a perfect oval with high cheekbones. She was about twenty years old, but her hair was a white silvery color that she wore bond in the back into a roll as curling tendrils framed her face. Strangely, her cat-green eyes had recently started to turn the same silver color as her hair, which gave her an ominous look.

"Shalyndria, what have they done to your hair? It does not suit you," Marsalis said from his throne, looking down at her with his head held slightly to one side as if he were trying to figure out what was wrong with her look.

He had allowed her all the privileges of a woman much higher than her status as a slave. In short, Marsalis treated her like a queen. She was by far the most beautiful woman in the palace for her unique features set her apart from everyone else. Her gowns were made of the finest silk clothes. She was showered with jewels and valuable trinkets. Her suite alone had cost him a fortune. It consisted of three large rooms, including a built-in bathing pool. She slept in a large beautiful bed, the frames of which were made of pure gold.

She pulled the pins out that held her hair up and let it fall down her back like water being released from a dam. He controlled every other aspect of her life. Why not her hair as well?

"Does this suit you better, my lord?" she asked, lowering her gaze so he would not see her nostrils flare with irritation.

Hair as beautiful as yours should never be tied up, he thought. He'd known her long enough to know when she was angry, especially when she tried to hide her face from him, but all he said was, "Indeed it does," with a smirk.

She had been sold away from her family at age ten when her master learned of her ability. Even though he was only fourteen at the time, Marsalis knew the power such a person could bring to him, and he ordered that she to be sent immediately to the palace. When she had arrived, he was shocked to find that they were just about the same age. The servants that brought her meals and her lady's maids were forbidden to speak with her because the king wanted her powers all to himself, and with death as a penalty, no one ever did.

The king had told her when she first arrived that her abilities had saved her from death and that they had been the only reason he had decided to spare her. As long as she used them to aid him she was safe, but since she was a slave he couldn't allow her to defile his home with her presence, so she spent the days of her life locked away in her rooms until he came to see her or sent for her as he had done this day to ask his question.

He had given her tapestries and looms to relieve her boredom, but she longed for a friend. She remembered what it was like to have a family. She remembered what it was like to love someone and to get their love in return, and to not be able to at least speak with another person was tearing at her soul.

"My question is: When would be the best time for me to attack Theslia?" he asked. Shalyndria's eyes grew wide, and her hair started to fly behind her. She stretched her arms out over her head as her body lifted effortlessly from the pillow. When she spoke, the sound seemed to be carried on the wind as a distant echo.

"The best time for you to attack Theslia would be on the night of the royal naming ceremony. The king's men will be full into their cups and off guard, but they will be the least of your problems. For within the Theslian castle walls a child will be named, a Pheolatian child. This child will grow strong with powers like no other and will one day bring about your downfall," she said in a hollow voice that was not her own, her face lighting up in a smile at the news.

"Take her to her chambers! Messenger, take this down and send it to my man in Theslia: On the night of this royal naming ceremony, whether it is to be tomorrow or years from now, I want every child within the castle walls put to death," he declared, then stormed from the hall.

Despite his order to keep Shalyndria's vision a secret, word spread from the palace and across the lands of Marsalis's foretold demise. The slaves rejoiced and called the vision the prophecy of the coming savior.

At the news of Marsalis's foretold demise, Laven finally saw a possible solution to his problem. If this prophecy was indeed true, he would only have to keep Marsalis from producing a legal heir and the kingdom would be his in no time. He would never name any of the bastards he had made with his concubines heir, but he worried about the admiration his cousin seemed to have for the seer.

His posture became nervous when he was around her, and that was telling. Marsalis was his father's son; ruthless, cunning, and arrogant with a regal grace, and his body language reflected it. And if he hadn't been studying Marsalis's body language over the years, looking for any weakness in the impermeable shell he'd wrapped around himself, he might have missed it. Perhaps the seer was that weakness he had been searching for all these years.

CHAPTER 2

A Child Is Born

Five years later, Royal Fortress of Theslia

The candles burned low in the sconces along the wall. The windows were black and frosted over with condensation. King Alosis Shakur paced back and forth in the great hall of his castle. He nervously rubbed his hands together. His brow furrowed into deep grooves as he turned toward the entry again. He stood there for a moment, expressionless, waiting. When nothing happened after a few seconds, he turned and marched back down the aisle toward his throne.

His knights carried on loudly, celebrating their latest victory against the Lavitians to the north. Benjamin Casesar, his first knight, noticed their leader's troubled mood. He couldn't imagine what the burden must be like to bear the well-being of an entire country, even a country as small as Theslia, on his shoulders, but at least he could lend an ear to his friend. He got up from the bench and approached Alosis as he headed back toward the throne.

"Sire, why such a gloomy expression on such a wonderful occasion? We have claimed victory over our enemies and we await our country's first heir," Benjamin inquired.

"I have had troubling dreams concerning the birth of the child. They are all different, but each wakes me up in a dreadful panic. Now, the day is here and I …I know not what to expect, to be honest. I'm a little scared," the king replied. Casesar had been by his side since this whole ordeal began, back when they were slaves hiding in the woods, secretly recruiting men to their cause. He had always been able to confide in him.

"It is only nerves, Your Majesty," Benjamin said, placing his hand on the king's shoulder. "I had those same worries when my own son was born. It is normal to be a little nervous about the birth of your first child.

"When Rosaly carried Alexander, and I feel a little guilty about admitting this, I resented him. I mean, I loved him, but I didn't know him. What I did know was that he could take her away from me. I was only concerned for Rosaly. I had never been so scared in all my life. She is so small, and the baby grew so big. I had terrible dreams that the child would tear straight through her stomach and kill her." Benjamin shuddered as he recalled his anxieties.

"I worry for the queen as well. Then I worry that I will drop the baby. What do I know about children? And then after all that, I am responsible for making this child into a good ruler," Alosis said turning back toward the entrance again.

"Fear not, my lord…" Benjamin started.

Just then, the queen's lady-in-waiting appeared in the doorway. The king started toward the stairs as the woman turned and walked back toward the royal bed chamber. He rubbed his hand down his face, pushed it through his hair, and then followed her to his chambers. She stopped at the door and held it open for him.

Queen Tess looked up and smiled. And all at once all his worries went away and were replaced by a calming peace. He could never doubt their happiness when he gazed into her face. She had big bright amber eyes. Her thick black hair, which she usually kept neatly arranged, was wildly tossed around her face. He still thought she was the loveliest woman he'd ever known. The candlelight turned her golden skin into liquid honey, but the dim light they provided was nothing compared to the brightness of her smile in this moment. She looked down at the child again that she held securely in her arms and announced that they had a baby girl.

"I'm sorry, my love… she is not a son," she said, lowering her head, feeling as if she had somehow failed him. Alosis breathed in a sigh of relief at that news. He lifted her chin with his forefinger and smiled at her. Then he took the baby gently from her arms, turned, and sat next to her on the bed.

"There is no need to apologize. There will be lots of time for sons. I am only amazed… I never dreamed I would ever love someone as much as I love you; and for no reason at all, the knowledge that I have created this life is… overwhelming," he said as he rocked the small child gently back and forth in his arms.

"She has your nose," the queen said as she peered at the child over his broad shoulder. "What will we call her?"

"I have not thought about it. I was so worried about what her arrival would bring that I forgot to think about the proper names for our child," he answered.

"Well, we have eight days to come up with the perfect name for our little angel," she replied.

"Alexander, get down from there before you fall and hurt yourself," Benjamin said. He picked his son up after he jumped down from one of the trunks that lined the wall of his bed chamber. He threw him into the air and smiled as he laughed and squirmed in his arms. "I leave now for the ceremony. Are you sure you don't want to come?" he asked his wife.

Rosaly walked toward him and smiled. "You look very handsome, but I cannot," she said. "I promised the little munchkin I would take him to the gardens tonight to see the winter pixies. You go. Have a good time, my love."

"Very well. Don't stay out too long. It is cold tonight," he said. He pulled her in his arms and kissed her passionately, ruffled his son's head, and left the room.

Alosis stood outside the doors to the great hall as his wife adjusted his banner on his shoulders. He twisted from side to side, adjusting and readjusting his tunic. She looked up into his dark brown eyes smiling at his nervousness. He was a brilliant thinker, but he still needed work when it came to public appearances.

"I hate these formal ceremonies," King Alosis said as he pulled at the banner draped across his right shoulder.

"Will you stop fidgeting and smile?" the queen said, turning forward again when the doors opened.

The king and queen entered after being announced to their court. The hall was decorated with the royal colors: crimson red and forest green. Benches and tables lined the walls. His soldiers stood near the dais while the courtiers stood on both sides of the hall, creating an aisle down the middle of the room. They bowed, creating a slow wave as the king and queen walked by.

Kalina, the queen's lady-in-waiting, followed behind them, carrying the child. She placed the baby in a large white bassinet that was covered with a translucent chiffon cloth accented with gold trim, then took her place behind the queen on the large platform next to her throne.

The king stood to address his audience. "My queen and I would like to welcome you all on this special day. We would now like to introduce you to your heir," he said, stepping down from the platform and picking the sleeping baby up from the bassinet. Then he turned and held the child aloft for all to see. "Theslians, I give you… Princess Saroja Minunette Shakur!"

He walked forward and placed the child on a large altar that resembled a steel drum in the middle of the floor. He bent and kissed his daughter on her forehead before returning to his throne. The queen took his hand and watched nervously as four men in white robes and two healing women approached the altar.

They placed a circle of candles around the child after setting the pit of coals on fire. They chanted softly and placed a long, thin iron post with the royal seal attached to the end into the fire. One of the men removed the child from her blankets while another placed red and green dust on her left ankle to lock in the colors of the roses. When the end of the post glowed bright orange, the holy man removed it from the fire then turned to the king. He, in turn, turned to his wife and noticed her eyes were glassy and slowly filling with water. He patted her hand to reassure her that everything would be alright, then nodded to the man to proceed.

Two of the men held the baby while the other held her leg still. The iron post had already cooled to a dark red color when they held it inches from her skin.

"I brand this child with fire, the truest purification. Let her reign bring prosperity to our kingdom and may she be a blessing to our country. She shall be called Princess Saroja Minunette Shakur. Let her name be known to all those who are loyal to king and country. Let it be written in the archives and remembered through all time as the first heir of King Alosis and Queen Tess of the house of Shakur," the holy man said, touching the iron rod to the child's leg.

At the child's sudden scream of pain, King Alosis had to restrain his queen to keep her in the seat. The holy men filed out with their oils and candles. The royal nurses moved forward to administer herbs to the child's wound. The baby continued to yell at the top of her lungs as they treated the burn which had immediately begun to blister.

The two intertwined roses were now large bubbles on the infant's small ankle. When the nurses were done, they placed the screaming infant back in the bassinet. The queen, now also crying, stood and removed the child from the cradle and held her to her chest, rubbing slow circular patterns across her back, trying to offer her some comfort. She turned, bowed low to the king, and carried the child from the room. Kalina followed close behind.

"Let the celebration begin!" the king announced, stepping down from his throne. The room erupted in applause.

"I did not realize this would affect the queen so. She's been looking forward to the naming ceremony since the child was born," he said when he reached Benjamin, grasping his forearm as he grabbed his. He turned and took the goblet of ale the servant brought to him.

"The deliverance of the family crest is always difficult for the mother. She will be fine, You're Majesty," Benjamin said.

The servants entered and removed the ceremonial pieces, then more arrived, wearing festive costumes with trays bearing ale and wine, while another train of servants arrived with an entire roasted pig and several other dishes. The food was placed on a long table that was set just in front of the dais. The musicians entered with the dancers.

The festivities went on late into the night. Finally, filled with ale, the king bid his guests good night and to continue to enjoy his hospitality. Then he turned and headed up the stairs to his bed chamber.

Cain finally saw his opportunity when he saw the king leaving through a sliding door behind the throne alone. Marsalis had sent him years ago to penetrate the rebellion by becoming a soldier in their army and acting as a spy to keep the king informed of their army's strength and new tactics. If Laven couldn't provide him with the rewards he deserved, surely a king such as Marsalis would pay him handsomely for his particular skills. He would never forget the look on Laven's face when he had walked into the hall that day.

"Your Majesty, Sir Cain Sisemour," the herald had said. The doors were opened and he proceeded nervously forward. When the messenger had arrived at his door with a parchment explaining that the king demanded an audience with him, his first thoughts were to run. He escaped through the back door only to find his home was surrounded by soldiers. He was certain his luck had run out.

He thought Laven had become a turncoat until he saw how his eyes almost exploded from the sockets when he looked up from his perch next to the king and saw who stood before him.

"You are the mercenary, Cain Sisemour?" Marsalis asked. He spoke with confidence and was certainly assertive, but he was just a boy.

"Yes, Your Highness," he answered. His voice squeaked to an unusual octave, and he repeated himself to correct it. "Yes, Your Majesty, I am." There was no fear in this child's eyes, but he was just a child no less. Laven should have been ashamed to have let someone so much younger intimidate him, but the king's next words changed those thoughts.

"Why did you attempt to escape my summons?" Marsalis asked looking up at him for the first time. He sat straight up on a large pillow with one hand braced against his knee, the other held a parchment. Perhaps it was the thought that this boy would have you killed and not think twice about it.

Cain was a tall, middle-aged, slim man. , but he looked to be about twenty-five. His skin was a pale white alabaster color. He had long golden hair that he secured at the nape of his neck with a leather cord. His eyes were a stormy grey with a hint of blue. He wore tightly fitting brown pants, tall dark boots, a white linen shirt, and a brown leather vest.

"I…" Cain started.

"Do you fear me, Cain Sisemour? I thought a man such as you would welcome death," Marsalis asked, sizing up the man.

"Every subject should fear their king, Lord. As for death, when he comes knocking, he better be prepared to fight for his prize," Cain said, picking his words carefully. He had gotten himself out of worst situations with just a little charm and finesse.

"Only the subjects that have broken the laws should fear me. Have you broken any of my laws, Cain Sisemour?" Marsalis asked in a patronizing tone, sitting up tall and straight on the dais.

"I am a mercenary. I've probably done countless things that Your Highness would not approve of," Cain replied.

"Your reputation as a mercenary is the very reason you have been brought before me," Marsalis had explained.

The grunt of a shutting door brought him out of his reverie. He backed out of the crowd of men, pulled the hood of his cloak over his shaved head as he walked slowly toward the king, and followed him up the stairs, looking over his shoulders to make sure no one noticed. He crept close to the walls, keeping to the shadows. As Alosis opened the door to his bed chamber, Cain covered his mouth and pushed the sword slowly through his back. His muffled whimpers went unnoticed as he slowly lowered Alosis's body to the floor and pulled the door closed. The queen slept peacefully in her bed only yards away. He tiptoed around to her side of the bed and slit her throat as she slept. He wiped his blade off in the sheets and moved to the small bassinet set off to the side. He looked away and stabbed his sword down through the center then peeked into it. The small bed was empty. The door to the chamber was slowly pushed open.

Kalina screamed loudly at the sight of her king lying face down, covered in blood. She clutched the precious bundle to her chest when it started screaming. She had come to deliver the child to its mother to be fed. Suddenly, she noticed the assassin moving toward her. The hood came down low over his face, shielding his identity from her. She turned and ran, pulling the door closed behind her.

Kalina's screams had alerted the soldiers in the great hall to his presence. Even now, Cain could hear the rumbling of footsteps coming toward him. He went to the window and gave the signal for his men to attack. The portcullis was raised, and the soldiers poured into the castle. He left the room and stepped into the hall in search of the woman with the child. He looked left and then right, but she was no longer on the hall. He swore loudly and decided to go the opposite of the way he had come. He had to find and destroy the child.

The sounds of battle cried out loud through the castle halls. Kalina thought she should leave now before someone found her hiding place. She pulled her finger from Saroja's mouth and slipped from behind the large drapes that covered the windows right next to the royal bedchamber and headed in the opposite direction than the one the murderer had taken. She crept her way pass the kitchens and slipped behind a large tapestry that concealed an escape passageway. She moved quickly down the dark hall filled with cobwebs, holding the child securely to her chest with one arm as she cleared them out of her path with the other.

Benjamin disarmed and killed the solider he was fighting. He stopped and looked around to assess their situation. Most of his soldiers who fought near him were holding their own, but he saw that a lot of good fighters had fallen. There were over a hundred soldiers in the castle, but most were probably drunk from the celebration. Their enemy had chosen the perfect time to attack, he admitted to himself. Thinking of the families that lived within the castle walls, he finally accepted the fact that the castle would fall. He turned suddenly, killing the Lavitian that tried to take him from behind.

"Theslians retreat!" he yelled loudly. The thirty or so soldiers that fought near him defeated their opponents and followed Benjamin down the west tunnel. He gave them orders to collect their families and to report to the Great Oak that divided the river by dawn. Then he turned and took the stairs that led to the south tower.

"Simo, we will collect the royal family," he said to the soldier that ran up the stairs behind him. They took the left bend of the stairs and headed to the royal chamber. Benjamin saw Alosis's body as soon as they stepped onto the hall and hurried quickly to his side. He knelt down next to him to see if he was alive. Simo moved by him and stepped into the room. Queen Tess's eyes were closed and her head was slumped to the side as if she slept. The pillows and sheets were soaked with blood, and it drained into a large dark pool on the floor.

"She is gone, Sir Benjamin," Simo said. He kissed his fingers and touched her forehead, silently asking the Great Creator to grant her peace.

"Retrieve your girls. I will meet you at the Great Oak," Benjamin said. He grasped Simo's forearm and took the opposite direction to retrieve his family.

We will regroup and retake the castle. Stopping suddenly, he backed up into a corner. Five Lavitian soldiers ran by him. His heart jumped five beats ahead. The veins pounded at his temples. When he opened the door to his chamber, his heart sank.

"Rosaly," he murmured breathlessly. She was covered with blood. He crumbled to his knees beside her. An agonizing pain crept slowly into his throat as he fought to swallow the screams that tried to escape. He gently picked up his wife's body and held her against his chest.

"Rosaly…no no no no," he said.

"I knew you would come," she answered in a strained whisper. Benjamin's eyes flew open. He thought she was dead. "Take care… of the munchkin." She lifted her hand and gave him a key. Benjamin took it in his hand. His tears fell silently onto her face. He smoothed them away with his finger. He placed the key on the floor. Then slowly bent and kissed her, caressing her cheek with his fingers.

"I love you," he whispered against her lips.

She sm iled and said, "I know." Her eyes closed then opened again slowly. She laid her head against his chest and stared at his face.

Benjamin held her tightly, holding her hand until it went limp. He held her for a few minutes and cried. He brushed the hair from her face and gently closed her lifeless eyes. He kissed her lips and hugged her tightly again, taking a deep breath and storing her smell in his memories. Silent tears spilled down his cheeks as he placed her body back gently on the floor.

He looked around panicked. *Alexander*.

"Alexander…Alexander," he called, thinking the worst. Then he heard a tapping sound and a muffled voice coming from one of the trunks that lined the wall. He went back to his wife's body and got the key he had placed on the floor. His son was curled into a ball with tears streaming down his face. Alexander wrapped his arms around his father's neck and clung to him.

"Mommy locked me in the dark," he said between sobs.

"No, son," Benjamin remarked as he stepped around his wife's body, shielding his son's eyes so he would not see it. "Mommy saved your life." He looked back at her one last time before he fled from the room and the castle.

CHAPTER 3

Matilda

Kalina ran frantically through the woods, trying to find the road that led to the village. The castle had been built on top of one of Theslia's many hills. After nearly sliding down the hill and crossing the valley floor, it was surrounded by a thick forest. Kalina held the baby tightly as she entered the dark woods. A bird screeched in the distance, answered by a wolf's howl, sending a shiver up her spine. Kalina tripped and stumbled around the trees. The shadows seemed to close in all around her. She nearly jumped out of her skin when a loud snap cracked through the silence until she realized she had only stepped on a stick. It startled Saroja awake and she released a piercing wail that echoed through the night.

The winter pixies celebrated the season's first snow dancing through the dark night's sky. They flitted around her head, leaving glowing sparks of pinks, blues, greens, and gold in their wake. Kalina wished they were bigger so they could provide her with some better light, but the butterfly-sized entities only left trails of light that dissipated after a few seconds.

"Hush, little one. I know you're hungry and cold. I'm cold too," she said as she paused for a moment, trying to wrap the small blanket more securely around the child when a blast of cold wind rushed passed them. Kalina regretted the thin night shift she had changed into. Her gown had been much heavier.

A little pixie suddenly darted toward them and landed on the child's forehead. Kalina gasped; she had never seen a pixie come so close to a human before. It looked like a tiny little naked woman. She was the color of the new snow, shiny white, with dusty pink wings. Her hair was the color of clear crystal. It hung into her eyes in the front but was cropped short in the back off her neck. Her tiny little wings fluttered, giving off a tinkling sound as she hovered in the air inches above the child. Dust from her wings flipped pink sparks of light around her. She looked up at Kalina with brilliant grass-green eyes and smiled. Then she bent toward Saroja and kissed her on the cheek before she flew off into the darkness.

Kalina stood, stunned. She shifted her weight and fell on her bottom; her feet had sunk several inches into the snow. Now on top of everything she would be wet, she thought, holding Saroja in one hand, brushing the snow from her shift with the other. She trudged along, lifting her knees high into the air, moving slowly through the trees.

"If only I could find the road… I hope I'm going the right way," she said to herself, looking up at the sky only to find no stars there this night to guide her way. She was suddenly surrounded by glowing pixies. They swirled all around her then shot off to the south. She shrugged and headed in the direction they had indicated.

After about a miles journey, the trees began to thin and the road appeared before her eyes. She turned east and continued through the dark along the shoulder of the road. She had walked for what seemed like forever when she caught a strong scent of smoke in the air. She hastened her steps, trying to get to the village quicker. She didn't risk running and waking Saroja, who no doubt would remind her very loudly how hungry she was and that she had nothing to feed her. When she reached the village, her knees nearly gave out beneath her.

The village was covered in a scorch of bright orange flames. Roaring fires stretched to the sky line in front of her. *Mother!* Without any thought, she instantly raced through the inferno, dodging people and falling structures. Was it a coincidence that the castle was attacked and the village burned on the same night?

The people ran frantically with buckets of water in a hopeless effort to save their homes. Men shouted instructions, women scurried about carrying their meager possessions clutched to their chests, and the children huddled together in a clearing, trying to keep each other warm.

Kalina continued to run. Her feet felt like they were being held down by iron weights. Her chest heaved up and down trying to keep her lungs filled with air. The small baby she carried in her arms got heavier and heavier with each step and she still had a ways to go. Her mother's cottage wasn't exactly a part of the village. It was set off into the woods that surrounded it. She had argued endlessly, trying to get her to move into the castle with her, but Matilda had refused. The village, the outskirts of it at least, was as far as she would come.

She pushed through her exhaustion when she noticed the wind blowing sparked embers toward the woods. When she reached the forest, she stopped, bracing herself up against a tree, breathing deeply to catch her breath. She could only make out the outline of the cottage from where she stood, but she felt relief wash over her to find that it was still intact. She pushed herself off the tree and into the dark forest, trying to be careful of her footing.

She tapped on the door, then turned the latch and pushed it open slowly. The old rusty hinges gave an irritated groan as the door opened. The warmth of the cottage sunk into her bones, and she instinctively drifted to the hearth. She pulled the edges of the blanket away and was amazed to find Saroja was still asleep. Maybe the myth about pixies being able to put you to sleep for a hundred years was true.

Her mother slept soundlessly on her bed with her back to the rest of the room. It was a small wooden cottage that opened out into one large room. Matilda had her bed and personal belongings on one side. There were trunks on the floor against the wall, shelves lined with books and small trinkets, and of course, candles. Candles of every size and every color, tall ones, small ones, short ones, and fat ones littered the room. There was a tall bookstand set off in one corner, like the kind a holy man would use, with a large black book on the podium, which Kalina knew from her childhood was not to be touched. The other half of the cottage was the kitchen/pantry/dining room. There was a large square table with jars and stacks of bowls with two sturdy chairs pushed under it. There was one window and a back door by which logs were neatly stacked. The fireplace set into the wall a few paces from the back door with a large black pot hung from the iron arm attached to the hearth. The rest of the room was empty.

Kalina sat on the edge of Matilda's bed and gave her a gentle shake. She moaned in her sleep then slowly turned over in the bed.

"Kalina," her mother called out, sounding confused and surprised to see her daughter at this hour of the night. "What brings you here, child?"

"Mother," Kalina said, standing again when Matilda sat up and swung her legs over the side of the bed. Her hair was a mixture of black, silver, and white. It hung lose down her back. She wore a white long nightgown that fell to her ankles.

"You must be cold," her mother interrupted. "Come, warm yourself by the fire."

"Mother," Kalina tried again as Matilda crossed the room heading for the wood stack. She picked up two logs and threw them in the fire.

"Did you walk all this way alone? It is not safe out this—"

"Mother," Kalina yelled loudly, finally getting her attention, but waking up the child at the same time.

"What is this?" Matilda asked, taking the baby from her daughter's arms. She looked at Kalina with a brilliant smile on her face. Her skin was smooth with deep grooves from years of wear. The green eyes that mirrored Kalina's twinkled as she held the baby to her chest.

"Is this your baby, Kalina?" Matilda asked, admiring the crying child.

"I've been trying to tell you. The castle was attacked and I had to escape," she explained, speaking loudly over Saroja's screams.

"The child is wet," Matilda said, taking the baby to her bed and laying it down.

"*The child is wet*. Is that all you're going to say? I just told you the castle was attacked. The entire village is burning to the ground and your only concern is that the child is wet. You've cut yourself off from everything, hiding away in this little cabin—"

"And it would seem that was for the best or you would have no refuge this night," Matilda explained nonchalantly. Kalina released an irritated sigh.

"That child is our queen. Her parents are dead. She's probably hungry. I can't even feed her. What will we do?" Kalina rambled as tears began to fall from her eyes.

"Calm down, child," Matilda said digging through one of her trunks. "First, we will tend to the child, and then we will figure out what to do."

"She will be in danger. No one can know who she really is," Kalina said.

"I have it. Tomorrow we will journey to Gativa. No one will know us that far away from the capital. We will change her name and raise her as our own," Matilda said.

"What about the mark? She bears the royal seal. People will recognize it where ever we go," Kalina explained. "It probably needs to be cleaned again."

"She's a girl. No one will ever see her ankle, but what new name will we give her?" Matilda said as she moved her hands in a circular motion around her water bag. Lights flashed and moved through Matilda's hands as she conjured a baby's bottle out of thin air.

"Mother, what are you doing?" Kalina exclaimed, coming to take the bottle from Matilda's hands. "We are not going to use witchcraft to take care of this child. It will only get us in trouble!"

"Child, I have been using magic every day since I was fifteen years of age and it never caused me any trouble," Matilda explained taking the bottle back again. "You have been blessed with natural powers and what have you done with them? You've neglected everything you've been taught to play nursemaid to the queen. To be a servant. Why? For the life of me, I don't understand you. Your sister wasn't able to hide her ability as you can," Matilda said.

"And look what happened to her," Kalina said, starting to cry again.

Matilda filled the bottle with the milk she had collected that morning as well as some water to dilute it, disregarding Kalina's comment.

"And for your information, Mother, Tess was my best friend. She was the only one who was nice to me when you sent me away."

"I didn't send you away. I wanted you to learn everything you could about your powers. I thought you would like having other children around after what happened and I knew Lady Lynea could teach you more than I could," Matilda explained, sitting down with the baby in her lap.

"Please, don't lie to me. I know that's not why you sent me away. You just couldn't stand the sight of my face. I should never have come here," Kalina exclaimed. She stood from the table and crossed the room, holding her arms out for the baby. Matilda placed the bottle on the floor and laid the baby down and got up from the bed. Saroja squirmed then let out an irritated wail at this treatment.

"Kalina, don't go. I have missed you. Look," Matilda said, waving her hands in front of her, pointing out the empty space. "I was planning to journey to the castle to visit you. Look." She walked to the back door and opened it. There was a wagon piled high with her mother's belongings. "I was going to the village tomorrow to buy a horse, but now I don't know where we're going to get one. No one will be there to sell us anything."

Kalina stood in the back door. Matilda always did this; she could have just conjured these things a moment ago with all that hand waving, but Kalina wanted so badly for it to be true and that her mother had truly missed her. She pulled the door closed and nodded her head.

"I'll stay. Gativa will probably be a safe place for her until we get all this straightened out," Kalina said.

"Good. Let's get some sleep then," Matilda said. "After we get this little one fed, of course."

CHAPTER 4

Broken and Defeated

Benjamin pulled his horse to a stop. He looked into the blackness of the forest as Bear nervously pawed the ground, tired shots of white smoke released into the air as he stammered and tried to catch his breath. The winter pixies were everywhere, filling the sky with burst of colored lights, but he couldn't enjoy their beauty tonight; those bastards had taken away his angel. Benjamin adjusted the fur cloak tightly around his son. Alexander slept in the saddle before him. He twisted and turned, snuggling closer to his father's warmth.

He had about two hours before dawn. He had been riding at a slow trot, but he feared his son would have to be awakened. He would never make it to the Great Oak by dawn at this pace, so he kicked the horse in full gear. He arrived after an hour, making good time. His men were nowhere in sight, perhaps they had already entered. It would be awhile before he could, considering the entrance was now under water.

The great river split around the huge oak tree that would once again be used as their people's sanctuary. King Alosis had never told him the story of how he had discovered such a place—perhaps the wood nymphs had blessed him for some deed—but he was glad it existed or there would be a lot of families without shelter on this cold night. The tree was nearly the size of the great hall in width and it towered above all the other trees in the area. Now they would have to wait until the water was low enough to enter.

He got down from his horse and Alexander woke up, looking around confused. Benjamin carried and laid him down under a nearby tree. He tucked the fur around his body then started gathering sticks to make a small fire.

"Father, where's Mommy?" he asked. Benjamin paused and looked down at his son.

"Mommy's gone to live with the Great Creator," he explained in a somber voice.

"When is she coming back?" Alexander asked.

"She's not coming back, son. She will be with you always, but you won't be able to see her."

"Is she with us now?" he asked.

"Yes, and right now she wants you to go to sleep."

"But, Father… I *want* to see her," Alexander said as he began to cry. Benjamin picked him up and hugged him tightly to his chest.

"I know. I want to see her too. Don't cry, don't cry," he cooed softly. He wiped away the tears that fell onto his own cheek. He held Alexander until he fell asleep again in his arms then laid him down again when he started to shiver.

After getting the fire started, Benjamin sat down next to him and leaned back against the tree looking down at his son.

He looked just like her. At least he'd be able to see her every day. They had been married for five years and he couldn't think of a day when she wasn't smiling. She had had a perfectly round face, beautiful nose, and perfect lips. He would miss looking into her brown, almondshaped eyes that seemed to capture the light even in the dark and the feel of her soft caramel-colored skin. Her hair was black as the night but it shimmered when she moved. She had the most beautiful voice when she sang their son to sleep at night. She would even sing for the king's court sometimes. It always made him proud. Their marriage had been arranged, but he remembered falling in love with her the moment she had smiled at him.

He remembered that day like it was yesterday. It had been a warm summer night. His father came to his chamber just before evening meal. Kirk Casesar was their clan's leader. He stood about three inches taller than Benjamin, which was always intimidating when he stood directly in front of him as he had that night, giving orders in the deep commanding voice he used to speak to his men.

"The Teal family has arrived, Benjamin. Are you ready to do your duty, my son?" his father asked. He looked him over and nodded with approval.

"Yes, Father…but what if…what if I do not love her?" Benjamin asked. He had only been eighteen years old at the time. He wasn't disturbed about the idea of marriage, but the idea of marrying a girl he had never even seen before had him literally shaking in his boots.

"Son, we have talked about this. Love is not an issue nor is it a necessity. An arrangement has been made and Casesars do not go back on their word," he had said.

Benjamin straightened his shirt again for the hundredth time and pulled on the bottom of his vest. He pushed his fingers through his curly black hair, pulled himself up tall, and then followed his father from the room. The entire clan was gathered in the meeting hall, carrying on loudly as usual. His father led him to the long table where his family sat with their guests. He took his place next to his younger brother, ignoring the huge smile he wore—no doubt at his expense—and tried to concentrate on the meal.

The Teal clan mixed in with his cousins at the opposite side of the table. There had been four women among them; one was grey and wrinkled so he disregarded her. The other three all bore a striking resemblance, each bearing big brown eyes and round, heart-shaped faces, but he knew there were only two children so one must be the mother. He sat looking from girl to girl when his father came to stand over his shoulders.

"Come, my son, it is time to meet your future bride," he said. Benjamin stood up slowly from the table, his nerves settling into a jumbled knot in the pit of his stomach, and followed his father around to the other end of the table.

"Lyle, this is my eldest son," Kirk said, standing behind Benjamin with both his hands on his son's shoulders. Lyle turned and waved the girl forward. Benjamin looked up at his father. Kirk looked down at him and gave him a reassuring nod.

"My daughter," Lyle said as the girl reached his side. She looked up at Benjamin, then gave him a formal bow and said in the sweetest voice he'd ever heard, "Hello, my name is Rosaly." Benjamin bent and took her hand as she stood up straight again.

"I am Benjamin." The smile that lit up her face at that moment touched his heart with a kind of warmth that seemed to completely fill him. Over the years, he had come to love her—truly love her. She had become a beacon from which he drew his strength. Now she was gone, and at that moment he knew that life for him would never be the same.

When he thought of the Lavitians all he felt was rage. Guilt washed over him as he thought over the night's events. He should have been watching over his king; instead he had let his guard down. They had become too comfortable in their newfound freedom. Now they would have to start over, and this time it would be without their great leader.

Who would the people turn to now? How had the Lavatians found out about the naming celebration? An occasion such as that was not an ordinary thing.

A traitor.

The sound of horses approaching brought him back to reality. He got to his feet, kicked out the fire, and backed around the tree, cupping his hands around his mouth.

"Hoo…hoo," he called, imitating an owl. He stepped into the clearing when a wolf's howl was returned. He was amazed by the number. Maybe he had underestimated his men. "Maybe we left too soon. I thought most of you were dead," he called in a humorous tone, trying to hide the burning turmoil that was stirring up inside him.

"It was your wise thinking that saved us. It seems they were after our women and children. They kept us busy in the great hall while they went through the castle, murdering innocent little girls," Simo said in a defeated voice.

"I walked in on one of them as he slit my boy's throat as he slept. What kind of monster would kill a sleeping child? Luckily, I was able to save my wife," Creagar added, staring off into space.

"Well, we were not all that fortunate," Benjamin replied.

"I'm sorry, my lord, I…I'm sorry," was all Creagar could think to say.

"What of your boy?" James asked, getting down from his horse.

"He is there," he said gesturing toward the tree where his son slept. "Rosaly locked him in a trunk."

Creagar helped Filine down from the horse. She walked passed Benjamin in a sniffling daze, tears slowly trickling from her eyes, then went and sat down beside the sleeping child, longing to hold her own.

"If you had not sent us to retrieve our families, Filine would be dead right now," Creagar said.

"Lots of people have died this night, but fear not. Our country will not be taken again. We will regroup and burn Lavitia to the ground. Only then will we have peace," Cain said.

"No. We will not kill innocent women and children. To do so would make us no better than them," Benjamin said.

"You are right," Simo said, now allowing the tears to fall freely down his face.

"Look there…the steps," Thulamnul cried out.

"Come, we must move quickly," Benjamin said, walking to the edge of the river. He reached into his pocket and threw in six clear crystals. "Don't forget your offerings to the river nymphs. We don't need any more trouble tonight." The soldiers each stepped to the edge of the river, depositing the crystals. Moments later the river started to glow. The bleak water turned bright gold then faded back to normal.

Benjamin ran and picked up his son. He adjusted him in his arms, placing his head securely over one shoulder. He picked the blanket up and threw it across Alexander's body, then bent and helped Filine to her feet. Creagar was there to take her arm. Benjamin stepped into the river, moved quickly down the stairs, and paused briefly when he came to the waterfall before stepping through it. He came to two large wooden doors with an emblem of a star surrounded by five rings etched into the wood between the double doors. When everyone was inside, Benjamin had a positive feeling for the first time since this ordeal began. A group of soldiers had already arrived and had lit a few torches, but the light in the room was still very dim. He could barely see the large roots and vines that snaked up and down the walls of the tree.

Filine took Alexander from his arms and cradled him in her arms. She took him to a nearby table and stared at his face as he slept. Benjamin decided now would be a good time to meet with his officers and the five soldiers gathered at a table in the back corner of the large room.

"I think we have enough men for a siege of the castle, but I think we should move now before they have time to send for reinforcements. What say you?" Benjamin asked.

"I agree," Simo said.

"I think we should send to the village for reinforcements first, that way we will have the strength to guarantee our victory. That is what Alosis did the first time," Cain added, trying to buy some more time for his soldiers.

"Then we would have to waste more time training. That situation was different. The enemy was already here. Besides, Cain, this meeting is for my officers. You go see to the people," Benjamin said as the soldier walked away. "It would be foolish for us to wait until they are able to send more men to outnumber us," Benjamin said.

"Benjamin is right. We should move now," James agreed.

"What is your plan?" Creagar asked.

"Thulamnul, organize the archers. You will enter first through the south postern. Follow the passage north to the old soldiers' barracks. That should lead you directly over the courtyard wall. Wipe out the sentries and replace them. James, you will lead your cavalry to flank the courtyard. Try to keep the horses quiet. Simo, you will divide the infantry into three groups." Benjamin set up a diagram of the castle on the table and continued to explain his strategy for retaking the castle.

"We will attack in three days' time. Let's let them think they have won for a little while," Benjamin added when they had all come to an understanding about what was to be done.

"What about the princess? I did not find her body when I swept the royal chamber," Simo said.

"Do you think they would take her captive?" Creagar asked.

"They killed the other children. I'd think they would kill her too if their goal was to eliminate our families," Simo said.

"They will pay for what they have done," Benjamin said.

Cain found an empty table off near a wall. He sat down and looked around at all the grieving families that had lost loved ones this night. They were mostly lone soldiers, some women, and to his dismay, children. This would be the second time he had failed his mission. He still had time to fix this problem, but if he had succeeded in wiping out the Covax bloodline years ago he would be in Lavitia right now, living like a king, but here he was, a lowly spy acting as an even lower soldier in this dreadful army.

He was pulled away from his thoughts by a whimpering sound coming from behind him. He turned to find two small girls sitting off alone with their arms wrapped around each other. He scanned the room, feeling a brief moment of guilt. A woman sat looking off into space, slowly rocking back and forth with a child's doll clutched tightly to her chest. A soldier was turned into the wall of the tree, trying to shield the fact that he was crying.

It was their fault for keeping their families inside a castle in the first place. They were the ones that put them at risk. He was merrily a mercenary doing his job. If Vyner had not held out on his payment all those years ago, he wouldn't be forced to murder helpless children. How could he have known the prince would be away from the palace when he made his move? That's what he got for not doing the deed himself.

CHAPTER 5

Queen Nasci

Kalina slept on the furs her mother had given her on the floor in front of the hearth. She dreamed she was back in the castle. She pushed a large wooden door open and the assassin was there, slowly moving toward her, but this time her feet wouldn't move. The cloaked man slowly walked around her. A chill swept through her, starting at her toes and traveling its way up her body. She started shivering as the dark figure wrapped a hand slowly around her neck. At the same time the cold blade made contact with her skin. Fear had crippled her body's responses, though she knew she should move to the side or put her hand up or scream or anything else except just stand there waiting. She couldn't move. The blade slid into her throat, but instead of the sick gurgling sound she had expected, she got a groan followed by a solid thump.

Her eyes popped open scanning the room. She immediately jumped to her feet.

"Mother!" she screamed. "The baby's gone." She didn't wait for Matilda to respond. She slipped her shoes on quickly, grabbed her mother's shawl, and snatched open the front door. A golden cloud was carrying the furs the baby had been wrapped in high in the air heading towards the depths of the forest. Kalina ran to catch it.

Matilda called her name, but she didn't respond. She was almost in arms' reach when the golden cloud lifted higher than her extended hands could reach. That's when her focus turned to what was carrying the baby instead of the baby itself.

"Fairies," she whispered and paused in astonishment. Fairies never came out at night, some believed they couldn't, but Kalina had never cared enough about it to concern herself with finding out. She knew now that they could. They were "the keepers of the flowers." They chose the colors, the shapes, the length; they even opened and closed them. You only saw them early in the morning and just before sunset, but never at night, and certainly never in the winter. Fairies didn't hide their existence from humans, but they didn't frolic among them like pixies and nymphs tended to do.

Kalina shook her head and started to run after them again. She didn't care what they were. She would not let them take Tess's baby. She ran and jumped at the bundle they held just over her head as if they were taunting her. She was well past annoyed and vurgeing on rage when a little burst of pink light flashed before her eyes. Her mother caught up to her just as she raised her hand to swat the little pest out of the sky.

The pink flash passed again then it fluttered directly in front of Kalina for a moment, then moved slowly to stand on her nose. Kalina recognized the pixie as the one that had kissed Saroja. She looked down her nose at the little pixie then pulled her face away when her eyes became unnaturally crossed. It fluttered inches from her, pink dusty light flashing. With a little zip of movement, she flew to Kalina's ear.

"Greetings, I am Princess Meredith. My mother wishes to see the child. We must obey," she said in a tiny, high-pitched voice. Kalina could hear the tinkling of her wings this close to her ear as she hovered in the air. "You may follow," it squeaked again.

Kalina looked to her mother as she turned and looked at her.

"She says we can follow them," Kalina explained. Their eyes met and Matilda nodded.

"We will follow, but let me carry the baby," Kalina said loudly. *Follow indeed.* If she had not woken up, they would never have seen that child again. The fairies continued into the darkness of the forest. She huddled close to her mother, wrapping the wool shawl around both their shoulders and followed the little pixie as she zipped away into the night.

The forest was alive with sounds: the squeaks and squawks of the animals, the howl of the wind, the rustling of the trees, and all kinds of different sounds coming from all around them. They couldn't see anything until it was directly in front of them. The baby's image had disappeared; the dark color of the fur meshed in with the night. Now there was only the bright golden beckon the fairies created.

They led them to the edge of the river and down a slight incline. Kalina moved slowly, helping her mother through the dark across protruding sticks and rocks, being careful as they continued after the light. She could hear the rushing sound of water and felt its spray on her face as the roar grew louder. Then they were walking through a narrow stone passageway. The light ahead of them left a dark shadow into the cavern. The wall was wet under her hand when she put it against the wall to steady herself.

The passageway opened into a whole new world. The cold winter night transformed to a warm breezy day. The grass was plush and green. The air smelled of springtime, a mixture of grass, pollen, rain, and sunshine… if sunshine had a smell, it would smell like this place. The path they were led across was made up of flowers, the likes of which Kalina had never seen before. They were so beautiful it was difficult to walk on for fear of destroying them, so instead she stepped out of her shoes. The flowers had long white petals and they were soft and silky under her feet as she continued after the fairies. The walls of this place were the same hard stone they had walked through. Kalina could see the water trickling down it into a shimmering pool that covered the entire middle of the floor. Were they somehow under the river? Vines and flowers snaked down from the ceiling. The flower path continued across the pool without the help of any manmade bridge. The ceiling was high and dome shaped, which made her wonder where the light was coming from; she didn't see any candles or sconces on her way in. But then if everything that lived here glowed what would they need of sconces?

They had to duck low to enter the next room. This section was covered with a floor of grass. Pixies, fairies, nymphs, and elves were all gathered in a semicircle, facing them. The pixies were all naked with clear, crystal-colored hair, but while the winter pixies were snowy white with wings of pinks, blues, greens, and gold, the spring pixies were light green, almost yellow. Their wings were brilliant reds, orange, green, and purple. The autumn ones were brown. Their wings were the colors of fallen leaves: rusty reds, brownish orange and dull yellows. The summer ones were a rich grass green with bright blue, violet, and pink, almost red wings. The fairies were next to them on the left. They were the size of small birds. They looked like tiny little humans with different skin, hair, and eye colors, and clothes; even though they seemed to be made of flowers and parts of the forest, they covered what needed to be covered, but all their wings were gold. The nymphs were perhaps the size of the average toddler. Some were the brown color of trees, some were green as the grass they sat on, and some were white as snow. Their eyes were all a solid, glassy blue, with no white at all. The elves, which sat next to the nymphs on the right, were gorgeous humans with sharp, pointy ears. Most wore their hair long down their backs. Kalina had to turn away when she realized she had been staring at them.

In the middle sat a large golden chair. At a second glance, she noticed it truly wasn't a chair at all, or not a traditional chair anyway. It was made up of large, sturdy vines, which shot directly out of the ground and had twined and twisted together to create this shape. In it sat a lady. Light seemed to emanate from her; Kalina had to squint to look directly at her. She had long yellowish-green hair, and it had blossoms of white flowers growing from the tendrils. Her eyes were a sparkling crystal blue. Her skin was white as the snow that covered the ground. Her dress was indigo and it fell around her bare feet like flower petals. Kalina wondered if it was as soft as it looked. Suddenly, the lady spoke. The sound was like nothing Kalina had ever heard before in her life. The lady's voice was rich and full and it rose and fell like a song being sung.

She said, "You were right, Merry. I can feel her power even from this distance." The little white pixie with the pink wings was suddenly there again. She landed on a blue flower and bowed to the woman then she was gone again. Kalina saw her moments later in the pixie section.

The fairies carried the baby directly to the lady and she took her in her arms. She took Saroja from the furs and held her up. Her little white gown fell past her feet.

"Mestopholes's blessing has come full circle," she said, cuddling the child to her neck. "Do you know who I am?" she asked, turning her attention to Kalina and Matilda for the first time.

"Are you the Queen of the Fairies?" Matilda asked.

"I am queen of fairies, pixies, nymphs, elves, sprites, trolls… My name is Queen Nasci, but your kind might know me as Mother Nature."

Matilda's eyes widened in amazement. She slowly got to her knees and touched her nose to the ground.

"What would Mother Nature want with Tess's baby?" Kalina asked.

"Kalina, show some respect," Matilda whispered, pulling at the hem of her dress. Queen Nasci smiled. She leaned her head to one side and looked Kalina over.

"Where is Tess—the child's mother, I presume?" she asked, with Saroja sitting in her lap.

"She was killed tonight, along with her husband," Kalina explained, then wished she hadn't the minute the words left her mouth because while Nasci solemnly shook her head, her eyes told another story.

"That is unfortunate," she said, looking down at the baby. "Well, it is good that the entire forum has gathered this evening, for it would seem we have very pressing matters to discuss."

"Coincidence, indeed," Kalina mumbled under her breath, crossing her arms over her chest. There was little about the human world that the "Element Handlers" or "Mystical Ones" didn't know about, and just as Saroja's presence had been reported, she was sure the attack on the castle had been as well.

"My children," Nasci said, lifting her heavenly voice across the room. "We must decide who will care for this special child."

"Wait, wait, wait," Kalina said, stepping forward. "I am her lady's maid. I will take care of her. No one asked—"

"What my daughter means, Your Highness, it that Queen Tess left the child in her care," Matilda interrupted. She looked absolutely terrified. "Kalina," she called like a mother would do if their child was misbehaving in public. "Show some respect."

"That may be true, but we must consider the child's powers. She must be properly trained. I would care for her myself, but I have so many responsibilities that I fear I would be unable to give her the proper attention she would require. But my children are all capable."

The pixies started twinkling excitedly. Princess Meredith and three other pixies took off into the air, a streak of pink, blue, gold, and green light buzzing in a trail leading to the queen. She tipped her head to one side as she listened to them.

"Interesting, but I fear it will not work. She is small now but she will grow to elf size."

"We will take and care for the child, Mother, and teach her how to contain her powers," a tall elf said. His voice was deep and commanding. His eyes were a beautiful hazel color that matched his long, straight hair. He had a masculine square face that contained a hard nose, square chin, and thin lips that were framed by a dark brown goatee. His skin had a soft olive tone, and he had a very serious look about his face.

"You brutes will try to turn her into a weapon. That's the only thing you're good for," said a little brown nymph. He had spiky green and black hair. His blues eyes bore into the elf that had spoken.

"And what would your kind teach her, Stencil? How to be greedy, cruel, manipulative, and mischievous? Shall I go on? At least we can teach her to be an asset as opposed to a hindrance."

"Children, do not quarrel," Nasci started.

"Your Majesty, I think that we should take her. My mother is more than qualified to teach Saroja everything she must know about her powers, and it will be her only chance to have a normal life. She is Pheolatian after all, she should remain among her own people," Kalina explained. She bit down on her lower lip when Nasci started shaking her head.

"This child's power will be like nothing you and your kind have ever seen before. Matilda, you are a powerful sorceress, but I—"

"If we raise her, she will have a chance to have life beyond her own. Isn't it true that *your children* are created, not born, and you can check on her from time to time?" Kalina continued.

"You will speak to Mother with respect," the elf that had spoken said, glaring at Kalina.

Nasci disappeared from the throne.

"Father, I have the child. Please, may I keep her? I can feel her powers even now."

"And why would I do such a thing? Give her back to the Pheolatians and leave them alone."

"But Father, this child has my powers," Nasci chided like a spoiled child unable to have her way.

"A mere coincidence, I assure you. Now do as you're told," the Great Creator boomed.

"Yes, Father," she said, vanishing in a shimmer of light. She appeared once again at the forum as if she had never left. Two elves held Kalina as she struggled against their grip.

Nasci held up her hand for silence. "I like the woman's plan. You will take her and I or one of my children will drop in from time to time to make sure she is developing properly, but if at any time I feel she is a danger to my world…I will destroy her and you two as well.

"Prince Stagg, take our guests to your dwellings and give them shelter for the night. Escort them to their cottage in the morning."

"Your Majesty, may I also ask that when you check on her—I mean you no offense, of course, but will you—can you appear human around the child? Pheolatians are not very popular right now, and children don't understand that some things must be kept secret for their own safety," Kalina said. She watched Nasci closely as she mulled over her words with an exaggerated expression on her face. She wasn't even sure if it could be done, but she couldn't have fairies and nymphs over for dinner. The "Elements" usually didn't mingle in the human world. She had never even seen an elf before tonight.

Queen Nasci nodded and then curtly waved them away. Stagg moved forward and ushered the ladies toward another narrow stone passageway. Nasci stood gracefully from her seat and disappeared into her own light with Saroja cradled in her arms.

"She said we could take the baby," Kalina said to the elf standing beside her. His skin was black as the sky this night. His eyes were gray, almost white, with wisps of blue swirling in and out of the irises. His nose and cheekbones were perfectly set to give him a most distinguishing masculine look, which was good because he had the loveliest hair. It was long, white, and spun in long spirals down his back. He was the most beautiful being she had ever seen before in her life. She stood in silence, mesmerized by him, until Prince Stagg spoke, close enough to her ear she picked up a soothing, rich tenor, but she understood no words. She blinked and shook her head and tried to concentrate on what he was saying as opposed to how attractively he was saying it.

"Mother will bring the child to me in the morning before you leave," he replied.

"I didn't hear her say that," Kalina replied, hurrying to keep up with his pace.

"I heard it," he said, glaring down at her.

He led them to a village made out of what appeared to be tall trees. Honeycomb-shaped crystal dwellings sat high among the limbs. Some of them shone bright green while others had no light at all. Stagg led them to one of the trees then stepped up on a white, oval-shaped disk and gestured for them to follow him. When they were both on the platform, it started rising into the sky. Matilda grabbed hold of Kalina at the same time she grabbed hold of Stagg.

"Calm yourselves," he said with a look of disgust on his face as he stared at them.

"How is this possible?" Kalina asked, looking all around her. She had seen barrel pulleys lift several barrels into the air before, but they had been operated by ropes and men, this thing was moving in midair with nothing attached to it.

"I am moving it with my mind," he said, stepping from the disk onto a huge branch. It was the size of a small path. He led them to one of the honeycomb-shaped structures. Up close it looked to be made of glass. It was one of the dwellings that cast no light, but even in the dark she could see that it was a dark green color. He stretched his arm out to touch it. Before his fingers came in contact with the structure, it peeled opened like a flower. In the middle was a bright white light.

Kalina held her arm up to shield her eyes. Stagg started moving forward and Kalina held on to her mother as she followed Stagg into the light. Instantly they were inside of the dwelling and it closed up around them.

He led them through a large empty room down a hall and stopped at the wall. He did the same reaching action he had done before and an opening appeared in the wall.

"These are your quarters for the night. If you have need of anything simply touch the wall and someone will appear to you. I will be back in the morning," he said, turning to leave.

"Gideon, the river nymphs are demanding that the mountain fairies pay a toll for collecting water for their flowers," a female elf with flaming red hair said.

"I will be right with you, Saline," he replied and walked away in the opposite direction.

He walked into a dome-shaped room and sat cross-legged on the floor. "Mother, I have arrived." Nasci appeared before him, cradling the sleeping child in her arms.

"Before first light, return the humans to their world. Once there, I want you to destroy the women and the child. Make it appear as if the soldiers are responsible," she said, handing the sleeping child to him.

"It will be as you command," he replied as she disappeared.

Kalina turned inside the room for the first time and was stunned by the tranquility of this place. There was an actual cloud floating in the middle of the room. The walls seemed to be made up of moving whispers of the night sky. Orange flames flickered opposite the bed of clouds. The whole place smelled like a mixture of mint and pine. She helped her mother onto the cloud and then crawled in behind her. She had never imagined anything so soft. She was so comfortable she didn't remember falling to sleep, only the deep voice saying, "It is time to rise."

Prince Stagg stood in the doorway, holding Saroja cradled in his arms. Kalina sat up and moved to stand. The cloud disappeared and what had appeared to be the night sky the night before had transformed to a bright winter day. She walked toward him with her arms stretched out in front of her, reaching for the baby, when he turned away, leading them back into the room with the now empty golden chair in it. They traveled back down the narrow stone path that led to the room with the shimmering pool, but this time there was no pool. They were outside, surrounded by large white boulders. He led them along a thin ledge to an opening behind a roaring waterfall. They walked under it and down into the valley that led into the forest.

Stagg shifted the child in his arms and she woke up. Moments later she was crying. He looked down at her pinched red face and frowned. Why was it creating that awful noise? He tried putting her back in the original position but she continued to wail at the top of her lungs. He pulled her blanket closer around her. His finger gazed across her palm and she closed her tiny hand around it, then closed her eyes and was asleep seconds later.

Kalina nearly collided into him when he suddenly stopped dead. He peered at the tiny child as if seeing her for the first time. He stroked her cheek and smiled when the babe nestled into his chest.

"Is she wet? Do you want me to take her?" Kalina asked, waking Stagg from his stupor. He continued moving through the woods. They reached Matilda's cottage just as the light touched the roof. Stagg stood at the edge of the forest, looking from the two women to the child he held in his arms.

"Journey to Gativa as you planned," he said. He held his hand out straight and two horses appeared before them. "Stay on the main road. Keep the child from the forest." Quickly he pulled his finger free from her grasp, dumped Saroja in Kalina's arms, and then disappeared in a streak of white light.

CHAPTER 6

A New Beginning

enjamin watched the flame flash across the sky twice. He and his soldiers moved quietly from the forest, quickly across the shallow valley floor to line the outer wall of the castle. He stepped away from the wall, swinging his grappling hook around at his side before releasing it into the air. It flew high and hit the stone with a clank. He pulled on it to be sure it was secure then looked down his line of men, silently signaling that they should wait until he reached the top before they followed. He scaled the wall in seconds, followed by a handful of soldiers. He crept silently to the middle, coming up behind the patrolling soldier. He grabbed him from behind, placing his hand over his mouth, and then cut his throat and proceeded to raise the portcullis. The soldier behind him handed him the flaming sconce. He waved it across the sky twice, then turned toward the main building as the remaining soldiers waiting in the forest raced toward the castle. Moments later the sounds of battle filled the quietness of the night.

The Lavitians were quickly subdued. Benjamin's soldiers had them disarmed and surrounded. He was appalled that they didn't fight to the last man. They had the audacity to surrender after murdering sleeping women and helpless children. Twelve soldiers that claimed they had no knowledge of what the mission entitled were hung. The six commanders were beheaded after they refused to give up any information, and their leader was to be boiled alive feet first.

"Wait, wait," he screamed as the rope began to lower him into the bubbling water. "Please, I will tell…" he started then fell into the boil with a splash.

"What happened?" Benjamin demanded.

"I'm sorry, my lord, the rope slipped," Cain said.

"He was about to give up the source to all this. Do you realize what you have done?" Benjamin exclaimed.

"I thought I had it secure, sir. When he started to speak, I released my hold on the crank thinking it was locked, but it wasn't. I'm so sorry."

Benjamin grunted, shaking his head, and marched from the room. No wonder the enemy kept infiltrating their defenses; with incompetent soldiers like Cain in their army they would never succeed.

The soldiers all gathered in the meeting hall to decide what would be done next.

"We should declare a new king!" Someone shouted.

"King Benjamin," someone else said.

"Yes, Benjamin," someone else agreed. The entire hall started shouting Benjamin's name. He stood up and moved slowly to the front of the room. Could he lead these people as Alosis had? What would he say to them? How could he keep them safe? He reached the platform and raised his hands. The hall fell quiet.

"I will lead you," he said. The hall erupted in applause.

"This calls for a celebration," Cain said.

"No. No celebration. We have lots of work to do. This castle will never fall again. Simo, take a regiment of soldiers to retrieve the people from the Great Oak."

The next night his son was branded on his left arm with the royal seal and declared their next heir.

Castle Covax, Lavitia

Marsalis read the message from Cain, then crushed it between his hands. Cain reported that the king and queen were dead, but that some of the children had survived. Marsalis had said nothing about killing the king or the queen; he had wanted to kill Alosis himself. His orders were to kill every child. This news scared him. A Covax should never be afraid of anything, but he had cursed the Great Creator and now he feared death. Shalyndria's visions were never wrong. But there was time; he would not let a descendant of slaves destroy him.

"Messenger, send word to Cain. Tell him I want him to hold his position until I contact him again," Marsalis said as he walked away. He stopped suddenly. "Also add that if he ever fails me again or misinterprets my orders to carry out his own agenda, I will rip off his head and feed it to my dogs." Then he marched off down the hall. He came to Shalyndria's chambers and opened the door. The girl was nowhere in sight.

"Where is she?" he asked the servant girl that stood near the bed, bowing her head to him.

"She is in the bathing pool, sire," the girl answered.

Marsalis walked into the other room and ordered Shalyndria out of the water. She swam to the edge and walked slowly up the steps. She pushed the water out of her face. It slid down her body as she walked slowly toward him. She brushed away the yellow flower petals that clung to her wet skin and took the towel from the servant and wrapped it around her body, covering her nudity.

Marsalis could not deny her beauty. Her skin was the color of gold and it glistened in the candlelight. Her breasts were large and round. She had a small waist that led to a triangle of dark curls. Her hips were well rounded and fit perfectly with the shapeliest legs he had ever seen. The sight of her made his loins ache. There was something about her that made him want to dismiss the fact that she was a slave. Lately, he found he had to remind himself of that fact just to keep his hands off of her. Even his advisors suggested that he take her as his queen so the child they created would possess her powers, but his cousin had advised against it, reminding him of how beneath him she was.

Suddenly, he pushed the thoughts from his mind. He could not believe he was actually thinking of taking a slave to his bed, and worse, sharing his throne with her. His father would never forgive him.

"Yes, Your Majesty?" she asked for the second time.

Marsalis suddenly struck her hard across her cheek with the back of his hand, knocking her to the floor. She looked up at him shocked, eyes wide with confusion. He had never hit her before. What had she done?

"Do not use your trickery to bewitch me. I have come to seek your advice. Get up. Now!" He grabbed her arm and pulled her to her feet. He pushed her onto the bed and dismissed her servants.

"How may I serve you?" she asked, holding her face. She glared up at him, wondering what she had done to bewitch him. What had happened to this man to make him so mean and cruel? He was tall and strong. He rarely wore a shirt and carried the extra material that hung from his pants over one arm. His eyes were light blue. He wore his golden-brown hair long onto his shoulders and kept it combed to the back off his face. He had a nicely shaped face and a stern, attractive nose. His chest was oiled and it shone in the light the candles provided, giving his tanned complexion a yellowy hue. Most women would find him attractive. Shalyndria thought he was gorgeous, but his heart was dead.

"Do not look directly into my eyes. Your kind is unworthy to look upon the face of a king," he said, watching her as she looked down at her lap. She wiped the tears from her eyes as they slid down her face.

"How may I serve you, Your Highness?" She repeated quietly.

"Was the child you spoke of killed during the naming ceremony attack?" he asked.

Shalyndria's hair began to fly freely as she lifted her head.

"No, my lord," she replied, wishing he would leave now so she could cry in peace.

Marsalis stormed from the room and slammed the door behind him. He stopped and leaned back against it, thinking of her. What was wrong with him? Why did he deny himself when she was right there? Maybe it was because over the years she was only one he truly trusted and he thought that if he truly possessed her, mind, body, and soul, she would soon become his undoing.

He walked directly to the hall of concubines. He peered through their windows but could not find one that aroused him as Shalyndria had. Finally, he entered the room of the twins. They were not that beautiful, but they had the capacity to drain him of all his strength, allowing him to sleep peacefully through the night.

As he entered, they immediately stopped working on the tapestry that was set between them and came to him. Ayanna, the oldest of the twins, took his hand and led him to the large bed in the center of the room. Sonya unshackled the chains that held his pants up. Marsalis sat back against the pillows and closed his eyes. Sonya took his manhood into her mouth as Ayanna kissed his neck and nibbled on his earlobes. Marsalis took Ayanna by the hair and kissed her fiercely. Sonya slowly crawled around him, using her hair to caress his stomach and his chest.

He sat up straight in the bed and pushed Ayanna down completely onto his throbbing shaft. Sonya pulled him back onto the pillows and used her tongue to tantalize his nipples as her sister moved slowly on top of him.

Marsalis flipped Ayanna in the bed and used hard, fast thrusts to push into her body. She moaned as she whipped her head from side to side. Suddenly Marsalis stopped and separated their bodies. He pulled Sonya down onto the bed and pushed into her. Her sister curled up next to them on the bed and watched. Marsalis finally sated himself after switching between the two girls. Drained of his earlier frustrations, he laid back against the pillows. The girls draped themselves across his chest, but Marsalis pushed them away. He suddenly rose from the bed, put his pants back on, and left. Shalyndria instantly came back to his thoughts.

Part Two

CHAPTER 7

The First Encounter

Gativa, Theslia
Eighteen Years Later

Mirage wondered across a field of wild white and yellow flowers, wondering what it would be like to live on one of those mountains in the distance. She longed for adventure, but at this point in her life she would settle for just a little change. She was tired of doing the same things day in and day out. There was nothing in Gativa but farms and fish. There had to be more to her life than this dull, boring place. Her aunt Lina never let her go anywhere on her own. Her best friend Lidia had been married for nearly a year now and had moved away to live with her husband's family. She was the only girl of her age unmarried— not that she had ever met anyone she wished to marry anyway.

She looked back over her shoulder and watched her aunt carry a bundle of clothes into the house. She walked slowly toward the wooded area nearby then ran through the trees until she couldn't see the farmhouse anymore. She ran up fallen logs, twirled around trees, skipped across stones, and danced to the music the wind made. The forest seemed to come alive. A little yellow-and-green butterfly zipped by and buzzed around her face, then zipped away again. She giggled quietly to herself, and then ran through the forest to find her favorite little spring.

The butterfly followed, and then landed on a thin limb high above where she sat. In a twirl of white light, it turned into a little yellow green pixie with pale blue wings.

"There is a stream through these woods. We can water the horses," James said.

"When was the last time you've been home, James?" Alexander asked in an irritated tone.

"I haven't been here since…I buried my mother ten years ago," James answered. He looked at Simo, wondering if he had also noticed the prince's attitude on this journey.

"Then how do you know the water's still there?" he snapped.

"Some things you just know," James replied with a shrug.

"Your Majesty, is something bothering you?" Simo asked. "I have noticed a change in you this journey. You travel with us, but your mind is obviously somewhere else."

Alexander glared at Simo. Besides the fact that he'd been in this saddle for almost two weeks and that he thought this journey was a complete waste of his time, he didn't want to be in these dreadful woods looking for water.

"I apologize for my rudeness, but Father has gone too far. Before we left he called me into his chambers and announced that he had no choice but to deceive me. He had promised me when I came of age that I would be allowed to choose my own bride. He explained that his concession could never be a possibility because I have been betrothed to the late King Alosis's daughter since he found out she survived the invasion all those years ago.

"He told me of the night my mother died and how the true heir of this country had been secretly taken away to save her life, and now it was time to restore her to the throne by having her join with me in marriage. Her name was Saroja Minuo—or *something*—and she will be arriving at the castle soon. Then he has the audacity to send me on this journey to collect a maid that has been specially chosen to serve the princess. I would rather go to the frontlines to aid in our country's defense than retrieve some farm girl to serve this stranger I'm being forced to marry. What did father tell you about this mission?" Alexander asked as they moved slowly through the woods.

"Only that we are to watch over you and to find and give this message to Lady Kalina," Simo answered.

"Well, I think the two of you could find and retrieve a woman on your own. Every time I ask Father to join the forces near the border he comes up with some excuse or task for me so I won't have to go," Alexander said.

"We have been at war for decades. There will be plenty of time for you to fight," Simo said.

"Why can't I find my own bride? He should trust me enough to make a wise choice for our country. I want a woman that can think for herself, not some puppet wrapped in silks."

"Have you given any consideration to your father's dilemma, Your Highness? The man gave us our freedom. His blood must be restored to the throne. Trust that your father has your best interest in mind," Simo responded. Over the years, He had watched over Benjamin's son as if he were his own. His twins would be about his age now had they survived that terrible night.

"I had not thought about that, but why did he have to lie to me?" Alexander asked, wondering how Simo would answer that question in his father's favor.

"As I remember it, you plagued him for weeks to change his mind. You of all people should know that your father does not change his mind. Perhaps he gave you the answer that you wanted to hear for a little peace and quiet," Simo replied.

"There is your water," James announced, "but I don't remember the spring looking like this."

"I think we've found something better than water," Alex said, nodding his head in direction of the girl. She sat on the ground near the edge of the water, her face angled up to the sky with her eyes shut. The sunlight broke through the trees, shining a cascade of light down on her face. There were flowers and butterflies all around her. The trees seemed to lean in toward where she sat. The water seemed unnaturally clean, as it lapped over jagged slates of rock. The birds flew in toward her, then flew away again. She paid them no attention.

What is she doing out here all alone? Alexander thought. She was beautiful. Her hair was as black as night and it fell onto the ground. Thick lashes lay against her cheek. She had a stern nose that fit her face perfectly. The white dress she wore made her golden-brown skin glow. Perhaps she was an angel set in this peaceful scene to taunt him, or maybe a wood sprite of some sort. Her ears seemed too small for her to be an elf, but she was unnaturally beautiful; there had to be some super natural forces at work.

The horse's neigh woke her from her daydream. She opened her eyes to find three men approaching. She got up quickly from the ground and started backing away. Then she turned and ran as fast as her feet could carry her deep into the shadows of the forest. Alexander kicked his horse's flanks and followed her. Simo and James glanced at each other, then followed him.

They caught up with her in no time and surrounded her. Her heart slammed in her chest as she came to a halt, slowly turning so she could see them all at once. Her eyes shifted from man to man nervously.

"We mean you no harm," Simo said.

"Then why did you chase me? What do you want?" she asked nervously.

Alex smiled, pleased by the sound of her voice. It was pure and strong, but sweetly feminine; not like the women at court that whispered and held their heads down and away so he would have to lean in to hear what they were saying. Her eyes switched from man to man then settled on him when he spoke; their amber glow completed the picture and emphasized her appeal to him.

"We are heading to Gativa. We thought we should have arrived there by now. I just wanted to know where we are. Do you live around here? Well, you must, I see no horse. Can you help us?" he asked.

"This is Gativa. The village is just outside these woods," she said, walking past their horses.

"Will you show us the way? We have business there," Alexander said. James and Simo turned and looked at each other.

Mirage looked them over and then said, "Very well, you may follow me." She led them to the edge of the field and then pointed to the village down the hill.

"Thank you, my lady," Alex said as he watched her walk away down the hill toward the farmhouses in the distance. She turned, gave him a formal bow, and then continued down the hill.

"May I at least have the honor of knowing your name before we depart?" Alex asked.

Mirage turned back around and smiled. "And what, sir, would you do with my name?" she asked, looking him over. He sat up straight and tall on a gray horse. His hair was black, short, and slightly curly. He had a pleasing smile and large brown eyes. His clothes were very fancy, telling her that he was someone of importance. He had on tall black boots, tightly fitting black brocks, a loosely fitting silver shirt that moved with the wind, and a dark blue-and-silver cloak.

"I would keep it as a tool to remember you by," Alex answered.

"You don't need my name to remember me. When you're thinking of this moment, sir, give me whatever name you wish. It will make for a more interesting thought," she said, heading back down the hill.

"Mirage," Kalina called. "Come in now."

"Well, it would seem the Great Creator would give me your name despite your objections," Alex replied.

Mirage looked back at him and smiled, then ran down the hill to her aunt.

"What have I told you about strangers? I give up on warning you of the dangers of the forest. Why were you talking to those men?" Kalina asked as she watched the men ride off toward the village.

"They were looking for the village. I simply gave them directions," she replied.

"Do you know them?" Kalina continued, coming to stand her, lifting her chin.

"No, but—" Mirage started.

"Then that would make them strangers, wouldn't it?" Kalina interrupted.

"Well, I'm not dead, am I?" Mirage said with a quiet giggle.

"You can take your breakfast to your room and remain there for the rest of the day as punishment for disobeying me," Kalina said sternly.

Mirage shrugged and went into the house. She marched up the stairs and went into her room. She closed the door behind her and sat down at the table. She touched the candles with the tip of her pointer finger and lit the flames. She looked down at the large book before her and released an irritated breath. *Maintaining a Large Household* was the title of the book. She had no desire to live in a house of any size. She just wanted to travel all over the land, discovering new things. She would spend her days sleeping on the ground with the sky as her blanket.

Why did she need to know about the history of the country, or diplomacy, or any of the other nonsense her aunt made her learn? Her lessons with her grandmother were a different matter. She loved using her powers. She wanted to know everything there was to know about them. Auntie Lina's lessons made no sense. She would always tell her, "Your mother would want you to be a lady," when she complained or asked why she had to study any particular subject, but her mother wasn't here.

Her mother had married a wealthy man and had a very privileged life, from what she had been told, and her aunt had promised that she would see to it that Mirage had the same opportunities, but all she wanted was to be just like everyone else.

They lived in a small village and she couldn't go anywhere by herself. She could never visit her friends at their homes. The only reason she had friends at all was because Matilda was the teacher at their school for girls and Kalina had allowed her to go, even though she insisted on giving her additional lessons in certain subjects. She wasn't allowed to even have any male friends, which she thought was completely unfair.

She was strictly forbidden from the forest, but it seemed like the only place she could be herself and for some reason she was drawn to it. She would start off tending the horses and end up in the woods. Now she could only go outside when she was there too. All these rules had made her a prisoner and this farmhouse was her jail. And it wouldn't stop until she was confined to this room to wither and rot away.

She stood up from the table, breathing deeply, her arms stiff at her sides. She walked to the window and climbed up into the window seat. She had to tiptoe to reach the latch. She bent down and inched the squeaky window up slowly. She stopped at about a third of the way up and slipped through the opening. The thick green ivy growing on the wall was her ladder. It had yellow honeysuckles twined through it, filling the air with a rich sweet smell. Once she hit the ground she ducked under the kitchen window and ran to the back of the house and circled to the barn on the other side.

"Shshshshsh," she whispered as she walked in the stable. She lifted the latch and pushed the door open slowly. Midnight rubbed his nose on her shoulder as she saddled and bridled him. She climbed on his back and raced toward the village. Auntie Lina was still on the other side of the house, tending the laundry.

She rode through the village, past the market and shops, past the docks with the busy men and their boats and nets, women with bins, fish, and birds, and raced down the shoreline. She pulled the horse to a slow trot and climbed down when she reached a secluded inlet near a pile of large granite rocks. She climbed up to the top and sat down cross-legged.

Alexander, Simo, and James walked into a tavern and everything went quiet. The chatter started up again as the three men walked to the bar. The bartender walked over after a while and asked, "What can I get for you gentlemen?"

"We need some information. We seek—" James started.

"We'll have two ales and a goblet of water," Alexander interrupted.

The men took their drinks and followed Alexander to one of the empty tables.

"My father said to use discretion," Alexander said, answering their unasked question. "We will observe them first, then choose a trustworthy person to help us."

Simo and James carried on a quiet conversation while Alexander sat quietly, twisting his mug of ale around and around on the table. He watched the people at the tables and the ones standing at the bar. He tried to stay focused on the task at hand, but he couldn't help thinking about the girl. *Mirage.*

That was a good name for her. He wanted to see her again. The gods were truly trying to torture him by putting this woman in his path at this point in his life. If he had a choice, he would choose her. After just a moment's encounter he could tell she was simple, witty, strong, and absolutely beautiful. He wanted to know her. There was something about her that seemed familiar to him, as if he had seen her somewhere before. His father would probably think a farm girl would not be a good selection for a bride, but at least he'd believe her when she spoke. He was fed up with the wiles of the women at court and he wasn't looking forward to meeting this princess. She was probably spoiled beyond repair with a fake smile that hid a deceitful heart.

After watching the bartender settle a dispute between two customers, Alex decided it was time to handle his father's affairs so he would be free to deal with his own. Maybe he was moving too fast, but he wanted to get this over with so he could find the girl from the woods. After all, he knew where she lived and it wouldn't hurt to see her again before he left for the castle.

"Simo, ask the bartender if he knows where we can find her," he ordered.

Simo rose from the chair to do his bidding. He returned a few minutes later with the information. "I have the directions, my lord," he said, sitting back down at the table.

"James, see if there is a decent inn nearby. We will get rooms and seek her out in the morning," he said.

"Are you alright, sire?" Simo asked when James left. "You seem distracted today. Are still thinking about your father's decision to choose your bride?"

"I'm fine," Alex answered.

"Good. Besides, it has been decided. Trust in your father, he will not disappoint you," Simo said.

He trusted his father, but he still thought any decision concerning his life should be made by him and him alone.

Mirage sat back with her arms stretched behind her holding her up. Her head lay on her left shoulder. She wanted to cry. She wanted to yell. Kalina always said, "The world is a terrible place if you get to know it." Well, she wanted to judge for herself. How could something she found so alive and so beautiful be so bad?

She sat there for hours, staring at the ocean. She loved the way it sparkled. The air smelled like salt and it was wet when the wind blew. The sun was hot on her shoulders. She shifted her weight and found her neck was sore. She must have been here longer than she thought. She was in trouble, anyway. What was the worst that could happen? She stood slowly, deciding it was time to face the gauntlet, and climbed down.

When she reached the farmhouse she saw Kalina looking out through the kitchen window. She rode slowly through the yard to the stables. When she got there, Kalina was standing at the door.

"Get down from that horse right now," she said with her arms crossed. Mirage climbed down and put Midnight back in his stall. She walked right past her aunt, determined to ignore her.

"I have come to tell you that you have been chosen to serve the crown. You will be lady-in-waiting to the new princess. This is a wonderful opportunity and look how you behave," Kalina said.

Mirage stopped in her tracks and spun around. "What if I don't want to be a servant?" she asked.

"I'm sorry. It has already been decided. Your escort will arrive any day now to take us to the castle," Kalina explained. She hated deceiving Mirage this way.

"Why do *you* get to decide what I am to become? I don't want that life you had to give up to take care of me. I'm sorry that happened to you, but I'm not your second chance at happiness. I'm eighteen now. You can be free of me—you don't have to pretend anymore."

She took two steps backward, her chest heaving as she tried to catch her breath. Tears were rolling down her cheeks. She couldn't believe she just said all that.

"Pretend what?" Kalina said softly. Mirage could tell she had hurt her feelings, but she had said too much already. Now was the time to speak before she was cast away to some bigger stone jail.

"Pretend—pretend that you—that you love—" Mirage said in between sobs. She was a terrible mess when she cried. Out of nowhere, the clear sunny turned black and the rain poured down from the sky. She and Kalina raced to the house. She got inside and ran up the stairs, her nerves washed away by the rain. She stretched out across the bed, and moments later she was asleep.

She dreamed she was on her horse in the forest. It was dark and airy. A thin fog moved through the trees, which were packed in close. Then a grey shadow started to approach her. Her horse moved toward it and she pulled the reigns tightly to stop, but Midnight kept walking forward. As the shadow grew closer she recognized the image to be a man on a horse, then it was *the man* on the grey horse. He rode slowly toward her. And then they weren't in the forest anymore. They were in her room, and he was walking her to her bed. They sat down in the middle with their legs crossed, facing each other.

"May I have the honor of knowing your name?" he said. His voice was warm and soothing. His eyes were deep and brown and they flashed with light as his mouth slowly moved to smile at her. He reached out to touch her face. His hand rose ever so slowly. It was inches away when she closed her eyes and bent her head to meet it. Then she woke up.

She looked around the room. It was dark outside. She had never closed the window. The candles were blown out. She sat up, feeling disorientated. She stood from the bed and relit the candles and went to the window seat. She had never had a dream about a man before. Right now, her stomach was in knots and she couldn't seem to collect her thoughts or think about anything but him. She peered out at the mountains. She would probably never see him again anywhere.

After a while she laid down, bored with her own company. She fell asleep again on the seat under the window. Moments later she was awakened by the creaking of her door. Matilda opened it, bearing a tray of food. She got up and cleared off her table so she could set it there.

"Is the prisoner hungry?" the old lady asked, placing the tray on the edge of the bed.

"Thank you," she said.

"What have you been doing up here all day by yourself?" Matilda asked.

"Nothing, just thinking," she answered quietly.

"Was it thinking or dreaming?" Matilda asked.

"Auntie Lina didn't even tell me I was a candidate to serve the crown. Why does she feel my life belongs to her? I am eighteen now," she said.

"She is only trying to give you the best, my child. Don't be angry with her. Think of the balls, the tournaments. Kalina knows how bored you are here. Living in the castle will be like a new adventure every day," Matilda said.

Mirage gave her a grunt, tore a piece of bread in half, and handed it to her grandma. She had not thought about it that way. Her grandmother was her best friend now, and she was easy to talk to. Her eyes were always so kind and her long silver hair gave her an air of wisdom. She was always able to cheer her up when she was upset about something, just like she was doing now.

"But I won't be able to enjoy the balls or the tournaments. I'll be holding a tray of fruit or retrieving a shawl. I want my life to have some purpose. The only time I feel content is when I'm outside, in the forest. What will happen if I'm cooped up in a castle all day? Surely I'll lose my mind," she said, laying her head on her grandmother's shoulder.

"Everything will be fine, you'll see," Matilda said, trying to reassure her. She thought she was old enough now to be told the truth, but Kalina insisted they follow the king's commands by keeping her identity a secret until she was safe in the castle. Matilda sighed and wrapped her arms around her.

After they had shared the whole pitcher of wine, she kissed her goodnight and left the room, pulling the door closed behind her.

Theslian Border

Benjamin watched as Marsalis's soldiers descended from the hills in the distance. It looked to be about five hundred men or so. He wondered why Marsalis insisted on sending his men to slaughter. He had two thousands soldiers at his back. They always saw them coming and could easily prepare for the skirmish. Then he noticed about two hundred more men descending from the other side of the hill. Benjamin got down from his horse and went into his tent and set up a strategy for defeating the soldiers as quickly as possible. He had matters to attend to at the fortress. He decided he wasn't going to keep risking the lives of his men just because this king refused to give up these vain attempts to reclaim lands that he didn't need.

Marsalis's army reached them as the sun went down. Benjamin and his soldiers had spread tar over the ground. When the handful of soldiers crossed the oiled area, Benjamin gave the order and five flaming arrows were shot. The ground blazed with fire. The air smelled like fuel, charred meat, and smoke. The soldiers screamed and ran in all directions wrapped in orange, angry halos of rage. Benjamin's men easily dispatched the others. They killed the soldiers that had escaped the flames, but kept one alive.

"You will take a message back to your king," Benjamin said. "Tell him that I tire of his lack of effort. Tell him that perhaps he should give up and allow our countries to live in peace. I admit that the land does legally belong to him, so perhaps we could parley. Theslia is willing to pay an annual fee to him in order to end this war. His lands are very large. He has no need for Theslia and as long as I live he will not touch her. Now go."

They took the soldier's weapons and gave him food and supplies so he could make the journey back. Benjamin wanted Marsalis to know that he was in control of his country and that he wasn't afraid of him.

He dismounted from his horse and went back into his tent.

"Evard, inform my personal guards that I am ready for the journey back to the castle," he said rolling up his maps and collecting his strategic books. Evard bowed and turned to leave to deliver the king's message.

CHAPTER 8

The Give and Take

Gativa, Theslia

The next morning Mirage woke up refreshed. She walked through the house, lighting the candles with the tip of her finger.

"Stop it, child," Kalina said from the bottom of the stairs.

"Pay her no mind," Matilda piped in from behind her.

"Grandma Tilda, may I feed the chickens for you this morning?" she asked, standing in her grandmother's doorway.

"No," Kalina answered. "You have History, Diplomacy, and Etiquette lessons this morning."

"Why can't I feed them first?" Mirage asked, coming down the stairs.

"Because I am in no mood to scour the forest looking for you," Kalina answered. "Now have your breakfast so we can get started."

Suddenly there was a tap on the door. "Mirage, answer the door, please, my hands are filled." Mirage pushed back from the table, upset about never being able to enjoy even the simplest pleasures of her own life. She opened the door and was shocked by the face that stared back at her.

Alex looked down at her just as dazed, but his face slowly grew a very pleased smile. Simo looked at the two, wondering what was going on until he realized this was the girl they had met yesterday in the forest.

"We're looking for Lady Kalina," James said finally. Mirage stood glued to the spot, not hearing a word he said.

"Mirage, who is at the door?" Kalina asked.

"It's…it's the stranger. The strangers I met in the woods yesterday," she answered, never taking her eyes from the man who gazed at her with the darkest brown eyes she'd ever seen.

Kalina came to the door and slid Mirage out of the way. "Who are you? What do you want? Why have you come here?" she asked.

"We are looking for Lady Kalina. We have this message from the king," Alexander said, bowing slightly, handing her the parchment. Kalina apologized as she asked the men to come in while taking the parchment from his hands.

"Mirage, take your breakfast and go upstairs," Kalina said as she broke the seal on the king's message.

"Why?" she asked.

"Just do as you're told," Kalina said without looking up from the note.

She walked to the top of the stairs and sat down so she could listen to what they were saying. Matilda walked by and touched Mirage's ear then snapped her fingers and suddenly Mirage could hear the conversation as if she were seated in the chair beside them.

"Prince Alexander," Kalina said, bowing to the young man she had been so rude to moments before. "I can't believe the king sent you to escort us to the castle. We are honored to have you in our home," she lied. The king had explained in his message that Alexander didn't know who Mirage was and he wanted them to use this journey to get to know each other.

Alexander was nervous about being around this girl, but at the same time he was excited. It would take weeks to reach the United Rose Fortress and he would have all that time with her. His father must not have known how beautiful this girl was.

From the top of the stairs, Mirage listened. She didn't know he would be her escort, or that he was the Prince of Theslia and now unavailable to her. She couldn't wait for her journey to begin though. She thought she would never see the world outside of Gativa, and here she was about to journey to the castle. She got up and ran to her grandmother's room.

Matilda was busy placing candles around the circle she had drawn in the middle of her floor. Mirage started to light them while she explained what she had learned.

"We are leaving on the morrow, but, Grandma Tilda, I don't want to be anyone's servant. Am I strange for feeling this way?" she asked.

"No, but fear not, life at the castle can be very rewarding. Try not to worry about it so much. Take the opportunities that come to you. Now is your chance to escape to the barn," Matilda said. She had never agreed with Kalina's plan to isolate the child from the world. Mirage wasn't able to enjoy her childhood as she should being so closely guarded, so Matilda took it upon herself to help her experience life whenever she could.

"I'll stay and help you call the corners," she said.

"Fine, but we should probably close the door," Matilda said.

"I don't think we will journey as far as the mountains, but I know we will have to cross the great river. We might even see the Great Oak Tree Grandma Tilda told me about. We'll be able to visit lots of different villages and people. Auntie Lina told me I am to be Lady-In-Waiting to the new queen. I don't know if I want to be a servant for the rest of my life, but it's got to be more exciting than living here. I am a little nervous about life at court, but I'm excited at the same time. There will be tournaments, balls, and ceremonies. Are you excited, Midnight?" she asked, brushing his hair until it shone.

Alexander stood in the doorway of the stable and listened to her one-sided conversation. He thought he was the only one who spoke to his horse like that. She was absolutely gorgeous and even though he knew he should not, he wanted to know her.

"Well, boy, I have to get back before Auntie Lina comes looking for me. I'll see you later," she said, putting the blockade back up behind her. She turned and jumped at the sight of Prince Alexander standing in the doorway.

"I'm sorry. I didn't mean to startle you. I brought JeNi an apple, but I didn't want to intrude. What a massive horse, for such a tiny girl," he said as he walked to the silver horse across the stall from the black stallion she was talking to. He stroked JeNi's head as she ate the apple from his palm.

"I am of average size for a *lady* my age. Perhaps I'm normal and you're the one who's too tall. Judge me not by my size, Your Majesty. That would be a mistake. You must think me foolish, talking to an animal like that," she said as she turned to leave.

"On the contrary, my horse is my best friend and confidant. She also knows how to keep a secret, and she's the fastest horse in all Theslia. Isn't that right, girl?" Alex said, nodding his head.

"This is the first time you have journeyed to Gativa, is it not?" Mirage asked.

"Yes. This city borders the ocean. I will see it before we leave," he answered when she stopped in the doorway.

"Well, then, I would not say all Theslia, if I were you. I should get back. You should come in as well. Auntie Lina doesn't like when you're late for dinner," she said.

At dinner, Mirage ate quietly. She tried not to look at Alex because when she did she ended up staring like an idiot, but she couldn't help it. He was so perfect, his manners, his posture…his eyes. It was like Kalina had been his strict instructor all these years.

Alex tried to concentrate on his dinner. He didn't want to look like a lovestruck fool by drooling over her. She wore a light blue gown, and her hair was down over her shoulders. The light from the fireplace behind her made her look like a portrait come to life. If only he could be alone with her. Simo, James, and Kalina were talking about something that held little interest to him. And just when he had built up the courage to ask her to accompany him for a ride after dinner, the older woman called her up to her room.

Matilda had not taken her meal with them. She had claimed she had things to tend to before they left tomorrow on their journey. Mirage excused herself with a slight bow and went upstairs to see why Matilda had called her.

"Yes, Grandma Tilda," she said as she entered the room. "Are you alright?"

Mirage knew Matilda was old but she had never looked elderly until this night. She looked weak. There was a spark missing from her eyes. She seemed distracted somehow.

"I'm fine, just a little tired I guess," Matilda answered. "Are you enjoying having company to visit with?"

"I would be if I didn't feel like such a fool every time I opened my mouth. What is it about this man that has me all tongue-tied?" She asked falling backwards on the bed.

"Come here, child, I have something for you. Take this book with you on your journey. You may need it if you run into any trouble," Matilda said.

"You're not coming with us?" Mirage asked, holding her grandmother's thick black book. There were no words on the cover, only two large gold bands wrapped around the seam and linked together at a buckle in the middle. In the center was an impression of a small star with five circles around it.

"No, my child," she said as she sat down in her chair before the fireplace. "My old bones could not handle such a journey. Come, sit before me."

Mirage placed the book on the stand and sat down on the floor before Matilda and laid her head in her lap. "I don't know what I'll do without you," she said.

"Give me your hand," she said. Mirage held her right hand out. "*Lacigam emalf etaerc eht sserecros rats dna tsac a kcolb, yam siht dercas yek reven eb dekcolnu.*" A flame ignited in the palm of Mirage's hand.

"Ouch!" she exclaimed, trying to instinctively close it, but Matilda held it open. When the flame burned out, a four-pointed star was left imprinted in her palm.

"What is it?" she asked, tracing the star with her finger.

"It will protect your powers, my child. Remember that," she said.

"And the words you spoke?" she asked, turning her back to Matilda when she picked up the brush.

"The words are the original tongue of our people. The magic is stronger when you use the ancient tongue," she said.

"Pheolatian people?"

"No, Veagan people," Matilda said.

"I only know a few spells that require the power the ancient tongue offers. The spells are in my book along with the translations."

"I understood the words. You said, 'Magical flame create the sorceress star and cast a block. May this sacred key never be unlocked." The words sounded very strange, but I understood them."

"You must change your mind and come with us; there are so many things I don't know. Who will teach me? What will I do?" Mirage pleaded.

"You understand a language that has not been spoken for nearly two hundred years after hearing it spoken once. You don't need to be taught. You must remember to always be strong. Your powers come from within. Look to them when you have any doubts, they will not fail you. This is not only a book of spells. It is a journal, a personal diary passed from person to person, of their own magical experiences. It will help you understand your powers and how to use them fully. There are empty pages in the back. After you've read over the entire book, you will be able to add new things that you discover, and I think that with powers like yours there will be much more to add. When you become one with the magic, your thoughts will be all you need to control your powers," the old woman explained. "And you'll be fine without me. Use this journey to get to know that young man you're so fond of, and be patient with your aunt. She loves you."

"Sometimes I don't think so. And I can't get to know him. He is to be wed when we reach the castle," Mirage said.

"Oh, I almost forgot," Matilda said, biting her tongue. When she finished braiding Mirage's hair, she took a gold necklace from around her neck. It had a charm at the end of it that was similar to the impression on the book. She placed it around Mirage's neck.

"It's beautiful. Why haven't I seen this before?" Mirage asked, admiring the jewelry.

"It is not for decoration that is why. That is the symbol of our kind. The star stands for the individual light in every Pheolatian person. These four circles stand for the four winds from which we draw our internal energy, and this band that stands straight up and down symbolizes the essence of life. Without it there would be nothing." She held Mirage's hand open and touched the different points on the star. "The individual light, the winds, the essence of life, and purity of heart," she said, placing her hand over her heart, "are what makes you magical. The necklace is also the key to open your book. It is to be worn on the inside of your gown always. Do you understand me? Always, Mirage. People have been killed," Matilda explained.

"Killed…why?" Mirage asked.

"People destroy what they do not understand," Matilda said. "Now off to bed. You have a long day ahead of you tomorrow."

"I will rise early to help you call the corners before we leave," she said, getting up from the floor. "I love you, Grandma Tilda, I'll visit you someday."

"When you leave this village never look back. There is a whole world out there for you to explore," Matilda said as she got up slowly from the chair and walked over to the bed.

"But I'll miss you too much, and you will be all alone," Mirage said, sitting near her on the bed.

"No, I'll be with you, right here," she said, touching Mirage's chest. "Now give me a hug and stop all that silly crying. People come in and out of our lives all the time. Remember the balance, the give and take, and don't worry so much. Kalina is starting to be a bad influence."

"Good night, then, I'll see you in the morning," Mirage said, trying to smile as she left the room, clutching the book to her chest.

She took the book to her room and opened it to the first page. The first letter on the page was written in intricate calligraphy. It read *Rules and Consequences of Magic*, written by Mestopholes Delong.

Mirage read the three rules and the consequences, then she closed the book and placed it on the top of the things she had packed for her journey to the castle.

She lay down across the bed, but she wasn't tired. She got up and went to her window seat and stared out at the mountains. She was glad she was leaving, but she would definitely miss Gativa. She leaned forward on the window sill and braced herself up on her elbows. She watched the riders in the distance get closer and closer until she recognized the beautiful silver horse. The moonlight made the horse's white hair glow. Alexander pulled his reigns and looked back over his shoulders to taunt James and Simo about losing another race to him. Mirage wished she could ride her horse at night. Maybe now she would be able to. She got up and walked back to the bed and crawled under the covers. She swept her hand through the air, making a fist, and all the candles in her room blew out. She closed her eyes and asked the Great Creator to bless their journey.

The next morning Mirage danced from one corner of the room to the next. Excitement and the overwhelming urge to leave Gativa seemed to fuel her. After washing up, brushing, and braiding her hair, she picked up the light blue gown she had worn the night before and laid it on her bed. She chose a dark green feather from her bag and placed it on the dress, turning it instantly to a dark forest green. She pulled at the cuff of the long thin sleeve until it was nice and wide. She grabbed the middle of the outer cuff until the sleeve came to a chevron point. For decoration, she chose a black feather. She touched the collar and made two stripes to circle the cuffs of the sleeves. She tapped the middle of the dress twice with the feather then rubbed the black spot until it became a long smooth, silky sash. Finally, she held the dress up and looked it over. Her favorite part of the gown was the silk black sash that covered her waist and tied into a large bow in the back. She pulled the dress on and went to Matilda's room to ask her help with her bow.

She knocked quietly then pushed the door open. "Grandma Tilda," she whispered. "We have time to call the corners before I leave, but first I need your help with my bow. Do you like this dress?" She turned when she got no answer and noticed her grandmother was still asleep. She tiptoed to the trunk in the far corner of her room and started to set the candles up for the morning ritual.

Grandma Tilda must be really tired. She's usually the first one up in the morning. I'll give her a little more time. She set a red candle up around the circle, to favor the eastern wind.

Alex rose from a restless sleep. He had dreamed they had reached the United Rose. As he opened the door to the great hall, the room erupted with applause. The hall was decorated for a wedding and near his father on the throne stood a holy man and a veiled bride. But it was just a dream; at least he prayed it was just a dream. He wanted to be able to at least get to know this woman before they were made to marry.

He got up from the bed and got dressed then went outside to feed, JeNi. He trusted her care with few people. She had been a gift from his father, and the key to his freedom when he wanted to be away from the courtiers and tutors that plagued his days. Sometimes he wanted to run away to a place where no one knew who he was.

After lighting all the candles, Mirage lit the sweet grass braid that would be offered to the winds. She put it on the bookstand where Matilda usually kept her book of spells. Then Mirage turned to wake her. When Mirage stepped closer to the bed she noticed how ashen and pale Matilda's face looked. She touched her forehead then withdrew her hand quickly as if she had been burned. She felt so cold. When she finally realized what had happened, she crumpled to the floor and burst into tears.

Kalina had just got her dress on when she heard Mirage crying. She ran to her room, but found it empty. She left and opened Matilda's door. The room glowed with light and a sweet smell filled the air, but the picture that she stepped into made her heart sink. Her mother looked dead in her bed and Mirage was on her knees with her head on the floor, crying. Kalina fell beside her and gathered her up into her arms. She hugged her close and told her everything would be okay.

The soldiers had been loading the cart for the journey when they heard the commotion and came quickly up the stairs. Kalina heard their hurried footsteps. She closed her eyes and waved her hand in a circular motion; instantly a breeze followed the motion and the candles disappeared. James and Simo came to the door with their swords drawn. After seeing what had happened they put them away.

"We'll send to the village for the steward," Simo said.

"That won't be necessary," Kalina said, wiping tears away. "Will you give us a minute?"

"What about the body?" Simo asked.

"Please…please leave us," she said. Mirage was still crying and rocking back and forth in her arms. The soldiers went back down stairs to inform the prince of the situation.

"Mirage….Mirage," she said quietly, lifting her head up so she could see her eyes. "This is life. She was old. She lived a wonderful life. We will honor her memory by remembering her life, not by being devastated by her death."

"She knew this…was going to…happen. She gave me…her spells last night. She could have warned…me—or at least let me say good bye," Mirage whispered in a defeated voice around her sobs as the tears continued to roll freely down her cheeks.

"Will you help me send her to our ancestors?" Kalina asked.

Mirage nodded and stood, sniffling, wiping her face. They conjured a black candle and a white one, lit them, and set them down on the floor. They cut a lock of Matilda's hair and placed it in a bowl of oil, then added three drops of water. Then they got on their knees and chanted the words: "Away from this world; we send her into the wind; as this life ends, let another begin," over and over again. Twinkling white lights surrounded Matilda's body and the room filled with thick white fog. When the fog dissipated only a few twinkling lights remained.

James found Alex in the stable brushing his horse. He looked very menacing dressed in all black. He wore no cloak, but it was warmer in Gativa than it was in the capital city. He planned to ride to the ocean before they left for home. Maybe Mirage would want to come with him. He could just picture her aboard that enormous horse of hers, her hair blowing in the breeze, her bright smile lighting up her face.

"Sire, the old woman is dead. I don't think the young lady will want to go to the ocean. She is very upset," Simo explained.

Alex thought for a minute and decided he would ask her anyway to take her mind away from her pain. If she said no, then at least he had tried.

Kalina pulled Mirage to her feet. "There are some things I need to explain to you about living in the castle. There will always be people around—courtiers, servants, soldiers—so that means no magic, no spells, and no conjuring. No one can know that we are Pheolatian. They would have us arrested and put to death. Do you understand me?" she asked.

Mirage looked into her golden green eyes as new tears formed in the corners of hers.

"So…Grandma Tilda…really is….dead," she said, then ran from the room. Kalina did not follow her; she'd give her some time to be alone. She looked around the room and thought about her mother, then walked to the door and closed it behind her. She headed down the stairs, intent on going about the day as they had planned. Matilda would have wanted it that way.

The men were seated at the table. Simo and James looked at each other when Kalina started cooking.

"Lady Kalina," Alexander said. "I'm sorry for your loss. If there is anything we can do, please let me know."

"You need not worry, we will proceed as planned. Mirage is upset, but she is strong. She will be alright. She was very close to my mother," she explained.

"Then do I have your permission to send for the steward?" James asked.

"That won't be necessary," she said.

"But we just can't leave the body here," Simo said. He was shocked by her composure. Her mother had just died and she went on with her chores as if nothing had happened.

"I've already sent the stable hand for the steward. He probably won't be able to come until after we have left," she said after thinking of a quick explanation. "Mirage, come down now. Breakfast," she called, turning and placing the platters on the table. She fed the men and left for a moment, returning with a large book. "Mirage. Now!" she called.

Mirage came down the stairs slowly and sat at the table before her food.

"Now, where were we?" Kalina asked, opening the large book to the spot she had marked. "Here we are. *Lethargic*."

"Unnaturally drowsy; sluggish, dull," Mirage whispered.

"Lethe—" Kalina started.

"Do we have to do vocabulary right now? Today?" Mirage asked, staring down at her plate of untouched food.

"Why wouldn't we?" Kalina asked.

"Why? Because Grandma's dead!" she screamed and ran from the house.

She ran across the field and up the hill into the forest. She ran until her chest burned and her legs felt like lead. She sat on the ground and breathed deeply, trying to catch her breath. She pulled the necklace out and held it tightly in her palm. She felt so alone. The clouds drew in overhead and casted a dark shadow over the land. Matilda had said that Kalina loved her, but she only loved the fact that she had molded a perfect puppet to follow in her footsteps. She would not be a servant for the rest of her life. Her life would have some purpose.

"Are you alright?" a deep voice asked from behind her. She turned as Midnight brushed his nose against her shoulder. She reached up and stroked it. For a moment, she thought the horse had spoken. Alexander dismounted from his horse and sat next to her on the ground.

Mirage put the necklace back on the inside of her gown and said, "I'll be fine, I guess." She looked down at her hands, then nervously back at him. She couldn't believe he would be concerned about her.

"Your aunt reminds me of my father," he said.

"It's like that every day. If it weren't for Grandma Tilda, I'd probably have lost my mind by now. Being with her was always like an adventure; you'd never know what she'd do next," she laughed, remembering the fun they would have playing tricks on Kalina.

"The only time I ever have to myself is when I'm riding my horse, but then I usually have two guards trailing close behind," he said, looking over his shoulder. James was standing against a tree while his horse grazed. "At least you get to be alone."

"*Alone.* If it weren't for those stupid vocabulary lessons, I wouldn't know the meaning of the word. She never lets me out of her sight for more than a moment, but I'm getting better at sneaking away. Hopefully, I'll have a little privacy when we reach the castle," she said.

"Don't except too much privacy living in the castle. What have they told you about why you are going to live there?" he asked curiously.

"I was only told that it's going to be my new home. I'll be lady-in-waiting to the princess. Auntie Lina used to live there in the same position before my parents died, and then she had to leave to care for me. Are there lots of girls living in the castle?" she asked.

"Umm, I didn't notice this when I sat," Alexander said picking the violet flower that swayed between them and handed it to Mirage. She smiled as she took it from his hand. Slowly the clouds moved away, letting the light through. Alexander looked up at the sky.

"For a moment, I thought it was going to rain. Now the sky is completely clear," he said, looking down on her. The sun lit up her face and her golden eyes sparkled as she looked up to meet his gaze.

"Sire," James interrupted, "we should get started if you still wish to see the ocean before we leave."

"Thank you, James," he said, getting up from the ground. "Will you accompany me? It will take your mind off your troubles for a while, and we will finally know for sure who has the faster horse," he said, offering her his hand.

She took it and pulled herself up from the ground. She looked up at his face to see his eyes. From this distance she realized how much taller he was than her. The top of her head came to his shoulder.

"I already know who has the faster horse." They traveled through the village and stopped at the docks. "No, follow me," Mirage said, leading them to her secret place past the homes on the out skirts of the town down the shoreline of the ocean to the secluded inlet. The sun set high in the sky and it made the ocean sparkle like a jewel.

"Well, what do you think? It's beautiful, isn't it?" Mirage said.

"Not as beautiful as you," he said.

Mirage blushed, lowering her head. "I'll race you to those rocks. Ready. Take your mark. Go!" she said, ignoring his remark, kicked Midnight's flanks and took off like a shot. Alex followed behind her, not really concerned about the race. When they reached the large rocks, she jumped down and climbed up one of them, declaring herself the winner. Alex dismounted and followed her.

"Only because you cheated," he said.

"Don't pout because your horse wasn't able to catch us," she giggled. "Just take your defeat like a man." She hopped down and walked to the shore. "It will probably be a while before I see this again."

"The castle is not the dungeon. Most of the servants just ask the chatelaine when they want to leave to visit their families or go other places. Maybe someday you could come back," he said.

"What will I be coming back to?" She asked quietly.

"Your Majesty, we must get back. It is time for us to get started for home," James said, looking up at the sky. He didn't like the look of the clouds that had suddenly moved in over them.

Mirage walked to her horse and climbed aboard. Alexander took JeNi's reigns and walked to the shore. He looked at the ocean and wished he had a choice in the path his life would take and followed Mirage back through the village.

CHAPTER 9

A Wet Spark

The group traveled quietly through the woods that led to the northern road. Kalina watched Mirage on her horse. She was a beautiful sight. Tess would be pleased with her. She had turned out to be a lovely woman, and she would make a great queen, but she grabbed at every leaf and watched every bird until it disappeared. Maybe she'd been wrong about keeping her so isolated.

She had stopped letting her play alone when she was about seven. Mirage had not come in for lunch when she had called. She had gone outside and the child was nowhere to be found. She had followed her obvious path through the woods and found her near a shallow stream. Two wood nymphs held her hand. Hopping, skipping, and laughing they lead her toward the water. She caught up to them just before the child placed her feet in the water and snatched her away.

"But Auntie Lina, I want to play in the water," she said.

Kalina scooped her from the ground and balanced her on her hips. "I will tell the queen about this," Kalina said backing away as the two nymphs grew to four and then six. She turned to leave and there were two more standing behind her.

"We only wanted to visit with the child. It was her idea to play in the water," a little grey nymph with what looked like green moss for hair said.

"She is only a child. She doesn't understand the rules, as you well know. If she had touched that water, you would have charged her, knowing she couldn't pay. Does the queen know you're here? I have ways of communicating with her," she lied. "She will know it was you if something happens to this child." Kalina spoke quickly as she slowly moved away from them.

Suddenly they were upon her. They snatched Mirage and started pulling her into the depths of the forest. She was crying and reaching for Kalina. That was the last thing she remembered after being blinded by a bright white light. She woke up later in the yard on the edge of the forest next to the farmhouse. Mirage was asleep next to her.

The nymphs were gone, but she knew that they would try again. She remembered how scared she had been. Since then she had never let Mirage enter the forest alone.

Alex also watched Mirage. He admired her free spirit. She seemed to become a part of her surroundings. But then that familiar feeling came back. He was sure he had never met her before, but there was something in her face, something in her eyes that he'd seen before. He wondered what it would be like to see her every day. He wouldn't mind living at the castle if she was going to be there.

He couldn't believe his father would deceive him this way. If they knew he had to marry this woman since he was five years old, then he should have been able to meet with her from time to time.

Mirage found the forest enchanting. For some reason, she felt it was where she was supposed to be. It was so alive with activity. She wanted to see what everything was doing. But despite her need to be away from Gativa, a part of her hated the fact that she was riding into a future of servitude. She was finally putting the final pieces of her life together. She always wondered why she was made to sit up straight and take walking lessons with a book on the top of her head.

None of the other girls in their village ever talked about politics or cared anything about their etiquette. Their only concerns were finding husbands and having babies, and most of their fathers had them married by the time they were sixteen. Lidia had been promised to the man she married since her naming ceremony. She turned in the saddle and looked at Kalina, then turned back around again.

"All this education for a servant. It makes no sense," she mumbled to herself. The group came to a shallow stream and took the opportunity to rest the horses and have lunch.

"Do you feel better now?" Kalina asked, sitting down next to Mirage on the ground.

"A little, I guess," she replied. "I miss her so much."

"It will get better with time," Kalina assured her.

"Don't you miss her?" Mirage asked.

"Of course. She was my mother," she said. "I've just been taught that death is not something you can change. It comes to us all."

"Yes, but Grandma Tilda was special to me. I just can't let her go so easily," Mirage said.

"You never let her go. She'll always be here with you. Now put a smile on that pretty face," Kalina said.

"Do you think there are tadpoles in that stream?" Mirage asked suddenly.

"Why don't you go see?" Kalina said.

"Prince Alexander, would you like to go tadpole hunting with me?" she asked from the other side of his horse's saddle. He had been tightening the straps under JeNi's belly.

"Sure, but what is tadpole hunting?" he asked as she grabbed his hand and dragged him toward the stream.

"They are like children," James said, shaking his head.

"Very important children," Kalina mumbled under her breath. James waved Simo to follow the couple as they disappeared through the bush.

"Here, this is a tadpole," Mirage said, moving slowly toward Alexander with the wiggling creature cupped in her palm. "Hurry, before it gets away."

He took her hands and looked the creature over. "So, this is a tadpole. It's the strangest little fish I've ever seen," he said as she placed it back in the stream.

"Prince Alexander, it's a baby frog," she said, giggling. "They really have been lacking in your education concerning our country's forest creatures."

"My father probably didn't think I would need to know about frogs to rule the country," he said.

"Prince Alexander, what is the princess like?" she asked.

"Actually, I don't know. I've never met her," he answered. "And you can call me Alex."

"Are you sure, even after we reach the castle?" she asked.

"Sure, why not? My father might not like it, but it will serve him right for lying to me," he said.

Shocked by the suggestion, she turned and suddenly tripped over some stones. She tried to grab onto his arm for support, but ended up pulling him down with her. They laughed as he helped her to her feet. Alex looked at her and at the same time she lifted her head and their eyes met. He felt a strange wave wash over him. It started at his feet and rushed through the rest of his body. Mirage blushed and looked away as she saw Simo approaching them.

"Come, Your Majesty, we must move on," Simo said.

"Yes, but I think we should get dried off first," Alexander said. "My lady, I apologize for what I said earlier. I wouldn't want you to get in trouble at the castle. If someone else is around, call me Prince Alex." Mirage looked down at her hands and nodded.

After they had changed, they rode on, sometimes on the road and sometimes through the forest, "Mirage, look," Alexander said, pointing at a deer eating grass along the road. This action put a huge smile on her face.

"I want to touch it," she said pulling the horse to a stop and swinging her leg over the side. Alexander was pleased by that smile, knowing he was the cause of it.

"It will only run away," he said.

"It will not," she said softly, walking slowly toward the animal with her hand out in front of her. Everyone watched as the deer lifted its head. Mirage continued slowly toward it. Alexander drew in a shocked breath when the animal started toward her. Mirage stopped and let it smell her hand. The fawn lowered its head as Mirage gently stroked it as if it were a pet instead of a wild animal she'd never met before. Kalina looked at the soldiers nervously.

"Mirage, let's go now," she said. She left the animal and climbed back on her horse and continued down the road.

In a flash of light the deer was gone. Stencil sat down on the grass as the group disappeared down the road. There would come a time when she would be alone. The forest called to her just as it called to the rest of them; only she was free to come and go as she pleased and they were trapped by it. The queen should have never allowed her to live and he would prove to her just how dangerous a human with such powers could be.

That night Alex woke from his sleep after dreaming he had returned home to find the veiled bride waiting for him again. He got up from his cot and stepped outside of the tent. James was seated on the ground, playing a solitary game of dice. He walked to his horse, "Father wouldn't do that to me, right, baby?" he asked the horse who stared back quietly.

"Wouldn't it be wonderful if they could talk back?" a soft voice said from behind him.

"You should be asleep at this hour," he said.

"I've got too many thoughts in my head. They won't shut up and let me sleep. Have you seen the moon?" she asked, pointing at the sky. "It looks bigger out here, don't you think?"

"Are those the thoughts that keep you awake?" Alex asked, looking up at the sky then down at her.

"Not exactly. The closer we get, the more frightened I become. I know Auntie Lina did it, but I don't think it's the life I want—no offense to you or your father," she said.

"And I don't want to marry a stranger," Alex said, looking down at her. "But what can we do?" He turned back toward camp.

"We could run away," she said, grabbing his arm.

"Where would we go? My father would find us in a day," he said.

"I could make it so no one would ever find us," Mirage said.

"What do you mean?" he asked, looking puzzled. The weird look he gave her made her rethink telling him the truth.

"Never mind. It was silly, anyway," she said as she turned to walk back to the tents.

Alex caught her arm as she turned and pulled her to face him. He looked into her eyes and saw a spark of innocence. She looked down, trying to avoid his gaze and the way he was making her feel. He used his hand to lift her chin. The look in her eyes made him smile.

"Are you afraid of me?" he asked, pushing a stray strand of hair back from her face. He used his hand to caress her cheek. Mirage pulled free of his touch.

"No. Should I be?" she asked, looking down at her hands. She was a little afraid; she had never had these feelings before and she didn't know how to respond, or if she should at all. He stepped toward her and lifted his hand toward her face again. It was like the dream she'd had as his arm lifted slowly toward her. And like the dream she closed her eyes and leaned her head to meet his hand. He caressed her cheek softly, then took his other hand and held her face gently as he slowly moved closer to her.

It seemed like an eternity passed before their lips touched. Even the air seemed to slow down as it moved pass them. Mirage never imagined a man could be so gentle. His lips were soft and smooth and they moved with just the right amount of pressure. She took a deep breath and was filled with his heady scent. She felt a strange sensation that started in the pit of her stomach and spread through her body, down to the tip of her toes then back up to the top of her head. She moved her hands up the front of his chest, loving the feel of the firm wall of muscles that tightened and flexed in response to her touch.

Alex felt her hands moving up toward his chest and he waited for her to push him away. He was amazed by his body's reaction to that simple touch. When she pulled him toward her, he kissed her like he'd never be able to kiss anyone ever again. She was sweet and savory. Her hair smelled like wild flowers and sunlight. Her lips were so soft and she was so passionate. He took a deep breath and was swept away.

Mirage wrapped her arms around his neck and held on as he sent her spiraling into another world. His arms wrapped around her small waist and he lifted her slightly into the air.

It ended just as it began; the spinning began to slow and he set her feet back on the ground, but he couldn't bring himself to let go. He separated his lips from hers and looked deep into her eyes. He could honestly spend an eternity in her eyes. They sparkled like precious jewels as she smiled. He took deep breaths, filling his lungs with the cleansing air, trying to clear his head. Slowly Mirage's smile faded away.

Suddenly, she pulled away and backed up from him.

"My Creator, what have I done? I'm sorry, Your Majesty," she said and bowed as tears started to stream from her eyes. She turned and ran back through the trees.

"Mirage, wait—Damn!" he exclaimed, following her through the trees. Just then, four men in dark robes rode by on horses like the woods behind them were on fire. They kept looking over their shoulders as they disappeared. James was on his feet at the edge of the camp when Simo stepped out of the tent with his sword in his hand. Alexander caught up with Mirage, took her by the arm, and led her quickly back to their camp.

"What was that?" Mirage asked when they reached the campsite. Kalina stepped out of tent and pulled a shawl over her shoulders.

"What happened?" she asked, walking toward Mirage.

"I don't know, but we should move," Simo said.

"I agree," James replied. "Whomever they were running from will track them through here. We don't need that trouble."

"Get dressed. Start taking the tents down," James ordered.

"Your Majesty, we must move the camp from here. It is not safe," Simo informed Alexander.

"As you wish," Alexander said, walking Mirage to her tent.

When they reached it, he kissed her palm and said, "Until we meet again, my lady." Then he bowed and watched her slip through the tent opening.

CHAPTER 10

Truths Revealed

Castle Covax, Weeks Later

Marsalis sat at the head of his dining table on a pile of pillows, entertaining the new ambassador, when one of his servants entered the room. He bowed low and waited for Marsalis to wave him forward.

"My apologizes, Your Majesty, but one of the soldiers has returned from Theslia with an urgent message from their king," he whispered.

"Excuse me, Ambassador, there is an important matter that requires my attention," he said, getting up from the table. He followed the servant from the room. The boy walked by, intending to lead Marsalis to the soldier.

"This way, Your Highness," he said.

Marsalis punched the boy in his stomach, knocking him to the floor. He turned on his side, clutching his stomach, gasping for the breath that had been suddenly knocked from his lungs. The king stood over him with an angry look on his face and crossed his arms over his chest.

"When I say that I do not wish to be disturbed, that is exactly what I mean," he said sternly, then he stepped over the boy and marched down the hall to hear this message.

When he entered the hall, the soldier was seated at one of the tables. He immediately stood and bowed to the king. His face was blistered from the icy winds of the mountains. He had scratches and bruises on his arms. He moved slowly toward Marsalis with a slight limp.

"What message do you bring?" Marsalis asked, crossing his arms over his chest.

"King Benjamin says—" the soldier started.

"He is no king," Marsalis said bluntly. "A man is born a king. You cannot be elected to the office. To be royalty is a state that must be learned from birth," he explained as he paced back and forth. "Now speak." He listened to the message of how his men were so easily killed. After the soldier had spoken, Marsalis ordered that he be fed and bathed.

As he walked back to his guests he thought about Benjamin's words. An annual payment might be considered if the inhabitants weren't murdering, deceitful Veagans. Did they think they were of the same class as him that he would accept money from them? They underestimated him if they thought a few mountains would stop him from ruling over lands that were rightfully his. If he could not go over the mountains, he would go through them. He would burn the entire country to the ground and rebuild it as a treasure city. He would name it after his father and his image would be carved into every wall.

"Your Highness, may I speak with you?" Laven said, walking up the hall toward him, followed by a parade of the fanciest men he ever cared to see. Some of them could almost pass for women.

"Yes, Cousin, but be quick about it. I have important matters that I must attend to," he replied, continuing down the hall.

"That is exactly what I wished to speak to you about. Perhaps the time has come for me to take some of the pressure from your all but capable shoulders. Perhaps I could rule over one of the eastern provinces, reporting directly to you before any decision is made, of course," he said, looking up at Marsalis to see his reaction.

"I will think about it," Marsalis said, wondering where this was coming from.

"Thank you, sire. I was just thinking…we are family. We must be there for one another. How can I spend my days in leisure while you are burdened with the responsibilities of the entire kingdom? I just wanted you to know that I am here if you need me. I love you, cousin," Laven said. He grasped Marsalis' forearm, bowed, and walked away down the hall.

Marsalis stood staring after him as Shalyndria's words came back to him. *Those closest to you; that claim to love you, see you through green eyes and speak to you with a forked tongue.*

Aden, Theslia

"You're quiet this morning," Kalina said, watching Mirage as she gathered the plates from Kalina's bundle. She was usually singing and dancing when she woke up in the morning, twirling from corner to corner with a huge smile on her face. How she envied her. "Mother would not have wanted you to mope around like this."

Mirage had thought about Matilda when she first woke up. Usually, they would "call the corners" together, but she had only thought about that for a moment. Mostly she thought about Prince Alexander. He had kissed her last night and she had been foolish enough to kiss him back. Actually, she really couldn't help herself. She had never been kissed before and it had been so wonderful. She never knew such pleasure could be found in a man's lips, the warmth and security found by being held tightly in his arms. She was nervous about seeing him this morning. Now things would be so different.

"Come, Mirage. Prince Alexander will be awake by now," Kalina said. At the mention of his name she dropped all the dishes she had stacked up to carry outside.

"Mirage," Kalina said, dragging her name out.

"Well, if I could conjure a tray or something, that would not have happened," she snapped.

When the group set off again, Alex rode beside Mirage, but he noticed a change in her today. She wasn't her usual carefree self. When he tried talking to her earlier, she had blushed and turned away. Perhaps he had been wrong to kiss her, but she had been so beautiful bathed in the moonlight, those golden eyes of hers sparkling with white light, and so close that he could smell the fragrance of wild flowers in her hair. He just couldn't help himself.

"Are you angry with me?" he asked quietly.

"Yes—no. I don't know, but now is not the time to discuss it," she whispered as she looked over her shoulder.

"Why?" he asked, confused.

She ignored him and continued to ride forward as if she had not even heard the question.

He kicked his horse forward and blocked her path. "Tell me why you are angry with me," he said.

"Because you kissed me knowing you would be going home to marry another, I may be a simple farm girl to you, but I will not be made a fool of. I have feelings and I will not allow you to play with them for your own amusement," she said, guiding Midnight around him.

"What are you talking about? I was not trying to deceive you," he said, following her down the road.

"Shh," she said, looking at her aunt. Alex pulled his horse back to a slow walk and let Mirage ride away.

He would speak to her later, and she would listen.

Castle Covax, Lavitia

"Come, Lamar, you must not fear your master. I will not hurt you," Laven said as he sat down beside the boy. He put his hand on his leg and started gently rubbing his thigh. "You must be hot in all these clothes," he continued. He unbuttoned the boy's shirt and removed one of the sleeves from his shoulder gently rubbing his back.

"I want my mother," Lamar said as tears started to fall. Laven wiped them away.

"Your mother would be pleased if you brought back these five gold pieces, would she not?" he asked, holding the coins out to the child. Lamar nodded and wiped his nose on his sleeve. He reached out to grab the money Laven offered him, but he snatched them away at the last minute. "I will give you them to you, but first you must be my friend."

Suddenly the door was pushed open and Marsalis walked in. He was disgusted with the scene he walked in on. His cousin sat in the nude on the edge of his bed with what appeared to be a six-year-old boy. The child was crying and looked frightened out of his mind.

"Boy, return to your mother, quickly," Marsalis said, sitting down on of his cousin's couch as the child ran from the room. "I came to speak to you about your request, but how can I trust you with matters concerning my kingdom when you insist on engaging in these unspeakable acts?"

"Cousin, I'm sorry. Sometimes, I don't know what comes over me," he tried to explain, feeling embarrassed.

"For the Creator's sake, cover yourself. This palace is filled with beautiful women. Why do you prefer children, and male children at that?" Marsalis asked, confused. "This impurity that creeps through your veins must come from your father's side of the family."

"It will not happen again, my liege, I give you my word," Laven said, wrapping his robe around himself, fearing the look on Marsalis's face.

"It better not. I will not allow you to dishonor our family. If I even hear of such a thing again I will disassociate myself from you the best way I know how. Is that clear, Cousin?" Marsalis said, rising from the chair.

"Yes, Your Highness," Laven answered, bowing low.

Marsalis left the room. Laven walked into his sitting room and poured himself some wine. He paced back and forth then stopped as he passed the mirror. He stared at his reflection, remembering the first time his father had joined him in his bed. He must have been six or seven. He remembered how awkward and confused he had felt, and he remembered how safe he had felt when he had told his mother. She promised him it would never happen again. She, in turn, told his uncle. Hector had his father beheaded, but that wasn't what he had wanted. He had loved his father; he only wanted him to stop hurting him. Marsalis was there when his father was executed before the entire court, but he was too young to remember. Now if he couldn't get this madness out of his system Marsalis would kill him. He hated him just as he hated his father and he couldn't wait until Shalyndria's prophecy came to pass.

Aden, Theslia

Later, as the sun went down, the group came to a small clearing. Simo decided this would be a good place to stop for the night. It was back off the road and slightly uphill. Kalina noticed the distance between Mirage and the prince. She thought they had come together nicely when they had first met. Now there seemed to be some tension between them. Mirage had the tendency to avoid confrontations instead of working through them. Her moods were easy enough to read. She would get quiet and withdrawn, found wandering around the yard with her hands held behind her back, remaining in an aimless silence for days until she forgot what she was originally bothering her. They had no time for that now. After they had dinner, Kalina had a wonderful idea.

"Mirage, will you honor us with a song?" she asked.

"A song," Mirage said, caught off guard by the suggestion. "What should I sing?" she asked finally.

"Sing Mother's lullaby," she suggested.

Mirage got up and sat next to the fire they had built. She looked at Kalina, her brow furrowed in confusion, and sang the song her grandmother used to sing to her when she was a child. She imagined she was at home again, sitting at her feet as she brushed her hair. She could almost feel the brush running through her long strands and it made her smile, but she could also feel her eyes welling up with tears. Her grandmother would never brush her hair again. She closed her eyes to fight back the tears and sang her grandmother's lullaby with all her heart. The fire flickered and grew larger as her voice filled the clearing.

Alexander was awe struck. Her voice was so pure and sweet. It echoed through the trees and filled the air all around them. It made him think of his mother. He could remember her singing to him when he was a child. Actually, it was the only memory he had of her. He leaned back on his arm and sipped his wine. She looked at him and smiled; he couldn't help smiling back. He looked up and noticed the wood sprites had come to hear her sing as well, creating dots of light all along the tree limbs, casting a warm glow through the forest. Tonight he would speak with her, and he would make her understand that he would never hurt her.

She sneaked out of the tent, tiptoeing so she would not wake Kalina. She just wanted to be alone for a little while. She had to think of a plan. She ran to her horse and climbed aboard.

"Going somewhere?" Alex asked from behind her.

"Maybe," she said, grabbing the reigns and leading the horse away from him. He stepped in front of the horse's path pulling the reigns from her grasp.

"Get down," he said sternly.

"Don't give me orders. I don't have to listen to you, and in this forest, you're just like everybody else. Now, release my reigns." she said.

"Little one, these are my forests. Get down!" he said, pointing at the ground. She jumped down from the horse and walked toward him with her hands on her hips.

"Why did you kiss me? To see if I would allow it?" she asked, poking him in the stomach.

Alexander could not help but smile. She was a fiery little thing when she was angry. He was excited by her spirit and how open she was with her feelings. At court the women were all smiles; he never met one that ever disagreed with anything he said. And they would not dare argue with him. They all knew that a union with him would give them a seat on the throne, so he never believed their affections to be genuine. He did not have to guess when it came to Mirage; how she was feeling was usually there on her face.

"Am I amusing you? Answer the question," she said, crossing her hands over her chest.

"I kissed you because you fascinate me and because you're extremely beautiful, and I had no doubt that you would allow it," he said, caressing her cheek. Mirage pulled her head away and turned her back to him.

"I will not be your mistress, Prince Alexander," she said. She turned back and looked up at him.

"But I desire you more than any maid I have ever met. What if that is our only option?" he reasoned.

"It is not an option for me. I'm sure the castle is filled with lots of girls that would not mind such a position, but I am not willing to share with another," she explained, standing before him, crossing her arms over her chest.

"If only I'd met you weeks ago," he said, moving toward her.

"Weeks ago, you still would have been promised to another. Your father won't let you disobey him, and why would you want to? I'm sure he has chosen a beautiful bride for you," she said, holding back the urge to cry as one tear rolled down her cheek. She turned and wiped it away. She didn't want him to see her cry.

"She could never be as beautiful as you, little songbird," he said as he walked up behind her. "Look at me."

She looked down at her hands, then turned and glazed directly in his eyes. "Do you say these things in earnest, or is your flattery a weapon used to seduce me?" she asked.

"My lady, if I were to seduce you, there would be no question that I was doing it," he said arrogantly. "And I never lie. But I do have a question for you. Why did you return my kiss if you thought I had ill intentions?"

"Because…because it was the first time I had ever been kissed and I enjoyed it when it was happening. I was all caught up in the moment, but then I remembered that you have been promised to another," she said, looking down again when his smile made his eyes twinkle with light.

"I have promised nothing to anyone. If you liked kissing me? Prove it," he said, lifting her chin.

"No, I will not," she said, backing out of his grasp.

"Why not? Are you afraid?" he asked, pulling her toward him.

"I'm not afraid," she said grabbing the end of her braid and twisting the end nervously. "I have just been taught to value my virtue. Kissing a married man…"

"A betrothal is just as binding as the actual marriage itself." She stepped toward him and placed her hands on his shoulders. She pulled her body up to her tiptoes. She closed her eyes, knowing that her virtue hung in the balance despite what he told her and touched her lips to his softly. He let her control the pace. He did not want to force her. He would prove to her that she desired him just as much as he desired her. When she wrapped her arms around his neck and increased the pressure to his lips, he leaned away, causing her to stumble into his arms. She looked up at him, confused, and new tears began to form in her eyes. She wrapped her arms around his neck and buried her face in his chest.

"Why are you crying, little one?" he asked, stroking her hair.

"I don't want you to marry another. I know I have not known you very long, but I think it would hurt to see you kiss another woman in such a way," she said, feeling foolish for admitting the truth.

He had no words to comfort her. His father was a stern man and he very rarely changed his mind, especially when the matter concerned Theslia. Alosis was dead, but his father was still loyal to him.

So, he bent down and picked her up to comfort her. It felt so natural having her in his arms. She released a stunned gasp when he suddenly pulled her into the air. He spun her around and around with her feet swinging. She wrapped her arms tightly around his neck and buried her giggles against the smooth column of his neck.

"We should get to bed. It will be light soon," he said. "Will you meet with me tomorrow night?"

"Yes, but we can't do this every night. They will discover us," she said.

"You think they don't already know," he asked putting her feet back on the ground. "And don't you think it strange that your aunt allows you to meet with me every night, thinking I'm to be married?"

"She was asleep when I left the tent. She doesn't know I meet with you," she explained.

"Believe me; she knows you're not in that tent. Something is amiss. I can feel it," he said.

"I'll see you tomorrow," she said.

"Good night, little one," he said as he kissed her one last time before reluctantly letting her hand go.

Alexander could not sleep. His mind was plagued with thoughts and worries. He was trying not to think about it, but one thing was certain: the more time he spent with Mirage the more he absolutely adored her. *Mirage*—her name said it all. Maybe she was an illusion. But she was right, his father had chosen his bride, he would have no choice but to obey his orders and be miserable for the rest of his life. He wanted to make his own choices concerning his future, and that was exactly what he intended to do.

CHAPTER 11

When Death Comes Knocking

Covax Castle, Lavitia

His servants held trays of fruit and wine as his favorite dancers twirled around him. He was seated on several furs surrounded by pillows on the floor near the pool. He swirled the wine around in his goblet and the servant poured more into his glass. A light, dizzying haze settled over him after he took a sip. He watched Adreana shake and giggle from one side of the room to the next, trying to get his cousin's attention. Finally, she just pretended to trip over a pillow and fell into his lap. The look on his face was laughable. Laven laughed and smiled as he held her uncomfortably, looking around nervously.

His advisors discussed the costs his wars were causing the country loudly to his left. It was an annoying nuisance when he was trying to relax. He had so many things on his mind.

"Come, Adreana, you are not my cousin's taste," Marsalis said as the voluptuous golden-haired girl left his cousin's lap to come sit in his own. "He prefers the much younger, more masculine type," Marsalis whispered in the girl's ear, making her laugh.

"Your Majesty, something must be done. Perhaps we could raise the land tax again to pay for this new campaign," one of the advisors suggested.

"We are losing more and more soldiers every day. We need to think of a plan to insure our forces remain strong," another said.

"Perhaps the Veagans could be made to fight," another suggested.

"I thought the idea was to make the army strong," Marsalis said, eating a piece of cheese from Adreana's hand.

"Your Majesty, perhaps the time has come to concentrate on our own country. Poverty and starvation are at an all-time high because of continuously raising the taxes. The task of recruiting soldiers to the army becomes harder and harder because the men don't understand what they are fighting for. Perhaps we should end this war. The Pheolatians have been nearly wiped out. I think that as long as they don't cross into our lands we should allow Theslia to live in peace," an older advisor by the name of Galius Freemond said.

He was tired of this needless fighting. Most of the people in the land didn't even know what they were fighting for. They had no use for the lands anyway. Marsalis was simply being selfish. He wasn't thinking of what was best for the country. His hatred for these people was now blinding his reasonable judgment.

Marsalis stood from his seat on the floor and pushed his hair back from his face. He walked slowly toward the advisors and stabbed the elderly man in his stomach with the dagger he was using to cut his food. The room fell silent. The women gasped and turned to each other, shielding their faces. Galius clutched his stomach and fell to his knees on the floor. He remained there for a moment, his eyes glazing over with shock and pain. Finally, he fell forward as he died. Marsalis walked back to the pillows and seated himself.

"Musicians," he said. The music started again and the girls returned to the dance. "Will someone clean that up before his blood stains the marble?"

The servants came in and removed the body. The advisors were awestruck at what had just happened. They remained silent, each afraid of what to say for fear of the consequences.

"So, from your silence, I would take it this meeting has ended. Very well, gentlemen, you are dismissed. Send for Shalyndria," he said, pulling one of the girls into his lap.

"Your Highness, perhaps the time has come for me to join your royal council, now that there seems to be an opening," Laven whispered with humor in the king's ear.

"I thought your wish was to rule over the eastern provinces, Cousin. I have no need of your advice. You will leave in three days' time. I suggest you prepare yourself," Marsalis said while sipping on a goblet of wine. He decided he would honor his cousin's wish by heeding Shalyndria's advice and send him away; usually he would kill a member of his household that was not to be trusted, but Laven was the only family he had left.

The advisors filed out of the room as the girl entered. He pushed the dancer from his lap as Shalyndria approached his dais. She was wrapped in gold silk clothes. She held her head up high and Marsalis couldn't help but think that she would indeed make a beautiful queen.

"Shalyndria, when you first arrived and explained that you could only answer one question a year, I agreed because I was more delighted with your ability, but now I must ask you why," he said.

"Your Highness, it is because each time I look into the future, I lose years of my life. I suggested that you only ask one question a year so I would be around longer to serve you, my lord," she said softly, bowing slightly.

Marsalis thought about what she told him. That would explain why her hair was the color of the elderly.

"Well, in light of this news I have decided to honor our agreement. Besides, after I destroy Theslia, I will still be in need of your services. My question for today is: where is the child of the prophecy, right now?"

"My lord, I cannot see where she is right now, but the child will be traveling east toward Thedan, soon, with four other travelers, a woman, and three men," she replied after a short time.

Marsalis dismissed her with a curt wave of his hand.

"One more thing before you leave. I have decided that we will be wed." Laven's face fell flat of expression, his arms went limp at his sides, and he suddenly dropped his goblet on the floor. It clinked loudly as it rolled to a stop against a pillar. A servant raced forward to clean up the mess. Marsalis looked in his direction briefly before returning his attention to Shalyndria. "I will give you two days to prepare yourself to be my queen," he said, watching her reaction.

"As you wish, my lord," was all she said before she turned and walked away. "Messenger, get a message to Cain as fast as your horses can carry you, I want a flock of assassins sent to Thedan. When this group arrives, I want them disposed of," he said, thinking it would be an easy task to ambush a group of weary travelers.

Shalyndria walked slowly back toward her chambers. The servants opened the door, and she walked into the room. She dismissed them and undressed. She pulled the pins from her hair and set them down on the table. She took the nightgown down from the dressing screen and slipped it over her head and sat down before the fireplace with a goblet of wine. She had no idea where this marriage thing was coming from. She had never seen any glimpse of a union between them before.

She put the wine down and held her arms up to the ceiling. Her eyes glazed over and her hair lifted from her back, flipping and twirling around her face. She saw Laven, holding a dagger, moving toward her. She dropped her arms and ran to the doors. She had sent her servants away. She pulled the door open and came to an abrupt halt. He was standing there with his hand in a motion to knock on the door. She backed away from him as he moved into the room and pushed the door closed behind him.

Laven looked around the room and was shocked to find it was empty. He had intended on calmly asking if they could speak in private. Her parade of servants was almost as large as Marsalis's. So, he came straight to the point.

"I have come to demand that you break the spell that you have placed on the king. I know my cousin would never choose to marry a slave of his own design," he said, standing before her.

"My lord, I promise you that I have done nothing to influence His Majesty," she said, slowly moving away, looking around for something to protect herself with.

"You think I have not noticed the way he watches you?" Laven said, glaring at her, slowly inching toward her. "Your time with us has run out, but you already knew that, didn't you? What an awful thing, to see your own death…"

"The king hates me, my lord. You don't have to do this," Shalyndria said desperately.

"I will not let you take this kingdom from me. You or that mongrel you would create together," he said, slowly closing the distance between them. She moved to the hearth and grabbed a gold chalice from the top. She held it with both hands as Laven crept forward. He had an evil look in his eyes as he approached her. His face was creased with an angry scowl.

He smiled at her then revealed the long, thin dagger he carried at his side. Shalyndria dropped the chalice and grabbed the dagger she used to cut her food from the side table.

"Please, my lord, I will not marry him. I'll run away. You could help me run away," she pleaded.

"You idiot. He loves you. You're a slave and he loves you. That's why he doesn't want you around him, you know, that's why you're not allowed to look at him. He was ashamed of the way he felt about you, and well he should be, falling for a slave girl; it's ridiculous, and now he's decided to have you and I cannot have that. If you ran he would find you."

He swept the dagger through the air and cut a long slice down her forearm. She swiped at him with the dagger she held, but it wasn't as long as his and he dodged it. He started slowly circling her. When his back was to the pool she made a dart for the door. Laven caught her by her hair and dragged her across the floor. She reached backwards with the knife. He winced when it nicked the back of his hand and released her.

She struggled to get up from the floor but ended up tripping over the extra material of her nightgown. The next thing she knew she was rolling onto her back after being kicked in the side. She clutched at her stomach as the pain seemed to spread through her stomach. Then he was standing over her. She rolled slowly to her knees, attempting to get up, but instead stabbed the dagger into his foot and crawled away from him.

She realized too late she had crawled in the wrong direction when she found herself at the pool's steps again. She climbed down into the water. If she could make it across there was a door on the other side. Then a scorching pain shot through her skull as he grabbed hold of her hair again, pulling her back up toward him. He turned her around to face him, then struck her hard across her face, leaving a blaze of fire where his fist made contact. She spat in his face staring into his eyes.

"He will kill you for this," she said hoarsely against his strangling hold on her throat. He tightened his grasp around her neck so she couldn't scream and plunged the dagger into her heart.

A blinding pain ripped through her as she stumbled backwards into the water. She looked down at her chest. Thick red blood slid across her fingers. She looked up at Laven with tears trickling down her cheeks. He stood at the edge of the pool cleaning his blade off in her towel. Then he tossed it to her. "Shalyndria, you are a mess," he said, then turned and ran limping from the room.

She crumbled weakly to the pool's steps. The pain had already begun to fade just as the light in the room started to blur. It became harder and harder for her to breathe. Blood dissipated through the pool. She wished she could be there when the king was told she was dead and she wondered if he would be happy or sad. Then she closed her eyes and sank into the darkness.

Later that night, a servant boy entered the chambers to throw logs onto her fire and found Shalyndria's body floating face down on top of the water. They immediately reported to the king that she was dead. Marsalis was infuriated. He put on his pants and marched to her room. The servants had pulled her from the pool. The floor was covered in blood. The pool water was red. Some tables and candles stands had been knocked over. At the sight of her dead body, Marsalis fell to his knees beside her. He pulled her onto his lap; the servants gasped and lowered their heads to the floor. He gave them a fierce glare. "Who did this?" he asked.

"We don't know, Your Highness. I was only away from her door for a moment. I didn't see anyone coming or going. She has been sad, Your Highness. Perhaps she killed herself," the servant said.

"Killed herself? Incompetent fools," Marsalis whispered. "I suppose *she* cut her arm, inflicted these bruises on her face, and pulled out her own hair as well. Get out. Get out, all of you!"

He pushed the hair from her face and kissed her lips. She was the only woman he'd ever desired that he was unable to have. He would have shared his throne with her.

"Who would have done such a thing?" he said in a defeated voice, putting her back on the floor. Then he noticed the trail of blood leading to the door. It streaked across the handle. He got up and followed it to the closed door and ripped it open. Fury washed over him in a red haze; the servants were on their knees cleaning the blood up from the floor.

"You idiots, where did the blood trail lead you?" he yelled. They looked around at one another with blank expressions. "Guards, take them away." He left her chamber and retreated quickly to his own suite. The closer he got the angrier he became and then he was running. He reached the chamber and pushed the doors open before the servant standing there had a chance to.

"Get out!" he bellowed. The servants and the three women in his bed quickly filed out of the room. He threw the chalices from the tables, flipped those over, and kicked over the furniture. He was angry and confused and he screamed with frustration. He didn't know whether he was upset because he could no longer see into the future or because Shalyndria was dead.

A sinking feeling swelled up in the pit of his stomach and he fell to his knees from exhaustion. His chest burned as he tried to catch his breath. He pulled his chin off his chest and pulled in a lungful of air, staring into the flames of the fireplace. This pain was familiar. A shadow seemed to close in slowly around his heart; he had felt this way only once before. His chest heaved up and down settling into its natural rhythm. He took deep breaths trying to focus, but he lacked the effort and a single tear lid down his cheek. He could hear his father's voice—"*Kings don't cry*"—but it didn't matter. Nothing mattered.

He was alone. *Again.* His sat there on the floor in a trancelike state, breathing slowly, staring into nothingness. He thought of her pretty green eyes. They had changed over the years from a golden green to a wintry mint, but they had been gorgeous. They used to turn completely white when she used her powers to look in to the future for him. Her hair was white as fresh snow. She was the only one who didn't fear him. She was smart enough to respect him, but there was never fear in her eyes like the others. *She was gone.*

He had never seen her smile. She was going to be his wife, his queen; he would have made her smile. She had been his treasure, his most valuable possession. There was no other woman like her in this world, and she had belonged to him. She might have been his treasure, but it had been wrong to keep her locked away. He had been foolish for not making her his queen a long time ago. Now it was too late.

Rage burned away the shadow that had covered his heart. His mind saw Shalyndria lying in a pool of blood. Someone had dared to touch her. They would die.

The next morning, he had her nightly servants put to death. They should never have left her alone. He arranged a funeral for that afternoon to be held in the courtyard. Every human soul in the palace was to come before him personally to express their condolences.

Shalyndria's body was placed on top of a high dais. He had chosen the wedding dress he had made for her. It was white silk with gold threads, and it was wrapped around her like a second skin. Lavatian flower blossoms wrapped around her coffin. The servants had placed vanilla seeds and lavender flower petals inside to be offered to the Gods.

The procession started slowly, but started to move along in a regular motion as Marsalis waved them by.

"Lord Kail, is everyone here?" Marsalis asked, waving the people by.

"Yes, Your Highness. Even the servants, my lord," Kail said, standing at his right shoulder. What was the purpose of all this anyway? Most of the people had never even seen Shalyndria before. Perhaps the king's grief at his loss had influenced this strange funeral. The girl had given him great power. It was right of him to mourn such a loss. He had advised him to marry her years ago, but he had not listened. Hopefully he wouldn't let this incident affect all that he had accomplished.

"Where is my cousin?" he asked. He was probably still in his chambers trying to choose the right thing to wear.

"Lord Laven has already left for the eastern provinces, my lord," Kail said.

"Bring him back here immediately," he said sternly. Laven left early. He would find out why.

The procession ended and a servant stepped forward, holding a lit torch, and bowed to Marsalis. He sat up nervously as the servant moved toward the platform with the fire. Marsalis stood as he started up the ladder.

"Stop," he yelled. "Bring her down," he said.

"My lord, is this wise?" Lord Kail asked, quietly leaning over his shoulder, then followed him when he rose and headed back to the hall.

"Do not forget yourself, Kail. Now be gone. I want to be alone," he said and stormed off to his chamber.

CHAPTER 12

Beauty: A Gift or a Curse

Thedan, Theslia

After weeks of travel, the group came to a small village. As they rode through the cobblestone streets, Alexander couldn't help but think something was not right about this place.

"Where is everyone?" he asked.

Kalina couldn't care less. She was just glad for the opportunity to take a real bath. She was tired of washing in cold streams with no privacy. She had a terrible feeling inside. Last night she was unable to sleep. She had lain awake all night with chest pains. Today she felt like a part of her was missing. She pulled her cloak tighter around her shoulders, trying to shake the airy feeling.

"It's about to be dark soon. Perhaps everyone has gone home," she said.

They continued down the narrow street until they came to a tall platform sitting in the middle.

"What did they do to deserve such punishment?" Mirage asked horrified by the display. Four men had been burned until no flesh remained on their bones and left on display in the middle of the streets. The bodies were black and still smoking and there was an awful smell of burnt meat in the air. "Who would do such a thing?"

Alexander rode closer to the platform and looked up at the men.

"Perhaps these are the men that passed through our camp some nights ago," Simo said.

"They have been burnt at the stake for the crime of witchcraft," Alexander said after reading the plague in front of them.

"Witchcraft," Mirage repeated quietly to herself, putting her hand over her mouth.

"We should leave here. I don't want to see it anymore," Kalina said with tears running down her cheeks. Alexander rode away and the others followed him.

Kalina's mind went to another time as they left the awful scene in the distance. She would never forget that smell. She was just a girl in love with a wonderful boy. She had met him soon after she had arrived at Lady Lynea's school. Degar had been everything to her; they had been inseparable.

Then the new laws came down from Lavitia and everything changed. Anyone possessing any magic or abnormal abilities were arrested, tried, and executed. It got so bad that the healers had to hide, for the soldiers were ruthless.

After classes one day they had journeyed into the forest so he could help her with her conjuring, despite Lady Lynea's warnings that they were not to practice their magic outside, but they were just children and didn't understand how serious things were, until these men in black hoods surrounded them. Degar pushed her into the darkness and screamed for her to run. She ran through the trees into the woods and hid under a nearby fallen tree where she watched as they beat him until he couldn't get up from the ground anymore. Then they tied his hands and hung him from a limb and set him on fire.

She couldn't contain her screams and she couldn't move from her hiding place to go to him. The hooded men could hear her screams but were unable to find her. They gave up their search after they realized she was not to be found. Later she realized that Degar must have placed a spell on her. Sometimes she wished that he hadn't and she had died that day with him. Simo's comment pulled her back to reality.

"Most of the people executed for witchcraft aren't witches at all. The magistrate wants the family's land, or something of that nature. They refuse to sell, so they trump up charges against them. They are killed after being tortured to make a confession. It's a terrible matter, really," Simo said as they continued down the street.

"Yes, a terrible matter, one that should be taken before the king," Alexander said in an angry tone. He had no idea his people were being made to suffer such unjust treatment.

James found a small inn just before dark. He paid the innkeeper for three rooms; one for the women, one for him and Simo, and one for Prince Alexander. They would take turns standing guard. After a while, a slender maiden came to lead Kalina and Mirage to their room.

"May I stay, Auntie Lina, while you have your bath?" Mirage asked. The inn was full of different people, even though they were the only women.

Kalina thought about it as she looked from Alexander to the soldiers before saying, "Very well, I will come get you after my bath."

"We will let no harm come to her," Simo said. "James will escort you safely to your room."

Mirage watched everything. She was fascinated by the little birds that played cheerfully together despite the fact that they were in separate cages.

"Look, at those strange little birds," she said to Prince Alexander, nodding toward the animals.

"Those aren't birds. You've never seen a fairy before," he said, looking at her.

"No. What are fairies?" she asked curiously.

"Surely you jest," he said, but the look on her face told him she wasn't kidding. "They are small entities with wings that create flowers and other things that grow. Your house is surrounded by flowers. How is it you've never seen one?" Alexander asked, confused.

"I don't know, but if they are what you say, they shouldn't be in cages," she said, climbing up on top of the table. Alexander stood from his seat, shocked and looked around the room. Everyone was watching her. Mirage grabbed one of the cages and held it steady as she unlocked and opened the door. The little fairy inside backed away from her hand as she reached into the cage. This fairy appeared to be female. She had tan skin and short black hair. Her eyes were grey and her wings were dusty gold. "Come on, I won't hurt you." The little fairy looked at her and then climbed into her hand. She moved to the other cage and opened the door. This fairy was almost black with shiny white hair and green eyes with the same dusty gold wings. He climbed into her hand and let Mirage take him from the cage.

"Get down from there at once and return my property," the small innkeeper exclaimed with his hands on his hips. Mirage hopped down and glared at the little man. His skin was so sweaty it seemed to be covered in a lacquer of some kind. His eyes were sunken in with dark circles around them. His nose was long and narrow and protruded awkwardly from his face and a thin crescent of white gray hair stretched from one ear to the next.

"You ugly little troll, these are living creatures. They are not your property. How dare you cage them?" she asked, marching to the door. "Can you fly, little ones?" she asked, holding them up to eye level. They each flipped their wings in answer, and they came alive with gold light. They nodded to Mirage then fluttered into the air.

The black fairy flew to her ear, "Thank you, Princess," he whispered, then flew into the night, leaving a trail of gold light streaking across the dark sky.

She shrugged on her way back to the table. The fairy must have recognized Alexander and assumed she was his wife. She sat back down in the chair next to him as he reattached his purse to his waist.

"Please tell me you did not pay him because I released those creatures," she said.

"I had to, especially after you called him an ugly little troll," he said with a crooked smile. "And besides it's too late to find another place to sleep," he said, smiling as she crossed her arms over her chest.

Just then a stout man stumbled up to their table. He had a round fat head and a face full of hair. He wore a white turban on his head, large gold earrings, and several large gold necklaces with colorful stones hung around his neck. He wore a fancy burgundy tunic that was left open to display a round hairy stomach, big billowy gold pants, and shiny gold shoes that turned up in the front. Mirage had never seen such clothes; she thought he looked very funny. He tapped Alexander's shoulder then walked near Mirage.

"I have a profitable proposition for you. I will buy this beautiful girl from you for ten purses of silver."

Alexander glared at him with a look of disbelief. Surely this man was not offering to buy a human being in the middle of a busy inn. He knew such things were done, but he didn't know it was such an open practice. By the look of the men standing behind him, this was merely a ruse. He shook his head at Mirage when she opened her mouth to speak. He was a little surprised when she remained silent.

"Not enough? How much do you want for her? I am very wealthy, just name your price," he said, reaching toward Mirage trying to touch her face. She turned at the last minute, avoiding his touch. Her eyes squeezed together in angry golden slits.

He had been paid to ambush the group and kill them all, but when he saw how lovely the women were, he decided a little change of plan was in order. After all, the Great Hi'Sserad was known for owning the most beautiful concubines in the land, and a live, breathing woman in Thedan was worth much more than a dead one.

Alexander dismissed his remark with a curt wave of his hand. "She is not for sale."

"Hah! Silly boy, everything is for sale," he said, laughing. "You have two lovely women. I try to be generous by offering you a fair price for one and you refuse me. Perhaps I should order my men to simply take her then you will have no woman and no money."

"Perhaps your men should try," Alexander said, sizing up the two taller men that stood behind their drunken master.

"Do you have any idea who I am? I am the Great Hi'Sserad, the most powerful mercenary in Tribeca," he said.

At Alexander's order, Simo stood, removed Mirage from her chair, and escorted her to the stairs.

"Wait. You should not leave him alone to be slaughtered—one against three," she whispered, watching the scene unfold as she was led up the stairs and across a balcony that looked down on the large room below. Simo came to a halt when she stopped and leaned against the banister.

"After I kill you, *boy*, and your men, I will take both of your women as my newest concubines," Hi'Sserad said, laughing as he held his large round stomach.

Alexander was still seated in his chair looking up at the foolish man, "No, Great Hi'Sserad," he said sarcastically. "After I kill you, the innkeeper will probably ask me to leave."

Hi'Sserad was taken aback by this boy's arrogance. No one had ever dared to speak to him that way, and this foolish boy would be the first and the last to make such a mistake.

"Kill him!" he ordered.

At his order, Alex stood up quickly, using his forearm to push Hi'Sserad into the others. Caught off guard by the sudden move, the three men fell backwards, breaking one of the tables into pieces. Alex drew his sword so fast Mirage would have missed it if she had blinked, and then he spun to the left and sliced one of Hi'Sserad's guards across his chest and stomach. He punched Hi'Sserad in the face as he struggled to get up from the floor, knocking him down again. He turned around just in time to cut the other guard's hand off, causing the man's weapon to fall uselessly to the floor in his twitching appendage. The man wailed in pain clutching, his arm to his chest. Finally, Alexander turned as Hi'Sserad came running toward him with a dagger, bringing his sword's tip to the man's throat. He instantly came to a halt.

Simo watched from above and nodded his approval when Alexander said, "Drop it." The weapon was instantly released from his hands and fell with a clank to the floor. "Now, I have a profitable proposition for you. You can either leave this inn right now with your life, or you can stay and I will open your throat and spill your blood all over this floor. What will it be?"

"I will leave...I will leave," Hi'Sserad conceded, holding his hands up in defeat.

Alex slowly lowered his weapon and watched as the man walked backwards toward the door. He turned and headed to the stairs, looking up at Mirage on the balcony. He had ordered Simo to take her to her room.

"Alexander, behind you!" she yelled.

As Alex turned around, he watched as Hi'Sserad suddenly flew into the far wall so hard he fell forward again, coming down on the dagger he had just picked up from the floor. He turned over and pulled the weapon from his chest, causing the blood to flow freely, creating a dark purple pool around him on the floor. Mirage put her hands over her mouth and ran down the hall. Alexander walked over and stood above him. Hi'Sserad stared lifelessly at the ceiling.

Alexander looked around the room, wanting to thank the man who had come to his aid. The innkeeper came over, wringing his hands, frantic and upset with the mess they had created. The prince apologized for the trouble and offered to pay the man for the table that was destroyed and the expenses needed to dispose of the bodies.

"Did you, by chance, see who came to my aid?" he asked the innkeeper.

"No one. Your praise should go to the Great Creator. Was he who sent a strong force to save you," the man said, bowing several times when Alexander gave him the entire pouch of gold.

He walked up the stairs and met Simo on the balcony. "I thought I told you to take her out of sight. I did not want her to see that. Where is she?" he asked.

"My apologies, sire, the girl feared for your life. I let her watch so she could see that you could defend yourself. She ran away...down there ...at the sight of the blood. I beg your forgiveness," Simo said, lowering his head.

Alexander dismissed him with a curt wave of his hand and walked down the hall to find Mirage. She was crouched in a corner with her head on her knees. Her shoulders convulsed every now and then, telling him that she was crying. He hated her tears.

"Mirage," he said quietly, stooping down to her level. Big golden globes of amber looked up at him. "Come, my sweet, you have had a long day." He pulled her to her feet and guided her down the hall.

"I—I didn't...mean—I was only trying—you were...and he was coming...he's dead. I killed him. I'm sorry," she said in between sobs.

"It was not your fault. You didn't ask him to come over. Your only crime is being a beautiful woman," he said, tapping on the door to her room. "Have your bath and relax. I will see you in the morning. We will leave at first light. I have a feeling we should be away from here."

He kissed her on her forehead and used his thumbs to wipe away her tears. She turned her head into his palm and he wrapped her in his arms and gave her a comforting squeeze. He loved the feel of her in his arms. He had an overwhelming desire to protect her. As Kalina opened the door he released her and watched her walk inside.

"What's wrong?" Kalina asked.

"I just killed a man," she answered as she crawled onto the bed and curled up into a ball.

"What do you mean you killed a man?" Kalina asked. She paused with the brush in midair, turned, and looked at Mirage on the bed. "What happened?"

"A man tried to buy me and there was a fight. Prince Alexander fought them and told the man to leave. He turned to walk away and the man came up behind him with a knife. I called out to warn him and suddenly my powers pushed the man back into a wall. He fell on his knife and died. I didn't mean to push him. It just happened. I wasn't even thinking about my powers. Now a man is dead and I am to blame," Mirage said.

"The magic did not kill him. Remember the laws and the consequences. What did the Prince say?" Kalina asked.

"They didn't know I caused the man to hit the wall," she said.

"Come, I will assist you with your bath," Kalina said, relieved. "I know you didn't mean to kill that man, and if he did not have a knife, he would still be alive, but you have to be very careful. Think of those men we saw today."

"They were Pheolatian, then?" Mirage asked.

"I think so. There were four of them. Some people must form a coven of four to use the magic, and then it still won't work unless at least one of them has natural powers.

"Remember what Mother told you. Your powers come from within. They are linked with your emotions. If you lose control of your emotions you lose control of your powers and that is very dangerous for someone like you."

"I have no control of my emotions when… What should I do?" she asked as she stepped out of the water. Kalina handed her the towel. Mirage sat down near the fire as Kalina brushed the tangles from her thick hair.

"I can't answer that. Just don't let your feelings rule over you and you'll be fine," she said.

"Easier said than done," Mirage said under her breath as Kalina finished braiding her hair. "Let's just go to sleep so this awful day will end." She had to start reading that book.

CHAPTER 13

Simple Desires

"When will we reach the great river?" Mirage asked.

"Tomorrow or maybe tonight if we hurry," he answered. Alex looked over at her and he couldn't help but smile. She was wearing a brilliant smile that lit up her face. Her eyes were closed and she held her arms up to her sides as the wind blew.

"We don't have to hurry. I want to see it in the light of day," she said as their horses moved through the trees. She loved the sound of the forest; the flittering of the birds flying by, the voices of the animals in the distance, the whisk of the wind through the trees, and the faint trickling of water, she could feel it inside.

It enchanted her, the things she could feel that no else seemed to; that sometimes made it scary. She had realized for some time that she wasn't like other Pheolatians. Such powers should not be controlled by someone like her.

"See what?" he asked.

"The Great Oak," she said.

"I almost forgot. It is massive; that tree's base stretches from one side of the river to the other! You won't believe how big it is. You can see the top of it from the castle," he explained.

"Tell me everything," she said excitedly.

"The base is nearly the size of the great hall. It shoots straight out of the mighty river like a grand tower. Some of the branches are as thick as my horse. It towers above all the other trees around it. The best part about it is," he said, lowering his voice, "that if you're there when the river is at its lowest, you can go down these steps, walk through a small waterfall and enter the trunk. Father said the room is for emergencies only, but I had to see it for myself. I tried to go one day when the tides were low but there were no steps. For some reason, the tree only allows you to enter at night.

"Roots and vines hang down like chandeliers. It's like somebody carved out the inside and it just kept growing," he explained.

"I can't wait to see it," she said, turning her horse off the road, following Simo.

"Will you sing to me tonight?" he asked.

"I will sing for everyone tonight, at dinner," she said as her smile slowly faded. The clouds moved in slowly over them and the bright sky suddenly got dark.

"No, I mean tonight…after they have gone to sleep," he explained. "I will take you to see it." He noticed the change in her expression. Her eyes were darker and she turned her head away. Then he noticed the change her in mood happened at the same time the sun went away.

"I don't think it would be a good idea. Besides, I think we should stop fooling ourselves. I mean, it's obvious the Great Creator has chosen different paths for our lives. You will rule our country. And I have to accept the fact that princes marry princesses, not farm girls. And besides, if we were truly meant to be together, we would not have to hide it," she said, leading her horse around a fallen log.

If only all women were so easy to read. He loved her wit, but her prudence was starting to bother him. He wasn't used to it. No one told him what he could and couldn't do except his father. If he wanted her to sing to him, she should just do it, but then that was why he liked her; she was the only woman he'd ever met that treated him like he was a man instead of a prince. She seemed to have her own opinion, but rejection— it was dry in his mouth.

The closer they got to the castle; the worse his dreams became. He wanted to meet with Mirage so he wouldn't have to sleep. The very idea that he had been deceived by his own father after all that talk about honor and honesty and being a man of your word. He had given him his word that he would be able to find his own bride. He would never trust him again. He had finally made up his mind. He would escape Simo and James, somehow. He wanted to take Mirage with him, but he would not put her life in danger.

When the group stopped to eat, Mirage went inside the tent. Kalina told him she wasn't feeling well, but he knew she was just avoiding him. When they started out again, she seemed a little distracted or maybe worried about something. She looked as miserable as he felt.

"Are you feeling better?" he asked.

"I'm fine. Or I will be fine," she said quietly. Why wouldn't he just leave her alone? Why was he torturing her?

"You looked a little flushed earlier," he lied.

"I'm just fine," she said, looking down at her hands.

Her tone was dry. She seemed distant and cold. He never had a woman avoid him before, but it was probably for the best. She was like forbidden fruit; sweet and tempting. Maybe that was why he wanted her so bad.

They rode on for hours. The setting sun had painted the pale blue sky with brilliant pinks and subtle purples. Alexander heard a faint rushing in the distance.

"Can you hear it?" he asked.

"Hear what?" She really wasn't listening to her surroundings. She hated it when they traveled on the road. It was dusty, dry, and boring. When she was bored she would become lost in her thoughts. A millions worries, concerns feelings…it was overwhelming.

"The river," he said. "We're probably just a couple of miles away."

"We should stop here, sire, before it gets too dark and set up camp," Simo said.

"Very well," Alexander replied.

Mirage dismounted and walked away. She helped gather wood to make a fire. She helped her aunt prepare the meal, then she retired to her tent. She had to finish reading the book. She had learned so much in just a few hours of reading. She never knew magic could be used to control the weather. She needed to practice the enchantments, but she couldn't risk doing it in camp, but then she couldn't just use her powers out in the open either.

She would have to sneak away, but she would have to be very careful of Prince Alexander. He never slept. For now, she would just focus her attentions on getting all the information inside of her head. Once she knew everything there was to know, she would find a place where she could be alone. It would have to be a place that she was sure would be private. Instantly, it came to her: the Great Oak.

If it was only a couple miles away, she could rise in the dead of night and journey there. She read until she couldn't hold her eyes open anymore. Then she put the candle out and went to sleep.

Alexander sat in a clearing while JeNi grazed nearby. He noticed the light go out in Mirage's tent. He wanted to take her with him, he wanted it more than anything, but he would be asking her to disobey her king. That act could mean imprisonment, banishment, or even death, and he would not risk her life just because he was angry with his father. Reluctantly, he rose from the ground and walked to his tent. This would be his last sleepless night.

Mirage woke up early the next morning and slipped silently from her cot. Kalina slept soundlessly. She took her book and stepped outside. She looked up at the sky. She had about four hours until daylight. She tiptoed around the tent, trying to keep out of sight by hiding in the shadows. She made it successfully to her horse and breathed a sigh of relief. She untied Midnight and led him slowly away from the others, constantly keeping an eye on Prince Alexander's tent.

After walking the horse until the camp was out of sight, she climbed aboard and rode hard toward the sound of the river. She only hoped it didn't take long to find the Great Oak.

When Mirage reached the river, she looked up at the line of trees and was amazed by the size of the tree that towered above the rest.

"Come on, baby, time to fly," she whispered in the Midnight's ear. He raced upriver. Mirage pulled him to a stop when she reached the base of the great tree. She prayed it wouldn't be long before she'd be able to enter or this whole trip would have been a waste of time. She watched the moon and the edge of the river. She watched the base of the tree.

"Please, Mighty Oak, let me enter," she whispered.

Strangely the river started to instantly go down. She moved the horse into the water and watched for the stairs Alex had told her about. When they appeared before her, she dismounted and led the horse down the steps. She stepped through the waterfall and saw the Pheolatian emblem on the door. She took the necklace from her gown and smiled.

Her kind was great indeed. She kissed it and put it back inside her gown and opened the door. She only hoped she would one day be powerful enough to create such a phenomenon. Her grandmother had told her that she was unique and her powers would teach her about herself. She hoped that was true.

She walked slowly into the dark room and wished she had brought some candles with her. She put her palms together, intending to conjure some up, when suddenly the roots that snaked up and down the walls of the tree started to glow. Mirage walked to the wall and touched it; the roots shone brighter and swept toward where her hand touched the wall.

"You can feel me too, can't you?" She shrugged and put the book on the floor and practiced the spells she had read about. She was amazed by how easy it was to master them. She quickly flipped through the pages. She wanted to know her powers as Matilda knew hers. She wanted to be in full control of them just in case she needed to use them on her journey, after all, now she would be traveling alone. She had gone through nearly the entire book of spells when she came to a page that read "Altering Time.

"Oh my, the time—Midnight, why didn't you remind me?" She closed the book and jumped to her feet. When she tried to open the door, it wouldn't budge. She pushed and pulled, but the door would not open. "I don't have time for this. The sun is probably up by now," she said. Then it came to her. The door didn't exist in the daytime. She was trapped.

She opened the spell book and flipped through the pages. She found an enchantment that was meant to open locked trunks without keys. "With these words and this slightest touch," she said, sliding two fingers down the door, "give to me nature's key. Open this door, immediately!"

The door clicked open, the water rushed in. It knocked her off her feet and pushed her back into the room. She struggled to keep her hold on the spell book as she tried to regain her bearings. The water flipped her over and over. . When she finally got her head above water, she took in a lungful of air, then swam to her horse. She put the book into her satchel and latched the clasp shut and held on to Midnight tightly as he moved through the water to the entrance. As soon as they passed the threshold, the two doors slammed shut. The small waterfall now meshed with the river. She kicked the horse forward. The water beat down hard on their backs. Midnight moved up the stairs.

Suddenly she was being pulled from the horses back under the water. She struggled to be free of whatever it was that was holding her, but couldn't get her arms and legs free. She sank down into the watery abyss. Her throat burned as her need for air increased. Then she saw what seemed to be blue hair floating in front of her. Then a woman's face appeared. She had large eyes, like that of a frog's, and thin lips. There was no nose on her face. Her lower body was that of a fish. A *fish*.

Is this what happened when a person drowned? Would she now be turned into this half-fish thing? She thought of all the possibilities. If there were entities that made flowers, perhaps there were half-human, half-fish things that lived in the sea. But why hadn't she ever heard of them before? Grandma Tilda had never told her about fairies, and she knew for a fact that they existed. What else had been kept from her? If fairies made flowers, then they were a part of the natural balance, and she should have been told about them. What place in nature did these things have, and what did they want with her? Seconds passed by as these thoughts flipped through her head.

She could make out a sparkling blue-green tail. Her arms were thin and long; they reached out toward her. Her image began to blur as the burning in Mirage's throat increased. Then the fish woman was kissing her. She lacked the effort to struggle anymore as the darkness seemed to close in around her. The fish woman released her and her body instinctively took in a lungful of water. It didn't choke her as it should; instead it felt like a breath of air had filled her lungs. She could feel a thin film fall over her eyes. It was cold and slimy, but as she blinked she found she could see better. It was like outside just after dusk. She could see, but the images were dark and shadowed.

Was this the beginning of the change? She looked down at her feet; they were still feet. She didn't think she would like the idea of having a tail, no matter how beautiful it was. Panic struck. She had to get away from these things. She snatched one of her arms away and was attempting to get the other released when she was subdued by another fish woman.

Now there was one holding her on both sides. The one on the left had yellow hair with a yellow-green tail and the other had silver hair with a silvery green tail. They pulled her quickly through the water, following the blue-haired one. The river opened out to the ocean and they dived deep through the dark caverns and trenches.

A faint glow could be seen in the distance. As they got closer she could make out a large palace rising up in the middle, surrounded by smaller buildings, creating a large city under the water. The half-human, half-fish things were everywhere. Mirage had never seen such a sight. It was like Gativa, but underwater. They swam into the buildings and along the paths in between them. Smaller ones, which she assumed were children, frolicked through the waters. They stopped and stared after her as she was pulled along through their city.

They took her directly to the palace in the middle. Everything was so dark, but she could see the dwelling was made out of shiny shells and stones. The walls of this place were encased with them. They entered a spacious room and brought her to stand before a fish man seated on a throne made of a giant clam's shell that was opened like a chair.

"I have been anxious to meet you. Nasci—" he started to say in a hollow singing voice.

"Who are you? Why have you brought me here?" Mirage interrupted nervously. She didn't recognize her own voice. It had a gurgled hollow sound to it. She knew she should be more respectful to someone sitting on a throne, but she was so scared she couldn't think straight.

"I am ruler of the Mer People. My name is King Aquius and you have been brought here because a river nymph sold you to me."

"There must be a mistake," Mirage whispered. Her hair and dress floated around her. Her braid must have come loose in the struggle. She wondered if she would sink into the dark murky waters below if her captors released her arms.

"Is it a mistake that you entered the river without paying the river nymph's toll?" he asked.

"No, I didn't know a toll had to be paid," she said desperately. *River nymph*? "Please let me go. I'm sorry, I will—"

"Your ignorance and apology is of no consequence. You were very expensive. He wanted to kill you, which is unlike a nymph. No profit, you see. But I convinced him that it would be in his best interest to let me have you; I had to swear you would never see the light of day again, and a king must keep his word after all, even if it is to a slimy little nymph," he said. "Now what am I going to do with you?"

A bright light flashed and rippled through the water. "You will release her, now, Aquius," a tall man with dark hair and pointy ears said. Behind him was a score of pointy-eared soldiers with weapons.

"Prince Stagg, it has been centuries since you have graced our watery haven with your presence. What brings you to my court?"

Aquius asked, flipping his tail, sending chilled rippling waves through the water. Mirage shivered as she looked from the king to these new creatures. They looked like humans, but their flawless beauty and perfect features were extremely unnatural.

"You know full well why I am here. The girl must be freed," he said.

"The girl is mine. What business is it of yours what I do with my property?" the king asked.

"I am no one's property, sir. I demand that you take me back to my horse," Mirage said sternly.

"Riparia sold her to me and I intend to keep her." He ignored Mirage's remark.

"Riparia cannot sell you that which does not belong to him. I have been charged to watch over her and I will not leave here without her," he said, moving forward toward Mirage.

"Charged by whom?" King Aquius asked.

"Mother, of course," Stagg said and looked nervously to his left. His soldiers believed he acted at the behest of the queen. If they found out otherwise, he would lose everything.

"Interesting," Aquius responded, tilting his head to one side. "Very well. I will allow you to take the girl…if she is able to complete a single task," the king said, rising from his throne.

"There will be no task—" Stagg started.

"You dare enter my realm and demand that I release my property to you without some form of payment? You think your meager forces intimidate me? I could have them all swept away with the flick of my wrist," Aquius yelled. His voice boomed through the water like an echo quaking through a cave.

"My soldiers and I are willing to die if that is what it takes, but know this—" Stagg started.

"Wait," Mirage yelled. "No one has to die for me. I entered the river without paying. I will complete the task to be released. It is only fair," she explained.

"Nothing this king does is ever fair. Let me handle this," Stagg snapped at her.

"No, I will not allow strangers to die because of my ignorance," she said.

"Then you must swear that if you are unable to complete the task you will then belong to me and remain in my watery kingdom forever," Aquius said, staring into her eyes. His were a translucent murky white color. He had broad shoulders and long hair that meshed in with the color of the water around them. His tail was large and silver and it glistened and sparkled as he moved. There were three dark slits under both of his arms as he crossed them over his chest.

"No," Stagg said just as Mirage said, "I swear."

"Very well, follow me," he said swimming into the darkness below. Stagg tried to snatch Mirage away from the mermaids that held her, but they were too fast as they followed Aquius into the depths of the ocean. He had no choice but to follow them.

"Do you know what you have done? You should have remained silent. The task will be impossible for anyone to perform. I will do what I can to get you out of here. Let me handle this, Princess," he said, coming alongside her.

"Is that why you're trying to save me? Because you think I am a princess? I'm not," she explained.

"Your powers call to us," was all he said as he took off after Aquius.

He led them to the wreckage of a ship. There were barnacles and algae growing all over it. Fish and other creatures had made it their homes. It was leaning against some large rocks. The ropes had been tangled on some plants and were green and mossy.

They entered through a jagged hole in the side. It must have been a state room of some kind. There was a rotting bed and remnants of what must have been furniture.

"This is what I want," Aquius said, pointing to a faded painting that hung on the wall.

"You want a portrait made?" Mirage asked.

"No, no, I want what is in the picture," he said, smiling at the two of them.

Mirage moved closer to get a better look at the faded images. It was a portrait of a woman seated next to a blazing fire.

"*Fire*," Stagg said. "You want fire. It is impossible."

"Yes, fire that is what it's called. It is said it warms you and provides you with light. If you can create the fire, I will release you. Come; let us return to the palace, so you can begin," the king said. This time he took Mirage by the arm and led her back to the palace.

When they reached his throne room he seated himself and said, "You may begin the task now."

Stagg shook his head. Mirage swam forward. How could such a thing be done? Stagg was right, it wasn't fair.

"Fire needs air," she said absently.

"Are you not breathing air right now?" Aquius asked. "The air that you need is all around us in tiny bubbles," he said, waving his hand through the water.

Bubbles. That gave her an idea. She closed her eyes, trying to think. Stagg moved slowly toward her.

"You stay where you are or the deal is off," Aquius said, pointing at Stagg. Mirage held her hands out in front of her and started moving them slowly in a circular motion. The water started moving with her hands until she created a swirling ball of water. She stuck her hand into it and said, "Water ball true and clear, empty out, leave nothing but air." The bubble of air was left suspended in the water. It drifted slowly to and fro as Mirage held her hand out to it. She very slowly touched the bubble, then slipped her fingers into it. She held her fist closed tightly as she concentrated. Slowly she uncurled her fingers opening her palm. A single flame danced in the middle. She placed it on the bottom of the bubble and removed her hand. She held her palms flat to the sides of bubble with her eyes closed. The flame grew and grew until it filled the air bubble with lapping flames of orange, red, and yellow fire.

Stagg was stunned. Aquius excitedly clapped his hands together and moved from his throne toward the bubble that encased the fire. Suddenly Stagg was there blocking his path.

"First, release her," he said, still unable to believe what he had seen. It had seemed so simple, but he knew it could not have been. He had never seen such powers in a mortal before.

"The girl is free to go," Aquius said—for now, anyway. He waved them away,, anxious to get a closer look at the fire.

The elves surrounded Mirage and started moving her away. Stagg moved out of Aquius's path as he moved closer to the fire. He held his hands out to it holding it inches away.

"Heat and light…they are finally mine, and Nasci said it couldn't be done," he said in quiet amazement, reaching forward to touch it. As soon as he made contact the bubble burst and the flames were extinguished by the water.

"Noooo," he screamed.

Stagg smiled and swam away after his soldiers. He moved through their ranks and came to Mirage's side. He couldn't help but stare at her.

Suddenly she started to wither and thrash at his side. He wrapped her in his embrace and in a flash of light they were in the forest. Mirage was unconscious in his arms. He placed her gently in Saline's arms.

"You and Carmilla, return her to her horse. I must go see Father," he said, disappearing instantly.

CHAPTER 14

Truce

Mirage woke up on the ground next to the river. Her dress was wet and dirty and it clung to her as she tried to stand. The light was blinding as she looked around the forest, confused by her surroundings. Then she saw Midnight grazing nearby, and she remembered being stuck in the Great Oak and nearly drowning. She got up from the ground and walked to the horse. She couldn't remember anything after being knocked around by the water and swimming to her horse, though she thought she should. She replayed the night before as she climbed onto the horse.

She remembered sneaking away to practice her spells. She remembered opening the door and being tackled by the water, but that was it. Maybe she had passed out and Midnight had pulled her ashore. She raced back down the river. Kalina was surely going to kill her. She looked down at her dress and pulled the horse to a stop. She jumped down from the horse and held her arms out over her head.

"Oh, great sunshine, I take you into my hands." She made a fist as if to hold onto to the light and bent to the ground and spun around. When she stood erect again, her gown was dry. She looked back at the tree, glad that she had the chance to see it. Now she would be free to leave. She would not journey to the castle to see the man she was falling in love with marry another.

Falling in love with. Was she actually falling in love with him? Was this love, this excruciating pain that seemed to be filling up inside her? She wanted to be with him all the time. It felt like something—some piece of her that she didn't know existed until now—had been missing when they were separated. She had never believed in love at first sight. How could you have such strong feelings for a person you knew absolutely nothing about? What did she know about Prince Alexander that would make her think she loved him?

Nothing, except for the fact that she had been unable to get him off her mind since the first time she'd seen him in the forest, and the fact that he had the most gorgeous brown eyes framed by the thickest lashes she'd ever seen before in her life had absolutely nothing to do with it, but when he kissed her…it felt like the whole world dissolved away into nothing and left just the two of them behind to carry on. She took a deep breath and climbed back aboard her horse and raced to the camp.

"There she is," Simo said as she rode up through the woods.

"Where have you been? I was so worried about you. Why do you do things like this?" Kalina asked as Mirage got down from the horse.

"There is no need to get down. We're leaving now," James said, shaking his head. If anything had happened to her the king would have his head. Perhaps he had been wrong to suggest they travel with no soldiers to appear less conspicuous. He and Simo would have to keep a better eye on things. Good thing they were almost there.

Alex said nothing. He climbed aboard his horse and followed the group toward the river. Mirage followed them quietly. She felt so embarrassed.

They rode quietly down the dusty road. Where would she go, and why would she go alone, Alexander wondered. She lived with her head in the clouds. She had no knowledge of the dangers of this world. Hell, she didn't even know what a fairy was, which he found confusing. What would she do if she came across a nymph or a troll? What would *he* do?

After a few hours of travel, Alexander pulled his horse up next to hers. He couldn't stand the silence anymore. "So, where did you go?"

"I just needed to be alone so I could think," she said, looking down at her hands. It was almost the truth; there was no reason to mention the fact that she had almost drowned.

"You will never do that again," he said sternly. "The forest is dangerous, especially at night. There could be strangers or wild animals or… Just don't go into the forest alone again?"

"Sire, you were concerned for my well-being, I'm flattered," she said, smiling sarcastically.

"You find this amusing," he said seriously.

"I find you extremely amusing, but I think you're overreacting," she said, smiling at him.

"I am trying to tell you things that will keep you from harm. You must obey me on this."

Mirage laughed. The clouds threw grey shadows across the forest floor.

"You are a naïve little child," he said quietly, shaking his head.

Her laughter ceased and her eyes grew wide. "I am not naïve, nor am I a child," she said, glaring at him. "I am not afraid of the forest and I don't remember asking for your advice or concern."

"Perhaps you should be, on both accounts. You think the forest if filled with deer and birds—" he started.

"You are an arrogant fool if you think I know nothing of the world. Life marching up and down castle halls with thousands of servants to grant your every desire must truly be difficult to endure."

"You will never speak to me like that again. Do you understand me?" he snapped, raising his voice. The others stopped and turned around to see what was going on.

"I beg your forgiveness, sire," Mirage said, bowing her head to him. The others rode on. When Mirage looked up at him again her eyes were glazed over with fury. The sky was clear and blue, but it cracked with lightening in the distance. She kicked her horse's flanks and rode away from him. How could she have fallen for such a pompous, arrogant, and conceited…

"There it is," he said to Mirage, standing at the edge of the river, pointing at the grand tree in the distance as if nothing had ever happened.

"Do we have time to go see it?" Alexander asked.

"No, sire. If we continue, we can reach the castle by tomorrow morning," Simo explained, anxious to get home.

Mirage said nothing. He had the audacity to treat her like a child in one breath then expect everything to be as right as rain in the next.

James found a place for them to cross and deposited the crystals into the river.

"What's he doing?" she asked Kalina quietly. Kalina looked at her, trying to think of something to say. "Tell me," she pleaded.

"It is an offering to the river," she said.

"River fairies?" Mirage asked, watching as the river glowed.

"No. Who told you about fairies?" Kalina asked nervously. She knew it would be dangerous to keep her in the forest this long without something happening.

"There were fairies in cages at the inn," she said, puzzled by the confused look on her aunt's face.

"Ladies, please," Simo said gesturing to the river. They crossed and set up camp near the shore to change their clothes.

"We will stop here for a while to give the horses a chance to rest. We must travel uphill from here on out. I would also suggest that everyone adorns a cloak," he said.

After changing their clothes, Alex walked over and sat down next to Mirage on the ground near the fire.

"You look angry," he said.

"Oh, wise ruler, how observant you are," she said, lowering her head and turning her back to him.

"Stop it," he said.

"No. If this is how you want me to behave, like a cowardly slave, then this is how I will behave, Prince Alexander," she snapped, folding her arms across her chest.

"I deserved that. I was wrong to raise my voice earlier, but you must learn the difference between serious conversation and jest," he said. He bent forward and kissed her on her forehead. "Let us be civil to one another."

"Do not kiss me. And I beg your pardon, Prince Alexander, but you are too confusing and I neither have the time nor the desire to get to know your many temperaments. First you tell me not to use your title, making me think you want us to be equals, then when I speak to you as my equal you get angry." The lightening cracked twice and the sky got darker. The fire flared and the flames flashed with brilliant blues and greens. Alexander held his arm up to his face as the fire grew hotter. He gave Mirage another glance then noticed the sky above them. She continued to yell at him and he decided it was time to test his theory. "Perhaps those smiles and gentle words were just your means to steal kisses in the night and admiration in the day. As we get closer and closer to your castle your affections for me seems to be fading away.

"Your father was right to choose you a bride. I doubt you would find another that would want to put up with such nonsense if they were not ordered to!" she said, getting up to leave.

"Stop this. My way is the only way I know. Am I to be faulted for being myself? Don't think you are without faults. You are a spoiled little girl who is used to having her own way. You live with your head in the clouds, thinking you can wipe all the world's problems away with a smile. I will not cower to you nor will I apologize for my title. I want to be your friend, but you will remember that I am Crown Prince of Theslia and you will respect me.

"And if I recall it correctly, all the kisses I have gained were given willingly. So, what will it be?" he asked, staring up at her. He gave her a smile and watched the sky slowly change back to normal as her temper cooled. The fire calmed and settled back to a normal size.

This was very interesting. The elements reflected her mood and wild animals approached her.

She looked down at him and extended her hand. "Truce," she said.

"Truce," he said, shaking her small, delicate hand.

"Come, sit beside me," he said. How were these things possible? Maybe he was just imagining things. No one else seemed to notice, so maybe it was just a coincidence.

"And just for the record, I never get my own way," she said, settling down next to him.

"You are unlike any farm girl I've ever come across," he said, relaxing back against a fallen log.

"And how many would that be?" she asked, looking at him with her arms crossed over her chest.

Kalina watched as Mirage and Prince Alexander sat down together near the fire. The king would be pleased to know his plan was working out so nicely.

"Sire," Simo said, standing over Alexander.

"Yes," he answered, looking back over his shoulder at the soldier standing behind him.

"We have decided to stay here tonight rather than taking the risk of being trapped on the mountainside as the sun goes down. James will accompany you if you still wish to see the Great Oak," Simo said. He looked at Mirage and was surprised when she shook her head no.

"We will stay," he said, dismissing Simo with a nod.

That night Mirage helped Kalina with their dinner. After they ate she got the wine from Kalina's sack and placed the bottle against her leg where it was engulfed into a pocket that appeared on the side of her gown. She turned and entered the tent as Kalina moved toward her.

She changed her clothes, took the wine from the dress pocket, opened it, and placed it on the floor. She kneeled before it, circled her hands around the opening, and said, "When at last they close their eyes, take them to the land of dreams. Keep them lost and drifting there, until the sun reaches its highest peak." Dark blue smoke circled around the neck of the bottle. Shards of light emanated from the smoke casting the bottle with a green hue. Then the smoke turned white and was sucked inside. She conjured a tray and poured it into the four goblets.

Kalina entered the tent. "Are you ready?"

"Almost. Will you take this out?" she asked. Kalina passed the wine out then took her mandolin from her sack. She sat down and waited for Mirage to emerge from the tent. She would dance the traditional flusha, a dance preformed at parties usually by four girls, to celebrate their last night of travel.

Mirage stepped out of the tent headfirst and then stood up straight. At the sight of her, Alex dropped the goblet on the ground, spilling the wine. He quickly bent to retrieve it, looking around to see if anyone had noticed. He shook his head, feeling foolish. She turned slowly, holding her goblet up high. "Let us drink to our last night of travel," she said.

Simo looked at his goblet as if it contained a serpent. He had not had a drink since the night of the naming ceremony when his daughters were killed. He had promised their mother on her deathbed that he would always watch over them. Tonight, he would forgive himself after all this time for not being able to keep that promise. He put the goblet to his lips and took a sip.

Alex pretended to drink, and then placed the empty goblet on the ground. He watched Mirage as she walked slowly toward them. He had seen this dance performed numerous times, but he never felt so stimulated by the dancer. His loins throbbed at the sight of her. She wore a light pink and white sheer costume that left nothing to the imagination. It was cut low, exposing the top of her breast. The material stopped just above her stomach where she wore a thin gold chain with dangling jewels attached to her navel. The translucent sleeves were comprised of long separate flowing pieces of silk that connected again at her wrist. The waistband of her pants was made of a shiny white material that came to a chevron point in the middle. It fit securely around her small waist and was lined with sparkling jewels. The legs of her pants were made of the same silky strips as her sleeves, but they hung loosely around her legs like a skirt would so they could fly freely through the air.

Kalina began to play and Mirage danced around the fire, twisting and turning while gyrating her hips erotically to the music. She used a magenta sash to play with the flames. She flipped her head from side to side, sending her long braid flying.

Simo and James clapped their hands and swayed to the music. Alexander crossed his arms, then stood up and left. He could not take it anymore. He wanted to grab her and carry her to his tent so he could release this burning desire he had for her. He wanted to shield her from the other men at the same time. He didn't want them seeing her that way. He watched as she threw the sash over Simo's head and had to fight back the rage that action made him feel. He turned away and walked to his horse, but he could not keep his eyes off her. Finally, he entered his tent just to be away from her.

Goddess in the Rain

er life had been moving in a dull, boring line until she met Prince Alexander. She had never felt so plagued and confused by her thoughts. Plans were always easier to make when they were wrapped with dreams and fantasies. Now she would have to see how strong she really was, or if she was strong at all. She would have to rely on her magic now and it frightened her. She had no guide to whisper in her ear to tell her to concentrate or back off.

Kalina's deep, steady breathing interrupted her thoughts. She got up from the bed quickly before she could think of a reason she should stay to endure the worst possible fate she could imagine. She would not accompany them and watch him be tied to his perfect princess.

He would slowly lose all interest as she faded into black and white; she would become a fixture on the wall, no more interesting than a candle or a chair. She walked to Kalina's cot. She was sound asleep. She put her book in the sack, gathered some things she would need for her journey, and then walked over and kissed her goodbye.

"I'm sorry, but I just can do it. I will think of you always," she said softly.

Alex got up from his cot and attached his sword to his waist. He was leaving and James and Simo were not going to stop him.

He removed his knife from his boot and slowly cut a slit in the back of his tent, if he could just slip away. Maybe if he didn't disturb his guard outside and he made it to his horse he could out run them. He slipped through the opening and put his back to the tent. He crept around the side and ran quickly to the guard's tent and stopped. This would be the hardest part; getting from the tent to JeNi. He peered around the side trying to see where the guard was exactly.

Mirage opened the flap to the tent slightly and looked around. James was asleep on the ground outside of Prince Alexander's tent. She looked at the horses just to be certain he wasn't there, and then she stepped outside into the night.

As Alex moved around the tent to get a clear view, he noticed Mirage walking quickly to the horses. He leaned back against the tent as she passed. Where was she going at this hour, and why didn't the guard stop her? He tiptoed out and was surprised to see James asleep on the ground. He walked slowly toward the horses trying to sneak up on her.

She attached the sack to Midnight's saddle and untied him from the tree. She thought for a second about going to see Prince Alexander before she left but thought against that idea. She put her foot in the stirrup. He would be asleep anyway, what could one last look hurt? She took her foot down and turned.

"Oh!" she exclaimed, shocked at the sight of Alexander standing right behind her. "How is it you are awake?" she blurted out without thinking.

"I was going to ask you the same question, along with another. Simo and James are two of my father's first officers and most trusted friends, which is why they were chosen to accompany me on this journey. They would never neglect their duties by falling asleep. What have you done to them?"

She thought for a moment, trying to think of a believable explanation, when she thought of the perfect answer. Lying shouldn't be so easy.

"Promise you won't be angry," she whispered.

"I will not make you that promise, but you still have to tell me," he said, crossing his arms over his chest.

"I drugged them. Well, I drugged the wine, which is why I'm shocked to see you awake right now, but they will be fine. The herbs will only make them sleep deeply. How is it that you are not asleep?" she asked, confused. Could someone be immune to a spell?

"I didn't drink the wine, and I see that was for the best. Why would you drug everyone? Where are you going?" he asked a little impressed.

"I did it because I'm not going to the castle. I'm leaving and don't try to stop me. By the way, where are you going with all your belongings?" she asked, noticing the sack he carried over his shoulder.

"I'm not going to the castle either. I planned to leave as well. I was not sure if I could do it with Simo and James watching me like hawks, but you have given me the means," he said, climbing aboard his horse.

"Where were you headed?" she asked, excited by the idea.

"Thedan. And you?"

"Where is Thedan? Can I come with you?" she asked.

"Women in Thedan are treated like slaves. They are bought and sold like cattle. I would not dare take you there."

"Well, if it is as bad as you say why would you want to go there?" she asked curiously.

"It would be the last place my father would think to look for me," he huffed. "Simo is the best tracker I know. Could we discuss this as we ride? Where are you going?" he asked, spilling six crystals into the river.

"Gativa for now," she said, speaking loudly over the rush of the water. "Will you come with me? Your father would never think you would go back there, either. We could get a boat and take to the sea. And we wouldn't have to worry about finding a place to stay because the farmhouse is empty. It's right on the edge of the village, so no one would know we're there," Mirage rattled off nervously, feeling awkward for asking him.

She had to admit she was a little frightened about traveling alone, and she was glad he would be with her.

"I think it is a sound plan. But it will take a longer time to get back to Gativa than it would to get to Thedan. We can only stay there for a short time. They might check there," he said as they rode hard down the road.

"Just as long as it would take to buy a boat," she pleaded. Alexander smiled at her then nodded his head and kicked JeNi's flanks.

They ran the horses on and off as the sun came up.

Kalina woke up in a pool of sweat. She had a terrible headache and a strange queasy feeling in the pit of her stomach. She stood up on wobbly legs and suddenly realized why she was sweating. The heat from outside seeped through the thin tent walls, creating a natural sauna. She could hardly breathe. She noticed Mirage was already up and wondered why she didn't wake her earlier so they could leave.

She staggered to the entrance and stepped outside. She became very nervous when she noticed James still sitting on the ground outside the tent with his head slumped to his chest. She walked slowly toward the soldier. *Please, let him be asleep, please, let him be asleep.* She touched him on the shoulder and called his name. James slowly lifted his head and looked up at Kalina. He tried to get up but stumbled to his knees. Kalina helped him to his feet and walked him over to one of the logs around the fire pit.

"My apologies, Lady Kalina, I didn't think one goblet of wine would affect me," he said, holding his head.

At that moment Simo stepped out of the tent, shielding his eyes from the sun.

"What time is it?" he asked. "It looks to be about noon. Why didn't you wake me, James? I thought we had agreed to leave at first light," Simo said, sitting down next to the others on the log. "I feel awful."

"I just now woke up myself," James answered.

"Where is the prince?" Simo asked.

"Where is Mirage?" Kalina asked.

"Their horses are gone, and that would explain why we slept so long. We've obviously been drugged," James explained, trying to stand on his unsteady legs.

"Why would they do such a thing?" Kalina asked.

"Who's to say why children do what they do. Alexander knows I'll find him. They just wanted a little privacy," Simo said.

"Hurry. We must find them," James said, mounting his horse.

Simo found their tracks leading into the river and the three of them crossed.

"We have to stop now, JeNi is sweating badly," Alex said, pulling her to a walk and then a complete stop. He jumped down and turned to help Mirage down.

"Well, I am a little hungry," she said, handing him an apple.

"After riding all night, you give me an apple," Alex said, looking at her as she walked to her horse.

"It's for the horse," she said with a giggle.

Alex sat down in the shade near a large boulder. Mirage walked by, intending to sit beside him, when he suddenly grabbed her hand, causing her to fall into his lap. She looked up at his smiling face and couldn't help but smile herself, but deep down her stomach was flipping and twisting inside her. She knew she should get up, but she just couldn't. She took a deep breath and tried to relax as he used his fingers to slowly unbraid her hair and spread it over her shoulders.

"I've been thinking this might have been kind of foolish," he said playfully, sifting through her hair. "Simo will just track us down and take us back. My father will be furious and your aunt will certainly be angry. You may even lose your position in the castle."

Should she tell him that she could help? Would he kill her if he didn't understand? She looked up at his face and took a deep breath.

"Prince Alexander, if I tell you a secret, will you promise not to be angry?" she asked, sitting up in his lap to look in his eyes.

"I promise. What is it?" he said nonchalantly.

"No, really, look at me," she said.

He noted the seriousness in her voice. "What is it?"

"Earlier when you asked what I did to make James and the others sleep, I lied. I didn't use herbs to drug them. I used magic to put a spell on the wine, and I can stop Simo from being able to track us because I am Pheolatian," she said in one quick breath, watching his expression as she spoke.

"Pheolatian… witches and warlocks with magical powers—Mirage, those are just stories."

Mirage got up from the ground and held her arms out to the sky. She closed her eyes and turned around twice. She clapped her hands together then opened her palms and spread her fingers wide. The clouds came together and the sky grew dark. Alex looked up, amazed. There were a crash of thunder and a bolt of lightning. "Send me rain and storm," she said loudly. At those words, the sky opened and the rain poured down hard. She put her hands down slowly and turned to Alexander who was staring at her, horrified.

"Alexander," she said, walking toward him. He stumbled to his feet and backed away from her.

"Please don't be afraid of me," she pleaded. Her eyes welled up with tears and they began to fall from her eyes down her cheek.

"Are you a witch?" he asked, looking her over.

"No, I am a sorceress. I was born with my powers. My people are known as the Pheolatians. Surely you've heard of us," she explained, feeling a little better when he stopped backing away, but the look in his eye was horrific.

"Is it your magic that makes me feel the way I do about you?" he asked accusingly.

"I doubt it, since I don't know how you feel about me," she said, glaring at him with her hands on her hips. But her anger was only a cover. His words pierced her soul and left her heart bleeding. "Well, of course, the only reason someone of your status would be interested in somebody like me was if you were under some powerful spell. But for your information, I cannot make people fall in love, take life, or bring anyone back from the dead. It is against the rules of nature. If any one of those three rules were broken, I would lose my powers forever and since I was born with them. I would die without them.

I would never put a spell on you, even if I could," she explained, unable to stop the tears from falling. Here she stood with her heart exposed, waiting for him to bury his sword.

Alex looked her up and down and thought about what she was saying. His father had told him about the Pheolatians, but he had always thought the story of Mestopholes had been a fairytale. He had never seen a human use magic before.

But he did know that he loved her and he didn't think she had anything to do with it because he had loved her from the moment he had first laid eyes on her. He didn't care if she had the power to make it rain. He didn't care that she yelled at him when she was upset. And he didn't care that she wasn't a princess. She would be his.

"I think you have got me under a spell," he said, crossing his arms over his chest.

"But I don't, I promise you," she said in a defeated voice dropping her head.

"You did it with your eyes that day at that stream, and I've been enchanted ever since," he said.

She looked up at him slowly. He loved the way her anger made her eyes flash with fire, the same fire that seemed to be running through his veins. Her hair was wet and dripping. The rain made her dress cling to her body, emphasizing her every curve. He pulled her slowly into his arms. The feel of her against his body made his manhood rise with desire. He kissed her gently at first until she pulled away from him using her hands to smooth the water away from his face.

"So, you believe me?" she asked.

"Yes, I believe you," he said, bending his head to kiss her again.

"And you're not afraid of me?" she asked, backing out of his embrace.

He answered her the only way he knew how. He pulled her toward him and wrapped his arms around the small of her back, lifting her into the air, then slowly lowered his head to taste her. She wrapped her arms around his neck and clung to him. He used his tongue to open her mouth, wanting to taste her fully. He kissed her neck and sucked gently on her earlobe. He whispered softly into her ear, but she was so caught up in the waves of his passion that she didn't hear what he said.

"Huh? What did you say?" she asked, quietly turning her neck to receive his kisses.

"Join with me," he whispered as he nibbled on her ear.

"What of the woman you are to marry?" she asked trustingly, looking into his eyes, waiting for an answer that would make the way he was making her feel be okay.

"I will have you as my queen or no one at all," he answered, looking deep into her eyes.

What answer could have been better? She believed him, believed that they would be together forever. She wrapped her arms around his neck and squeezed him tightly, burying her face in his chest. She took a deep breath and was filled with his scent.

She could feel her nipples throbbing. The tiny hairs on the nape of her neck stood up. It felt like spiders running up and down her back. He left a hot trail up the path he ran across her arms. Then he used his fingers to raise her chin.

He gave her that contagious smile and before she knew it he was kissing her again. Her heart pounded and her breath sent her heaving to and fro when she felt him pulling at the laces on the back of her dress. Between the rain and his kisses, she could hardly breathe, but she knew this could go no farther. She pushed herself from his embrace breathing hard staring into his eyes.

"Alexander, I don't know…I'm so confused. I…" she said, feeling foolish.

"I promise I won't hurt you," he said, closing the distance between them. He took her hand and pulled her toward him as she started to cry. "Don't cry, little one." He held her tightly against his chest and stroked her hair. The next thing he knew he was waking up with her cradled in his arms.

The rain continued to pour down from the sky. He had no idea how long they had been asleep. They had to get moving. He tried to rise but found he couldn't move. Thick green vines covered with pink and white blossoms with thick green leaves had sprouted from the ground. They wrapped around their bodies, intertwining between the two of them.

Alexander looked around nervously as he struggled to free himself. Something had ensnared them while they slept. Probably fairies; they were surrounded by wild flowers. Mirage began to stir in his arms. The vines adjusted to her, letting her sit up freely and releasing Alexander at the same time.

"What is it?" she asked, worried by the expression on his face.

"You do not see these flowers?" he asked, thinking maybe he was truly losing his mind.

"It happens when I sit on the ground for a long time. Grandma Tilda says—I mean, she used to say it's because so much power is inside of me that nature reacts to its presence," she explained.

"Just like the sky when you're angry," he said.

"What do you mean the sky when I'm angry?" she asked earnestly.

"The sky must respond to your power as well. You haven't noticed clear sunny skies filling with clouds when you're sad, like when your grandmother died, or flashing with lighting when you're angry," he said, getting up from the ground, pushing the water back from his face.

"I've never paid it any attention. It must have just started happening," she said as he helped her up from the ground.

"What do you mean?" he asked, watching her tug on the wet gown. She pulled her wet hair through her palm and to his amazement it was braided into one fat braid when she reached the end. She flipped it over her shoulder. He tied her horse to his, then he helped her climb into the saddle then mounted behind her.

"If you had met me three years ago, I would have been normal. My powers are just developing. You should have been there that day all the farm animals started following me around. I barely notice it now."

"So, that is why the forest creatures come to you…because of your power? We are the same in that regard," he said quietly, guiding the horse into the forest.

"You and the animals? The same? How so?" Mirage asked, looking up at him. He cleared his throat and pretended to concentrate on the path he was taking through the trees. "How are you the same?"

"We are all drawn to your power, little one," he said softly into her ear. She turned in the saddle and looked up at him. The words were familiar somehow, but the voice was all wrong.

"I'm cold," she said as the wind blew. She wrapped her arms around his waist and closed her eyes.

Alex pulled his cloak around her, thinking it wouldn't make any difference. It was soaked through and through. He looked up at the sky and saw no end to this storm. Then he remembered this was no ordinary storm.

"Mirage, I think our tracks are gone by now. Do you think you could bring back the sun?" he asked. She looked up at him and smiled.

"If Simo is as good as you say, it will take more than rain to cover our tracks. I have to get down, though," she said. He helped her down, then got down from the horse and watched as she used her hands to push the clouds away. She was like a God. The sun came out shining brightly. She made a fist, then swept her hands back and forth around Alexander, drying his clothes then her own. Then she bent down and put her palm flat to the ground. "May the path we've taken be erased, and those that track us find no trace." The ground gave a small rumble in response. Leaves and dust kicked up, sending a kaleidoscope of colors spinning across the forest floor then it settled back to normal. He helped her back on the horse and rode off down the road.

Kalina thought the sudden storm was strange, but when the rain suddenly stopped and the sun came out again, she knew Mirage had caused it. She was more powerful than she had ever thought. Her own powers were nothing compared to a sorceress that could complete the weather enchantment alone, but then she had known that for awhile now. Matilda had not even mastered the spells to control the weather. Even after being warned, she still found herself saying that phrase.

If Mirage was using magic to aid in their escape, there was nothing the king or Kalina could do—alone, anyway. She would need her sisters of magic to find her. The thought of telling the king about her powers made her head ache. She was afraid, but it was the only thing that would work. Suddenly her mind went to Degar. She could see his face. The thought made a tear fall from her eyes. The king would not burn her at the stake if she could help find his son.

Simo circled the ground, trying to find some trace of their trail. The running horses had been easy to follow, even in the rain. Now it seemed as if they had taken flight. He couldn't even find a broken twig that would indicate that they had passed by. He looked up at James and shook his head.

"We will return to the castle. The king will be furious," James said. How was he going to explain to the king that he let two children get the best of him? If anything happened to them he would never forgive himself.

"So, if you were born a witch, does that mean your parents were witches?" Alex asked as they traveled quickly through the woods.

"I'm not a witch and I never knew my parents, but from what I've been told, my mother had powers and my father's mother had powers," she answered, ducking her head under a low-hanging branch.

"Can you fly?" he asked.

"Do you think that if I could fly we'd be racing through this forest like this? The truth is I still haven't mastered the entire spell book, so I really don't know what I can do. Grandma Tilda did say I floated out of my cradle when I was a baby," she said, shrugging her shoulders.

"Look there. What's that?" he said, gesturing toward a half-standing hut. "We will stay there for the night. I know it looks kind of shabby, but we will be okay," he said, helping Mirage down from her horse. As he turned she waved her hands as she said some words he didn't understand and turned the shabby hut into a quaint little cabin.

"Looks fine to me," she said, walking into the room.

"We should get some rest. I want to leave before its light. We have to get as far away from Father as possible," he said, looking at her over his shoulders.

She was curled up into a ball on the bed, fast asleep. Alex crawled into the tiny bed and wrapped her up in his arms. They were making good time, but he couldn't help being nervous about running from his father. He had never disobeyed him before. He closed his eyes and fell asleep.

CHAPTER 16

Orders

The United Rose Fortress, Theslia

Benjamin sat back against his throne after being told that his son had run away. He couldn't believe he would dare disobey his orders. Alexander understood the importance of the chain of command; since he was a child he was taught to follow orders regardless of his own personal opinions and to always think every situation through. Alexander had been groomed to become the next ruler of Theslia, unlike himself, which meant he would naturally be better at it, but with such a job came responsibility and sacrifice. Why would he dishonor his family name by running away from his throne? Such an act could cause the fabric of their government to fall apart. Men might even try to challenge the throne.

He thought it would be a good idea for him to spend some time with the princess before they were married. Maybe he had been wrong to deceive him about the purpose of the journey, but he thought that if he had told Alexander he was going to meet his bride that he would have closed his mind to the situation and refused to get to know her. So, he had devised this plan that would allow him to meet the princess.

Kalina had sent him an annual report concerning the child over the years, from which he had perceived her as a lovely girl. Kalina had explained that she was smart, sincere, honest, and also very beautiful. He thought his son would appreciate those qualities in a woman, knowing his feelings concerning the women of the court. He could have allowed the princess to remain in oblivion, but he owed it to King Alosis to see to it that his blood was placed back on the throne. Their country would still be under Lavitian rule if it weren't for Alosis.

"I want them found and brought back here yesterday!" he said sternly. The soldiers filed out of the hall to follow his orders.

Kalina stepped forward and gave the king a low curtsy, then waited quietly until he addressed her. The king nodded toward her and she stood up to speak to him.

"Your Majesty, may I speak with you privately?" she asked.

"What is it concerning?" he asked in turn.

"Finding Mirage, sire—I mean Princess Saroja and His Highness," she answered.

Benjamin waved her forward and she walked quickly to the platform. She explained that she could find them but needed help. She gave him the three names and was surprised when he immediately dispatched the soldiers without any extra explanation.

Grecian, Theslia

Mirage woke up early. The sky was pale white through the window. Alexander still slept quietly beside her. They still had a few hours before dawn. She rose quietly so she wouldn't disturb him. She figured if she was going to use her powers to get them through this ordeal, she'd better start practicing her magic wholeheartedly.

She conjured the candles she would need to "call the corners.

She had them all in place and was about to begin the ritual when Alex asked her what she was doing.

"I have to ask the four winds to bless our day," she said, turning away from him.

"Where did all these things come from?" he asked.

There was a black circle drawn on the floor with a white diamond drawn through the center. Tall white candles circled the room.

"I conjured them," she answered while lighting the last of the white candles with her finger tip.

"Do you think you could 'conjure' some food?" he asked, rising from the bed, stretching his arms up over his head yawning. He walked up behind her. He wrapped her up in his arms, kissing the smooth column of her neck.

Mirage wiggled out of his embrace. "I will as soon as I'm finished with the ritual, but you must stop interrupting."

"I beg your forgiveness. Please, proceed," he said with a hint of humor, sitting back down on the bed, folding his arms across his chest.

There were eighteen candles in the room, one for each year of her life. All were white except the four that were placed inside the circle she had drawn on the floor. She knelt in the middle of the diamond and placed a candle at each point. One was white, one yellow, one red, and one black.

She lit the white one and said, "I call to the northern winds, invoking all the powers of sky and earth," she said, turning left to light the black candle. "I call to the western winds, invoking all the powers of light and darkness," she said as she turned to the left and lit a yellow one. "I call to the southern winds, invoking all the powers of spirit and being," she said, finally turning to light the last red candle. "I call to the eastern winds, invoking all the powers of past and present." She stood then and raised her arms high above her head.

The wind blew into the room and all the candles went out except the four on the floor inside the circle. The room was filled with a warm mist and it circled all around her.

Alex sat back on the bed behind her. He stood up and walked toward her, curious to find out how she felt, filled with so much power. She was a beautiful sight. Her hair had become undone as she slept and the raven-colored locks that hung down pass her small waist flapped rapidly in the wind, which encased her as it sped rapidly around her. He walked slowly toward her, starting to rethink his idea as he got closer to the circle she stood in the center of. The wind was strong and cold as he walked into it. It wrapped around him swiftly, making it hard to walk. He had to concentrate on each step.

Mirage stood with her eyes closed, concentrating on connecting the energy of the wind with her spirit. She practiced completely relaxing her thoughts which allowed the natural powers within to breathe as she had been taught. As she pushed her powers out, the winds started moving faster and faster around her.

Something grazed pass her arm and Mirage opened her eyes. She held out her hands to him as he walked toward her, wet and shivering.

He took hold of her tiny frame and wrapped his hands around her waist. She seemed so small and fragile, but he would never deny that she was a woman. He would make her his woman; the very idea made his heart warm inside his chest.

When she returned his embrace, instantly he was wrapped in a blanket of warmth. The hot air seemed to rise from the floor. Mirage wrapped her arms around his neck and closed her eyes again. He kissed her and held her tightly to his chest. She returned his savory kisses and allowed her powers to run freely between them.

The energy seemed to fuel the winds circling around them. Lightning flashed and flashes of light started to emanate from her body causing her to glow. Alex separated his lips from hers and noticed that their feet were no longer touching the floor.

"Mirage," he whispered, not wanting to startle her. "We're floating."

She opened her eyes and looked down. Slowly they descended back to the floor. The winds calmed and whistled out of the small cabin. Mirage was amazed; calling the corners had never taken her from the ground before. "Well, I guess I've found a new source of power," she said, wrapping her arms around him. "Maybe you have some powers too."

"No, I think that was all you, little one," he said. He hugged her and walked to the table. "Now can I have something to eat?"

She kissed him sweetly and went outside. She came back moments later with an arm filled with leaves and pine combs and placed them on the table before him.

"Surely, you jest," he said, looking up at her over his shoulder. She waved her hands, ending with a fist, and the candles disappeared. She touched the table then closed her eyes for awhile, and then she swept them over the table and a feast appeared before him. She walked back to the bed and spread her dress out on it. She cleaned it and turned it into a pale, yellow day gown, then pulled it on.

"Hurry, we need to leave," she said, braiding her hair and securing the end with a ribbon.

After eating and packing some of the food for the journey, the two raced through the forest as the sun came up.

Castle Covax, Lavitia

Marsalis sat in his study, planning his new strategy for taking Theslia, and for the first time in years he was sure that this was finally going to work. He would need lots of slaves to get things started. He would also have to find the country's best builders to fortify the tunnel he planned to run straight through the mountains.

After it was built he would lead the army himself that would crush Benjamin. Then he would climb to the highest peak in the land and watch as his soldiers set the land on fire. He drew the design for the tunnel that would lead to his new treasure city. He would draw the plans for the architects after the tunnel was built. He wished he could be there when his men finally broke through to the other side. He had fifty thousand soldiers waiting to pour into Benjamin's puny country. It would be a battle they never forgot. And finally, the Great Creator would know that he was born to rule this land.

A knock at the door disrupted his thoughts.

"Enter," he said loudly, sitting up straight.

"My lord, Lord Laven has arrived," the servant said from the doorway.

"Tell him to await me in the throne room," he said, rising from the pillows where he sat. He picked up his father's sword from its stand and removed it from the scabbard and marched slowly down the hall.

When he reached the throne room, Laven rushed to his side. Marsalis immediately noticed the slight gimp in his stride. *He had killed her.* The enemy had been staring him straight in the eye for years and he hadn't noticed. That mistake had cost him his queen.

"Cousin, are you well? The messenger said you needed me to return with all haste," Laven asked, hopeful. Marsalis did look a little flushed, though he'd never known him to be sick a day in his life; he could make any illness work to his advantage.

Marsalis said nothing. He continued silently to the throne. When he reached it, he stopped and looked at his cousin expectantly, then offered him the seat with a gestured wave. Laven's face went flush. He bowed to the king then backed away.

"No, cousin, I insist," he said, grabbing him by his robes and flinging him into the seat. "How is it? Are you comfortable?" he asked, moving up the two steps. He leaned over, placing both hands on top of Laven's hands, which were gripping the chair's arms so hard his knuckles were white. Marsalis's eyes were wide with the building rage he had repressed after he'd seen her lying dead covered with blood. "Are you comfortable?" he yelled when he got no response, causing everyone in the room to jump and turn their attention to the proceedings at the throne. The guards moved in closer but none interfered.

"Do you know what today is, cousin?" Marsalis asked, standing up straight again, staring down at him expectantly.

"Um, today, sire? Today is—" the words stumbled out of his mouth. Marsalis turned to the crowd.

"Today is my birthday. Did you know that? You are the only family I have and you've never once wished me a happy birthday since my parents died. Stick out your tongue," the king said, turning back to his cousin. "Now," he yelled. Laven slowly pushed his tongue from his mouth. Marsalis brought the sword he held behind his back up to eye level.

"A liar has no need for a tongue. Shall I remove it from your mouth?" Laven's eyes grew wide as Marsalis rested the sword against his tongue. The razor, sharp blade instantly drew blood.

Laven sat staring at Marsalis, terrified. His thoughts were coming so fast he couldn't catch one in time to throw it out. Should he say yes? Should he say no? Ask what he'd done? No, he dared not to ask that question. He dared not move. He was shaking as Marsalis pulled the blade away, slicing open the tip of Laven tongue. He started pacing back and forth, glaring at him, and waving his sword as he spoke.

"What happened to your foot?" he asked calmly. "My foot, my lord," Laven stammered, looking around nervously.

"Yes, your foot," Marsalis said as he walked over and stomped on it. Laven wailed in pain.

"There was—my king, there was—"

"There was what? A defenseless woman alone in her chambers? You can jump in at any time. Why did you kill her? Because I was going to marry her? Answer me!" the king yelled.

"What was the question?" Laven whispered. He was undone. Marsalis knew everything. It was only a matter of time before he pushed the sword through his heart. He shouldn't have touched the girl. Or better yet he should not have returned. He should have waited like he'd planned.

Marsalis rushed forward and brought the sword to his throat. "Why did you kill her?" He knew why. He wanted to see if his sniveling cousin would admit it.

"She was bewitching you, my king. I went to ask her to remove the spell she had placed on you and she tried to attack me…with her…her magic," Laven pleaded.

"You would dare look into the eyes of a king and lie. You think I would bring someone into my home that I knew nothing about. She couldn't cast spells on people.

"You don't seem to have a scratch on you, yet she was beaten like a dog. Today you will take her place. You will be the weak, I, the strong.

"Get off my throne! Guard, give me your sword. No one is to interfere," he said loudly, making a full circle until he faced Laven again. "You want my crown, cousin? Come, take it," he said, throwing the sword the guard had given him to Laven's feet. "Pick it up."

Laven looked around nervously. He bent slowly to pick up the sword. Everyone in the hall knew who would be the victor of a sword fight between these two. He had learned how to use a sword for defense, but his skill would be nothing compared to that of the king's.

Marsalis had been taught that the king should be the best. He should be stronger than the strongest soldier, better than the best fighter. Laven didn't stand a chance. He reached his hand out to retrieve the sword and he was suddenly kicked in the jaw.

Marsalis's roundhouse had landed square on his chin, knocking him to the hard marble floor where he hit his head. *Crack*. He slowly lifted his head. An unsettling wave moved through his head as he turned it. His fingers felt warm blood as he held it, getting up slowly. Through the haze he did remember to get the sword.

Marsalis waited as his cousin got to his feet and he was impressed when he displayed the proper battle stance. He engaged him as soon as he met his eyes striking his sword twice before he punched him hard in the face, sending him flying to the floor again. Marsalis started toward him. Laven turned to his stomach, trying to untangle his robes as he tried to crawl away. Marsalis kicked him in the stomach and slashed him across the chest. He yelped with pain and tried to dodge the next blow but ended up getting stabbed in the leg. Finally, Marsalis came to stand over him, placing his sword to his throat. He moved it slowly to his stomach and pushed it into Laven's shoulder, then leaned on it.

"Tomorrow at dawn you will receive fifty lashes before you are racked and beheaded. Take him to the dungeon," he said as he marched from the room.

The next day the entire court assembled to watch Laven's execution. Marsalis was in a foul mood. Even his advisors had distanced themselves from him. Only Lord Kail remained by his side.

"Bring out the prisoner," Kail called loudly. The drums rolled as they waited for the jailers to arrive. The guards returned moments later and headed to the dais where the king sat.

"My king, the jailers are dead and Lord Laven is gone," the guard said quietly, with his head down.

"Search the grounds and report back to me. I want him found and killed on sight," Marsalis declared, rising from his seat. Lord Kail followed him.

"Laven could not have escaped the jailers in his condition, my lord," Kail said to the king's back. There was a breath of silence.

"It is my fault that he escaped at all. I wanted him to suffer. I should have killed him when I had a chance, but you go find and bring his accomplices to me," he said, looking over his shoulder for a moment then continuing to the palace. "And Kail, do not fail me."

"It will be done, my liege," Kail replied. He bowed low to Marsalis's back then went about his task.

CHAPTER 17

Daybreak

Outskirts of Gativa, Theslia
Three Weeks Later

Alexander and Mirage rode hard down the road, trying to reach Gativa before dark. Suddenly the sky opened up and the rain started to pour.

"Can you do something about this rain?" Alexander asked, looking up at the sky. He pulled JeNi to a steady trot.

"I cannot stop a natural storm. I can only create and control my own powers. The Great Creator rules over the rest. Can you feel it?" she asked in an excited tone.

"Feel what? The rain?" he asked, holding his palms up as the rode slowly down the muddy road.

"The power," she said, looking over at him with a big smile on her face.

"Power? No, it just feels wet to me," he said, wishing he were as excited about the cold wet drops trickling down his back as she was.

"The world's power. It lives and it breathes. It is so strong. It makes my skin tingle," she said, hugging herself.

"I'm glad you're enjoying yourself," he said, smiling at her, shaking his head.

They rode on until they came to a small village just off the road and decided to find some shelter there for the night so they could start off fresh in the morning. As they entered the village, a tall man greeted them carrying an armful of wood.

He had a lean, muscular build. He must have been a soldier when he was in his prime; his arms and legs were so chiseled with muscles. He smiled and nodded his head in their direction as they approached.

"Greetings to you on this soft evening," he said as he walked back toward his cabin. They were a sorry sight. They were drenched from head to toe and covered with mud. He couldn't help but feel sorry for them.

"Sir, we are on our way to Gativa. Do you know a place where we could find shelter for the night?" Alexander asked looking up at the sky.

"You're welcome to stay here with us," he said immediately.

"Are you sure? We don't want to intrude," Alexander said.

"Nonsense. It would be our pleasure to have you and your lady stay the night. I couldn't leave you out in this weather and there are no inns in this village. Besides, we were just about to have dinner," the man explained.

"Thank you for your kindness," Alexander said, getting down from his horse. "My name is Simo and this is Sara."

"I am called Theyman. Please, come in out of the rain," he said, pushing the door open with his foot.

"Cassandra, set two more places. We will be having guests for dinner. They will be staying for the night," he said, getting a wary look from his wife that asked why he invited these strangers to stay with them. He shrugged, replying that they seemed nice enough and they were young, probably just starting off.

He remembered what that was like, though he couldn't remember anyone offering them shelter from the elements. She was right to be wary of strangers, especially in these trying times, but his heart had softened at the sight of them and he found himself compelled to help.

Alexander and Mirage came back into the cabin and sat down at the small table. Cassandra served them with a smile, then took her own seat.

"This is my son, Jesse, and that is my little angel, Jules," Theyman said, pointing to the children who beamed at their father over their plates. "Cassandra, this is Simo and his wife, Sara."

"Once again, thank you for having us. You have a lovely home and beautiful children," Mirage said, smiling.

"Theyman tells me you journey to Gativa. Do you have family there?" Cassandra asked.

"No, we're going to settle down there. We hear fishermen make a decent wage in that town," Alexander said.

"Well, the good news is you're almost there. Gativa is only a few miles away," Theyman said, getting up from the table after he'd finished his meal.

"Okay children, off to bed," Cassandra said. The two children kissed their parents, good night, then climbed up the loft to their beds.

Cassandra went up behind them and came down moments later with several thick blankets.

"I'm sorry, there are only three beds. You'll have to sleep on the floor," she said, handing Mirage the blankets.

"Its fine, my lady, I'm sure it would be much more comfortable than sleeping on a wet ground," Alexander said.

"Thank you again for allowing us to stay," Mirage said, spreading the blankets out on the floor. Theyman and Cassandra retired to the loft and Alexander lay down next to Mirage on the floor. He wrapped her up in his arms and they went to sleep.

Hours later they were awakened by a terrible banging on the door. Theyman came down the stairs and opened it. Four men in black hoods pushed their way into the cabin.

"Theyman, it is rumored that your wife has had some dealings in the black arts. We must take her away for questioning," one of the men said.

"That is a lie," Theyman said, shocked by the suggestion. "I know what this is about. I told Silus I would not sell. You will leave here now."

"Do you refuse to cooperate?" another man said.

"You have no authority here. You're nothing but thieves preying on the weak. Well, I'm not weak and I'm not afraid of you. Leave my home," he said, drawing his sword, prepared to die defending his family.

Cassandra held the children as she watched her husband face off against the men.

"That witch, is coming with us. If we have to go through you to get to her, so be it," they said, pulling their swords out.

"You will leave them be," Alexander said, pulling his weapon out and walking to Theyman's side. Mirage stood near Cassandra.

"Stranger, this is not your concern," the leader of the group said.

"He is right, Simo. I won't ask you to risk your life," Theyman said.

"You have showed us kindness and for that I stand with you," Alexander said.

"So be it," one of the hooded men said, charging Theyman.

Alexander pushed Theyman out of the way and blocked the attack with his sword. Theyman turned quickly and engaged with another man. Alexander twisted and turned around the man he was fighting, slicing him several times. He didn't want to kill anyone in front of the children. He was knocked off his feet and ended up cutting the man's leg to escape. The blood spewed from the wound. Theyman killed his attacker and turned to another man. Mirage and Cassandra moved the children up the stairs and watched from the balcony. The tallest of the men grabbed Theyman around the throat and used him to threaten Alexander after noticing his men would be beaten.

"Lower your weapon, or he dies," he said. Alexander slowly put the sword on the floor and stood up straight again. "Now back away."

He backed up and allowed the man to move to the door still holding Theyman hostage.

"Release him or I will kill you," Alexander ordered.

The man laughed and brought his sword to Theyman's throat.

"No!" Cassandra screamed from upstairs. Alexander threw his dagger quickly, striking the man in his eye. He screamed and fell backwards out of the door.

"We will return, Theyman! This is not over! The witch will burn!" one of the men yelled as he limped from the room, helping another fallen man.

"Thank you for your help," Theyman said as Alexander helped him up to his feet. "I can't imagine what would have happened if you weren't here. It would seem the Great Creator knew what he was doing when he sent you to my door."

Cassandra ran down the stairs and hugged her husband.

"You should come with us," Mirage said.

"No, our place is here. I have worked too hard for this land just to be pushed off," Theyman said.

"But those men will be back and there will be no one to stand with you the next time," Alexander said.

"Our village will stand together. We will be fine," he said, looking down at his wife. "Let us get some sleep."

The next morning Alexander and Mirage said goodbye to the family.

"Are you sure you won't change your mind? I can't help but worry what will happen to you when those men return," Alexander said.

"You have been a good friend. We will be fine. I will speak with the village council. If those men return, we will make our stand," Theyman said.

"Thank you for your kindness," Mirage said again. "Are you really Pheolatian?" she whispered.

"I used to be, but that was a long time ago. I can't even practice magic anymore. I left my coven to raise my family. I thought it would be too dangerous for them if I stayed, but I see my past has finally caught up with me," she said sadly.

Mirage hugged her and climbed aboard her horse. They waved good bye and started on their way.

"There it is," Mirage said from the top of the hill, looking down at the farmhouse she'd grown up in. "We made it, and just before dark."

"Let's walk," Alex said, getting down from his horse. "They have to be exhausted."

Alexander took the horses to the stable and fed them while Mirage went inside the house to make them something to eat. As he walked back around, he decided to close the windows. They were at the edge of the village, but it was getting dark and people could see light from miles away. He walked around the house and closed the shutters. He was stunned when he walked through the door. This magic thing would take some getting used to.

There was a fire humming in the fireplace on one wall, a table laden with food. The floor was covered with rugs and tall white candles littered the room. And Mirage was in the middle, bent over a large white tub filled with steamy water and soap bubbles.

"You have been busy. Is this what I should expect each time I enter a room?" he said, walking toward her.

"Then you would become spoiled, and we simply couldn't have that," she said.

"You forget I am a prince. I'm used to being spoiled," he said.

"I have prepared the water for you. Soak and relax your muscles," she said.

"Will you join me?" he asked, smiling down at her.

"I have my own bath waiting on me… upstairs," she said, walking by him. He caught her hand but she slowly pulled it away and took to the stairs.

He took off his clothes and stepped into the hot water, sitting down slowly. He pushed his head back against the rim and closed his eyes. When he was done he draped the towel around his waist and poured a goblet of wine for himself. He drank the contents then walked to the foot of the stairs looking up. She was awfully quiet up there.

He tiptoed slowly up the stairs and leaned against the banister. She was seated on the floor in front of the fireplace in a long white night shift, brushing through her wet hair. He watched her switch from arm to arm when one grew too tired to continue. He stepped up one more step. It creaked in defiance. He stood up from his crouched position when she turned to the stair. "Do you want to eat with me?" he asked awkwardly after having been caught.

"I'll be down in a moment," she said, rising from the floor. She looked up and tripped over the edge of the nightgown, falling to the floor again. Alexander was dressed only in a towel and it nearly fell away when he rushed to her side to help her up from the floor.

"Are you alright?" he asked, picking her up in his arms.

"I'm fine, I just scraped my knee. Put me down, Alexander," she said as he held her against his bare chest. "I can manage on my own. You should put on some clothes."

"I want to carry you and I prefer comfort over modesty when I sleep," he said, turning to the stairs.

"Put me down. I will make you something comfortable to wear," she said as he carried her down the stairs and placed her on the edge of the bed and started lifting the edge of her nightgown.

"What are you doing?" she asked, putting her hands on her knee to stop the action.

"I want to see the bruise," he said.

"There is no bruise," she said, allowing him to look at her knees.

There was a red mark on her knee from where it rubbed the floor, but besides that it was fine. Alexander bent and kissed it.

"Now are you going to pat my head and say all better?" Mirage asked, smiling down at him. "I need your pants," she said, rising from the bed. She spread it across the bed and turned them into loosely fitting linen pants. "There. These will be comfortable don't you think?" she said, spinning around to give them to him. Then she spun back around when he took them from her hands and let the towel fall to the floor.

"I'm decent," he said in a humorous tone. After they ate, Mirage cleared the table.

"Good night, Alexander," she said, heading for the stairs. He stood, blocking her path.

"Where do you think you're going?"

"To bed, if I'm allowed," she said. Her adrenaline had tripled in the seconds it took for him to reach out and touch her face.

"You can sleep next me. I promise I won't touch you."

"It's not that, I just didn't want to…you know…tease you. I should sleep upstairs," she explained.

"That was not a request and it's not like we haven't slept in the same bed before."

"Very well," she said, crawling into the large bed. She laid flat on her back, waiting for the bed to shift. She couldn't bear to watch him. The thought of his towel nearly falling away upstairs made her heartbeat quicken. His bare chest was covered with hard muscles. Moments passed as she thought what it would be like to sleep next to a half-naked man, but he didn't join her. He sat down in the chair next to the bed and watched her. "Aren't you going to sleep?"

"Rest your nerves, Mirage. I'll be right here until you fall asleep."

"You don't have to do that," she said, turning on her side to face him.

"I hate to admit it, but you were right. I don't think I could lie next to you without touching you." Mirage smiled and held out her hand.

"I think I can endure your touch for one more night, Alexander," she said. His name seemed to roll off her tongue, making it sound far more exotic than it really was. He took her hand and crawled into the bed next to her. She moved slowly toward him and kissed him softly on his forehead. She placed her head gently on his shoulder and then closed her eyes. He wrapped his arms around her and pulled her close to his side.

When Mirage had fallen to sleep Alex pushed back on the pillow as she lay sleeping on his chest staring up at the ceiling. He had never met anyone like her before, but if he wanted to keep her he would have to make amends with his father and he wasn't looking forward to it.

CHAPTER 18

Through the Looking Glass

United Rose Fortress, Theslia

"I don't even know why we're here," Maja Findi said, lifting the end if her gown as they walked up the stairs of the castle.

"We're here because the king ordered us to come," Claris Sise' answered.

"You both know Kalina needs our help. We cannot be selfish. If we needed her for something important she would come to help us," Kaemar Dante said.

"No, she would not," Maja said, leading the way.

"Well, I'm here to help the king find his son. We don't need her to do that. After all, she left us," Claris said.

"How can we help without her, Claris?" Kaemar said, giving her a side's glance. It had been nearly twenty-five years since Kalina told them she was leaving the coven. It had hurt, but that hurt had faded years ago. Right now, she was excited about seeing her friend and using her powers again, and she knew Claris and Maja were too; they just liked to complain. They entered the great hall and were told to wait. The king was busy talking to a large group of men.

As she scanned the room, glancing from face to face, a skill learned from years at court, Kalina noticed Maja in the doorway. She hadn't aged a day. She was still strikingly beautiful with her pale, regal looks. Straight black, shiny hair fell down her back. High cheekbones and crystal-blue eyes only added to the picture. She seemed to still lead the group. Claris and Kaemar stood to each of her sides slightly behind her. Claris was nearly the same height as Maja. Her skin was a deep mahogany and she had cut her hair to the shoulders. Kalina was surprised Maja had allowed that. Kaemar had always been the smallest most spirited member of the group. She wasn't as pleasing to the eye as Claris and Maja but where she lacked in looks, she made up for it with heart.

She swallowed her pride and started toward them. She slowed her steps when Maja's and Claris's heads went together. She stood up straight and held her head at a higher angle, then continued toward them.

"My sisters," she said nervously, hugging Kaemar. "It is good to see you after all this time."

"*Sister*," Claris said. Her nose wrinkled as her mouth turned to the side. "You are no sister of mine."

"You wanted a normal life, right, one free from persecution. Is that not what you said when you broke a blood oath?" Maja said, crossing her arms.

"I'm sorry, Maja, I'm a coward. Is that what you wanted to hear? I was tired of running, tired of hiding out, afraid to die," Kalina explained.

"You deserted your family; we were your family. We function in four, but you have natural powers. You didn't need us so you deserted us to enjoy life at court while our kind was persecuted and destroyed," Claris said.

"Ladies, please," the guard said when their conversation grew louder.

"I couldn't do it anymore after they killed him. I'm sorry. I need you to forgive me," Kalina pleaded, desperate for their help.

"Would we even be having this conversation if you didn't need us?" Claris asked.

"Maybe not, but I do, so here we are. Will you help me…please?" Kalina pleaded.

"This is not the time to discuss this," Kaemar said, wringing her hands frantically.

The king finally called the ladies forward and told them that he would meet them in his private chambers. Kalina, Maja, Kaemar, and Claris entered the chamber and formed a circle, holding hands. They started a low chant as they closed their eyes. "With the coming of days and everlasting nights, grant us the power of unlimited sight."

The king sat nervously, watching. He did not like not knowing where his son was. He knew Alexander could take care of himself, but he was an arrogant boy who believed he was invincible. He knew the world of magic. Years ago, the Pheolatians practiced it openly. Some believed it was evil, but if these women could use their powers to find his son, then there had to be some good in it.

"I see her," Kalina said.

"Is Alexander with her?" Benjamin asked.

There was no answer. Kalina saw Mirage in her mind. She was asleep on a large bed. She expanded her focus to look around the room. The light from the candles made the images dim and fuzzy.

"He is there," she said.

"Where are they?" The king asked.

"I don't know, I've never seen this place before," she said.

"You must look beyond the room," Maja ordered, taking charge of the circle as usual. It had been so long since she'd been able to use her powers that she had forgotten how good it felt. She would never understand how anyone could give up such a feeling. It was like being dipped in warm water but never getting wet.

Kalina used her mind to look around the room. She walked to the door and went outside. Those hills were so familiar. White fog started to cloud the images. She reached into the power of the coven. It was like pulling a tattered string, at any minute it could pop. She pulled a little too hard. The energy overwhelmed her, even though she had natural powers she very seldom used them as her mother had. She had learned over the years to do without them. She closed the vision from her mind and looked at the darkness behind her eyelids and allowed her mind to relax for a moment.

When she looked into the vision again, she still stared at those familiar hills and suddenly it came to her. She turned around and saw the farmhouse.

"I know where they are," she said, breaking her connection with the others. "They are in Gativa at the farmhouse. Right now, they are asleep."

The king rose immediately and left the room. He dispatched his fastest men to Gativa. When he returned to the chamber after some time, he explained to the women that he wanted them to stay at the castle just in case they moved.

Gativa, Theslia

Mirage lay flat across the bed on her stomach, flipping through the pages of the spell book. The first letter of each page had been drawn in calligraphy. Each spell had an extensive explanation of how in came to exist. It was a diary passed down from generation to generation.

There were spells that ranged from conjuring candles to absorbing fevers into them. If she memorized the levitation spell, she wouldn't even have to move her feet to walk. She read over a story about a man out at sea during a dry summer.

The sun beamed its scorching rays down on the ship. There had been no wind to move the ship for days. A journey that should have taken a week had been drawn out to three. His rations were depleting quickly. Usually he could conjure more by simply collecting inanimate objects, for nothing could be made from nothing, but all he had left were his sailing materials and the clothes on his back.

Naked and starving he turned to his training to take his mind off his stomach. Calling the corners one day, he prayed for the wind to move his ship. He would not last much longer. Suddenly a great gust of wind started the ship gliding quickly through the water. Now he feared he would be lost at sea because he had already eaten his oar, but with no interference from him the wind guided the ship directly to his dock on the border of his village. From that incident people began to manipulate the weather as was needed. During the long drought seasons, they would bring about rain for the crops.

Alex came back into the house.

"We must leave soon. We have probably been here for too long as it is. Come, let's take the horses to the ocean. You've had your head in that book for the last three days. I have to get out of this house or I swear I'll go mad," he said, pacing back and forth.

"What's the matter with you? Remember, the fisherman said we could leave on his ship at dawn, but I'd love to go to the beach," she said, closing the book and rising up to her knees. Something was bothering him, that much was certain. He paced and rubbed his hands together nervously.

Every day she spent with him she learned a little more about him. His mannerisms reflected his emotions. He was curt and used short hand signals when he was irritated. He smiled and his hand gestures were more graceful when he was relaxed. He gave her confidence and for some reason that made her powers stronger. She couldn't explain it. Maybe it was because she could finally use them openly.

They rode through the village to the ocean. When they reached the beach, they climbed off their horses and let them run free across the empty spans of the secluded shore. The sun was set low in the sky. They walked along the shore and watched the surf wash up over the sand then retreat back to the ocean. The seagulls drifted in the wind currents overhead.

"The easy part is over," Alexander said, taking her hand. "Now we will have to face the world. Are you ready for that?"

"I think so," she said, looking up at him. Then she stared out into the endlessness of the sea sparkling with oranges and reds reflected down from the colors the sun cast across the sky. "We'll be fine, won't we?" Was he worried about the journey? Was the world really the frightening place Kalina had described? It couldn't be.

"Sometimes I don't know. I've been feeling guilty about disobeying my father. I haven't just run from him, you know, I've also run from Theslia. Father always told me, 'Theslia is a child and it would one day be my responsibility to take care of her.' I love my country. I would die for her," he explained.

"Then maybe you should go back," she said, turning to face him. "Maybe the country needs you more than I do."

He stared at her for a moment. His brows pushed down in the center and rose slightly on the ends, creating thick wrinkles across his forehead. "If I go back to the United Rose Fortress, you are coming with me," he said bluntly.

The beautiful sky suddenly filled with clouds and covered the white sand with a dark gray shadow. Alexander looked up at the sky then down at Mirage.

"I told you before. I will not watch you marry another. Then I would be made to serve her. I just couldn't do that," she said, shaking her head.

"Well, what do you propose we do? You always have a plan. Are we to run for the rest of our lives? Where would we go? Lavitia, so we could be thrown back into slavery?

"I thought I could do this, but I can't neglect my duties to my country. I must go back and you're coming with me, but not to be a servant. You will be my queen. I will speak with my father and remind him of our agreement. He told me I would be able to find my own bride. I will not let him go back on his word, and once he meets you he will know I have made a wise choice. In fact," he said with a devious smile. The more he spoke the darker the sky became. The surf they once watched from about a six feet distance was now lapping at the edge of their feet.

"Do you really think it will be that easy? You will just explain that you had an agreement and the king will just disregard this woman he has chosen for you so you can marry me? A poor farm girl from Gativa? I'm nobody. She's a princess, Alexander. She was born to rule beside you. It's probably the only thing she knows how to do. Your father will not change his mind just because you ask him to," she said, pulling away from him, stepping back into the water. The waves reacted instantly to the contact and crashed violently into the large rocks she had once climbed on top of and declared Midnight fastest in all Theslia.

"Let me finish, little one," he said, dropping slowly to one knee before her. He took her hand and gazed up into her golden amber gaze. "I will not speak to anyone at all. It is my heart and I will not allow it to be ruled by my father. Will you have me? Will you be my queen? Marry me, Mirage, let's do it now. Then there will be nothing Father or anyone else could do to keep us apart," he looked up at her with pleading eyes as she stared down at him, her face was flat without any trace of emotion. He dropped his gaze, thinking perhaps he had been too hasty when she said, "yes," in a soft but firm tone.

"Are you sure? You won't look back on this day years from now and regret having thought of such a thing?" she asked, moving into his arms as he stood up before her.

"I promise I will love you from now until my heart ceases to beat. I don't want a woman whose only purpose is to sit beside me and be beautiful. I want the sorceress that enchants me with her golden eyes and makes lightening flash in the sky when I displease her. She is real.

She has substance, and that's the woman I want as my queen. Why should her lineage matter? Father is not the son of a king," he said. "Let's return to the village and find a priest."

She nodded absently as he turned to seek out their horses. Mirage sat quietly on her horse, following Alexander through the village. Was this the right thing to do? They would finally be together without worrying what the future would bring, but girls in her village that had crept away and eloped were disowned by their families and cast away. She certainly didn't have to worry about that; most of her family was gone already, only one aunt remained, but what would happen to him if he were ever to face his father again? Luckily, they would journey far from all worries of that ever happening. One day they would come back and the king would be so happy to see his son returned that he would not be so angry that he had taken an insignificant wife. Then she would prove to him how much she loved his son in hopes that one day he would accept her.

"You want to be my wife, don't you?" Alexander asked with his head inclined toward her. She looked frightened out of her mind while he was quaking inside with anticipation.

"Yes, of course I want to be your wife, it's just…a girl dreams all her life of what her wedding day would be like. I just never dreamed I'd be stealing away with my Prince Charming in some drab, empty church with no family or friends to witness or celebrate," she explained.

"How did you dream it would be?" he asked out of curiosity.

"Well, of course it was always outside, sometimes on the hill behind the farmhouse. The farmhouse decorated with flowers and ribbons. Auntie Lina fretting over the finishing touches of my hair. Matilda would come and get me when it was my turn. I walk out to find him waiting for me at the top of the hill, smiling brightly as I approach. Sometimes it would be on the beach struck between two white pillars, white silks flapping in the wind, the aisle covered with flowers petals. They would fill the sky as the wind picks them up but the village people would continue to throw them at my feet as I approach my groom. You know, regular fantasies. I guess things are never as we dream them to be."

"You could have any one of those weddings today if you wanted it so, except the celebration and the family part. And I am truly sorry for that. I would give anything to be able to bow to my father before I turned to take your hand, but this is the only way."

"I know, and it doesn't matter. Wedding vows are made between two people, not the whole village. All I need is you, the background is not necessary," she declared.

"Which wedding would you like, my little sorceress?" he asked, smiling at her. She looked at him with her brow wrinkled and then her lips spread into a mischievous smile as she caught on to his taunting.

"At the farmhouse on the hill, it would be a beautiful wedding." Her face lit up as she thought of the possibilities.

"Go to the house and prepare. I will find a priest and bring him in an hour. That should be enough time for you to get everything in order." She bobbed her head and kicked the horse's flanks.

"Mirage, wait, come here." She turned and rode back to him. He held his hand out to her. She took it and was pulled closer and closer until he was close enough to lean over and kiss her sweetly.

Alexander had no trouble finding a priest in the village, a tall but stout fellow called Father Tims. He paid him for his services and stood quietly in his small temple as he drew up the necessary papers. His wife, Marigold, promised to stand as witness, though Alexander wondered if she could manage it if she continued to bow every five minutes or so, exclaiming how she couldn't believe she was attending the wedding of the prince.

After the allotted time, the three journeyed to the farmhouse to find the two white- pillars Mirage had described standing like sentinels on the lone hill. Streaming silks flapped in the subtle wind. Green vines circled the pillars with white and pink cherry blossoms. White flower petals covered the ground and got stirred up by the wind when it blew.

Alexander smiled as he pictured the scene in his mind. He looked down at his clothes. He was clean, thanks to Mirage's magic, but he had had this same outfit on for three days. They were decent but they were so dark. As if reading his mind. Marigold ushered him into the house and into the kitchen. Mirage was nowhere to be found. The old woman carried a bundle under one arm.

"You did say this was a spur of the moment decision, and I didn't think even a prince would travel with the appropriate garments for wedding if it were not planned. These things are my son's." She continued to explain when she turned and noticed Alexander just standing there.

"Well, what are you waiting for? Take those clothes off and don't mind me. I've seen the parts of men before, being the mother of five sons. Luck is with us that I kept these things after my Kyle was married. They should fit you, you're a little taller, but we will manage."

The outfit was made of a white linen pants and shirt. They reminded him of the sleeping clothes Mirage had made. The pants were indeed too small so he adorned his own, thinking it would be fine with the white shirt. After he was dressed Mrs. Tims literally pushed him outside and sent him up the hill to her husband. Then she went on a search through the house for his bride to be.

She found her after a while, standing before a mirror in one of the rooms upstairs. Mirage had changed her dress into a long white gown that swept the floor around her feet. One sleeve had been removed so she could create a veil and the neckline crossed over her chest, leaving her left shoulder bare, but she was undecided as to whether she should wear the veil or not. After attending several of her friends' weddings over the years, she knew it was customary for the father to remove the veil as he gave the bride away to her new husband. Finally, she tossed it aside and picked her hair up from her neck and tried to arrange it on top of her head.

"Beautiful, my dear, you're just beautiful. I came to offer you some assistance, but it seems you have everything in order," Marigold exclaimed from the doorway.

"Really, what of my hair, should I leave it down or sweep it off my neck? What is the respectable fashion for brides?" Mirage asked nervously, turning from side to side as she stared at her image in the mirror.

"Leave it down. You look absolutely heavenly just as you are. The next part was the hardest for me, walking to my man, scared to death I'd trip over the dress and fall flat on my face and embarrass my whole family."

"Thanks, I hadn't thought of that," she said, looking down at the small woman. She had her grey hair swept into a bun on the top of her head. Her eyes were as blue as sapphires as she grinned up at her.

"Just take deep breaths and keep walking till you're standing before him. After that, it will be easy," she said.

She left her alone, standing in the mirror. Mirage took a deep breath and left the room. The door to the backyard had been left open and she spotted Alexander as soon as she reached the threshold. One more deep breath and a step forward and she was on her way to him.

He wore a brilliant smile as she got closer, and it only grew as she approached him, just like in one of her dreams. The priest told him to take her hand and he did. He explained about the duties of a husband and the responsibilities of a wife and asked if they both promised to fulfill these challenges. The talking went on longer than he thought was necessary, but when he finally said that they were lawfully husband and wife, a filling sensation swept through him. Mirage smiled as one tear slipped from her eyes. He swept it away with his thumb. He held her face gently with both hands and he leaned in to kiss her.

Mrs. Tims clapped her hands together and blotted at her own eyes with her handkerchief as she explained over and over again what an earnest marriage it was. "Each so truly in love with the other. You don't often get to witness that kind of wedding. Now off with you both. My part as witness is not yet over and I still have a supper to put on. Now off with you," she said, pushing the couple toward the house.

"Wait, Marigold, first these documents must be signed," Father Tims explained when they reached the house. Tims spread the parchment out on the table and signed it first, then handed the quill to Alexander. Mirage signed it next and handed the quill to Marigold, who in turn dropped it on the table, crossed her arms over her chest, and explained that she refused to sign any marriage document until the vows had been consummated.

Father Tims shook his head at his wife and sat down at the table. "Well, you two better get on with it, she won't budge till she gets her way."

Alexander looked down at Mirage and smiled; he took her hand and led her up the stairs.

"Well, I guess we better get on with it," he said, imitating Father Tims. Mirage laughed and moved into his arms as he pulled her into his embrace. "Just pretend they're not down there listening."

"Um…I made us a few things for…um… tonight. I wanted it to be special. There is bread and cheese, and, um, fruit and wine. Would you like some wine, *husband*?" Pouring two glasses of wine she handed one to Alexander then disappeared behind the changing screen.

She had decorated the room with candles and flowers. Red rose petals covered the white bed spread. After a moment and some flashing lights, she emerged in a long white night shift that left little to the imagination.

Alexander took another swallow from the goblet and set it down on the table. He wrinkled his pointer finger at her, beckoning her to come to him. She crossed the distance slowly and stood quietly before him as he caressed her face with his hands, looking her over. He bent and kissed her softly on her shoulder. She wrapped her arms around his neck as his other hand filled with the hair at the nape of her neck.

Suddenly she was swept up in his arms and carried to the bed. He placed her in the center then stood up straight again. He pulled the linen shirt up over his head, the muscles in his chest extending and retracting with the movement. He undid the ties on his pants.

Mirage gasped as they dropped to the floor. There was no denying the desire he had for her. His manhood extended from the junction between his leg like a branch on a tree and her pulse sped up with a mixture of fear and anticipation. He crawled slowly toward her. His hand settled on her thigh and it moved slowly up her body to come to rest on her shoulder where he pushed aside the lacy straps of chemise.

"Are you afraid, little one?" he asked quietly.

"Yes," she admitted solemnly.

"I promise to be gentle," he said.

"You've been making an awful lot of promises today," she said looking up at him and down at his manhood again. He didn't think it was possible for her to be more beautiful until she gazed up at him her golden eyes filled with sensual innocence. Her body glowed honeybrown bathed in the candlelight. Her skin was like silk as he swept his hands across the length of her. A primitive moan escaped her lips when his hand swept through the hair between her legs then down farther.

"I promise I will give you more pleasure than you've ever imagined possible," he whispered into her ear. His fingers were like an iron rod used to stir a fire to life as he stroked her. She arched into his caress. He pushed his fingers into her core, preparing her for what was soon to come.

"Do you like what I do?" he whispered against the column of her neck.

"Uh, huh," was all she could muster.

"Your body is ready. Tell me that you want me," he whispered as he watched her body react to his touch. He lifted her hips and held her still.

She wanted him more than she'd wanted anything. Her body reacted of its own accord arching into his touch as he stroked her.

Alexander drew her into a lulling trance and she just couldn't seem to break free. Her mind said *Yes, but not yet*. Her body said *Please, right now*. Her heart told her *He's the one*, while her soul whispered, *There could be no other*.

"I promise I will never leave you," he said. He kissed her gently looking deep into her eyes.

"Do you believe me?" he asked. She nodded like a small child. He kissed her as he moved to cover her body with his own. "You want me, don't you? Tell me that you want me."

"I ....want you," she moaned. It was the truth. She couldn't deny how much she wanted him. She wrapped her arms around his broad shoulders and pulled him to her.

He pushed his throbbing member into her slowly. She seemed to close in all around him as he tried with all his might to go slow. Finally, he came to the door of her love and savored the feeling that told him she was truly his. He closed his eyes, trying to remain in control.

He pushed gently at first, trying to make this experience as painless as possible, but he lost his control when she shifted her body beneath him. A deep groan escaped his lips and he instinctively buried himself inside of her but stopped moving instantly when she cried out in pain.

He kissed her forehead and whispered, "Nothing and no one will ever hurt you again. I promise, Angel."

"Something is wrong, we have to stop," she said, pushing against him.

"Nothing is wrong. It's normal to feel pain the first time," he said awkwardly trying with all his power to be still until her body adjusted to his invasion. "It won't hurt anymore, just lay still for a moment."

"But you're hurting me now," she said quietly, turning her head away to avoid his lips.

"It will pass. Trust me, my love. Please… let me kiss you, you'll see," he said, feeling uncertain about what he was telling her. He had never bedded a virgin before and wasn't really sure how long it took for a woman to get over the pain caused by her first taste of a man.

She shifted her hips as if to test his words and was amazed by the pleasure she got from that small movement. She started moving instinctively against him, telling him without words that he wasn't hurting her anymore.

He used rhythmic strokes to reignite the flames of her passion. Mirage was sent spiraling into a world of colorful adrenaline with each thrust. The rest of the room melted away, but the land could have opened and swallowed them up whole and they would not have noticed. Right now, he was a part of her and she was a part of him and the rest of the world didn't exist or matter as far as they were concerned.

He used his teeth to pull at her nipples. He pushed her knee up and locked it under his arm. She held onto his head as he kissed and caressed her breasts. His hair was so soft and silky. He moved slowly upwards until his lips were inches from hers. She opened her eyes and looked into his deep brown eyes. He kissed her then pulled away teasingly until she caught his head with her hands and kissed him fully. She used her teeth to gently hold onto his bottom lip. He pulled away and pushed his tongue into her mouth.

He wanted to taste her. He wanted to be buried deep within her. And he wanted to possess her mind as well as her body. He whispered into her ear.

"I've dreamed of this every night since the day we met, but never in my wildest dreams did I imagine it would feel so good. I want to touch you everywhere all at once."

This was her husband. This wonderful man was hers to love and have for the rest of her life and she basked in the knowledge as he moved within her. She wrapped her arms around his neck and held onto him as his thrusts came faster and more powerful. His body started to tremble and he slowed down to wait for her. Each thrust was long and powerful.

He pushed into her completely when her legs went limp and he felt her fingernails dig into the back of his hands. He stretched her arms out over her head as wave after wave of wet passion wrapped around his manhood. He pushed into her one last time, spilling his seed into her body.

Finally, they lay quietly, caressing each other. He watched her waiting for her reaction. Her passion-filled eyes opened and closed as if she wanted to go to sleep. Then she turned to him and kissed him.

"Can we do it again?" she asked. Alexander looked over at her and smiled. After that there were no words exchanged. They used their senses to communicate their feelings and desires. They spent the night bathing in each other's passions.

Later that night, Alexander went downstairs to see the Tims out. They had witnessed enough for one night, but the house was empty. The parchment was rolled up on the table. He picked it up and pulled it open. It had been completed and stamped with the priest's seal. "Well, its official," Alexander said. Rolling the scroll up, he headed back upstairs and crawled into the bed. "We should get some sleep so we can get started for the castle tomorrow."

"But I thought you said we would take to the sea. We can't go to the castle now. What do you think will happen if you return to the castle now with me as your wife?" Mirage asked. He gave her a look then shrugged his shoulders. "Tell me, Alexander."

"I don't know. Father will be angry. I'll probably be punished or something for disobeying orders and after his temper has cooled he will have no choice but to accept things as they are and we'll be fine."

"What kind of punishment?" she asked.

"Mirage, don't worry about it. I will take care of everything and in any event you'll still be my wife."

"That doesn't sound very encouraging. Why should we return at all? Let's continue with our plans and take to the sea. Time away will make any punishment you would receive less dramatic. What if he annuls the marriage or declares you unfit to rule?" she asked, truly frightened. They had made a terrible mistake and the king would be able to remedy it as soon as they arrived at the castle.

"We won't run anymore. The only way we'll have peace is if we face this now. Father won't renounce my throne. He'll probably just think up some punishment for disobeying him and after that's over I'll still have you. Don't worry about it, I'm not. Let's go to sleep."

"I'm not really sleepy right now," Mirage said, sitting up in the bed. It wasn't as easy not to worry about things as he said. This had all been a terrible mistake. Why did she always act before she thought things through?

"We don't have to sleep if you don't want to," he said, pulling her to his side. He turned her on her side facing away from him and framed her body with his. His hands gently swept down her arms and across the flat span of her stomach to the silky triangle of curls between her legs. She moaned seductively as he pushed into her. He stroked her slowly until she begged for release. Finally, she lay peaceful in his arms. She turned to him. After a while, her brow furrowed again.

"What is it, my love?" he asked, trying to smooth away her thoughts with his fingers.

"I'm scared, Alexander. I don't want you to be punished because of me. Maybe we should—" she said.

"Hush, little one. Don't worry. Everything will be fine. Don't think about it anymore," he said. "Are you hungry?" She nodded and he rose from the bed and bought the food tray.

"We should get some sleep. We have a long journey," he said solemnly. He couldn't help thinking she might be right and dreaded the meeting with his father when they got back, but he knew it was time to face his father. Mirage turned to her side as he placed the tray back on the side table. Alexander crawled in the bed beside her and drifted into a fitful sleep.

She lay awake, staring up at the ceiling. What if he lost everything because of her? Then he would come to resent her. The king would probably just annul the marriage or take away his throne.

What would he choose if given the choice? Would it be his beloved Theslia or the insignificant girl from Gativa? There was no contest.

She wiped the tears from her eyes and buried her head in the pillow. What was she going to do? She couldn't let him lose everything because of her. He wouldn't even listen to her. He said he wasn't worried but she knew he was. He hadn't stopped tossing and turning since he fell to sleep. She turned to face him.

He had the face of an angel when he slept. The sharp angles of his face melted away into soft curves, almost like an innocent babe with no cares in the world. He had been the most exciting thing that had ever happened to her, and she'd give anything to spend the rest of her life with him, but she knew that could never be, he would never change his mind, and he would never let her go.

She stroked his face with her hand and kissed him gently. He smiled in his sleep and wrapped his arm around her waist. She turned her face into the column of his neck and took a deep breath, trying to memorize his smell.

Then she rose from the bed. She had decided what needed to be done. She moved quietly around the room collecting items she would need for her journey. She conjured a purse of gold, wrote Alexander a message, and then she climbed back into the bed.

She slept for a few hours before she woke up again. It would be dawn soon. She reluctantly rose from the bed. She kissed Alexander lightly and left the house. She climbed aboard her horse and rode to the shipping docks.

When she arrived, the seaman they had spoken with recognized her as she approached. "Ah, there you are. I thought you had changed your mind. Where is your companion? We are ready to sail, but we can wait. I did say dawn, it is still early," he said, walking back up the gangway. Mirage followed him.

"He won't be coming. You can sail when you wish," she said sadly. The dark sky bellowed with thunder and filled with rain clouds.

"Very well. I will show you to your state room. But since your companion is not with you, I must ask that you try to remain there as much as possible. Days become long at sea and I won't be able to watch out for you. And you are the only woman on board. Well, here it is. It's not much, but you should find everything you need. My name is Excalibur. Call on me if you need anything," he said.

Mirage gave him three coins as she walked into the room. He seemed like a nice man. He was middle-aged with a slender build and he walked with a slight limp. His face was scarred across the cheek, but his eyes smiled when he did making him easy to look upon.

"Will you be in need of anything else, miss?"

"Mirage. And no, this will be fine, thank you. How long will it take to reach Merlot?" she asked then she thought for a moment. If Alexander decided to follow her, he would go to Merlot. "How long would it take to reach Wren Island?"

"It is about a three days' journey to Merlot and about four days to get to Wren Island if the sea is kind to us, but by the looks of things…" He looked up at the sudden approaching storm. Mirage looked up too. She would have to get this connection she had with the weather under control.

"I would put an extra two days on any estimation, and I hope you don't mind me saying this, but a lady such as you should not visit such a place as Wren Island. Nothing but drunks, pirates, and lowlife scum, trolls, and ogres and all kinds of evil creatures," he said with a look of disgust on his face. "Why don't you try Merlot? It is a nice place. The people are friendly and honest. I just recently moved my daughters there. After my wife died some years ago, I found it hard to concentrate on my work when I was away, with concubine collectors sweeping through these poor villages…"

"*Trolls and ogres*," she said, looking at him warily.

"Yes, ma' am," Excalibur said, bobbing his head up and down to emphasize these dangers.

"What are concubine collectors?" she asked, thinking she'd dwell on the possibly of trolls and ogres later.

"That's what we call the thieving bandits that plague our lands kidnapping the women to sell them as concubines in lands like Thedan and Lavitia. With them raiding our cities, trolls and ogres have become tolerable. That is why I was shocked to see you alone. It really is not safe," he said.

"I have no choice in the matter. Are there any other islands other than Merlot that would be safe to travel to?" she asked.

"There are a couple of barrier islands farther out, but it will take much longer to reach them. Are you sure you could handle being at sea for that long?"

"I'm sure I'll be fine. Thank you again for your kindness," she said. He nodded to her then pulled the door closed behind himself. She caught it before it closed and gave him three extra coins. He nodded to her again then left.

She tried to busy herself by taking the few belongings she had brought out of her bag and putting them into one of the trunks. She rearranged the furniture by pulling the table closer to the wall. She put one of the chairs at the table and one next to the bed. There was a small mirror on the wall. She looked at her reflection and pushed the hair from her face. She sat down on the bed then spread her body out across it. She turned her face into the pillow and started to cry.

Of course the first man she ever desired would be a prince and out of her reach. The sky erupted with rain. Mirage heard the sudden start of the downpour and remembered what Alexander had told her. She tried to calm herself, but she just couldn't seem to stop crying. Now on top of everything else she couldn't even cry when she wanted to. She shrugged her shoulders and let the tears and the rain flow freely down her face.

As the sun came shining through the window Alexander woke up. He stretched and yawned, then rose from the bed. He looked around the room, wondering where Mirage was this morning. Probably in the forest using her magic. She should have stayed with him this morning. He was a little hurt and surprised that she hadn't woke him up before she left.

He got dressed and decided to saddle the horses so they could get started for home. He looked out of the window. The sky was a pretty clear blue; at least she was happy today. When he reached the stable his heart dropped. Midnight was gone.

"Mirage!" he called. "Mirage!" he called again as he reentered the farmhouse. He ran up the stairs opening all the doors. She was gone. She had left him. How could he have been so naïve? He kept forgetting she was not the sort of woman he was used to. She had a mind of her own. She didn't follow orders, but she didn't understand. She was his wife now and she belonged at his side. His father would have no choice but to allow their marriage. He would never let him renounce the throne.

Then he saw the note on the table.

My Love,

Our stars have crossed for a brief moment in time and I would give anything to spend an eternity at your side, but it is not meant to be. Return to your father and live out the life the Great Creator has planned for you. I know you will be a strong king; our country is blessed to have you. Tell Auntie Lina that I am sorry to have disappointed her.

All My Love,
Mirage

He ran back outside to the stable and climbed aboard his horse and raced through the village. He had to get to the dock before the ship sailed. When he reached the docks, he watched the ship slowly moving toward the horizon. He was not shocked by the rain clouds that seemed to hover over it. She must have been very upset. He knew where she was going. He would find her and bring her back. He would make her understand how much he needed her.

He rode down the docks and tried to find out which ship would be the next to journey to or even pass Merlot. Soon he found a merchant that told him he would journey there at noon to deliver spices. He would be aboard that ship and he would bring her back. He thought she trusted him, but why would she trust him? She hardly knew him. He had counted on his word to be enough. Mirage would need more convincing than that, but she was his wife now and she would have to learn to obey him.

She lay across the small bed in her state room. She couldn't stop crying. Her head hurt and she just couldn't shake the feeling that she had made a terrible mistake. The ship rocked back and forth, causing a queasy feeling to rise in her stomach. She didn't want to leave him, but she had no choice. She would sacrifice her happiness for Theslia.

She rose from the bed and opened the door slowly to have a look around. The rain poured onto the deck as the crew ran around frantically, trying to keep the ship afloat. She closed the door back, determined to calm the sky. She would get this under control.

She sat in the middle of the small bed with her legs crossed and closed her eyes. She took slow deep breaths and tried to relax. She could feel the ship settling. She realized how dangerous it was for her to let her emotions get out of control on this ship. But that would never work. She was an extremely emotional person. She would have to somehow disconnect herself from the environment, but that was impossible. That would be like taking the sun out of the sky.

Once the ship started moving in a steady rhythm she got up from the bed and opened the door again. The rain had stopped. She closed it back and went to sleep.

Alexander was there in her dreams, reaching out for her. She saw his face drifting by in the distance. When she reached for him, he always seemed farther and farther away. He smiled at her and called her name. He looked around searching as if he couldn't see her standing right in front of him. Then he shrugged and walked away into a hazy mist.

"Come back. I'm here, Alexander. Come back," she called. Suddenly there was a loud splash and she sat up in the bed. She could hear the anchor lowering. She found a candleholder near the bed and touched the wick with her finger. Why was it so dark? She held it up in front of her and walked to the door. When she opened it a thick, dark fog covered the deck. She could barely see her hand in front of her. There was a flash of light to her left.

"What's going on? Why have we stopped?" she asked.

"Can't navigate through this, now can we. We will sail again when it clears," a deep male voice called as it moved away from her. She stared into the thick fog then turned and went back to the state room. Was this her doing as well? Did she subconsciously want Alexander to find her? Well, he couldn't. Her subconscious would just have to catch up with the rest of her way of thinking. She kneeled on the floor and set the candle in front of her. She concentrated hard on a beautiful scene with a clear blue sky and a calm peaceful sea. She took long deep breaths.

"I call to the northern winds, invoking all the powers of sky and earth." The wind seemed to enter through every crack in the room. It blew crisp cold air all around her in a circular motion.

"Commander of Sky and Earth, calm the sky and settle the sea. Calm the sky and settle the sea," she repeated it over and over again until the wind whistled out of the room. Slowly she opened her eyes and walked to the door. She had done it. She stepped out of the room to get a little fresh air and walked slowly to the stern of the ship. She leaned against it and watched as the wake started curling slowly away from the ship when it started moving again. She took in a lung of the salty wet air.

"You should not do that," a man called behind her.

"I was only watching the waves," she replied.

"Yes, I know, but the ship could hit a bump and cause you to fall over the edge," he explained.

"Very well, I will return to my room. Excuse me for disturbing your work," she said, walking back toward the cabin.

"You weren't disturbing me. Come to think of it, I could use your help. Will you hold this while I tie off the other end?" he said, handing her the rope. Aquius would give anything for such an opportunity.

She took the rope from him and held onto the end. "What is your name?" She asked.

"I am called Stagg. Gideon Stagg. And you are?"

"Mirage Gabby," she answered. She remembered what Excalibur told her earlier. She would help him do this one thing then go back to the room. She wanted to make it safely to her destination and she knew some strangers couldn't be trusted.

"You're very quiet. Is something troubling you, my lady?" he said, trying to make conversation. She was so intriguing to him. From the moment she had grabbed onto his finger, he had been unable to get her off his mind.

"I'm fine. I wasn't feeling very well earlier so I came out here to get some air," she said, watching him finish with his end of the rope. She handed him the other end then headed to her state room.

"Well, good day, my lady, and don't worry. The weather is usually not so unpredictable. You'll get your sea legs in no time," Gideon said as she walked away. He had felt when she pushed the fog clouds away. She could do things with her powers that no human was supposed to be able to do.

"Good day, sir," she said, opening the door.

"Perhaps we will speak again later," he said, smiling at her as she walked away.

"Perhaps," she replied, closing the door. Gideon smiled to himself then returned to his duties. She was alone now. He would watch over her and keep her from danger. Perhaps he would travel with her now and help her to understand the world that had been hidden from her.

She thought he was a nice-looking man. He had his long dark hair pulled back into a ponytail. He wore a white linen shirt, tan pants, and a hat that seemed too big for him. It came down over his ears. He seemed like a good person, but she didn't want to speak with anyone.

She just wanted to be alone. Alexander had been the first man that ever made her feel excited and confused, happy, and scared all at the same time. Now he was gone. She sat down in the chair in her room and read her spell book as the ship rocked slowly up and down, but she couldn't concentrate.

She flipped it closed and stretched out across the small bed. After all she would never see her husband again. Husband. She had always wanted a *husband*. The word itself appealed to her, grounded into her core as were so many other ideas.

She would have been a good wife to him. She had little skill in the kitchen, but then her powers would serve there. After thinking about it, Kalina always made sure she was able to manage without her powers, and she was quite handy with a flint and stone, which made no sense that she hadn't taught her to cook, but then the queen's lady-in-waiting would have little need for cooking skills. Did she never consider that she would find a husband one day, have children, and a home of her own? She couldn't have possibly thought she would spend her entire life in service to the crown.

Alexander's wife wouldn't need such a skill, but if he was banished and they had to live by other means, what would happen then? They would have to survive on her powers and risk detection. Then they would execute her. Alexander would be left ruined because of her. Yes, it was better if he went back without her.

She wouldn't think of it anymore; she might as well get over it and move forward with her life. Once she reached the island she would find a secluded area where she could make a place for herself. She would buy some animals and live quietly until she felt the need to do something else. She couldn't stay very long though. She would be a traveler, discovering new places while visiting different lands.

CHAPTER 19

What's Mine is Mine

Alexander packed his things and stepped out of the farm-house. As he pulled the door closed and turned around. He was immediately surrounded by soldiers. The leader rode forward, bowed his head to him, and handed him a rolled parchment. Alexander knew him well. His name was Ellison Craigon and he led his father's cavalry. He was a tall, burly man that took such things as orders and the chain of command as seriously as his father did. He had been Alexander's instructor on horseback riding over the years. Seeing him here now emphasized how much trouble he would be in when he returned home.

He read over the message. It said that he and Mirage were to return willingly to the castle or be placed in shackles then taken back.

"I will return, but first we must journey to Merlot to find Mirage, Captain Craigon," he said, getting a wary look.

"The king's orders are that we return as soon as you are found, my lord," Craigon said.

"The message also states that you are to return with both of us. Mirage has left. She's not here and I have to find her. Then we will return to the castle." Prince Alexander said climbing aboard his horse. He rode forward toward the soldier.

"Very well, but we must be quick about it. The king has given us a time frame that we must keep," he said, nodding his head to the runner who took two extra horses and headed back to the castle. "How long has she been gone?"

"I don't have time for this. A ship is leaving any minute now to take me to her. We must be aboard that ship. There is no telling what dangers will befall her out there all alone," he explained, turning his horse. The soldiers flanked him and they raced through the village toward the docks. The people moved quickly out of the way as the soldiers thundered through the narrow cobble stone streets.

When they reached the ship, Alexander explained who he was. The merchant bowed several times as the prince and the soldiers boarded his ship.

"How far is the journey to Merlot?" Alexander asked.

"It is only a three days' journey, Your Highness," the man answered.

"Is there any way for you to move the ship faster?" he asked.

"Perhaps if we sail continuously at full mast," the merchant answered. "But I need to deliver these silks to Caldrin first, your royal majesty."

"No, you must catch up with the fisherman that sailed at dawn as soon as possible. I will compensate you for any financial loss. Now set sail with all haste," Alexander ordered.

"All hands on deck," the seaman yelled. "What ship was it?"

"I'm not sure. I spoke with a slender man. He had a limp and a scar across his cheek," he explained, pulling his finger down his face to illustrate for the sailor.

"Excalibur. I know the man well. I will recognize his vessel," he said, nodding as he walked away.

Two days had passed when Alexander's ship finally caught sight of Excalibur's. He paced back and forth as their ship grew closer. They were making good time when it started to rain. The ship pitched from side to side. If she thought this rain would keep him from her she was wrong. She could probably destroy their whole ship if she had a mind to, but he knew she would never do that.

Mirage wished she could make this rain stop because the constant rocking was making her stomach and her head sick, but the Great Creator had sent it so it was out of her hands. She couldn't remember a time that she didn't enjoy the rain; perhaps the Great Creator was punishing her for some reason.

She closed her eyes and tried to focus on settling her stomach with her power, which she could do. She sat down in the corner of her cabin on the floor. She could hear the men yelling and running about as the waves crashed into the sides of the ship and she prayed to the Great Creator to give her courage. She blocked their voices from her mind and slowly used her hand to massage away the queasy feeling in the pit of her stomach.

After hours of being pitched and tossed about, the ship finally started to calm into its regular rhythm. She got up and went to the table, deciding it would be safe to eat now that the storm had passed. She conjured a simple bowl of stew and some bread to settle her stomach. She had just put a spoonful in her mouth when there was a knock at her door. She rose to open it.

"I was wondering if you would like to take your evening meal with me, my lady," Gideon said shyly. He adjusted his hat with his hand. It was scratchy and irritating. He hated covering his ears. They were very sensitive, but he had no choice.

Mirage smiled and looked down at her hands. "I was just having my dinner, but thank you for the invitation," she said, slowly closing the door.

"Wait, if you would like you could sit with us for awhile. You can't like being cooped up in this room all the time. I'll watch over you. I won't let any harm come to you," he said. She looked him over and started to shake her head. Where had she heard those words before?

"It's alright, my lady. You can come out if you like. I'm here," Excalibur said.

Mirage stepped out of the cabin and looked up at the sky. It was full of stars that twinkled and shone in the black sky. She smiled and walked over to the seamen. She sat down on a pile of ropes and listened quietly to their cheerful banter. Suddenly, the boy in the basket yelled, "Ship, due east! They're signaling us, Captain!" The men got up and ran to the side of the ship. The ship was using fire signals to communicate to them.

Mirage knew without being told who it was. She was sure when she heard the captain order the anchor dropped. She turned and went into her state room. She had to think of something before he got here, but what could she do? What could she do? She was on a ship in the middle of the ocean. She lay across her bed and drifted off into a fitful sleep.

Alexander watched anxiously through the captain's eyepiece as the anchor of Excalibur's ship was lowered into the water. They had stopped. He pushed it close and handed it back to the soldier standing beside him then headed for his state room. He sat on the edge of the tiny little bed that he wouldn't fit in if he tried.

Could he force her to return with him? What right did he have to tell her where she should go? He was her husband now but he didn't think he could order her to stay with him if she didn't want to, but he could not let it end like this, not when she didn't understand...didn't understand how much he loved her. He had never been in love before, but he knew deep down in the center of his being that he had to be. He longed for her touch, the sight of her face, her brilliant smile, and those gorgeous eyes.

Would he let her go if that was what she truly wanted? Was he that strong, that chivalrous, or would his selfish need to possess her cause her to resent him?

That night she lay awake all night, tossing and turning. She would fall to sleep only to wake up in dreadful panic moments later. The next morning, she woke up tired and worried; the ship would be upon them soon. She opened the door and walked to the stern of the ship. She paced back and forth nervously. She had to get away. Somehow, she just had to. How was she going to get away?

"My lady, are you alright?" Stagg said, coming to rest his hand on her shoulder. She jumped at his touch. "I'm sorry. I did not mean to startle you. You seem troubled. Is it this approaching ship?" he asked. Would she confide in him? If she asked for his help he could help her, but she would have to ask. She wasn't a child anymore. The time for secrets and discretion had long passed. These people had left her unprepared to deal with all the power coursing through her veins.

"Um… what? I—sorry, what did you say?" She felt like she was all bottled up on this ship, trapped off from any means of escape.

"I asked if you were troubled by this approaching vessel," he said, stepping closer to her.

"He comes for me. He will make me return with him," she stammered and went back to her pacing.

"And you don't want to go," he finished.

She wanted to go with him. She just didn't want to go to the castle. There was too much to explain. She was so nervous and confused.

Gideon stared at her expectantly. Then she watched as the large ship glided alongside theirs a few feet away. Men on the other ship began climbing into the small boats attached to the side. He would be here at any minute. She started wringing her hands, looking around anxiously as they were lowered into the water.

"I can help you, if you ask it," Gideon said, looking at the small boats crossing the distance.

"Help me? With what? How can you help me? Where could we go?" she said, waving her hands through the air. The soldiers were being pulled over the side of the ship one by one. She looked them over until she saw him climb over. He had a scowl on his face as he looked from her to Gideon standing by her side. Her breathing hastened as he approached her.

Stagg snatched off his hat and stepped in front of her, blocking her view of Alexander. "Tell me you want to be away from here and I will take you away," he said. Mirage stared at him, confused. Where could he take her? How could he help? She looked into his eyes and searched his face.

There was something familiar about him, his voice maybe, but she just couldn't place it. He turned to look behind him and she noticed his ears were long and came to sharp points at the tips. "Now is the time. Do you want to be away from this man or not?" he asked. "Do you want to go to his castle or do you want to be free?"

Freedom had taken on a whole different meaning. She pictured him standing near a holy man dressed in royal fineries. A gong sounded and the hall doors were pushed open and there she stood, his beautiful princess. And there she stood, bending to lift her train as she started forward to marry the man she loved. Gideon's words echoed in her head. *Do you want to go to his castle or do you want to be free?* She shook her head. "I want to be free," she said quietly, dropping her head in defeat. Tears pooled in the corners of her eyes. It was hopeless. Suddenly Stagg engulfed her in a tight embrace.

"No, let me go," she yelled, struggling against his hold. The anguish of seeing her in another man's arms swept quickly across Alexander's face, settling into an angry rage. He ran toward them, pulling his sword from the scabbard attached to his side.

"Close your eyes," Stagg whispered into her ear, but before she could there was a flash of bright white light and then darkness swallowed her.

"Mirage," Alexander yelled, turning around, confused. She was gone. Something magical had taken her away. Only an elf could pass for a man. There was only one place to seek out the Mystical Ones, and that was in the forest. "Take us to shore at once," he said.

Part Three

CHAPTER 20

Plateria a la Magos Incantare

Slowly the darkness receded into an awful, hazy fog. Her temples were slamming against the sides of her head, but she kept still on the bed. She had learned from Kalina's and Matilda's conversations about her when they thought she slept that if she laid still and kept her eyes closed and her breathing even that the whispering voices that she heard in the background would continue.

"What have you done?" a female voice said in an angry whisper.

"I had to do something. They have been leading her around in the dark. It is time she was told the truth. Everyone wants to rule over this child," a male voice responded. It was somewhat familiar, and thanks to Kalina's musical training, she was pretty good at recognizing voices she'd heard before.

"And what would you call what you're doing? We should have gone to council. The decision to bring her here affects all of us. It wasn't yours to make alone. When did you become so interested in the human world, anyway?" the female said. She was extremely angry. Mirage could hear the hurt in her voice. She sounded disappointed, but "the human world"? What were they talking about?

"No one knows she is here except you and me," he said.

"You and me…Mother doesn't know she's here! Are you mad?" the female said.

"Mother doesn't know she still lives. There is no reason to involve her. She won't be here that long anyway."

"*That long?* She has been here for one blooming and your chrysalis is glowing. You think someone with this much power can enter Incantare without Mother's knowledge? What is wrong with you? The entire Elves' Forest thinks you've finally decided to link. Have you?" she asked louder.

"Of course not. Is that what all this is about? We don't have time for your insecurities right now. I am making the chrysalis glow because I didn't want to be disturbed."

"My insecurities!" she screamed in his head. "This has nothing to do with you and me; you have disobeyed Mother. You bring this— this *human* into our world with no regard to anyone but yourself."

"I have everything under control," he responded telepathically.

"*You have everything under control.* Are you sure? Because it is not green as it should be," she said.

"What color is it?" he asked, confused.

She scowled at him, and using her voice, said, "It is white, bright white. You can see it for miles. She is too dangerous. I don't like this. Gideon, you need to fix this, you fix it quickly. She's awake," the female voice said.

Mirage slowly opened her eyes. She was in a dark room—no, she was outside. Wait, where was she? She was sure she was lying on a bed. She ran her hands along the sheets to be sure, but when she looked up she saw a dark night sky filled with twinkling stars.

"Are you alright?" the deep voice asked.

She sat up on her elbows and looked around. Gideon was standing at the foot of the bed. The female was gone. He was changed somehow. She recognized him as the sailor she had met but now he seemed extremely tall and handsome and beautiful and just perfect.

He no longer wore the torn shirt and shabby pants cut off at ankles as he had worn aboard ship. Now his clothes were made of the finest white silk, the likes of which she had never seen. The tunic fit loosely and opened at the neck. It dropped well past his waist. The pants had the same comfortable-looking fit, and the outfit shone silver in the moonlight.

His hair lay like a cape down his back. He moved forward and it flipped and curled with his movement. His eyes stared as if he saw through her. She blinked to start her thoughts revolving again.

"Where am I? What is this place? What are you? Why have you brought me here?" she asked, looking around the room.

There were trees and bushes as well as tables and chairs. She could even hear the sounds of the forest with the faint sound of moving water in the background. She had no idea what the floor was made of. It was misty and opaque. A dim glowing fog seemed to make out the walls.

"You are in *Plateria a la Magos Incantare*, the Place of Enchanted Magic. You are in the Elves' Forest. You are in my chrysalis—or my home, I should say, and I am an elf," he said with a bow, walking toward her.

"An *elf*? How did we get here?" He looked human. She closed her eyes to think. Memories of being on the ship as Alexander approached came back to her. She bolted upright in the bed. Her head started pounding at the sudden movement. She squinted her eyes and put her hand over her forehead. "Alexander—where is Alexander?"

"I know you are confused and you have a lot of questions, so I have decided to share my memories of our world with you, but you are human so it will be a lot to take in. I would prefer it if you rested a little while longer before we make the exchange. It will be better," he explained.

"I don't want to rest. I want to know where I am and why I'm here. You could just tell me. This memory exchange thing sounds a little complicated," she said.

"There would be too much to tell," he said.

"Very well, but perhaps you could give me a brief summary then I won't be so overwhelmed when I wake," she said, lying back against the pillows. She did feel absolutely awful.

"I am an elf, as I said. Actually, I am prince of the Elves. Incantare has many territories. You are in Elgar, or the Elves' Forest. We police Incantare and the lower creations: the trolls, ogres, pixies, fairies, nymphs, night riders… They each have a task in nature in which they must perform, given to them by our Queen Nasci, Mother of Nature.

"For example, nymphs have territories, such as rivers, minerals, trees… They protect the resources. Well, they were charged to protect the resources, but they have turned their task into scheming and treachery. They cause us the most trouble. As I said, it is a long story."

"Trouble? How so?" Mirage asked. It was all very colorful to her, like being told a fascinating bedtime story.

"Well, they toll the rivers, for one thing. Their job is to make sure the humans don't ruin them by building dams or filling them with waste.

They have taken it upon themselves to charge for access. Mother does not interfere as long as they take care of the latter, but she cannot be pleased by their behavior."

"Tell me about your mother," Mirage said quietly. Stagg took a deep breath.

"She is not my mother in the sense you are thinking. Well, she is in the sense that she created us, but not in a maternal sense. She is Mother Nature," he explained.

"You said she created you and the others, I guess, but I thought the Great Creator created all things. Now I am to believe fairies create flowers and nymphs patrol the forests. You are…a magical soldier, right?"

Stagg nodded. "The Great Creator did create the world, but in order to complete such a feat, he created lesser gods to delegate the work," he said.

"Why haven't I ever heard of these things before?" she asked, confused.

"Many things have been kept from you for your own protection. In both our worlds you are considered a woman. You should be told the truth before your ignorance causes you more problems," Stagg said.

"What city is Incantare found?" she asked.

"Plateria a la Magos Incantare is everywhere and nowhere. Humans can only see us if we want them to."

"So, they were there, they just didn't want me to see them. Why? What's wrong with me?" she said, thinking of the night she released the fairies at the inn. Alexander was so shocked that she had never seen one before, which could only mean that people saw them all the time. Why didn't she?

He moved to the bed and sat down next to her. She was so human. One of her eyes was slightly wider than the other. Her nose wasn't exactly centered. He could see her imperfections so clearly; it was in them that he saw her beauty. There was power in her innocence. What would her education bring?

"What are the other jobs?" she asked. Her lashes fanned out against her cheeks as she looked down at her hands.

"Well, pixies bring about the season, fairies bring about growth, trolls control the life cycles of trees and other plants—which is why they hate fairies, for making work for them. They are very lazy creatures. Ogres create the landscape. It is strenuous work and it makes them very grouchy. Night riders steer the winds…"

"You were right, this is a lot of information," Mirage agreed.

"Yes. You should sleep. I will return when you wake," he said, rising from the end of the bed where he had sat and started for the exit.

"Wait, one more question. Why have you brought me here?" she asked. There was silence and for a moment she thought he wasn't going to answer.

"When you wake, I will explain everything to you. When you wake, Prin—Mirage," he said, then turned to leave.

Alexander had the ship docked in under an hour. They did not bother looking for a harbor. They simply pulled in close enough and paddled the dinghies to shore. They dredged through high marsh grass until they entered a spacious wooded area.

"Chop these trees down," he ordered. A nymph would come, he was sure of it.

"But, Prince Alexander, we don't have axes," one of the soldiers said.

"Use your swords," he said vacantly. The soldier's eyes bulged as he thought of dulling his blade on a tree.

He had to find her. What did they want with her? What were they doing to her? He had to get her back. What if he never saw her again? No, no, no…he was going to find her. He had to find her.

"Even if we all chopped the same tree it would take hours for us to chop down one of these trees. Tell us what it is you seek and we will think of another way to get it done," Captain Craigon said, looking up the mighty redwood.

"Very well. I need to capture a mystical, preferably a nymph, so we can make a deal. A nymph will give us anything we ask for the right price," he explained.

"Best place to locate a nymph is at a river," one soldier said.

"The king should find another servant girl anyway. This one is too much trouble," another soldier said.

Alexander swirled around to face the soldier that questioned his father's orders. He didn't recognize him, but it was Craigon that spoke first. "It is our job to find her and take her to the king. The rest is not your concern, Phillip. Anyway, we have no way of knowing where the nearest river is. The Prince is right. Our best bet would be to destroy the trees, and then one will come to us." Craigon responded.

"Burn them," Alexander said absently. "Spread out and set them on fire." He normally wouldn't do such a thing. His father always stressed the importance of preserving Theslia's natural beauty, but this was a different situation. He only wanted to speak with one of them.

The soldiers set out using their flints to set the wooded area on fire. They had gone about a half a mile. The air was smoky and the ground was covered with black ash. Because of the heat Alexander and his soldiers had removed their shirts and were covered with ash and black soot.

Suddenly the fires went out. The wind swept through and cleared the smoke from the clearing leaving scorched trees and burnt black grass as far as the eyes could see. A sinking feeling of shame swelled in Alexander's belly. Look what he had done.

In the distance, a large animal was approaching quickly. The soldiers recovered their shields and drew their swords. As it got closer, it appeared to be a giant grey hare. It was as tall as a pony with long sharp ears and strong muscular legs. It was bridled like a horse and on its back sat a little brown nymph with glassy blue eyes and spiky green and black hair. He had a scowl on his face as he bounced to a stop in front of them.

"Just what do you think you're doing, burning my forest without permission? I will turn each and every last one of you into tree frogs," he said as he pulled his mount to a halt.

Alexander stepped forward and his soldiers lined up behind him with military precision. "I am Alexander Casesar, Crown Prince of Theslia. And I apologize for burning your forest, but it was the only way we could have a chance at an audience with you, sir. I have a problem and am in need your help. Any useful information you are able to provide me with would be profitable to you," he said charmingly.

"Profitable, you say. How so?" Stencil said, glaring at him.

"If you were able to help me, I will give you three hundred river crystals," he explained. It was half of what he had left the castle with. He always wondered what nymphs did with them and what they would do if they knew that fairies left them in the center of blossoms.

"Do I look like I have need of river crystals?" Stencil yelled furiously.

"Couldn't you trade them to a river nymph for something more to your liking?" Alexander continued in a charming tone.

"Perhaps," Stencil said, looking at him sideways. "What is it that you seek, that you are willing to risk your feeble lives to gain, willing to destroy centuries of work to achieve? Let me guess," he said, holding up his finger as he looked Alexander over. He rubbed his chin as if mulling things over. "You say you are a prince and you are willing to give me a handsome payment, so it is not riches you seek. I could have destroyed you instantly for this offence. You seem knowledgeable of our world, so I would assume you knew that.

Self-sacrifices, careless, hasty decisions. It can only be one thing. A woman. Am I right?" Stencil asked.

"The creature I seek is as tall as a man and has the ability to disappear in a streak of light." He knew an elf had taken Mirage. He just wanted to see how trustworthy this nymph would be.

"You are looking for an elf. Is that all? Because if it is I will give you hooves for feet."

"Where can we find them?" Alexander asked.

"For what purpose do you seek them?" Stencil asked, clearly interested now.

"One of them kidnapped my woman," he started.

"I knew it. And what will a puny human be able to do against the powers of an elf?" Stencil asked, crossing his arms.

"I will first try to persuade them to release her. If that doesn't work I am prepared to die to get her back."

"Is this woman worth the lives of you and your men? You humans and your silly notions of love. A female is for reproduction. That is all. Well, I will take you to the Elves' Forest only because I'm bored and have no wish to add you and your men to the creatures in my forest. And I think it will be interesting to see what elf would lower them self to the likes of a human woman. And what the mighty Prince Stagg will do to right this offense. Follow me and do try to keep up. We have a long journey," he said, turning back into the direction he had come. "My crystals, please," Stencil said, waiting with his stumpy little hand out as the soldiers pulled on the tunics and mounted their horses.

"I will give you half now and half when we get there," Alexander said, pitching the sack to him. Stencil tied it to his belt then grabbed his reins. The hare took off like a flash of light across the burnt field.

Covax Castle, Lavitia

Where is the king?" Lord Kail asked as he entered the empty hall.

"In his study, my lord," one of the servants answered.

"Ask him if I may have an audience with him," he said, coming to stand at the door. The servant tapped on the door and went in. Moments later he returned, allowing Kail to enter.

"What do you want?" Marsalis asked. He stood near the fireplace with his arms folded across his chest, staring into the flames which provided the light for the room. He wore a long black shirt and billowy black pants.

The king had been in a terrible mood since his cousin's escape; barking out orders, not attending court, remaining confined to his chambers or his study, but hopefully this news would brighten his spirits. "I have found those responsible for helping your cousin escape." "And have they told you under which rock the snake is to be found?" he asked.

"No, my king, I wanted to inform you first before we began the interrogation."

"Take me to them, Lord Kail," Marsalis said.

He followed Kail to the dungeon where five men were jailed. Marsalis recognized them all as members of his cousin's entourage. He should have known they would be the accomplices.

"You five are responsible for helping my cousin escape. He was a good friend to you and I understand your loyalty to him, but he has committed a terrible crime and even though he is my cousin, I cannot allow murders to roam free in my kingdom. So...the first man to come forward with the information will be spared all tortures and will receive a quick beheading. The rest of you will be boiled alive feet first. You have until nightfall to confess," the king said, then strolled away casually. Kail followed.

"Do you think they will confess?" he asked.

"It makes no difference to me either way. My men have already found Laven's trail and are tracking him down as we speak. He will die along with his friends."

They had just made it to the dungeon door when they heard loud shouting voices.

"I will confess!"

"No, I will confess," another said.

Marsalis looked at Kail and smiled. "So much for loyalty. Go get the information. I will be in my chambers."

"Yes, my lord," Kail said, bowing low.

"And Kail, I am impressed by the speed in which you were able to apprehend these men. You will be handsomely rewarded," Marsalis explained.

"Thank you, great king," Kail said, bowing low as Marsalis turned and walked away.

Plateria a la Mangos Incantare

Mirage woke up surrounded by small trees and bushes. She slipped from the bed and jumped as it disappeared. The room was empty, absolutely empty. No furniture now that the bed was gone, no trunks or armoires for clothes, no toiletries, nothing but trees and plants. It was extremely spacious as she moved along the wall, trying to get a closer look to see what it was made of. It was a cloudy green substance, but as she walked toward the wall it only seemed to move farther away. When she looked down she couldn't see her feet. A thin fog floated across them. She shrugged her shoulders, thinking she would never find her slippers in this haze.

Her stomach growled and she remembered it had been awhile since she'd had anything to eat. Was it safe to use her powers here? She wished Matilda was here so she could make some of her favorite stew for her. A sinking feeling settled in the pit of her stomach. Matilda would never cook for her again. She could see her chopping the beef as the vegetables simmered on the stove, filling the house with a delicious aroma. She closed her eyes and took a deep breath as she would if she were still there in the kitchen. Oh, how she missed her grandmother.

There was a sizzling sound and a bowl appeared, suspended in midair. She walked slowly toward it, looking around nervously, and took it in both hands. She brought it to her nose and took a deep breath. She would never forget that smell. It was Matilda's stew, steamy and hot. She moved the bowl slowly to her lips, thinking she should have thought of a spoon too. She sipped it slowly, smiling when the delicious liquid touched her tongue, sending a warm sensation down her throat as she swallowed. When she held the bowl upright again, there was a wooden spoon in it. She took it in her hands and sat down on the floor. She thought of fresh bread and it appeared before her. Maybe this place wasn't so bad after all. She was nearly finished with her meal when Gideon called out from outside the room.

"I'm awake," she called. She was still seated cross-legged on the floor, eating, when he appeared bearing a tray of food.

"Well, I guess I'm too late," he said. The tray disappeared from his hands.

"I'm sorry. I didn't use my powers. I was just thinking of my Grandmother's stew and it appeared to me," she explained.

"Then you did use your powers." He reached down for her hand and pulled her to her feet. A sturdy wooden table with two chairs appeared with her meal set on top materialized out of thin air. Gideon offered her the seat and sat down in the chair opposite as she finished. He could eat if he had a notion to, but it was not a necessity. The mound saw to all his needs. "You must be very careful with your thoughts here. Your powers are very strong. Most things in Elgar are controlled by the mind. Do you understand?"

"I think so," she said.

"You must not think so you must know. Have you finished with your meal?"

"Yes, I couldn't eat another bite," she said, leaning back in the chair.

"Come, I will show you." He walked toward her and took her hand.

"Close your eyes." He looked down at her face to see that her eyes were closed before he took her from the room in a flash of light.

"You can open your eyes now," he said. Mirage opened her eyes and looked around. She was standing on a cloud high in the sky. The blue stretched out before her brushing against the horizon in the distance.

The clouds were like the endlessness of the ocean.

"Where are we?" she asked, looking up at Stagg in awe. He looked down at her, his hard features relaxing his mouth into a peculiar smile.

"The Celestial Regions," he said, looking out at the horizon. "It is here that I will show you the extent of your powers."

"Are you sure? Grandma Tilda said a sorceress should learn over time," Mirage explained, bending down to touch the cloud she stood on, but she felt nothing. It felt like air, cooler perhaps, but absolutely no texture.

"I am sure that if you do not understand the extent of your power, you will make a fatal mistake. We must prevent this from happening. There are many that would like to see you destroyed, but first I will pass my memories to you."

The cloud shifted beneath their feet and Mirage grabbed hold of Stagg's arms to keep her balance. A cloud of grey smoke surrounded them. It faded away slowly, then came back together in the shape of a man—a man with wind for legs, but a man nonetheless. He had the indentations for eyes and the shape of a nose and mouth, but he was made of this smoky matter. There was a strong smell of ice and pine when he started to speak. His voice seemed to be coming from all around them.

"Greetings, Prince Stagg, what brings you to our realm?" he said.

"We were just enjoying your view. Mirage, this is Borealis. He is the night rider that steers the Northern Winds." He bent slightly in her direction.

"We have met before, though no introductions were made at the time."

"Yes, I remember," Stagg said. Mirage looked from one to the other, confused.

"Remember when you asked the wind to settle the seas? I felt your presence when you first entered Incantare. It is an honor to meet you, Prin—"

"Yes, well, we were in the middle of something very important," Stagg said, interrupting Borealis.

"It was an honor to serve you. Don't hesitate to call again if you need me." Before he finished the statement, he dissipated before their eyes. Stagg turned toward her.

"Are you ready?" he said.

"Yes," she replied, closing her eyes, trying to prepare herself for anything. Incantare would certainly take some getting used to with people appearing and disappearing with no warning.

Stagg placed both his hands against her temples. A sort of magnetic pull seemed to snap his hands in place and he was pulled toward her, closer and closer. He pressed his forehead against hers and exhaled slowly.

He focused on the things she had missed. He blocked the details of her birth from her; such realizations at this point in the process could be fatal. For now, he would just allow her to see the world again as it should have been the first time.

Moments after he touched her, she was a baby again, held tightly in his arms. There was darkness all around her, but she was warm and safe. There was a lady, "Mother Nature," his deep voice said in her head, encased in light with the purest blue eyes and green hair with blossoms hanging from the tresses. There were nymphs, thousands of fairies, pixies, and night riders. Then she was a child up in Kalina's arms, surrounded by nymphs. They were as small as Mirage was, but for some reason Kalina was afraid of them.

He passed her every memory he had of her. She saw herself through his eyes, playing in the forest as a child. Through his eyes she could see the pixies fluttering by. He shooed fairies from her windowsill in mornings before she woke.

Through his eyes there was no separation between the world she thought was the world of magic and everything else. It was all one, and it was spectacular. She could always feel it, but to see the energy in the air, the warm honey color of heat, the crisps grays and blues of cold. Life seemed to churn before her, creating that never-ending circle. It was like nothing she'd ever experienced before.

As the scenes of her childhood passed before her eyes, she realized that he had always been there watching, standing on the outskirts of her life. He was like her unseen guardian, or maybe an absent father. Her chest swelled as it filled with air. It was overwhelming to think that her private moments were not as private as she had thought.

"Are you alright?" he asked inside her head. She could hear his thoughts and feel his emotions. He was very content at this moment. On the other hand, she felt extremely uncomfortable. Then there was another voice inside his head, and then it was in hers. "Gideon, come quick," it said, and instantly the pictures were gone.

"Come, we must return to the Elgar. There is trouble." He grabbed her hand. "Close your eyes." When she opened them again, she was back in the chrysalis. Gideon's clothes had changed; now he wore a brown tunic that fit like a vest and opened in the front. He wore a white shirt under it and brown pants. He moved across the floor and a gold scepter with a large white diamond attached to the end appeared before him. He took hold of it and it lit up in his hand. It pulsed with light a few times, then faded back to normal.

Stagg returned to her then and took her hand. He moved to the wall and held his hand up toward it. The misty substance seemed to solidify as it peeled open before them. It was as if they had been standing in the center of a flower. He led her forward and they standing on a white disc, were surrounded by the tallest trees she had ever seen before. It started slowly descending and she realized she wasn't even on the ground. This realization made the trees taller even perhaps than the Great Oak, but before they reached the bottom the disk stopped and started back up to the top.

Saline was waiting there when it stopped. She wore a scowl on her face. Her lips were drawn into an agitated smirk. Her brilliant blue eyes could have been made of ice as they swept over Mirage. Her red hair was the color of the sky as the sun set. She stepped onto the disk, wearing the same outfit as Stagg but instead of pants she wore a long skirt. She turned her back to them.

"What's wrong?" Stagg asked.

"Princess Frill is headed to our border with the entire pixie nation, demanding that you release this Pheolatian. I tried to talk to her, but she says if she reaches our gates and the girl is still held captive, she will freeze the chrysalises. The elves are preparing for battle." The disk touched the ground and Mirage followed them.

"There is no need to prepare for battle. This is all a misunderstanding. Take Mirage to the mound."

"Are you sure?" she said, stepping in front of him, blocking his path. She discarded her voice to whisper into his mind. Usually she obeyed his orders without question, but he wasn't thinking as the Prince of Elgar. "*I don't think that's a good idea. It is one thing to have exposed her unusual powers to you and I, but the mound? I am already being drawn to her as you are. You have no idea what effect she'll have on the mound, the source of all our powers—it's too important.*" She looked over her shoulder at Mirage then back at Gideon. She shook her head and dropped it to her chest. There was no getting through to him.

"I agree with you," he said, lifting her chin. She lifted her head and met his eyes. They were hazel brown, stern and focused, filled with centuries of memories. He blinked and she saw her reflection in them, then he smiled at her. A warm sensation swelled in her chest. He was still there, still there amidst the poison. She jumped at the sound of his voice. "And she is getting stronger. Take her somewhere safe. I will return soon." Then he vanished in a flash of light.

When he reappeared, he was in the midst of Frill's forces. Millions of glowing pixies zipped through the sky, filling it with colorful streaks of light.

"Send Princess Frill forward," he said. Things had become complicated faster than he had expected. He would have to call the forum to order to fix this ordeal. Frill fluttered angrily inches from his face. Her arms were folded across her tiny chest as she jingled her argument to him.

"Frill, this is all a misunderstanding. I have not kidnapped her. She is here willingly," he said. Frill flew forward and touched Gideon's temple. "I was helping her escape the man. Here, see for yourself." He placed his forefinger against her head and allowed her to look into his mind.

"Very well," Frill jingled back to Gideon. "If she is here willingly, then why doesn't Mother know and why is the man coming for her?"

"If you know she's here, Mother certainly knows, and the man has no chance of finding Incantare on his own," he said.

"Yes, except for the fact that he's not on his own. Stencil is leading him here. Surely his intent is to irritate you, but that is another matter. You should not have interfered," she explained. She suddenly shot into the sky in a burst of pink light and disappeared into the flashes of color that zipped across the sky. There was a series of jingles before the pink light returned and the other pixies faded into the night. "What do we do now?" she asked as she landed on his shoulder.

"We set this thing right. Come. We will call the forum together before things get out of hand."

Saline took Mirage deep into the Elves' Forest into a dark clearing. "This is the safest place I can think of, as far from my people as possible, but we are still in the Elves' Forest, of course. We will remain here until Prince Stagg returns." Mirage sat down on the ground, Saline remained standing.

"What is your name?" Mirage asked, looking up at her. She folded her arms across her chest and looked down at her like a parent would a naughty child.

"Please do not speak to me. Introductions are not necessary. Try to keep your distance," she sneered.

"What have I done to make you hate me so?" she asked bluntly, shocked by this elf's rudeness.

"I do not hate you. I think the proper human emotion would be... *jealousy*. I have fought by his side for nearly five hundred years, waiting for him to make us one, and in less than twenty you have stolen him from me. We will never be as we should be because he has been poisoned by your strange powers. Already I feel its pull. I do not wish the same fate that my intended has fallen into," she explained.

Did Stagg follow her all these years because of her powers? Had she infected him somehow by being in his arms as a child? She picked nervously at her nails, trying to think. The first thing that came to her mind was Alexander. Was he being infected by her powers too? Her chest tightened. *He would certainly never find her here.*

She wanted him to find her. She wanted him with her, right now. She couldn't get him off her mind. She wanted to see his face, that glint he made with his eyes when he smiled like he was king of the world. She wanted him to pull her into one of those bear hugs of his and squeeze her tight.

Perhaps the elf woman was right. Her powers were unusual and she didn't like not being in control of them. She thought it had been this place, Plateria a la Magos Incantare, but perhaps it was her. For the first time in her life she was afraid, afraid she would do something wrong, mess something up, or hurt someone by mistake, and she needed Alexander to make her feel safe and secure again.

Was it security she sought? When she was very small she clung to Kalina to feel safe. When her powers started to work, Kalina had started the lessons. For every hour she spent with Matilda, she spent two with her, marching up and down the stairs. "Push your shoulders back, and hold your chin up, no lower." She felt like she was being punished. So, she had turned to Matilda for security, and she had been there to make her laugh and hold her when she cried.

Alexander had been there when Matilda left. He spoke to her like they'd known each other for years. You would think he knew everything there was to know about everything. He was arrogant and conceited. She should never have left him.

CHAPTER 21

I've Always Wanted Him

Alexander got up from the pallet where he slept. The night air was chilly so he pulled the hood of his cloak over his head. The soldiers slept around the fire they had created. Craigon and three other men stood guard around their camp. He sat down next to the fire and watched the dancing flames.

They turned into Mirage, twirling and twisting her hips, moving in a seductive rhythm to the silent music. She was in the clouds, smiling down at him. He couldn't even think the day it rained. He didn't know what he was going to do if something had happened to her. When they stopped to water the horses, he thought of the day he had first seen her. His mind was plagued by thoughts of her. Was she alright? Was she scared? Did she need him? What if she refused to return with him? What if his father annulled the marriage?

They had been traveling for nearly a week in what seemed like circles to him. The nymph was playing games. "Oh, Great Creator, what am I to do?" he said quietly. He pushed another log into the fire then stood up from the ground, heading to his horse. Craigon nodded his head as he passed. Suddenly there was a flash of light and he was gone.

"My word," Craigon said, rising quickly to his feet when Alexander disappeared into thin air. "Wake up! Wake up, men! They have taken him. They have taken the prince." The soldiers moved quickly, preparing their horses. Stencil rolled over.

"Why all the racket? Don't humans know night time is for rest? Quiet yourselves!" he said, irritated by the whole ordeal. There were other things he could be doing with his time than fooling around with these mortals.

"Rise, nymph, we must leave with all haste."

"The name is Stencil, Silva Stencil," he said, getting up from the ground.

"Why is it that you must travel like a man and an elf gets to go where he wants in the flash of an eye? Don't you have any powers?" Craigon asked.

Stencil jumped to his feet. "I have powers. I have more powers than you'll ever know. How dare you question my ability?"

"Well, then, use your powers and take us to our lord," Craigon said. Stencil looked around anxiously. All the soldiers were looking at him. "Yes, just as I thought. Why don't you climb aboard that beast of yours and make yourself useful? We must find the prince."

Stencil jumped to his feet, nostrils flaring. A human, this is where his people were now; so low and diminished from their former glory that a mere human would think to question their abilities. He remembered a better time. When Nasci had first created them, they were all like children in her eyes, no elves. Nymphs were the strongest, the most powerful, and dearest creations in the eyes of the queen.

Then his predecessor had found that if they cast river crystals into the mound it made their powers stronger. He came up with a plan to cast all the river crystals into the mound at once to make nymphs stronger than even the queen. He began to influence the other nymphs in an attempt to take Incantare from Nasci. What fools they had all been to think such a plan could succeed with so many involved.

Just as his master and his followers gathered to move to the mound Nasci appeared. One of their own people, that traitor Gideon

Stagg, had gone to the queen and told her everything that was being planned. She stripped the agitators of their powers and gave them meaningless tasks.

While the turncoat and the others that had refused to get involved were changed, right before their eyes he had watched as Stagg grew to the size of a human. His body had been encased in light. He fell to the queen's feet, expressing his gratitude. Nasci bent slowly and took his hand. He stood up straight beside her in all his newfound masculine glory as the queen glared at them and explained that Stagg and the rest of her loyal nymphs would now be called Elves and they would look over Incantare for her. And they were blessed to become gods after they had found their mates and created an offspring.

Nasci gave them great beauty and awesome powers. She made them the authority over Incantare by giving them the height of a human. But that was the past. He would create a whole new world for his people. No one nymph had ever had three hundred river crystals at one time. They were just too valuable to save. He would take these stupid humans to the Elves' Forest; once he was allowed to enter he would find the mound and restore his powers. He would be stronger than any elf, perhaps even the queen as well.

"I told you stupid humans we had a long journey. I told you to allow me to return to my home so that I could get each of you quobbits to ride," Stencil said, waving his hand, indicating the giant hare that hopped around the tree it was tied to, nibbling at the bushes. "But no, you are afraid I will not turn, even after I gave you my word."

"What is the word of a nymph?" one of the soldiers said.

"And we certainly can't let you go now that these creatures have taken our prince. You are the only one who knows where to find him," Craigon said.

"It would take months for these creatures you call horses to reach Incantare. They tire after a hard gallop. You must allow me to return if you want to find your prince."

Craigon looked the nymph over. "Very well, but I will go with you. We must have some assurance you will return. Can that thing carry two?"

Stencil looked up at him with a glare. "Yes, but it will slow her down. Come along then. Let me see," he looked from man to man. "We will need twelve in all. I shouldn't have a problem locating the quobbits, but it will cost me about fifty crystals. I don't think I should have to pay for them out of my payment for this task. If any of you could get any that would be helpful."

"Oh, get along, you. I will pay for the beasts," Craigon said, pushing the nymph toward the quobbit.

Stencil climbed into the saddle and Craigon sat behind him. "I don't think I will fit." The soldiers laughed and jeered as Craigon sat hunched on the back of the animal. Just hold onto the horn of the saddle, you'll be fine." Stencil wielded the quobbit around and snapped the bridle. "Off you go, Lit." The quobbit took off like a zip of light. It crouched its body low to the ground, bringing Craigon to an upright, comfortable position on its back. Craigon could barely see it legs moving. They moved across the land so fast the landscape was a blur. There was only the repetitive rise and fall like the rhythm a horse makes, but much faster.

After what felt like only minutes Stencil pulled on the reins. They were in a small village with tiny huts made from clay. They were painted and well kept. The little windows were all made of glowing colorful stained glass. The quobbit wobbled along to the corral. Stencil looked at Craigon over his shoulder. "Get down and stop gawking."

"Give me the crystals and I will return in a moment," he said, holding his hand out, looking up at the soldier.

"You are going nowhere without me at your side, little one," Craigon said in a dark tone.

"Very well, but you will cause a scene." Stencil said, shaking his head. *Stupid, untrusting humans.* He could have gone in, made the deal, and been right out with the herder to choose the animals. Now there would be questions and crowds. "Perhaps a little glamour then, sir," he suggested.

"What is it?" Craigon asked, crossing his arms over his chest.

"Well, I make you look like one of us, of course," he said, shaking his head. And these were the creatures the Great Creator chose to bless.

"Very well. You will change me back though," Craigon said.

"Of course," Stencil replied.

"Say it, then," Craigon said. He wasn't sure about this and he definitely didn't trust this nymph using magic on him, but he could understand the need for discretion.

"I promise I will turn you back into a stupid human before we leave Mullet's Grove. Now let's get on with it."

Craigon nodded his head. Stencil closed his eyes. He had to concentrate on this. He started with the eyes. They would be the easiest. All nymphs had glass blue eyes. Then he focused on the size. There, a little tall for a nymph, but it was as small as he could make him and have his proportions stay intact. He made his hair black and white and spiked it like his own. Now the clothes. He thought of brown corduroy overalls and a black cloak with a hood. "Now pull the hood lower and come on.

Give me the crystals and remain silent."

"You just hold your hand out to the side when you're ready for them and I'll act as your servant," Craigon suggested.

"Very well," Stencil replied. He was becoming annoyed with this human.

The two walked around the corner and entered the inn. It was like any tavern Craigon had visited. There was a low bar with nymphs leaning against it. The room was dimly lit and smelled of sour milk. There were tables placed across the floor and nymphs walking about talking and laughing. If circumstances were different he might have enjoyed this quaint little place.

Stencil looked around the room and headed to one of the tables where four other nymphs were seated. The serving maid collected the coins from the table and turned to leave as they approached. She peeked under his hood and winked at him. She had gray skin that seemed to have a hint of lavender in this light. Her hair was long and shiny white, but that was as far as details went to distinguish her from the males aside from the dress she wore. She swirled around when she reached the bar and smiled at him. He immediately dropped his gaze and looked back to Stencil. He had not meant to stare but he had been told there were no such things as female nymphs.

Stencil had approached a black nymph with white spots and green hair. He had a long face which reminded Craigon of a horse when he bobbed it up and down in response to whatever Stencil was whispering in his ear. He didn't like the whispering. What if he was plotting against him? He may look like a short stubby nymph but he still had his sword and would use it.

The two nymphs laughed suddenly then the black nymph grabbed Stencil around the shoulders and led him outside again to the corral. Stencil chose twelve quobbits from the herd and elbowed Craigon in his side holding out his hand. Craigon handed him his bag of crystals. He counted twelve into the grey nymph's hand. The two rubbed their bellies together, laughing. Then the black nymph hopped across the fence and went through the herd. He tied the animals together then went back into the inn.

"Quiet fellow, uh," Craigon remarked.

"He doesn't speak anymore. He's too old, just turned 15735— or 36. I forget. I was at the party. It was a good party," he said, tying the creatures to his quobbit. "Well, let's get back."

"First, you will make me a man again," Craigon said, drawing his sword.

"Oh, yes, of course. No need to get violent."

One moment he was headed for his horse the next he was standing in a dark clearing. He spun around, sword in hand, when he heard an intake of breath. His sword fell to the ground. There she was. Was he dreaming? His eyes were fixed on her as she stood up slowly from the ground with a stunned look on her face. She stood a foot away from him, looking confused and scared next to one of the thieving elves that had stolen her away. He instinctively bent for his sword.

Then she smiled at him. It was the face he had seen so many times in his dreams. His body froze and he stood up straight again.

"Alexander," she called and she took a step toward him. He immediately tried to close the distance between them and was knocked to the ground by an invisible wall. Stagg appeared standing directly in front of Mirage.

He looked to her. "You wish to be with him now?" he asked. There was a hurt tone to his voice that Mirage didn't understand.

"I've always wanted to be with him. He is my husband," she said. Saline smiled as Mirage walked to the man and placed her hand against the invisible barrier that separated them.

"Why can't I touch him?" she asked.

"Because he has not been invited into the Elves' Forest. He cannot enter," Saline said.

"Release her," he said. His voice bounced off the wall and echoed all around them. "Release her, now."

"You may enter the Elves' Forest, Prince Alexander Casesar," Saline said. The sooner this human was where she belonged, the better. If it weren't for this girl, Stagg would have linked to her years ago and they would finally be in paradise.

This existence had been fulfilling but she longed for the day she would lay beside her match and become the God she had worked all her life to become. Now he would join with her. The heavens would open and take them to the kingdom of the Great Creator. And he would bless them with a realm of their own as well as infinite power, and most of all she would finally be able to place her seed into a chrysalis and watch it grow from her pedestal in the sky.

Alexander stepped through the barrier and Mirage fell into his arms. He wrapped her up as tight as he could without crushing her. His arms ached as he attempted to release her, thinking this would be another dream and he would wake up all alone reaching for air. But he had to see her face. He swallowed his nerves and looked down. He met her golden gaze and their audience seemed to disappear as he slowly bent his head to kiss her.

She wrapped her arms around his neck and kissed him back. She didn't care anymore where he would take her as long as they were together. This was where she belonged, in his arms, by his side.

Suddenly there was a loud crack and a humming buzz filled the clearing getting louder and louder. There was a beam of light. It grew brighter and brighter until they could no longer look at it. Alexander moved Mirage behind him and bent to pick up his sword. Stagg and Saline went to their knees and bowed their heads. Then a woman appeared before them.

"Queen Nasci," Mirage whispered.

"Why are you absent from a forum you called to order, my son? My time is very precious. The entire court waits to hear what excuse you have for disobeying me, Prince Stagg," she said. She seemed to be made out of the light that encased her. As she moved in gliding, fluid motions, the buzzing seemed to move with her.

"Mother," Stagg said, standing up again. "Allow me to explain."

Suddenly there was a flash of light and then they were in a room surrounded by the element handlers. The woman was seated in the middle in a throne made of golden brown vines. Stagg, Saline, Stencil, Frill, Borealis, and the fairies that Mirage had released from the cages stood in front of the woman on one side while Alexander and Mirage stood on the next.

"Did I not give specific orders to each of you concerning this human? You, Princess Meredith Frill, were not to show yourself. You, Prince Gideon Stagg, were not to make direct contact with her. Saline, you should have come to me the moment she was brought to Incantare. Silva Stencil, I will deal with you later. Borealis, you knew she was here yet you failed to report it. As for you, Kenric and Amelia, I said she was not to be touched.

"I am truly hurt, children. Am I not Queen? Have I not been generous and loving to all of you? What have you to say for yourselves?" Everyone immediately started speaking, trying to explain themselves.

"Silence. One at a time. Stagg, you may start, for I am most disappointed in you."

"Mother, I could not complete the mission. She grabbed onto my finger and all I could see was her innocence. I just couldn't do it. She was so helpless—" Stagg stopped when Nasci held up her hand.

"You could have taken her anywhere, but you brought her here. If you felt you couldn't do as commanded, you should have said so, for I could have found someone who could. Step back. Frill," she said. The tiny pixie took flight and landed near the queen.

"I never showed myself. I only acted after Prince Stagg took her from the human world. I intended to retrieve her and take her back," she explained.

"Yes, you intended to retrieve her by calling forces to arms against Elgar without my permission. Saline, I know your excuse. It is hard to act against the one you are to be linked with, but you should have been strong enough to see past your infatuation to do what was right for your people. Rewards are not given without sacrifice.

"Stencil, your greed and mischievous mind has clouded your judgment once again. Before there is another uprising, I'm afraid you must be destroyed."

"M-my Queen, I have done nothing," Stencil stammered.

"Silence," Nasci's voice boomed across the room. "All those years ago you thought it was Stagg that informed me of Euthanasia's plan. Stagg informed me, yes, but it was only that act that saved him and the others from being punished as well. I hear your thoughts as you make them. You will be destroyed. The rest of you will be punished and you, Pheolatian, that has caused all this havoc, will be destroyed."

"No, Mother, that is not necessary. I will—" Stagg started.

"I have done nothing," Mirage said.

"You have disrupted my entire world. My children are making rash decisions. Men burn my forest in order to find you. Your power is out of control," Nasci said from her throne.

"It was your decision to bring me here as a child, knowing how my power would affect them. You sent the fairies for me. You placed me in Stagg's arms, knowing my power would call to him. You sent the nymphs for me when I was a little girl. You allowed the fairies to be caught so I would see them. If my presence was such a problem, why did you set so many in my path?" Mirage asked.

"You have been a weed in my garden for long enough. You were born with my powers," Nasci said, the rage in her tone turning her melodious voice into a high-pitched squawk. "I could not destroy you myself. My father would have punished me, but if you were a problem or interfered in any way I could have you destroyed. I should have destroyed you myself instead of giving the task to Stagg."

"Prince Stagg passed his memories to me and the rules of your world. No one acts without your orders. You knew any contact with me would compromise their instincts. You planned this whole ordeal, didn't you?" Mirage said.

Stagg stood stunned, looking at his brothers and his sisters. They had all been manipulated by their own creator because she was jealous of a human.

"Well, it makes no difference anyway. I will wipe you from this world now before you can cause me anymore problems," Nasci explained.

"You will not touch her," Alexander said, glaring at her.

"Silly human," she said from her throne. Thick green vines sprouted from the ground, circling Alexander's ankles, and started pulling him into the ground. Mirage fell to her knees and touched the vines. They instantly released him. Alexander drew his sword and Nasci burst into laughter.

"Wait, please—" Mirage started. She knew Alexander's skill with a sword would be useless here, yet she was afraid to turn to her powers. This was Mother Nature, after all, no matter how corrupted she had become. She was still the source. Stagg put the scepter on the ground and took hold of the diamond..

King Timerius

The room began to bend and twist, until slowly the world literally turned. Alexander took hold of Mirage and they dropped to their knees as the wind whipped around them with dizzying speed. Screams and shrieks were heard throughout the room as the pixies and fairies were pitched in the air and thrown in different directions. Saline closed her eyes and instinctively moved to Stagg's side and took his hand. After a few minutes, the spinning started to slow, then it stopped.

When the dizzying feeling started to subside, Mirage opened her eyes. Alexander stood up slowly and the two staggered to keep their balance. When they were able to stand without relying on the other for support, there was a man standing in front of Nasci. He wore a gold robe over his gold outfit and held a tall staff in his right hand that was similar to Stagg's scepter. He removed his hood, and shimmering, straight gold hair fell down his back.

"Timerius, what are you doing here?" Nasci demanded, standing up from her throne.

"Nasci, my queen, is that anyway to greet your husband after all this time, and in front of the children and guests, no less? You have not missed me," he said, moving forward, bending over her hand. She snatched it from his grasp.

"No, I have not thought about you. You can go back and hide under whatever rock you slid from under," she said, glaring at him.

His eyes were swirls of green and gold. He had high cheekbones and an attractive nose. Even his skin had a golden glow to it. He was young and virile with a slender body. He was at least five or six inches taller than her. He picked up his staff and Nasci flinched. He noticed and smiled and placed it back gently against the floor. The other hand he placed across his back as he started to pace slowly around her.

"You are looking well, just as breathtaking as I remember. I see you have redecorated. Incantare is as beautiful as it's ever been." He stopped and looked her over.

"Being Father Time, you should know mine is not to be wasted, so I will ask again. What are you doing here?"

"Oh me, I cannot complain. I was very busy. Time is a never-ending responsibility. So, there I was spinning the world when who should call on me but my son, Prince Stagg, with a very complicated situation concerning a nymph, the king of the seas, and my naughty wife. He needed my help, but after he explained what was going on I found myself just as baffled. I couldn't think of what to do so I went to my father," he said, stopping behind her, looking into her face from over her left shoulder.

"You didn't," she whispered.

"I did, my dear queen, and it would seem his orders were that you not interfere with these humans. And speaking of humans, I am King Timerius, Father of Time, and Keeper of the Creator's Clock. It is an honor to meet you," he said, bending over Mirage's hand. He kissed her knuckles. "I would also like to apologize for this entire ordeal. You look exhausted. Stagg, take them home. Children, you may all disperse. Except you, little Stencil. In your case I think my wife is correct."

"Do not come into my realm and start giving orders," Nasci reproached.

"Actually, it is my realm. And I have been instructed to return to your side, my love. He feels Incantare has become too much for you to handle alone," he said, walking slowly toward her. She stood with her mouth held slightly open. "You may retire to the palace if you like while I clean up this mess you have made. Don't worry. Your king will fix everything."

"I will not allow you to take over my kingdom, you arrogant, chauvinistic—" Nasci started. Timerius picked up the staff and Nasci went silent.

"I said return to the palace. You can continue your list when I join you."

"I'm not afraid of you. Incantare is mine. I'm not going anywhere."

"My love, it is not fear I seek. I will have obedience now. We will talk about your submission later."

"Don't flatter yourself, Time," she began.

"You know I grow tired of this conversation." He stamped the staff on the ground and Nasci disappeared. "Now where was I? Oh, yes. Stagg, return the humans to their world. Report to me upon your return, my son. I will be at the palace."

Stagg moved to obey his orders but stopped short when Saline would not release his hand. He gave her a reassuring squeeze and smiled at her as he pulled away. He went over and engulfed Alexander and Saroja in a flash of light, and they were gone.

Timerius took a seat on Nasci's throne. "Return to your territories, children. There will be another forum called after my wife and I come to terms, but before anyone leaves, stand and witness to consequences of treason.

"Stencil, step forward."

The little nymph moved forward until he stood inches from the throne.

"My Lord, I was corrupted as well, by the presence of the child. I was unable to control myself…because of the—the unbearable need to be near her. Please great king, show mercy."

"No," Timerius said. He twisted the staff in his hand and stamped it done on the ground. "I'm afraid your time has run out."

Stencil fell to the ground, shaking. His extremities began to fold in on themselves. He twisted and groaned on the ground. His body started smoking and eventually shriveled into a ball and disappeared in a puff of sizzling smoke. The room was silent as everyone stared at the black stain on the ground that was once Silva Stencil.

Nosto, Incantare

When she woke up she was laying on a small makeshift bed, looking around, disorientated. The last sane thing she could remember was being aboard the ship as Alexander's men boarded. Had the rest just been an elaborate dream? Imagination was a dangerous thing if reality allowed it to fester. She turned on her side and found Alexander lying there. She touched his face and he opened his eyes, looking around, confused.

"Where are we? What happened?" he asked. She started to say she didn't know, but Stagg's voice chimed in just as she was about to speak.

"I have brought you to Nostso. We are still in Incantare, but no one has been allowed to come here since the wars. I would have taken you to your own world but my powers have been restricted. I can… no longer visit your world." A solemn tone fell over his voice and he released a deep breath. "Rest for a while. You'll feel better. When you are ready to return, grab hold of this crystal at the same time and it will take you to your world. Stay where you are and you will rendezvous with your men." With that he faded away slowly, lifting his hand in farewell as he disappeared.

Alexander pushed back against the pillow. His head was pounding, but he had to get up and get her away from this place, from these creatures. He tried to sit up slowly but the aching in his head grew too unbearable. He let out a breath in aggravation and pushed back against the pillow.

"Alexander," Mirage said quietly, lying next to him, picking at her nails.

"Yes," he answered with his eyes closed.

"Are you angry with me?" she asked.

He opened his eyes and looked over at her. "You lied to me. There I stood bearing my soul, promising to love you forever, and all the while you were just looking for the first opportunity to be away from me."

"That's not true. I didn't lie to you. I left because it's more important for you to be king than it is for you to be my husband. I've never been in love before but I know I love you. I'm strong and complete when you're next to me and it hurt deep down inside me when you weren't, so much so that I couldn't care less what happens to this country without you. I need you. I'm a terrible person for being so selfish but I don't care anymore. I didn't think—" she started to say but Alexander suddenly turned over, covering her body.

His body pressed hard on her, stealing away her breath. The pressure eased as he covered her lips with his mouth and kissed her with an intensity that left her panting when he allowed her to breathe. "Never run away from me again. I couldn't bear it," he said sternly, inches from her face.

"I'm sorry. I thought—" she whispered. He kissed her again until he knew she would remain silent.

"Let me love you. I want you to let me take care of you. Will you do that for me? Will you?" he pleaded, looking directly into her eyes.

"I don't want you to be punished because of me. I don't want you to lose your throne because of me. Loving me will only hurt you, but…I want you to love me, Alexander. Love me right now and never stop."

Her words had him undone and for a moment he didn't breathe. He just stared at her. She opened her mouth to speak and he kissed her. He planted kisses across her face and down her neck. She slid her fingers into his hair and pulled him closer. He pulled the dress from her shoulder and kissed a path down her neck and across her chest. He cupped her breast in his hand and took her nipple into his mouth, then moved to present the other with the same kindness.

Mirage withered beneath his touch. Suddenly he was pulling her into a sitting position, tugging at the fabric of her gown.

"The laces, Alexander," she whispered, laying her head on his shoulder as he leaned across her, pulling at the ties on the back of her gown. When they were loose he pulled it over her head and rubbed a gentle path down her body.

"I had forgotten how soft you were, and so beautiful," he said as his gaze swept across the length of her. She blushed and smiled shyly. He used his fingers to lift her chin then kissed her sweetly before he pushed her back against the pillows. A chilling wind swept across the bed and a shiver ran across her body. "Are you cold? Damn elf didn't think of providing a blanket. Don't worry, I'll keep you warm."

"I don't think it is the weather that's making me shiver," she said, arching her body into his touch.

He slid his hand down the length of her then back up her thigh. He pushed them apart then moved to kneel between them. He kissed her mouth, then his face disappeared between her legs.

"Alexander," she exclaimed. She couldn't contain the sounds she made as his tongue darted across her most sensitive areas. She arched into him as he held on to her hips, keeping her just where he wanted her to be. Her head tossed from side to side as the sensations he created between her legs grew so unbearable she thought she would explode.

Then he stopped and pushed into her with one long thrust. His cry of pleasure was chorused by hers. He grabbed onto her buttocks and pulled her up against him. Her breast pressed against his chest. She wrapped her arms around him and captured his mouth for a searing kiss. He ran his hands up and down her back as he moved inside her. Alexander pulled the ribbon from her hair and it spilled down her back. She leaned backwards as he gripped her shoulders pushing completely into her, each time deeper and deeper until she was screaming his name.

He released his own cry as his seed shot into her womb. He laid her back gently against the pillow and stretched out next to her. He was exhausted, but he couldn't stop himself from touching her. He nuzzled into her neck and brushed his chin back and forth across her shoulder. She stretched her arms out over her head and released a satisfied yarn. Alexander's hand was on its way back up across her abdomen when he suddenly stopped.

"Look, sweet, your stomach is glowing."

"What?" she said, twirling her finger around the short locks of his silky hair.

"Are you hungry, my love?" he asked.

"No, I'm fine. Do you want me to conjure something for you?" she asked.

"No, I'm not hungry. But I think maybe you might be. Has this ever happened before?" he said, holding his hand over her stomach. Mirage braced herself up on her elbows with a stunned, confused look on her face. Her stomach was glowing. She sat up, staring down at it.

"I have no idea what it means. Oh," she exclaimed covering it with her palm.

"What is it? Does it hurt?" he asked, supporting her by the shoulders.

"No, there's a strange feeling inside me, like butterflies fluttering. I don't know what it could mean," she said, looking up at him. "Don't worry, my love, perhaps there is something in the spell book. I'm sure it's nothing," she explained, trying to wipe the scowl off his face.

"Well, in that case let's get you to your spell book and away from here. Are you alright to ride?" he said, rising from the bed.

"Yes, I can ride." At those words, the glowing dulled and her skin went back to normal. "Maybe your magic and this place…We should be away from here. Come," he said, standing in front of the large glowing blue crystal. Mirage finished the laces on her gown and got up from the bed. It immediately disappeared. She took hold of his hand.

"Ready," Alexander said. They both took hold of the crystal and in a flash of light they found themselves on a dusty country road with their horses grazing nearby.

Suddenly Stagg appeared before them as some sort of apparition, but his voice was clear and strong when he spoke as if were standing next to them.

"You are in Misakar. I have brought your horses to you. When you leave travel east, you will meet your men after a mile or so," he said solemnly. He lifted his chin and squared his shoulders, pulling himself to his full height. His dark hair waved behind him like a gentle breeze.

"Wait," Mirage called. "What will happen to you?"

"Don't worry about me. Just get her out of the forest," he said, looking to Alexander. "Keep her safe."

"I will. I swear it," he said as Stagg disappeared. "Come, we should go." Mirage followed him and climbed aboard her horse.

CHAPTER 23

Home at Last

The two rode off down the road. Alexander swallowed the lump he had been holding in his throat and took a deep breath.

"This is the road that leads to the castle. My soldiers should be along soon," he said. "Can I ask you a question?" She nodded and looked over at him. "Why did you run from me?"

"Alexander, I…" She wanted to explain. From the look on his face she knew she had hurt him. She wanted him to understand that she never stopped loving him even when she walked out of the door and left him behind. She took a deep breath.

"For eighteen years, Auntie Lina has controlled every aspect of my life—what I could wear, how I should walk. I could not even play as the other children did. I found out the day before you arrived that I had been chosen to serve the crown. And now after all this time I learn that I have been deceived.

"The real world was hidden from me. I…I don't want to be controlled. I don't want you to give me orders or assume that I must do what you say. I have my own mind and I intend to use it. I will honor you as my husband and I will try to obey you as my king. I'm sorry I hurt you. I left because I thought you would be so angry you wouldn't follow, then you would return and the king would have no reason to punish you.

"I'm still afraid. I don't know what's going to happen with my powers if I'm trapped away in a stone jail," she explained.

"It's not a jail. It's my home. You were never meant to be a prisoner. As a candidate, you could have always refused the position, but you are mine now, so it doesn't matter anymore. I would love to take you to see the world as it truly is, but we must return. Father has ordered it and I must obey. It is my duty." He paused and looked toward the road. "What of your duty?"

"What duties do I have to fulfill?" she asked glumly.

"The duties to the heart for one. You want to be with me just as I want to be with you. Put everything else aside for once and listen to your heart it will never fail you. Father taught me that."

"I don't know how to do that. I've been lied to by those closest to me. How can I trust myself? I don't even know the world as it should be," she said, dropping her head to her chest as she wiped away the tears that fell from her eyes.

"I will teach you. You just have to relax and let me in, into your heart. Please stop crying, little one. In this clearing, a storm could be very dangerous."

"I won't cause anymore unnecessary storms. I've already fixed that," she said.

"I wish you hadn't done that," he said. "I like being able to look up at the sky and tell what you're feeling."

"I'm not supposed to be the one that controls when it rains or when it's cloudy. I'm too emotional for such a power," she explained.

Castle Covax, Lavitia

"My lord, we are doing all we can, but the priests won't let us enter. They say we will be cursed if we forcibly remove anyone under sanctuary," the soldier explained.

"The best horses, the best trackers, the finest soldiers, and my sniveling excuse for a cousin is still able to escape punishment. I am tired of the excuses. Tell that monk that he is wanted for murder. Give him my seal and explain that I would hate to destroy the temple that would dare give sanctuary to such a man."

"We have done all these things, but he says that his orders come from the Great Creator and it is his duty to provide sanctuary to any soul that seeks it. He says that if Lord Laven is guilty of the crimes he is accused of the Great Creator will punish him so Your Highness can rest at ease."

"I want the monastery surrounded. If that is the jail he chooses then he will meet out his end from there. He is to be arrested and brought directly to me if he sets foot outside of its walls. Is that understood?" Marsalis said, turning to the soldier.

"It will be done, my king." He bowed low and backed out of the room.

Misakar, Theslia

The soldiers thundered down the dusty road. Alexander pulled the horse to a walk. Craigon held up his hand and the group came to a stop.

"My lord, you are safe," he said. "We planned to retrieve reinforcements from the castle when the nymph disappeared. How did you escape?"

"It is a long story, one which we will discuss later. For now, let's go home." They traveled hard and fast, never stopping for more than a moment to eat or rest the horses until finally they came to the top of a hill.

The United Rose Fortress rose from the top of the opposite hill like a commanding force. Mirage never imagined it would be so big. A high white stone wall wrapped around the entire fortress, making the details of its layout impossible to see from where they were. She rode through the gates, looking around nervously. The place seemed so cold and gloomy, just as she'd always imagined a castle would be. She felt as if she were riding into a tomb. There were no trees and no people, just guards. They lined the walls and stood at every doorway.

The group dismounted in front of the large white stairs that led to a stone drawbridge. All the soldiers bowed as they walked by. Mirage immediately took Alexander's hand and moved closer to his side. He looked down at her and smiled. She was not comforted by that action. Two soldiers led them to one of the inner rooms and told them to wait. Alexander removed his cloak and sat next to Mirage on a couch. The vest he wore complemented his chest and left his strong arms bare. Mirage had her head down and picked nervously at her nails. He patted her leg, trying to ease her nerves, but he was nervous as well. He stood and began to pace back and forth.

Mirage stood and walked toward him. She rubbed the mark on his arm, then looked up at him, confused. She had noticed his family crest before, but never paid it any attention. Everyone in Theslia had one; men wore them on their arms while women usually wore them on their legs.

It was a custom her people had developed during slavery. Men would give their wives and children distinctive marks that declared their parentage; if they were separated the family would not be broken.

"I didn't notice you had this. How is it you bear this mark?" she asked. Kalina had told her that her parents were killed before she could be branded and the mark on her ankle was given to her by Matilda. She always thought it had something to do with her powers.

Alex looked down at it and shrugged. "It is the royal seal of our country," he said.

"How can that be?" she asked, sitting back down on the couch. She bent to the floor and lifted the edge of her gown, revealing the same exact mark on her ankle.

"It is given to the firstborn child of the royal family," he said, confused. He kneeled before her to see if it was identical to his, taking her small ankle into his hand. He stood up and stared at her confused when he saw that it was.

"Does this mean that we are family?" she asked.

"Even if we were, only one child would bear this mark. The others would have the father's family crest," he said, showing the Casesar brand on his other arm. "I don't understand this. Unless…"

"Unless what?" she asked.

"How could I have been so stupid? I should have guessed it," he said, staring at her.

"Guessed what? Tell me, Alexander," she said, placing her hands on his shoulders.

The door was pushed opened and the guard walked in. "The king will see you now, Your Highness, in the great hall," he said, standing at attention with the door held open. Alexander took Mirage's hand and led her out of the room. The soldier fell in step behind them as they walked down the hall. He stopped them in front of the great hall.

"Whatever happens, we will deal with it together," Alexander said.

"Do you really think your father will allow this marriage?" she asked nervously.

"My father always listens to me and when I explain to him what benefits your powers would bring to the kingdom—"

"You will not tell your father I am Pheolatian. They will kill me. Promise me that you will not," she interrupted.

"No one will touch you," he said, taking her in his arms. "You can trust me. I won't let anything happen to you. I promise. Do you believe me?"

"I'm scared," she said, but looking in his eyes she had trouble doubting anything he said. "Okay, but if they decide to pitch a fire, grab hold of me and don't let go," she said, grabbing his hands. He giggled and lifted her chin to kiss her. She turned away from him and laughed.

"Stop it, you might be my brother," she said.

CHAPTER 24

You Lied to Me

Claris, Kaemar, Maja, and Kalina sat at a table in the great hall. Mirage and Prince Alexander entered from the left, hand in hand. Alexander walked directly to his father and bowed. Mirage curtsied to the floor and waited for the king to speak.

The room filled with hushed whispers and the king held his hand up for silence. "It would seem my disobedient son has found his way home. What do you have to say for yourself?" he asked.

"Father, I apologize for disobeying your orders. We intended to return. You must believe me," he explained. Mirage stood up straight again. She watched the king's mannerisms, seeing Alexander in his movements, but she kept her head slightly bowed. He was a powerfullooking man. He had the same dark brown skin as Alexander, but the lines in his face were harder. His eyes were brown with a hint of gray. He looked over at her at that moment.

"Well, I think you were obviously going through some sort of phase. You have never disobeyed me before. I am willing to forgive this one transgression if you swear to me before this audience that it will never happen again," he said, feeling a bit sorry for him.

"I promise, Father," he said, bowing low.

"I would like to thank these ladies for coming so quickly to aid their king. Tonight's banquet will be in their honor," Benjamin said, rising from his throne, holding up a goblet of wine.

Kalina ran to Mirage and hugged her.

"I've been so worried about you. Why would you run away from me like that? Are you alright?" she asked quietly, looking her over, patting her face, moving down, squeezing her arms, making her usual examination.

"I'm fine, Auntie Lina," Mirage answered, brushing her hands away.

"Father, I need to speak with you about an important matter when you have the time," Alexander said into his father's ear as he took his seat next to him. He knew those few words were said for their audience and that this matter was far from over. The look Benjamin gave him confirmed that. Mirage sat with her aunt, not saying a word. Alexander winked at her when she looked at him. The act made her smile and for the first time since she had gotten to this place she was able to relax.

"Come. We will speak in my private chambers," Benjamin said. Alex rose from his seat, went to Mirage's table, and took her hand.

"Come, we will speak with my father now," he said. Mirage got up and Kalina followed. The four entered the king's private chambers and seated themselves around one of the tables.

"Father, this is—" Alexander started.

"I know who she is," Benjamin interrupted.

"No, you don't understand. She will be my queen," Alexander said nervously.

"Yes, she will be," he said, crossing his arms over his chest, unmoved by the conversation.

"She will be?" Alexander repeated, shocked by his response. "No, Father, you don't understand. She is already my wife," he said, then cleared his throat. "And she will be my queen or I will not be king." He took the scroll from the pocket in his vest and handed it to his father. Benjamin pulled it open and scanned the document, then tossed it into the fireplace.

"Father, that is a legal document you cannot just toss it away. I will have it duplicated."

Mirage sat quietly, watching as the scroll curled up and slowly turned black, then crumbled into black ashes. She dropped her head and stared at her lap so they wouldn't see her cry.

"Alexander, that document has no legal standing because the information on it isn't correct. Her name is not Mirage Gabby. This is Saroja, Alexander," Benjamin said, waiting for his son's response.

"I thought so," Alexander said, rising from his chair.

"What are you talking about?" Mirage asked.

"Alexander, sit down. I will explain," Benjamin said.

"No. I will not sit down, Father. I'm tired of being treated like a child."

"Whether you choose to sit or stand, you will still listen."

Alexander crossed his arms over his chest. Benjamin turned his attention back to the women and began his story. He told them the story from the beginning. Alexander and Mirage listened in amazement. Kalina explained that she changed her name to protect her. Now all the lessons and strict rules that had made her childhood a living hell made sense.

"Well, I guess that explains why we both bare this mark," Alex said looking at Mirage. She looked from Benjamin to Kalina, shaking her head. She was hurt and confused. It made no sense at all that they would keep something like this from her for so long. She was shivering and those dreadful tears were sliding rapidly down her face. He couldn't imagine how she must be feeling. They had only lied to him about the purpose of his journey. Her whole life had been a lie.

"What's my real name?" Mirage asked quietly.

"Your name is Princess Saroja Minunette Shakur. It was given to you by your father, King Alosis, eight days after you were born," Kalina said, rubbing her back, trying to comfort her.

She shrugged Kalina's hands away and wrapped her hands around her stomach, rocking back and forth. "Don't touch me. My whole life is just one big made-up story. My parents were murdered; you told me they got sick and died from their fevers. The only family

I've ever known are really my parents' servants." It was more than she could bear. There was a loud boom of thunder and a crash of lighting that sounded like it had actually struck the castle. She bent forward and threw up on the floor, then got up from the chair and ran from the room. Alex rose to follow her but was stopped by the king.

"Kalina, you go. I need to speak with my son," Benjamin said. Kalina left to find Saroja.

"What were you thinking, running away from your guards that way? You placed yourself and the princess in grave danger by disobeying my orders," Benjamin said, rising from his chair. No doubt Craigon had already given him a full report of their journey.

"I'm sorry Father, I thought—" Alexander started. .

"I don't care what you thought. You were given specific orders, to retrieve the women and return to the castle. That is what should have happened. Never disobey me again. Is that clear, Alexander?"

"Father, I'm not a child anymore. Why didn't you just tell me I was going to meet my bride? I'm tired of everyone playing games with me."

"I give the orders. You follow them, end of story. Is that understood?"

"Yes, Father," he said lowering his head.

"Your duties on the training grounds have been doubled for the next two months."

Alexander looked up with wide eyes. He already put in six hours a day. Doubled, he would be exhausted. He cursed and mumbled under his breath, but stayed quiet as his father continued to speak.

"While you've been away, Marsalis's soldiers attacked our western border. We were able to beat them back, but several villages were burned. We are now forced to send men to rebuild those villages as well as soldiers to protect them," he said.

"There are other problems that need to be addressed, Father. The cities are plagued with tyrants, evil soldiers prey on the weak. They burn them in the streets, attack their homes as they sleep in their beds. I have witnessed these things with my own eyes, Father. Something must be done," Alexander explained.

"All these things will be dealt with in due time," Benjamin said.

Kalina found Saroja at the end hall, sitting on the floor.

"Sweetheart, are you going to be alright?" she asked.

"Why didn't you tell me? I always asked you about my mother. You didn't trust me enough to tell me where I was truly from. How will I know where I'm going if I have no idea where I've been? Just a couple months ago I was a farm girl, now I'm a princess, I—I— it can't be. So, Grandma Tilda's not—" Saroja started sobbing. Her voice was pained with confusion.

"I was protecting you and I also had orders from the king to make sure you were safe and protected. I had to change your identity in order to do that, as well as making sure you were prepared to help Prince Alexander run this country. I'm sorry I lied to you. I hope you will one day forgive me," Kalina said.

"Yes, but when I was old enough to understand, you could have told me then. Lessons wouldn't have been so hard if I knew why I was forced to learn them. Will you just leave me alone for a while?" she asked.

"Would you like for me to take you to your chambers, Mirage— Your Majesty?" Kalina asked, offering her a hand up from the floor.

Saroja looked up from the floor with disdain in her eyes. She wiped her face and got up from the floor without her assistance. She wished Matilda was here instead of her so she could hold her, tell her everything would be alright, and brush away her worries as she brushed the tangles from her hair. She adjusted her gown and followed Kalina down the hall to a large room.

"This will be your room until you are married. These things once belonged to your mother," she said, pointing to the hand mirror, combs, and brushes that were set up on the vanity table.

"Are those my parents?" she asked, looking up at the painting on the far wall.

"Yes. You have the look of your father with your mother's complexion. Dinner is at six. The banned candles will keep the time for you. I will return to help you dress," Kalina said, turning to leave.

"Auntie Li—Kalina, I—" Saroja called behind her. "Never mind."

Kalina bowed then turned and pulled the door closed behind her.

Saroja looked over the trinkets on the table wondering about what kind of woman her mother had been. She stared up at the strangers in the portrait, wishing she had some memory of them. They looked so happy. There was a light tap on the door.

"Come in," she said quietly, lost in her thoughts. The second knock brought her back to reality.

The door was opened and Alex walked to her. She wrapped her arms around his neck and squeezed him hard as new tears formed in her eyes.

"Everything will be alright, little song bird," he said quietly, stroking her hair. "Everything will be alright."

"Well, at least I get you. I won't have to be your servant," she said, looking at the bright side of the situation. She sniffled and wiped her face.

"Unless of course I want you to be, my love," he said, smiling down at her. "Come, I will take you to a place that will make you smile, maybe even tingle," he whispered in her ear. Saroja smiled, took his hand, and followed him from the room. They walked for what seemed like an hour through halls and down stairs, but Saroja was overjoyed when they finally reached it.

The garden was a maze of beautiful flowers in every color she could imagine. Statues and fountains littered the grounds. Secret paths snaked in and out of a thick green labyrinth. Birds sang in the trees, rabbits hopped about eating the plants, and butterflies were everywhere. It was like an image from one of her dreams.

"I had a feeling you'd like it here. Are you cold?" he asked. When she nodded, he draped his cloak around her shoulders. "This is where you belong. I should have known you were royalty. There was always something familiar about you. You look like King Alosis's portrait. The one in your room used to hang in the great hall. I hope you will be happy here," he said, thinking about how much her life would be changing. She remained silent as he talked. It was very unnerving. "I told my father about your powers."

"What did he say?" she said, standing to face him with a blooming violet tulip in her hand. She had been trying to imagine what it would be like to have grown up here. The butterflies fluttered closer to her, the birds zipped by and hovered in her face. The rabbits crept toward her slowly sniffing at her feet. And to her amazements a handful of pixies flew by and hovered near her face. They bowed to her and zipped away again.

"He knows a lot about the history of your people. Everything will be fine. This does not bother you?" he asked, backing away as her new subjects gathered around her to pay homage.

"What?" she asked, looking around. "Oh, them, they're just saying hello. I don't pay them any attention anymore." Alexander took the flower from her hand and threw it away.

"Here this one suits you better," he said handing her a brilliant white rose. She took the flower from his hand and held it to her nose. "Come, dinner will be served soon." As she walked forward the animals parted and let her pass.

He took her back to her chamber and kissed her on her forehead. He was just pulling the door closed when Kalina walked up.

"You are feeling better?" Kalina asked.

"Finally, everything seems to make sense," she said, thinking about her childhood.

"Are you ready for this? The king will announce you tonight to the entire court. Proclamations announcing your marriage to Prince Alexander will be sent out to all the villages and the united provinces of Theslia," she explained, feeling a great deal of pride.

"I'm not sure. I've never been a princess before," she answered.

"You've been a princess since the day you were born. Just remember what you've been taught and you'll be fine," Kalina explained.

After she was dressed in a lovely pink gown, Kalina brushed her hair down and placed a thin gold band over her head. It sat low on her forehead. Then she arranged her hair elegantly up off her neck and used several pins to secure it.

"The prince will be here soon to escort you to the dining hall," Kalina said, pulling the door closed.

"Auntie Lina, thank you for taking care of me all these years. You didn't have to." Kalina curtsied low to the floor then left the room.

Alexander arrived and the two walked to the dining hall followed by Saroja's newly appointed guards, Cash, a tall burly man and Isaiah, a tall skinny man. The servants opened the door and Saroja took a deep breath. King Benjamin stood at the head of the table and said, "People of Theslia, it is my greatest privilege to introduce my son, Prince Alexander's bride-to-be, Princess Saroja Minunette of the house of Shakur."

The people were quiet for moments after the announcement until Cain stood and started clapping. They all joined in on the applause. He pushed out of his seat and knelt before her. He took her hand and kissed it. "Your Highness, it is an honor to see you alive and well after all these years," he said, rising from the floor. He took his seat again, nodding to the king.

After dinner, the court turned their attention to the stage where a theatrical performance was taking place. King Benjamin was having a quiet conversation with some men near one of the fireplaces when he noticed Kalina getting up from her seat. He watched her as she walked toward the stairs to leave.

"Excuse me, gentlemen," he said. "Lady Kalina."

Kalina stopped then turned and bowed. "Your Majesty," she said as she rose from her formal curtsy.

"I would like to speak to you and your friends about what you did to find my son. Perhaps your coven will be able to provide our army with a little offense. I was thinking that perhaps you could use your powers to inform me of what Marsalis is planning or when he's coming. Then I would be able to send a messenger to the frontlines with the information. That way we will always have an upper hand over him," he explained.

"I think we will be able to help you with that, but Kaemar also has the ability to heal," Kalina added.

"She has the ability to heal wounded soldiers through a vision?" he asked, stunned by the possibility. Benjamin had decided that if his land was to truly be liberated from the rule of Marsalis then things would have to change. The people of Theslia would be free to live as they wished. Some of the people in his kingdom had extraordinary powers, but they were made to hide and keep their abilities secret. He intended to use the very people Marsalis tried to destroy to crush him.

"No, Your Highness," Kalina said with a giggle. "She would have to touch them in order to heal them."

"I had not intended for you to get that close to danger," Benjamin said, shaking his head.

"We will be able to help the soldiers and we will be there to tell them what we see instead of having to wait for a messenger to deliver the news," she explained.

"Yes, but Marsalis is treacherous. You must always be on your guard and I don't feel comfortable sending four women to the frontline of a battlefield," Benjamin explained.

"I am not afraid, and I know my sisters would do anything to serve the crown, but you are our king," she said, bowing her head to him.

"Very well. Speak with the other ladies and plan to meet with me tomorrow before midday meal in my study," he said. Kalina bowed and continued down the hall to her chamber.

CHAPTER 25

Royalty

The congratulations and well wishes went on late into the evening. Saroja thought she'd never get used to life at court. She was fascinated by the women's dresses and the entertainment that went on all around her. As the crowds began to disperse, she noticed that Alexander seemed distant or upset about something. She found his hand under the table and squeezed it. He looked at her and smiled, but it didn't reach his eyes. He leaned over and whispered in her ear, "Let's go somewhere."

She didn't say anything. She just looked at him and smiled. He pushed back from the table and suddenly the hall fell quiet. Alexander paid them no attention as he pulled Saroja's chair out she stood. She felt she needed to say something because everyone in the hall was staring at them. She looked up at him as he took her hand. He led her from the hall and the music and conversation started again as if nothing ever happened.

"Why did everyone get quiet like that?" she asked, confused by the crowd's reaction to their departure.

"They will do that when you stand, when you enter a room, even if you clear your throat. They wait for commands or for you to say something. Just don't pay them any attention. They're all puppets, disregarding the soldiers, trying to win favor from my father for some reason or another. You will get used to it," he explained.

"Where do you want to go?" she asked.

"Anywhere. It does not matter," he said.

"What's wrong?" she asked, concerned by the tone of his voice.

"Nothing. Let's just go somewhere we can be alone," he said.

"This is your home. Where is that?" she asked.

"The stables." He shrugged.

"Let's go to my room instead," she said.

"Okay, that sounds good," he said, looking at her.

They walked slowly down the hall, passing servants who stopped and bowed until they passed by.

"I think that is so weird," Saroja said, giggling.

Alexander stopped abruptly, turned to the girl and said, "Dora, bring some cheese and wine to Her Majesty's chambers."

The girl bowed again and hurried off down the hall to do his bidding.

"You know everyone's names?" Saroja asked, a little jealous, watching the girl walk away down the hall.

"They have lived here as long as I have. After seeing the same faces every day for a while, you will know their names too. Besides, we all grew up here together after the invasion," he explained.

"I think living here is going to be wonderful. I'll never be lonely again," she said.

They reached the chamber and Alexander opened the door, allowed her to enter the room, and then closed the door behind them. He kissed her hand and walked to the large chair that sat under the portrait of her parents. Saroja stood in front of him staring up at the strangers on the wall. Alexander pulled her into his lap. She turned in the chair, propping her legs over the arm. She laid her head on his chest and said, "Tell me about my parents."

"I don't remember them. They were killed when I was very young. All I know about them is what my father tells me," he said.

"You know more than I do," she replied, looking up at him. There was a light tap on the door.

"Enter," Alex called.

Dora entered the chamber with a tray of fruit, cheese, two goblets, and a pitcher of wine.

"Where would you like it, sire?" she asked, keeping her head bowed.

"The table is fine, thank you," he answered. The girl placed the tray on the table, bowed, and left the chamber.

"Would you like some wine?" he asked.

"No, tell me what you know about my parents," she said.

"First, let me get up," he said, trying to rise.

"Where are you going?" she asked.

"To get the wine," he replied, tapping on her legs so she would move them.

Saroja raised her hand and the jug lifted into the air and tilted over one of the goblets, pouring the wine into it. She motioned her hand down and the jug moved back to the table. She closed her palm and the goblet lifted into the air and moved toward them. She caught it with the other hand and handed Alexander the wine.

"Why don't you make a fire while you're at it?" he said, wrapping his arm around her waist.

"Fire was the first thing I learned to control," she said, holding her palm flat toward the fireplace and snapping her fingers. The logs ignited into flames.

"I will tell you the story of how your father won our country's independence," he said.

Alexander told her the story his father had told him countless times when he was a child. He told her of how King Alosis organized a handful of men to defeat the soldiers who literally forced their people into servitude. Everything they grew, gathered, and treasured was exported to Lavitia. On the brink of starvation, King Alosis's forces pushed the Lavitians across the border. As the army grew, he sent soldiers to the villages on the border to protect them from invasion. The Lavitians kept trying to invade but our forces kept them where they belonged.

"What about my mother?" she asked.

"I don't really know anything about her except that she would dance the *flusha* on the king's birthday. Father said she was the best dancer in the kingdom. Maybe you should ask your aunt—I mean Kalina. Father said they were friends before your mother married King Alosis. She knew magic too. Father said he was asleep in the great hall one night and he watched her light the torches with her fingers as you do," he said.

"How did all those soldiers allow my parents to be assassinated in their own home?" she asked quietly.

"The country was young. Our people had just come from the gold mines. They knew nothing of security and the thought that someone would betray Alosis was unthinkable; he had already done so much for our people. Simo talks about it all the time. It happened after your naming ceremony. The assassin was at the celebration. He must have followed your father to his chamber when he left the great hall. Simo said the Lavitians were after the families that lived in the castle. While the soldiers fought in the great hall, the Lavitians went through the castle, killing the women and children as they slept in their beds. A lot of people were killed that night, including my mother," he explained.

"And Kalina saved me," Saroja finished.

"My mother saved me too, and sometimes I cannot even remember what she looked like. Father says I look like her, but it is not the same. When I look in the mirror all I see is me. Father sees her though. Sometimes when he looks at me he has a strange look on his face like he's looking through me," he said, drinking his wine.

"Be happy, at least you still have a father," she said.

They talked for hours until Alexander noticed how tired she looked. He carried her over to the bed and placed her gently on top of the covers. Saroja opened her eyes and looked up at him.

"I'll send someone to help you take those things out of your hair," he said, walking to the door.

"I can manage," she said sitting up in the bed. "I want you to stay here with me tonight."

"Tonight, I cannot, but do not worry. Soon we will spend every night together, and I am going to send someone to help you anyway. You must get used to being royalty. I will see you tomorrow," he said, bowing to her as he left the chamber.

A girl about Saroja's age arrived after a while. She was about the same height with long black hair. She took Saroja's hair down and braided it into one single fat braid. She set towels and scented soap on the table before the fire. Soon two male servants arrived and placed a large tub before the fire, followed by a train of servants carrying buckets of steaming water.

"Would you like me to assist you with your bath, my lady?" the girl asked while looking down at the floor.

"No, thank you, I can manage," she answered.

"Just pull the white cord near your door if you need anything and someone will come to assist you," the girl explained, walking to the door.

"What is your name?" Saroja asked, studying the three cords that hung by the door. She followed them up to the ceiling where they disappeared.

"My name is Sasha, Your Highness," she answered, looking back over her shoulder.

"What are the other two cords for?" Saroja asked.

"The black one rings the kitchens and the red is for emergencies. It connects to the king, the prince, and the soldier's barracks. King Benjamin had them put in every room after the invasion years ago," Sasha explained.

"Have you been in the castle for a long time?" she asked.

"Yes, Your Highness, since we were girls. I mean my sister and me, Dora and me, I mean Dora is my sister—" Sasha stammered.

"I understand. You and your sister Dora have been here since you were girls," Saroja said.

"Yes, my lady, our parents were killed during the invasion. My father had been a soldier in King Benjamin's army before he was King Benjamin," she said.

"Will you stay and tell me about the people living here and what they do?" she asked.

Sasha nodded her head and walked behind Saroja to undo her bodice. It was unnerving to have someone other than Kalina or Matilda help her with her bath.

War, blood, assassins, murder…these were things she knew existed but could never picture in her own mind. She thought of her grandmother's body, cold and empty. She pictured the man in the inn, twitching and gasping for breath, the salty smell of blood in the air. She closed her eyes and saw the couple in the painting lying still, covered in blood. She squeezed her eyelids tight together and shook her head. She would not think of such things. She had to speak to Kalina.

Saroja lowered herself slowly into the hot water and listened to Sasha as she rattled off the comings and goings of the castle. She turned out to be a natural gossip. She told the princess about everyone, even who some of the girls desired to marry. It had been a long time since she had a girlfriend to talk with. It was nice to relax and giggle at simple things. She had longed for adventure; she certainly had quite enough of that for awhile. It wasn't long ago that she would have considered herself simple.

"What do you know about Prince Alexander?" Saroja asked.

Sasha paused as if pondering the question then said, "There is not much to tell. He keeps to himself. The only people I have ever seen him talking to are his teachers and his father. He likes horseback riding. Horses, too, I guess. He spends a lot of time in the stables and on the training grounds. He wins lots of tournaments. He does not like the courtiers. Dora says he blames them for his mother's death because the assassin was disguised as a courtier. That is all I know. He is very polite. He says please and thank you when he does not have to. Oh, and Olivia worships the ground he walks on," Sasha said.

"Olivia is the cook's daughter," Saroja said quietly to herself.

"You need not worry, Your Highness," Sasha giggled. "He doesn't even know that she's alive."

Saroja stood up and stepped out of the water. Sasha dried her off then pulled the nightgown over her head. She was fluffing the pillows on the bed when Saroja walked to the chair and sat down. Sasha poured her a goblet of wine and gave it to her. Then she moved the table closer to the chair so she could reach it. She picked up the clothes thrown on the floor, folded, and placed them in one of the trunks along the wall.

"Do you need anything else before I leave?" Sasha asked.

"No, I'm fine, thank you," Saroja answered.

"The servants will come to take the tub away. Good night, Your Highness," she said as she curtsied and left the room.

Saroja sat back in the chair and sipped her wine. She never dreamed in a million years that she would end up here, on the brink of inheriting a country—a country always in danger of being invaded. They had the ocean at their backs and their enemy in front. The villagers constantly needed protection. The castle was always on alert in case of siege. She thought the alarms were a wonderful idea. Her parents might be alive if those bells were there that night.

She got up from the chair and crawled into the bed. She swept her hands around the room, extinguishing the light.

"Not the fireplace," she said when it blew out. The fire in the fireplace suddenly relit itself. Saroja sat up in the bed shocked by what had just happened. Then her grandmother's words came to her. *When you are one with the magic your thoughts will be all you need to control your powers.*

"Fire, go out," she said testing her newly found ability. The fire went out and Saroja flopped back against the pillow, laughing. She relit the fire and closed her eyes.

Covax Castle, Lavitia

Marsalis sat on his throne, speaking with the generals of his armies.

"The soldiers leave, but they do not return. We must recruit more soldiers, Your Majesty," Garth, the general of his army, said.

"Sire, we must find another route into Theslia. The mountain range is too cold and too vast to cross," Silus added.

"There is no other route," Marsalis said from his throne. "Do you think me a fool? Do you think that if there were another way to cross into that land that I would not have tried it years ago?" Marsalis asked as he walked to Silus standing in his face.

"Of course not, Your Majesty, I was just thinking that maybe we should try going around them and entering by the sea," Silus said, backing away.

"No, we have tried that. The journey by sea would take the same amount of time and causalities as crossing the mountains would. The ocean narrows into a small river that slides under a rock shelf for miles then drops back to endless ocean," Marsalis said, pacing back and forth. "I have it. Garth, go to all the villages in my realm, every boy from the age seventeen to forty-five will be taken and trained. If they refuse, they die. We will not cross the mountain range. Instead of attacking Theslia, we will set up a training camp and wait. The slaves are digging a tunnel through the mountains as we speak. When it is complete, as one large force, we will move on them. Not even the Great Creator himself could stop us," Marsalis said, making a fist to emphasize his point.

"That is a wonderful plan, Your Majesty. I will be honored to lead our men into victory once and for all," Garth said.

"No, I will lead the army. Your incompetence has already been proven. If this matter is ever to be settled, I must be the one to do it," Marsalis exclaimed.

CHAPTER 26

A Concert in the Garden

The sun shone in through the window. Saroja rolled away from it and bumped into something on the edge of the bed. She opened her eyes to find Alexander smiling down at her.

"Good morning, little one. I have come to tell you that I must ride to the villages near the border today. Some of them were attacked and burned while we were away. Father has ordered that I lead some men to take them food and supplies to rebuild their homes. He says that the sight of me will prove to the people that we haven't forgotten them in their hour of need," he explained.

"Can I come with you?" she asked, sitting up in the bed.

"No, my love, you should never be that close to the border. It is still very dangerous. Father and I have discussed moving the villages farther away from Lavitia so they would be better protected, but I don't know. This war has gone on for too long. When will our people be allowed to sleep in their beds without fear?" he said, looking down at his hands. "I will return before dinner. I have planned a private meal for us tonight," he said, rising from the bed. "Have a lovely day, Your Highness."

Saroja sat up in the bed wondering how she would spend her day without Alexander. She had become accustomed to having him at her side, and one thing was certain: this place was most certainly not a jail. What would she do to occupy her time? It would be a task just finding her way to the kitchen. She thought answering the rumbling voice of her stomach, and in that she found her answer. She would explore the castle today until Alexander returned.

She found her things in one of the trunks and was about to create a new dress using her powers when someone tapped on the door.

"Come in," she called.

Sasha opened the door and curtsied. "Your Highness, King Benjamin has ordered that I stand as your lady-in-waiting. If it suits you, I am here to help you dress."

"I think that would be lovely. We will be good friends, you and I," Saroja said. "I was just trying to decide what to wear."

"Your Highness, you need only pick a color," Sasha said, opening the door behind the dressing screen in the adjacent room and pulling the rack of gowns out for the princess to see. Saroja walked into the room and looked around. She had not even realized the door on the wall was there. Perhaps she should take a few hours to explore her own room first. This room was filled with different-sized chairs and couches. There was a loom and supplies for a tapestry, along with other things for her to entertain herself.

She turned her attention to the gowns, fascinated by the collection. Creating different fashioned gowns had always been a hobby of hers. There were gowns of all fashions and all colors on this rack. Some were decorated with lace while others were encrusted with jewels. They ranged from simple day gowns to fancy formal ones. She chose a formfitting sky-blue gown after looking over several beautiful ones. The skirt had pink and white cherry blossoms stitched on it intricately with silver thread.

Sasha nodded and took the dress from her and laid it on the bed. Then she pulled a chair out from the table for Saroja to sit in. She unbraided her hair and brushed the long strands until they shined.

"How would you like to wear your hair today, Your Highness?" Sasha asked, pushing the gold band down over her head.

"I don't know. I usually just braid it into one," she shrugged.

"Very well, but I am able to style your in many different ways," Sasha said.

She braided the princess's hair and helped her dress. Dora arrived moments later with a tray of food. The girls moved around the room, cleaning and rearranging the furniture as Saroja ate.

"Would you like some juice, Your Highness?" Dora asked, standing over the table.

"Yes, thank you," Saroja said. After breakfast, she left the room.

Sasha followed on her right as the two guards fell into step behind them.

She explored the castle for hours, amazed by the wealth that was displayed on every wall. The beams that held the ceiling together were hand carved with different images. Beautiful hand- woven tapestries were found throughout the castle. She peeked into the kitchens and was amazed by how busy they were. She turned and left, not wanting to disturb their work. She didn't like the silence she stepped into when she entered the great hall; all those eyes following her around the room. She stayed long enough for Sasha to get her a goblet of wine. She walked down a long hallway and stopped in front of a portrait of Prince Alexander on his horse. He was much younger than he was now, but she still thought he looked very proud. She followed the hall to the end and opened the double doors of a grand ballroom. She twirled and spun around the room gracefully.

"Your Highness, I am Cain, a member of His Majesty's high council. I just wanted to greet you and to let you know how wonderful it is to have you back in the castle. Your father and I were very close. I wish the same friendship for you and me," he said.

"I am pleased to meet you. Are you a priest?" she asked, slowly walking toward the doors. He was making her very nervous. His eyes shifted up and down as he spoke. He seemed to be looking her over, but he stopped suddenly when he heard her question meeting her gaze head on.

"No. It's the bald head, isn't it? I get that all the time. I cut it off when it started falling out to save myself the embarrassment. Have a nice day, Your Majesty. If only your father were alive to see how lovely you have become," he said as she walked away down the hall. Saroja looked back over her shoulder and gave him a slight nod.

Covax Castle, Lavitia

The messenger arrived with a parchment from Cain. He informed the king that Alosis's heir had been restored to the castle, but he knew not if the girl possessed the powers that the prophecy spoke of. Marsalis returned the messenger. He wanted Cain to keep an eye on the girl. If she showed any sign of magic, he should be informed before any move was made.

He found it interesting that this so-called princess would be kept a secret after all this time. Shalyndria's last vision had informed him that the child of the prophecy was on her way to Thedan. Perhaps this princess had nothing to do with the vision. He realized how much power Shalyndria had truly given him. Now she was gone.

Perhaps he had been wrong to keep her locked away. She was young when she had arrived. He could have trained her to be anything that he desired, but the time for regret and what ifs were long gone. Now he would have to wait for messengers before he could make his move.

United Rose, Theslia

Before midday meal Kalina, Maja, Kaemar, and Claris walked hand in hand to the king's study, their sudden usefulness restoring the bond that had been destroyed years before. They rapped lightly on the door and it was suddenly opened by one of the king's personal guards.

"Ladies, please come in, have a seat," Benjamin said. He stood and walked around his large desk and leaned against it. He crossed his arms over his chest and looked down at the women.

"I have decided that you will go to the army. This is Galithe, he will accompany you. You will report anything that you feel is of any importance to him and he will in turn transfer the message to me or the generals. You will leave on the morrow," he explained.

The women looked at each other and smiled. They each knew how important this step was for their people. If they were successful, maybe the king would see their value and realize how much power Pheolatians could bring to the country.

"Well, thank you, ladies. I have another matter that needs my attentions," he said as they rose from their seats.

Saroja took her lunch in the solarium. Then she decided to walk to the stables to find her horse. When she reached the stables, a young boy was giving him a bath. Saroja missed Midnight, but she didn't want to get wet. The air was much chillier than she was used too, so she decided to go back to the main building. Alexander told her that sometimes in the winter it would snow. She wasn't looking forward to the cold, but she had never seen snow before.

She walked across the bailey then stopped suddenly when she reached the inner hall. She looked left, then right, but she just couldn't remember which way she should go. She started to ask Sasha, but then her eyes glazed over. Her vision seemed to change. It was like she was looking down a lighted tunnel. In her mind, she saw herself with Alexander walking down the halls. She felt his hand in hers leading the way. Slowly she opened her eyes, finally hearing Sasha's voice.

"Are you alright, Your Highness? For a moment there, you seemed to be lost in thought," she said.

"I'm fine," the princess said, heading off down the hall that led directly to the gardens. She could not wait to see the flowers. She would contemplate what just happened when she got back to her room. When she reached the gardens, she took a deep breath, clinging to the scent of the air. She sat down on a bench near a large fountain, intrigued by the sculpture. The stone was a light grey, almost white color. A woman kneeled humbly, offering a flat bowl to a man standing above her. The water continuously flowed over the bowl, spilling over the top into the pool below. She moved to the pool and sat near the edge. White water lilies floated on the surface. She held one up to her nose to smell it then placed it back in the water and pushed it around, creating ripples in the pool.

Saroja enjoyed the quietness of the garden. It wasn't like the forests she was used to. She felt as if she had escaped into her own little world. She hummed softly until she heard her voice echo off the stone walls. She sang in earnest, reveling in the sound projected off the walls. Sasha followed close behind her with a huge smile on her face as she walked through the trees.

Soon the guards that lined the battlements came looking down on her. Three gardeners mysteriously came into view, holding shears as two others came out of the nearby shed. Servants working nearby came and stood, stunned by the power of her voice. It echoed through the castle, running up and down the halls and dancing through the rooms. Benjamin opened his window and peered out, trying to figure out where the sound was coming from. Moments later she ended the song softly, when the sun started going down, and turned toward the archway to leave. Her face lit up with a brilliant smile when she saw Alexander leaning in the doorway, still dressed in his armor.

She ran to him as if she had not seen him in years. He held his arms open, engulfing her in his embrace. All encased in iron, he was careful not to squeeze her too tightly. He looked around after he put her back on the ground and noticed all the people that had gathered and all the flowers that had sprouted in the paths she had taken. She was absolutely gorgeous, surrounded by all the green. The flowers that seemed so beautiful before seemed to fade in brilliance next to her.

"Back to your duties now, everyone," he said, looking up at the battlements. "I heard there was a concert in the gardens, so I came to see for myself. You have gathered quite an audience," he said, escorting her back through the entrance.

He led her to his chamber and gave the white cord near his door two pulls. His chambers were much larger than the ones she occupied. The mantle above his fireplace was filled with trophies for horseback riding and swordsmanship. The large bed was surrounded by a sheer dark blue canopy that matched the covers. Some of the pillows were the same dark blue, some were black, and some were gold. Thick rugs covered the floor as several trunks lined the wall. There was a shelf with books over a table in one corner and to Saroja's surprise a golden harp was set in the other.

Alexander's attendants removed his armor and threw some logs into the fireplace. He held his arms up as they worked. His squire started tapping his leg when he wouldn't lift it for his straps to be released from under his boot. He was too busy watching Saroja. She sat on the stool in front of the harp and started to play a soothing melody. He smiled and shook his head. When the attendants finished he dismissed them.

"Is there anything you cannot do? Enter," he said to whomever was tapping on the door. A line of servants entered, carrying the tub and buckets of steaming water. Alexander pointed toward his inner room. The servants followed the unspoken instruction. "I will return in a moment," he said to Saroja. She nodded and continued to play her song. Moments later there was another tap on the door.

"Come in," she said. Three women entered the room with trays. They set them down on the table and removed the items. There was wine and bread, apples in sweet syrup, roasted corn, and a thick stew with beef, potatoes, and vegetables in a rosemary sauce. Saroja played softly while the women set up the meal. When they were done, two of the women bowed and left while the other went and stood behind Saroja.

Alexander emerged from the inner room moments later, walked over, and took her hand. He was casually dressed in a loosely fitting white linen shirt and black brocks. A bright smile covered his face as he escorted her to the table. The woman sat down on the stool and continued to play. He pulled out her chair then sat in the seat across from her.

"I explored your home today," she said.

"And does it meet with your approval?" he asked.

"I cannot believe you were willing to give this all up to be with me," she said.

"Why is that so hard to believe? You are worth more to me than these trinkets. Paintings and tapestries can be replaced. You are one of a kind," he explained.

She blushed at his comments and finished her dinner. Alexander dismissed the musician with a curt wave of his hand. He walked up slowly behind the princess and unbraided her hair. He took her crown off and placed it on the mantle. He massaged her head and her neck, letting her silky hair slip through his fingers. He pushed her chair back from the table and kneeled before her on the floor.

"I know it is not necessary, but I would like to formally ask you if you would bless my kingdom by becoming my wife…again," he said looking up at her. "Father gave me this when I told him I was going to ask you. He said it belonged to your mother."

Saroja sat silently, looking down at the beautiful ring he offered her. She smiled at him and said, "It would be my honor to marry you again, Your Majesty, but you will have to show me how to rule a kingdom."

"It will be my pleasure, Your Highness," he replied, slipping the ring on her finger.

Alexander had intended to have a ring specially made for her, but when he had spoken to his father about his intentions he informed him that the most beautiful ring in the kingdom was found among Queen Tess's possessions. When Benjamin had given him the ring Alexander agreed that it was perfect for Saroja. The gold band was designed to resemble the royal seal. The two blooming roses wrapped around the clearest crystal which was cut in a circular shape. The surface was flat with a beautiful star etched into it.

He pulled her from the chair onto the floor where he kneeled and wrapped her into his embrace and kissed her fiercely. He pressed her body against his until she was as close as he could get her. He stopped kissing her for a moment to look at her perfect face. When the marriage certificate had been burned it had felt like he was punched in the stomach; that he was losing her, again. Now she would be truly his once and for all, and he vowed to himself that he would never let anyone or anything take her away from him again.

Saroja was amazed by this man. She would have happily married him again when the king told her that she must. He had taken it to another level with this unexpected proposal. She looked into his dark eyes, trying to figure him out.

"You truly love me, don't you?" she asked softly.

"More than you will ever know," he replied.

"I think I'm going to cry," she said, wiping the tears from her eyes.

He picked her up and carried her to his bed. He swept the canopy back and placed her gently on top of the covers. She sat up and placed her hand on his shoulders.

"What's wrong?" he asked, noticing the serious look in her eyes.

He sat back against the pillows and pulled her into his arms. She laid her head back against his chest and admired her ring. She noticed the magical emblem etched into the stone and knew it was a sign.

"I haven't done anything to deserve a love such as yours," she said.

"I love you because the love you have for me is written all over your face. I can see it in your eyes. I don't have to guess what you're thinking because you will tell me what is on your mind, whether I want to hear it or not. You amaze me. Since the day I met you you've been showing me things I've never seen before. There is nothing you have to do to receive my love. I give it to you freely," he said.

"I've been thinking about our country and about my powers. They're getting stronger. New things are happening. I've always had to use hand gestures to control the magic. That is how I was taught. Now I can make things happen with my mind," she explained. "What if I could use my magic to protect us? We could think of a way that would liberate the country from the Lavitians without any bloodshed," she said.

"Tell me your ideas," he said, thinking she would need little help being a great queen.

"First, I thought I could conjure a wall around the country, but we'd still have to constantly defend it from invasion. Then I was thinking I could put a shield over us, but that would only make us prisoners in our own land," she said.

"What things can you control with your mind?" he asked.

Saroja made the fire burn out in the fireplace. Then she dosed all the light from the candles and pushed a cool breeze through the dark room. She relit the fireplace and handed him a long-stemmed red rose.

"So, you just think of something and it happens," he said, taking the flower. "Do you think you could just move them away from us?"

"The whole country!" she said. "How would I do that?"

"I don't know. Maybe you could find the answer in that book of yours," he suggested, moving her hair off her shoulder to plant kisses along her neck.

"When will you tell your father?" she asked.

"Tomorrow, we'll tell him tomorrow," he said, unbuttoning the back of her dress.

"What do you think he will say?" she asked, bending her neck slightly as he slowly moved his tongue up toward her ear.

"Shh…" he whispered against her skin. "We have more important matters to attend to at this moment."

She smiled and raised her arms as he slipped her dress over her head. He pushed her back against the pillows then took the rose she had given him and swept it slowly over her naked body. She cupped his face in her hands and kissed him. Slowly he aroused her body's sleeping passions, making her moan and plead for release.

Saroja could take no more of this exquisite torture. She pushed against him switching their position. She mounted his throbbing shaft, feeling somehow refreshed when he filled her completely. She moved instinctively against him. He held her small waist to push her down completely each time. She was like a warm glove; she held him securely as he slipped in and out of her. He caressed her thighs and tantalized her with his fingers as she moved against him. Suddenly he picked her up and moved to the edge of the bed with her straddled in his lap. His thrusts came harder and faster. She sucked on his neck and nibbled on his earlobe. He turned and laid her down on the bed when she pushed her tongue into his ear and whispered softly that she loved him too. Her breath was cool against the wet skin.

Saroja began to tremble as Alexander spilled his seed into her body. He separated himself from her and fell next to her against the pillows, drained of all his energy. She moved slowly into his arms and laid her head against his chest. She smiled at him when he looked down at her, then she closed her eyes and fell asleep. He kissed the top of her head and closed his eyes.

CHAPTER 27

Look to the Sky

Saroja wandered down the long hallway with Sasha, Dora, and her guards. Over the past few weeks she only saw Alexander during the private evening meals they shared in his chambers. As the weeks passed he had stopped joining with her. After he ate, he climbed into the bed, pulled her to his side, and fell asleep. She wondered what he did everyday that would make him so exhausted. Usually when she woke up he would be already gone. She missed him and she found herself extremely bored with her own company. Sasha and Dora carried on a quiet conversation but she barely heard what they were spoke of.

She passed through the doorway to the gardens and immediately felt better. She sat down on a bench near a part of the wall that was covered with thick ivy. She leaned back against it and was comforted by the thick spruce. It seemed to massage her back and her shoulders. She got up after a moment and stood up on the bench, trying to peer over the top of the wall. She had to jump and pull herself up to see what was beyond it. She plopped back down, unable to hold herself up anymore, and ended up nearly falling off the bench.

Beyond the wall was a shallow valley that led to the forest. She looked for her maids and her guards. They stood near the door, talking. Could she get over the wall without them noticing, perhaps if she used her powers? She turned and leaned against the spruce again. She grabbed on to the vines with both hands.

"Carry me to the other side," she said quietly. The vines slowly circled around her body and started lifting her to the top of the wall. When she reached the top, she sat on the edge and swung her feet across the top. The vines cradled her body like a swing made of ivy and slowly lowered her to the ground. "Thank you," she whispered as it unwrapped itself from her. She touched the wall again then lifted her skirts and ran toward the forest. When she entered the trees, she stopped and looked back.

The castle seemed so far away. She wouldn't stay long. She ran into the woods and disappeared in the darkness the trees created. The sunlight broke through the trees throwing light here and there. She called the corners when she got deep enough into the woods that she couldn't see the castle anymore. When she was done she sat on the ground and listened to the music the winds made for her.

Alexander walked slowly to his chambers. He was glad this torture was finally over. He would definitely think twice about disobeying his father again. He rang the cord for the servants to bring his tub, then sunk slowly into his chair and pushed his head back. The door was suddenly pushed open.

"Your Majesty," Sasha explained in a panicked voice. "The princess is gone. We were in the garden and she just disappeared, Your Highness. We never left her I swear to you…" Sasha rambled, quickly getting nervous as Alexander rose from the chair calmly and started toward her with his sword still strapped to his side.

"Where were you? How was the weather? How long has she been gone?" he asked as he walked past her out of the door. She followed, answering his questions.

"As I said, Your Highness, we were in the gardens. She's been gone for about an hour now. I've been looking everywhere for her," she replied.

"And the weather?" he asked.

"The weather—the weather was fine," she said, not understanding what that had to do with anything.

"Is her horse still in the stable?" he asked.

"Yes, Your Highness."

When they reached the gardens, Alexander stopped in the door way and looked around. Then he followed the trail of wild flowers to one of the benches near the wall. Then he had an idea. He took the side entrance that led to the stables and released her horse.

"Find your mistress, boy. Will you do that for me?" he asked, looking into the horse's eyes. He really wasn't worried. He knew it would be a simple matter for Saroja to escape her guards if she wanted to. He would find her. He knew she was alright where ever she was unless she had succeeded in disconnecting with the elements, but the day they had arrived proved that she had not. Midnight lingered in the doorway of the stable. Alexander saddled JeNi and pulled the other horse behind him. Then he let him go. Midnight trotted along slowly then ran down into the valley. Alexander followed him from a distance. He entered the forest and moved deep in through the trees. He stopped to graze near a patch of land covered by wild flowers, Saroja's flowers. She was nowhere in sight. Alexander got down from his horse.

"Saroja," he called but got no answer. He called again a little louder.

"I'm here," she said.

He turned and looked up. She was up in a big oak tree. The vines snaked in and around her, creating a natural hammock.

"What are you doing up there?" he asked, even as he figured it out for himself. She sat up, wiping her eyes, then she stretched and yarned.

"I must have fallen asleep, but I don't remember climbing a tree. I'm sorry. I didn't mean to stay this long," she explained. "How did you find me?" she asked.

"Midnight," he said, nodding his head in the direction of the horse. "Come down from there."

She placed her foot on one of the thicker vines that hung from the tree and grabbed it with both hands.

"Take me to him," she said. The vine started moving slowly, lowering her to the ground and placing her on the horse before Alexander. He circled his arms around her to reach the reigns, then turned the horse back toward the castle. Saroja kissed at Midnight over her shoulder.

"Come, baby," she said. The horse lifted its head and followed her.

Alexander took her to the stable and gave the horses over to the stable hands. Saroja followed Midnight to his stall then stuck her hand in her pocket and pulled out an apple that Alexander knew could not have been there before because he would have felt it pressed against him when she was on his horse. She kissed the horse then walked back to the entrance and collapsed moments later in the doorway.

Alexander ran to her side and picked her head up from the ground.

"Saroja, little one…wake up, my love." He placed his hand over her forehead and breathed a sigh of relief. She wasn't fevered. "Fetch the healer to Her Majesty's chamber at once," he said to no one in particular. The stable hands had created a small circle around the prince and the ailing princess. One of them ran off to do his bidding. Alexander gathered her up in his arms and carried her to her room.

"Um," she murmured and slowly opened her eyes.

"Are you alright, my love?" he asked.

"What happened?" she asked, groggy and flushed. Her color seemed washed out and she squinted when she looked up at him.

"You collapsed in the stable. Did you eat today?" he asked.

"Yes. I had porridge, fruit, and juice for breakfast, and then I had mutton, bread, sweet peas, and wine for midday meal."

"Well I have sent for the healer. Perhaps you should finish your nap until he arrives," Alexander said. When he reached her door, Cash pushed it open. Sasha was seated in the foyer with twelve other girls.

"What is this?" he asked, walking past them. He laid Saroja on the bed as Sasha came forward.

"The king has sent them for the princess to interview to service her chambers," she explained.

"Well, she will have to choose another day. Send them away," Alexander said, turning back to the bed. Saroja flipped her feet over the side and stood, but sat back down again when Alexander scowled at her and pointed at it.

"Alexander, I feel perfectly fine. Perhaps I had been in the sun too long."

"The sun could never make you weak, my love. Just relax yourself until the healer arrives."

Just then Cash entered and announced that the man was there. He entered, dressed like a monk in all black with a hood pulled over his head, and bowed to the prince.

"Your Majesty, I am Carmichael Lio, here to serve you," he said. Saroja's eyes widened at the sight of him. He carried a box full of jars filled with plants and different-colored liquids, strange-looking instruments that looked more fitting for the garden than a person.

"It is the princess that requires your attention. She just recently swooned in the stables. It may be nothing serious, but I wanted to make sure," he explained. Lio placed the box on the floor and asked Alexander to wait outside. He moved and stood by the foot of the bed with his arms crossed over his chest. Lio shrugged his shoulders and started his examination.

He asked her a million questions before he even touched her, which suited her just fine. His hands were cold and dry when he finally placed them against her throat. He tilted her head back and asked her to open her mouth. From there he moved slowly down her body, pressing firmly here and there. His questions had stopped and he now worked in silence.

Alexander cleared his throat when he pressed around her breast. This action he paid no attention to but instead asked her, "When was the last time you bled, Your Highness?" Saroja's face turned red and she wished Alexander had indeed gone outside. She looked at him then back at the healer. After some thought she realized that with everything going on she hadn't realized that it hadn't happened since she her attempt to reach Merlot and that had been almost two months ago.

Then she thought of their last day in Incartare. Her womb had started glowing right after she and Alexander had joined. She should have figured it out by now, but with everything going on she hadn't given much thought to her monthly cycle. There could be a child inside her and she was unwed. She would be a disgrace.

"Yes, that is the answer. She is weakened by a child, Your Highness. She will be fine once her body becomes accustomed to it. She will need to eat more to retain her strength," Lio said, gathering his box in his arms. He stood and bowed, then turned and left the room.

Saroja turned to her side and buried her face in the pillow. Alexander just stood glued to the spot, staring at her.

"Well, say something, Alexander," she said, her voice muffled by the pillow.

"A child," he whispered to himself. He moved to the bed and sat on the edge. Saroja's sniffles brought him out of his stupor. "Why are you crying, little one?"

"Because now there will be scandal and…"

"Hush now. There will be no scandal. You have been promised to me. That is as legal and binding as a marriage. Our child will be legal heir to the throne. Come here, little one." He turned her over in the bed and placed his hand over her abdomen. "I can't wait to see you swell with my child."

"You won't mind if I'm fat and walk like a duck?"

"You will be the most beautiful duck ever," he said, smiling down at her.

The next day Kalina was packing a few essential items that she would need for her trip when Saroja came to visit her. She sat down in front of the tapestry she was working on earlier and started to push the needle through it.

"How have you been?" Kalina asked, looking her over. She looked absolutely radiant. Her caramel-colored skin seemed to glow. Her face lit up when she smiled and hugged her. She sat down in the chair next to her wearing a lovely white-and-green gown.

"I have been fine, and you?" Saroja said. Actually, she was happier than she'd ever been in her life. "I have missed you."

"I have missed you as well. You have not been at dinner. You should come to the banquets. Let the people get to know you," she said looking at her.

"Alexander and I have private dinners. Right now, I'm trying to get to know him, but that is not why I came."

"There will be plenty of time for you to get to know your husband. The important thing is to get to know your country. Meet the people. Find out who they are and what they want. The one thing I regret about my past was that I had to start all over when trouble came. I had no one to turn to."

"I had something important to talk to you about. We have figured out—well, we were trying to figure out a way to protect the country from constantly being invaded by the Lavitians. I need your help. Alexander thinks I should separate the land," she said.

"Do you think you are strong enough to separate the entire country?" Kalina asked, continuing with her task.

Saroja had always been impressed by her composure. She was like a rock. She was rarely moved by anything. Saroja sat back in the chair with her hands folded neatly in her lap. She used her mind to pull the needle from Kalina's hand. Then used her powers to punch the needle into the tapestry and push it away.

Kalina turned to her with a look of amazement on her face. Degar had been the only other sorcerer she had ever met and even he used hand controls.

"Where did you learn that?" Kalina asked.

"It just happened one night," she explained.

"If you have this ability to control your powers with your thoughts, you may not need practice. Just command it done and use the magic to make it happen," she explained.

"Would you like to visit the gardens with me?" Saroja asked, getting up from the chair. She wanted to tell her so badly about the child she carried, but the king had ordered that it remain a secret between the three of them until they were properly wed. Sasha pulled the chair out and placed the shawl around her shoulders. Kalina rose from the chair and followed her from the room.

"I would love to, but we cannot stay long. The king is sending my coven to aid the army near the border," she explained.

They walked and talked. They talked about the future and had conversations about the past that they had never been able to have before. Kalina told her stories about her mother and explained how much they were alike.

"I think that's the reason your powers are so strong," Kalina said. "Your mother's powers were passed to her from three generations earlier. Your father had powers, but after he was named king, his mother thought he should refrain from using them to protect the family. Your grandmother, Lady Lynea was the most powerful sorceress I had ever known. She taught me how to use my powers. When she died…it was like I had lost my own mother. Some say she is responsible for the Great Oak. There is more power running through your veins than you will ever know. My mother was the only one in our family with powers and they were passed to me and my sister," Kalina said.

"What sister?" Saroja asked.

"I have a twin sister. Her name is Shalyndria," Kalina said.

"What happened to her?" Saroja asked, wondering why she had never heard about this mysterious sister, not even from Matilda.

"She was sold away from my family when we were slaves. We were only ten, but the estate was failing and the merchant was able to get a lot of money for her because of her special skill," Kalina explained.

"But if she was only ten, how did the merchant know she had powers?" Saroja asked, taking the shawl off her shoulders.

"She didn't have powers like you and me. She had the ability to see things in the future. She really couldn't help it. If you said, 'I wonder if we'll get rain soon,' her hair would start flying and she'd give you the answer. Her hair started turning colors. Mother was devastated when they took her away. Our father had been killed a month earlier. People thought it would be the end of her, but she just focused all her attentions on me. She found me a coven and left me with them to learn magic under Lady Lynea," Kalina continued.

"If it wasn't for Grandma Tilda, I would know nothing of magic," Saroja said.

"So many horrible things happened to me when I tried to be magical, so I just turned away from my powers. Sometimes I go so long without using them that when I do it's by accident," Kalina explained.

"I don't think anything could be that horrible. I have never used a flint to light a candle. Besides it feels so good when I'm all filled up with power, don't you think so?" she asked.

"Yes, but when I was growing up we had to hide the fact that we were Pheolatian. It just got easier being normal. Perhaps this is the Great Creator's plan for you. Besides, saving our people tends to run in your family," Kalina said, smiling at her.

"I am supposed to meet with Alex and King Benjamin before dinner. Will you accompany me? King Benjamin makes me nervous. It's like he's looking straight through me," Saroja said.

"That's just how he has always been, dark and menacing. He is probably seeing Alosis when he looks at your face. They were very close," Kalina said.

"Do I really look that much like him?" Saroja asked, looking at Kalina as they left the garden.

"Your size and your color come from your mother. She was small, demure, beautiful, and quite charming. Everything you could ever wish for in a queen. Your eyes have the same amber glow when you smile as hers did. The rest of your face was given to you by your father, your nose, your chin, even the set of your cheeks. Don't you see, Mirage, their memories will never be lost because you exist. That's what children are for," Kalina explained, secretly wishing she had a child of her own as she walked down the hall. Mirage was all grown up now.

"You called me Mirage," she said with a giggle.

"I've been calling you that for so long. I'll get used to Saroja again as I hear it more," she said.

When the women reached the king's private chamber, Sasha was made to wait in the hall. The guards pulled the door close. Alexander stood and walked to Saroja and escorted her to her seat.

"My son has been telling me of your idea to make Theslia into an island," Benjamin said.

"Your Majesty, I have no power over the Great Creator. He made the land as it should be. I cannot change it, can I?" she said, looking over at Kalina who shrugged her shoulder in response. "I have to honestly say I don't know if I can do it. I haven't even finished Grandma Tilda's book. There are still a lot of things about my powers that I don't know, that I'm still learning." She remembered when Matilda started being unable to answer her questions. She was all alone with this incredible power with no one to guide her. She shook her head and looked down at her hands laid neatly in her lap.

"That is true, sire, she is young when it comes to the world of magic. Her powers will be fully developed when she's twenty-five," Kalina said.

"Well, I think it is worth a try. You will finish the book and work with Alexander. Kalina, you should report to the galley. Galithe has been ordered to leave when the sun goes down. You should be better protected under the cover of darkness. Inform the other women and I wish you luck on your journey." Kalina stood and bowed to the royal family. She stopped and gave Saroja a hug and a kiss then left the room.

"How long do you think it would take before you finish the book?" the king asked. Finally, he could see the end of all this madness.

"Maybe a month if I work every day. Sire, am I allowed to freely use my powers around the castle?" Saroja asked, concerned about the idea.

"No. For right now you will confine your work to your chambers. We will reconvene in a month's time to see what you will be able to do," he said, looking at the two of them. "Now if there is nothing else, I'd like to get something to eat."

He got up from his seat and everyone else rose. They walked to the door and headed to the great hall. Alexander held Saroja's hand as they walked down the hall. She looked up at him and smiled. He gently stroked her palm with his index finger. Benjamin pulled them apart when they reached the doors that led to the great hall.

"Public affection should not be shown to the courtiers. You are never sure whether the guests are friends or foe. Never let them know more than they need to," he explained, then backed up from them. Alexander looked down at Saroja. She looked up at him and smiled. He was embarrassed by his father's remarks but he hid it behind the half smile he returned to her.

They entered the great hall and had dinner. Four girls performed the *flusha* for the king, but Saroja thought it needed more practice. She looked at Alexander. At the same time, he leaned over and whispered, "You would have done a much better job."

She looked at him from the side of her eye. "I thought you didn't like my dance," she said quietly.

"I loved it, I just couldn't see you that way without wanting to reach out and touch you. I couldn't see you that way in front of Simo and James. I didn't lie when I told you I was enchanted by you; it is a powerful lulling force that draws me near you when you move that way, and I don't want anybody else ensnared by it," he whispered in her ear as he used his hand to tickle her side under the table.

"So, you were jealous," she said, looking at him with a big grin on her face. The king tapped him on the shoulder at that moment and he turned with a great grin on his face.

"I hope you are not letting your new infatuation of your bride cloud your judgment. Affections between you and your bride should be kept in the privacy of your chambers," he said quietly to his son, always aware of their audience.

"But, Father," Alexander started.

"When you have an audience, she should be treated like a well-respected courtier, nothing more," Benjamin said.

"Yes, Father," Alexander said, sitting back in his seat. "Let's retire," he said, rising from his seat.

"Alexander, come with me," Benjamin said, rising from his throne. The room fell silent and everyone bowed as the two walked through the side doors to Benjamin's private chamber. "Speak to me, son," he said, leaning back against his desk.

"Father, when I'm around her, she is the only one in the room. I find it hard to think of anything but her when she's away from me.

What am I to do? I don't understand why we just can't send these people away if we don't trust them," he said.

"The problem is not the courtiers. They have always been a part of your life. The princess is the new factor in this equation. You are about to become a father. Now is the time for you to step up and prove to this kingdom that you deserve to rule. Besides, she is not your first woman," Benjamin said.

"She is unlike any woman I've ever met," he explained.

"I'm glad you have found love, but if you love her you can't let the love you have for her disrupt your better judgment. Don't let your love for your queen become a weakness. Your enemies would use it to break you. You still have a job to do. Do you understand me?" Benjamin asked.

"Yes, Father," Alexander answered. Benjamin nodded his head, giving Alexander permission to leave the room. He stood behind Saroja's seat as she rose and formally escorted her from the hall. Sasha and four guards left the room behind them. They walked to her chamber, quietly talking over their plans. When they reached the chamber, Saroja dismissed Sasha for the rest of the night then went inside.

"Now about this jealousy thing," he started.

"My love, you will never have to be jealous again. I never have to do that dance again if you don't like it," she said.

"You do, actually. You will have to perform it before the court at the wedding ceremony. Listen, I have no problem with the dance, I just don't want anyone else to see you do it, but if they must, may I ask that the costume not be so revealing?" he said, smiling and nodding his head.

"I will wear what I think will be pleasing to your eyes, my lord. The others do not matter, and if they do, my exquisite taste will be a reflection on your exquisite taste." By now she had crossed the distance between them and was now standing directly in front of him, her head tilted back so she could look in his face. He smiled down at her and caressed her cheek.

"Get your book so we can go."

"Where are we going?" she asked.

"We are going to my chambers because my inner room has no windows, so we won't have to worry about the spying eyes, and because I think your skin will look better against my blue sheets than it does against your burgundy ones," he said, wrapping her in his embrace and kissing her sweetly several times before opening the door.

When they reached the chamber, he let her read her book while he went over some parchments in the other room.

"Alexander, look!" she called. He entered his study to find Sasha standing in the middle of the floor.

"Is that you?" he asked.

"Yes, what do you think?" she asked, spinning around.

"You look just like her, that's amazing," he said, leaning against the door frame. "You should finish up, it is getting late."

Saroja closed the book and closed her eyes. Alexander watched as the image of Sasha got almost blurry, then it started to flip back and forth between the two, until finally Saroja stood before him. She followed him from the room to an alcove in the other where he sat down in front of some parchments.

"I'm almost done," he said when she touched his shoulder. She leaned against his back, rubbing her hands across his shoulders, and rested her chin on his head.

"If I stay here tonight, can I call the corners in the morning? It will help me to be as strong as I can be," she explained.

"You can do whatever you like, princess," he said, looking up at her. She kissed him then walked back to the other room. She took off her clothes. She slipped the silk chemise on over her head and slipped under the covers.

Moments later Alex joined her in the bed and pulled her to his side. She turned to him and placed her head against his chest where his heart beat strong inside. She closed her eyes, feeling complete, and exhaled. She had waited so long for this feeling. She was amazed at how easily he gave it to her. This was the first time in her life she was not wishing she were somewhere else. She was satisfied just lying next to him.

CHAPTER 28

A Monster with a Heart

The next morning before dawn, Kalina's campsite was attacked by twelve men on horseback. Galithe ordered the women to run and hide. Kaemar, Claris, and Maja ran. Kalina stood glued to the spot. This would be the second time someone would stay and die while she ran and hid. She just couldn't do it again. She backed into the circle. The soldiers formed and used a strong burst of wind and light to push the men away from them. Galithe and the other five soldiers fell after cutting their enemy's original number in half. Kalina was hit over the head from behind. She fell to the ground unconscious. Kaemar and the other women ran until they came to a nearby farm that had recently been burned. They found some old mules in the barn and rode them back to the castle to inform the king.

"Take the weapons and horses," one of the bandits said.

"She is beautiful," another said. "We'll fetch a good price for her."

"I am keeping this one," a small man said, jumping down from his horse. He walked over to Kalina's body and flipped her over on the ground. Her face was smudged with dirt and blood trickled down one side.

"No," their leader said, walking forward. "Marsalis will pay a full sack of gold if not more for a woman such as this. Bind her and put her in the cage with the others. Kiylar, get those horses secured. We must move on."

"We have sold thousands of women. When will we be able to sample one for ourselves?" Normen remarked.

"Wulf, their uniforms…I didn't notice as we approached. These are royal guards. You ordered us to attack royal guards, man! Are you mad?"

Livideon asked frantically. "The king will have our heads."

"Calm down, Brother. With all the gold we will receive when we reach Lavitia, no one will be able to touch us," Wulf explained.

United Rose Fortress

Saroja slipped quietly from the bed before the sun came up. She conjured the candles needed for the ritual and called the corners. Alexander woke up when the chamber grew too cold for him to sleep. He opened his eyes and watched as Saroja floated into the air and the wind rushed around her. Her hair swirled through the air as if she were underwater. The banded candle told him that it was still early in the morning. He pushed back against the pillow and watched as she descended slowly back to the floor. Quickly he closed his eyes and pretended to be asleep. She relit the fireplace and crawled slowly back into the bed. She tried to get back under the covers without disturbing him. She had gotten one leg successfully under when he grabbed her and started to tickle her.

She laughed and squirmed, trying to break free of his grasp.

"What do you want to do today?" he asked, moving his hand slowly across her womb.

"I need to finish the book. I've already been able to add some things on the blank pages. Sometimes I think I don't really need my Grandmother's book; the spells and enchantments are so easy. Do you know I can even stop time? That spell was very complicated, but I did it. I think messing with time is dangerous." She got up from the bed to get the book off the table. She climbed back under the covers and started flipping through the pages she had already mastered. Alexander sat back in the bed and watched her practice making flames of fire in the palm of her hand, with the flick of her wrist she tossed them into the fireplace.

Sasha arrived at the door later with a fresh gown and slippers. Dora carried the breakfast tray. After she was dressed, she dismissed Sasha for the day, claiming she would be staying in Prince Alexander's chambers for the day and she would ring if she needed anything. She followed the same routine for the next few days while she read over the spells and practiced them until she mastered them all completely and could do them with her mind.

Later that night the women of Kalina's coven arrived at the castle. They explained to the king that Galithe and Kalina were probably killed by bandits. Benjamin blamed himself. He had thought from the beginning that it would be a bad idea to send the women to the border alone, but Marsalis had not been the attacker. His country was in serious need of order. Now he would have to explain to the princess that Kalina was gone.

"Can you use your powers to see if anyone survived?" he asked.

"No, sire," Kaemar said. "We don't have natural powers like Kalina. We can only work as four. I'm so sorry."

"We shouldn't have left her," Claris said sadly.

"Do not fret. Perhaps the princess can help you" Benjamin said.

He immediately dispatched four groups of soldiers to search for Kalina. First, they would search their campsite. Then they had orders to search in a circular motion, meeting back at the castle if the bodies weren't retrieved. Every city was to be searched and Thedan was at the top of the list.

Now, after all she had been made to endure in the last few months, he would have to tell the princess that she had lost yet another loved one, and once again it was his fault. Benjamin dismissed the ladies and paced back and forth across the room. Then he opened the door and told the guard to send for the princess.

Saroja tried to focus all her energies on even the smallest hint of Kalina. She tried holding one of her gowns but it just would not work. She could feel her but she just couldn't create a vision to see where she was. When she tried working with Kalina's coven, the magic wouldn't work.

"She is a sorceress, Claris, look," Kaemar said, holding Saroja's hand up.

"Who did this to your hand?" Maja asked.

"Grandma Tilda. She said it would keep me safe," Saroja explained.

"That is a sorceress's star. It keeps you from joining a coven, but you can override it if you cut it with a knife," Kaemar said.

"No, Grandma Tilda said it would protect my powers and I believe that. I will not cut it," Saroja said.

"Does Kalina's life mean nothing to you?" Maja asked, confused and upset. "You have the power to save her life. How could you refuse after she saved yours?"

"I have tried, but I cannot. How dare you say I care nothing for her? She is my mother and I love her, but I will not allow you to steal my powers. Not for anything...not for anyone!" she exclaimed and ran from the room.

"Leave her be," Benjamin said. "If Lady Kalina is alive, I will find her and punish those responsible. And one more thing," Benjamin said rising from his seat. "Lady Maja, you will never speak to a member of the royal family like that again. Is that clear?" he said, walking slowly toward her. She bowed her head and took a step back.

"Please accept my apologies, Your Majesty. I never meant to hurt the princess. I was only trying to get her to realize her full potential. In a coven, her abilities would be endless," she said.

"And if she joined your coven so would yours. Perhaps Matilda was right to prevent such a thing from happening," Benjamin said, leaving the room.

Castle Covax, Lavitia
Weeks Later

"Sire, a wagon has arrived with new women for Your Highness to choose from," the servant said from the hall.

"Have them cleaned and taken to the great hall. I will be there momentarily to look them over, I hope they fare better than that last batch they brought," Marsalis said from his study.

After what seemed like an eternity in a filthy, damp wagon, one of the men that had captured them, the scraggily little one called Sam, who seemed to have some kind of deviant attraction toward her, opened the front flap. The girls were untied and taken out one by one. Kalina held her hands up over her eyes to block the force of light then fell in line behind a child that looked to be no more than fifteen years old. They were led across a long hall to a grand, open bathing room. The sun glistened off the pools, filling the room with light and warmth. A breeze blew in through the open balcony. It would have been a beautiful place if it didn't reek of unwashed bodies and stagnant water.

Young servant girls littered the room, carrying towels and stacks of silk clothes. The girls were stripped and made to stand in a line. A broad woman walked by, looking each girl over. She had a stern look about her. Her height and large build gave her an intimidating quality. Her eyes were a kind of gray with a hint of green. She wore a gold silk wrap that started at one shoulder and ended up being tossed over the next. She was also the only servant in the room that wore hers as a gown. The other girls had pulled the middle of their gowns up between their legs and secured it in the back as if they wore pants like a man. The woman's hair was in the same style the other servants. It was pulled back off her face and bond in the back by silver bands that made her white hair seem to gleam in the light that lit up everything.

"See to her bruises, here and here on the shoulder. I want the redness covered here on her face. Where are the silk wraps, Agnes? Let's try pink for her, lavender here. White for you, princess. Marsalis will like you," she said, lifting Kalina's chin, holding her face to the light. She pulled it from the woman's grasp and gave her a fierce emerald glare. "Cecile, bring in the soaps. What is wrong with you girls today?" Miriam said, dismissing Kalina's reaction to her touch. She was used to having them angry and scared when they first arrived. The king would break them of their insolence in no time. "Now let's get them cleaned."

Kalina was bathed by two servants and wrapped in silk clothes. They wrapped up her frostbitten fingers and put powder on her face to cover the redness and some kind of sticky paste on the bruise on her head. Her hair was cleaned and brushed with smelling oils. Then they added a strip of black-and-white beads to a lock of hair in the front and told her she was marked as a candidate, and if she was not chosen, she would be sold as a slave in the city. The rest of her hair they left spilling down her back. She was led down a long hall and placed in line next to another girl. She remembered standing in a line like this when she was very small. She remembered clinging to her mother's legs because she was so frightened. She remembered how her country had celebrated their liberation for seven days and seven nights. Now here she was once again standing on an auction block.

Moments later King Marsalis entered the room.

"Bow to the king!" Garth yelled in a commanding voice.

"Benjamin Casesar is my king," one of the girls said, spitting at Marsalis as he passed her.

"Have her racked on the charges of treason," Marsalis said, continuing to walk down the line of women, stopping in front of each one as he looked them over. He was golden from head to toe. His hair hung back off his face onto is shoulders. It was golden brown, a hint darker than his skin. He wore no shirt and large billow legged pants that fit securely around a small waist. The muscles in his stomach flexed as he moved down the line.

"I would rather die than bow to you!" the girl screamed as she was dragged away down the hall.

"Let that be an example to the rest of you. In Lavitia, life, love, and all of you belong to me. Serve and obey me and I will grant you your heart's desire. Disobey me and I will kill you," he said bluntly. All the women dropped into a low curtsy except Kalina. She stood tall and silent.

"I will take this one, this one, her, her, and….Shalyndria…" he whispered, stunned by the image that stood before him. "What is your name?"

Kalina remained silent. It had been a long time since anyone had mistakenly called her by that name.

"Answer me, woman!" Marsalis yelled, stepping closer to her.

"Kalina…. my name is Kalina. How do you know my sister?" she asked hopefully.

"Your sister…" he said shocked by the idea.

"Yes, I have a twin sister named Shalyndria. Where is she? May I see her? Please, sir! I would do anything to see her again," she said honestly.

"Anything…" Marsalis said, walking around her, looking her over. She looked exactly like his Shalyndria. Her hair was a wretched black instead of the shiny silver he preferred, but she was beautiful nonetheless, extremely beautiful. "Will you give me your word on that?" he asked, looking at her with an evil glare in his eye.

Kalina thought about it for a moment. She didn't trust him at all, and something in his tone made her think she would regret her answer, but she had no choice. If there was a chance that she could give her sister a hug and tell her how much she had missed her, she would do anything he asked.

"Yes, I give you my word. Is my sister here?" Kalina asked.

"Perhaps. Jason, pay the man for the five women. Have those four taken to the hall and given their rooms. No, take them to the harem. Tell Miriam I want them watched. You," he said, pointing at Kalina. "Come with me," he said, walking away quickly. Kalina followed him down the hall, then through a door, and down a winding stair well. Marsalis took a torch off the wall and continued down the stairs. They came to a stone wall with a single wooden door.

"Is my sister being kept a prisoner down here?" Kalina asked.

"Do you also possess her ability?" he asked, looking over his shoulder.

"No, I cannot see things to come. If I could, I would have been here long ago to save her," she said as Marsalis pushed the door open and let her walk in.

"Save her," Marsalis said to himself, leading her through yet another door. He started lighting the candlesticks around the room. Kalina started to faintly see what looked like a coffin of some sort. She held up her right hand and moved it in a circular motion, instantly lighting the rest of the candles, filling the room with light. Marsalis turned and stared at her, shocked by what had just happened before his eyes. She walked closer to the coffin.

It was white with a glass lid. Her sister was wrapped in a beautiful white shiny silk. She wore silver jewelry in her ears and on her wrists, and there was a string of silver beads in her hair. Her hands were folded over her chest and her eyes were closed as if she were asleep.

"How did she die?" Kalina asked, touching the glass top. She took a deep breath and tried to fight back the tears that she felt welling up in her eyes. She would not let him see her cry.

"She was murdered," he said. Kalina could hear the hurt in his voice.

He looked down at Shalyndria. He had realized how much he truly loved her after she had died. He thought the Great Creator had taken her away as a punishment for cursing his name. Now he had been given another chance. He would not let it pass him by.

"Who killed her and why do you keep her down here locked away?" Kalina asked, turning to him.

"Who, is of no consequence. Just know that they will suffer worse than any man has ever suffered when they are brought forth. He was jealous of her, for she had everything, everything a woman could ever want, but I don't want to talk about her. The gods have sent you to me to take her place. You have seen her, and you swore you would do anything to see her again," he said, walking toward her.

Kalina couldn't contain herself. She was tired of having everything she loved taken from her. She was angry and confused. Would the Great Creator never tire of seeing her dwell in sorrow?

"Were you taken from your family? Do you have a husband or children?"

"Why? Would you set me free if I did?" she asked, disgusted by this man's sense of superiority.

"Woman, you will learn quickly to answer my questions with honest responses, rather than giving me attitude. I do not tolerate insolence in this kingdom, especially from women."

"I would answer the question if I felt it wasn't a blunt attempt to mock my current situation," she said, turning back to her sister. He was trying to rile her. She would not give him the satisfaction. Marsalis smiled at her back. There was something about this woman that he found alluring. She was unlike any other candidate that had been brought before him. She spoke to him as if she was his equal and he saw no fear in her eyes. He walked up behind her and turned her to face him. He grabbed and held her by her biceps.

"You will be my queen and you will bear me a son and he will inherit my strength and your powers," he said, reaching up to touch her face. Kalina turned her face away at the last minute.

"I will not marry you! Will this child also inherit your prejudice, hate, cruelty, and thirst for blood? Will it steal innocent girls from their families in the dead of night and make them sex slaves against their will?" Kalina asked.

"Will you honor your word or would you rather be put to death for lying to your king?" he asked, using his hand to turn her face back so he could see her eyes. He held her chin firmly. Kalina thought about it for a moment. Death certainly looked like a better option, but now was not the time.

"I will honor my word, but I promise you this. I will never love you. You took my sister away from me. You are responsible for the death of my father, and the only man I've ever loved. I will never forgive you," she said walking toward him.

"Who said anything about love? All you have to do is obey me and come to my bed willingly," he said. "And of course, bear me a son. I will replace you if a girl is born."

"Very well, but you should know that I do not fear you and even though I look like my sister, we were nothing alike. Shalyndria is—well, was a very quiet child. I will speak my mind whether you want to hear it or not," Kalina said, staring into his eyes.

"Yes, I think you will do fine. You may await me on the stairs," he said, turning again toward the coffin.

"Wait. There is one more thing I must do before I leave," she said, walking back to the coffin. She reached down and unlocked it then pushed open the lid.

"No, you will let the air in and the body will begin to rot," Marsalis said, placing his hand on the top to stop her.

"You don't understand. This is not our way," Kalina said, pushing the lid open. She rubbed Shalyndria's hair and kissed her gently on her forehead. Then she swept her hands through the air and conjured a bowl of oil and allowed three drops of her tears to fall into the bowl. She took two candles from the wall and set one on the floor. She held the other in her hand and swept it through her palm several times, turning it black. She took a strand of Shalyndria's hair and placed it in the bowl. Marsalis crossed his arms and backed away from her. She fell to her knees and lit the candles with her fingertips, and then she turned to him.

"Would you like to help with the ritual?" she asked. "I see the love you had for her in your eyes. You do perhaps have a heart despite what people say," she said.

"You know nothing about me, lady. My heart died years ago when your kind murdered my parents. I will have nothing to do with your witchcraft," he said, standing firm.

"Yes, but you are willing to lay with me to create a child," she said glaring at him.

"That decision is made to benefit my kingdom. As king I must look beyond my own feelings to do what is needed for my country," he said, walking toward her.

Kalina turned forward and started repeating the chant over and over again. "Away from this world and into the wind; as this life ends let another begin." Suddenly white lights started to float all around Shalyndria's body as a wet fog filled the room. When it passed she was gone and only a tiny flicker of light remained.

"What have you done?" Marsalis asked furiously.

"I have sent her to our ancestors," Kalina said, rising from the floor.

"Bring her back, now!" he exclaimed.

"I cannot. She is dead. Let her go," Kalina said, walking toward the door. Suddenly Marsalis grabbed her by the throat and pulled her toward him, so close their noses touched.

"You will never give me orders. I am king here! I had given her immortality; she had risen above your weak ancestors. You sent her away, now you will bring her back, or I will choke the life out of you right now," Marsalis said, enraged. Kalina struggled against his grip.

"I cannot," she said in a hoarse, strangled voice. "She was not immortal. She was Pheolatian and so am I. If you can't accept that, then go ahead, kill me."

Marsalis glared at her. His eyes narrowed and shifted from side to side as he thought over what she was saying. Kalina closed her eyes so he wouldn't see how truly frightened she was. Then he dropped her to the floor and stared at her as she coughed and tried to regain her composure. She was right, of course. He had to let Shalyndria go. He would instead focus his attention on this new woman. She had a flare about her that he found fascinating.

"Come, I will take you to your chambers," he said, pulling her to her feet.

The next day they were married. There was no celebration, no *Flusha*, no kiss. After the quick ceremony, he had ordered that she be taken to his bed chamber. She had to get away from this man. The only emotion he seemed to know how to express was anger; she would not be used as a breeding mare. She opened the door slowly and peeked into the hallway. The four guards that escorted her to the room now stood against the wall staring straight ahead each holding a long Kwan Do knife. She closed it back and pressed her forehead against it to think. She grabbed the string of beads, which had been changed to a pattern consisting of a precious clear stone and pure gold bands which marked her as royalty.

In most royal chambers, there were secret passageways or trick doors installed to give the king and queen an opportunity to escape if the palace was ever under siege. A king such as Marsalis would certainly have one. She turned and took in the span of the room and her hopes dropped. The room stretched out before her and opened to a balcony that overlooked the grounds. Six pillars held up the ceiling. Sheer white curtains flipped and fluttered in the wind between them. She could already make out two doors and another double door which indicated an adjacent room. The furniture spread out across the floor and against the wall. The room was so big she'd never be able to find a way to escape before someone came. A bed that could probably hold ten people sat on a large dais in the middle of the floor between four separate smaller pillars that didn't connect with the ceiling as the others did. The covers were light blue, almost white. There were several long white and gray pillows on the floor all around it. Short white couches sat here and there. The wall bent a corner and a square trickling pool came into view as she walked into the chamber. The pool sat next to a black marble wall where a gentle waterfall spilled down into it. It was surrounded by shiny white marble. The rest of the marble floor on this side of the room was black with gold flecks.

She felt along the walls and looked behind the paintings and tapestries. She rubbed her hands along the furniture and pushed and pulled the fixtures. She lifted the candle sticks and rubbed along the shelves.

"What are you looking for?" A deep curious voice asked from across the room. Kalina jumped at the sound and turned to him.

"I—" she stammered.

"You cannot escape. Do not waste your time trying," he said calmly, dismissing the subject with a curt wave of his hand. He held his hand out and a servant that must have entered just as silently as he had along with five others that now lined the walls, came forward and placed a goblet in it. Moments later he was back pouring the wine. Marsalis offered it to her and waited for her to take it from his hand before he had another goblet poured for himself.

"What is it about you Theslians that make you so rebellious?"

"Perhaps it is because men cannot live free when they serve you. You want more than loyalty, you want to be worshiped. Do you think of yourself as a God?" she asked.

"And this Benjamin, he allows your people to live free, as you say?" he asked, ignoring the comment.

"He allows a man to govern his own household, but he also enforces the laws so that same man will be safe in his home. Theslia is not perfect," she said, pausing to drink from the goblet. "But I'd take my chances with them than you any day," she said, involuntarily backing away from him.

"Well, you would then find yourself on the losing side. My tunnel is nearly complete. Soon my army will march and Theslia will fall. But enough of this state's business. We have an heir to create. Come to me," he said, holding his cup out again for the servant to take it away. Kalina swallowed the rest of the wine from the goblet.

"May I have some more?" she said, gesturing toward the wine. Marsalis tilted his head in her direction and the servant started toward her with the jug. Then he held up his hand and the servant stopped.

"Use your magic," he said.

"He has to let it go," she replied. The servant looked back at Marsalis as he nodded his head. The boy turned back to Kalina and let the jug go. She held her palm flat toward the bottle catching it in midair.

She walked slowly toward him and made the bottle tip over her goblet. She drank the contents from the glass. Her heart pounded against her chest as she closed the distance between them. Marsalis walked toward her and took her hand. He held his hand up and waved quickly. The servants turned with military precision and filed out of the room. He led her to the bed and sat next to her.

"You may not have been afraid of me before, but I see fear in your eyes now," he said.

"Please, I cannot. I…please. This is all happening to fast," she pleaded.

"Hush, little one, I will not hurt you," he said.

Kalina didn't believe him. She couldn't get past the stories she had heard of his cruelty or the evils she had herself witnessed because of his orders. She wanted love and she knew this man could not give her that.

"I have never done this before," she said quietly, nervously picking at her nails.

"That is perfect. My queen should be pure. But fear not, Theslian. It is not something that you have to be taught. It will come to you naturally," he said softly next to her ear. He stood up from the bed and pulled her into his arms. He unhooked the clasp that held up her silks and let the cloth fall to her feet. He kissed her gently and picked her up. She trembled in his arms as he held her against his chest. He didn't want her to fear him—not just yet anyway. She would be his willing wife and perhaps if he gained her trust she would share some of Theslia's secrets with him.

He laid her down gently on the bed then kissed her slowly from her head to her toes. He used his hands to seduce her. He brought her body's passions to life slowly, trying to help her relax, but with every kiss Kalina felt like she was betraying her sister, her country, and herself. She turned her face away, but then he just kissed her along her neck. The tears she had fought so hard to conceal earlier started falling freely. Marsalis used his thumbs to wipe them away. The worst part about it was that deep down inside she liked what he was doing and she didn't want him to stop. How could such an evil man be so gentle?

He slipped his fingers into her body. Kalina arched into his caress. She allowed herself to think of nothing except what he was doing and how good it felt. Maybe for just a moment she could pretend that he loved her and she loved him in return. Marsalis opened her legs with his knees as he sucked on her nipples until they were hard with desire. He kissed a path down her stomach and used his tongue to tantalize her most sensitive part until she moaned for release. He looked up at her face. Her eyes were closed and she tossed her head from side to side. He pushed his throbbing shaft slowly into her body. When he came to her maidenhead he drew back then pushed pass the blockade. At the same time, he bit down hard into the top of her ear lobe.

Kalina cried out in pain, but as he released his hold on her ear, the pain passed quickly. He continued to move erotically inside her and at that moment there was nowhere else she'd rather be. Suddenly she felt like she was falling backwards and tumbling forwards all at the same time. The spiraling continued as wave after wave of wet heat, bright colors, and bursts of adrenaline washed over her. He filled her over and over again. It began to move faster and faster until there was an explosion inside her body. She couldn't remember anything ever making her feel so powerless and satisfied all at the same time.

Marsalis fell against her and separated their bodies. He raised her hands up over her head and kissed her gently, then got up from the bed to retrieve his wine. Kalina turned to her side and closed her eyes, trying to make the humiliation fade away into the blackness she looked into. She had betrayed her people for a few moments of pleasure. She had lain with the Dark One himself.

"What is the extent of your magic?" he asked between sips of wine.

"I thought you hated Pheolatians and our powers. You declared an ability that I was born with evil and illegal. You killed my father and he didn't even have the gift. You took my sister away from me, and the only man I loved was burned to death before my very eyes. Why do you want to know?" she said.

"I want you to answer my question before I get angry," he said sitting back down on the edge of the bed.

"I hate you!" she said. Marsalis turned and glared at her.

"I will not ask again," he said sternly.

"I can conjure objects from the air with the right spell, manipulate fire, and I can see things as they occur through visions, but I need a coven to do that," she said knowing someday he might use that information against her.

"You can see things as they occur and your sister could see things before they happened. What abilities will my son have?" he asked.

"I don't know," she said.

"But he will have them?" he asked, turning to see her face as she answered.

"Yes, the power is passed through our blood, but there is no way of knowing what powers a child will possess. But you are right. It is usually related to the powers of the parents. It depends on what you teach them, and even then they may develop their own special skill. When it is born, you can kill me?" she said. "I could not bear to watch you destroy my child's soul."

"It would be my pleasure, if that is your wish, but I had intended to allow you to raise the child for ten years. Who else would be able to teach him of his magic? Lavitia would be invincible with such a leader on the throne," he said, crawling toward her.

"I will tell you this, if you do not teach the child how to love, his powers will never develop," she said, looking at him to see his reaction.

He pushed her gently back into the pillows and made love to her again and again until he was so exhausted he couldn't move. He pulled her into his arms so she wouldn't find the escape passage she had been searching for earlier and fell asleep. Usually the queen would have her own chambers, but a woman such as this could certainly outsmart any guard. She would have to be watched until she learned to obey him.

The next morning Marsalis woke up with Kalina sleeping by his side. She looked like an angel and for a moment he thought of his parents and how much they had loved him. He placed his hand over her abdomen. His seed could be flourishing inside her. He would have a family again. He got up from the bed and walked to the door.

"Send for Lord Kail," he said to the guard. Moments later, there was a tap on the door. Marsalis let the advisor in and escorted him to one of his inner rooms.

"I have decided to push my plans to leave for the training grounds back. Instead of three days, I will leave in a fortnight's time. If anything happens to me, I want you to watch over her. Follow the royal protocol. Don't let my cousin near her until you are absolutely sure she doesn't carry my child," he said, pacing back and forth with his hands behind his back.

"My lord, nothing can harm you. You are a living God, blessed by the Sun God himself," Kail said.

"Care for her and watch over my child. That is all," the king said, dismissing the man from the room with a quick flick of his wrist. When he opened the door again, Kalina was sitting up in the bed, hugging her knees.

"Tell the servants to bring her some food," he said as Kail left the room. The women arrived and stood near the door, awaiting their orders. "These women will attend you. I will return to have midday meal with you, then you can finish telling me how much you hate me." Kalina wasn't surprised to see the large woman from the bathing room again. The other girl had shiny blond hair. She was slender and wore a pale green wrap. Her face was softened by her obvious innocence. She looked to be about Saroja's age.

"I would like to send a message to Theslia. I don't want them to worry about me," she said.

"No. You are to have no contact with that country. Is that clear? You are queen of Lavitia now, and we are at war with Theslia," he explained as he walked out of the door.

When he returned for midday meal he ate quietly.

"What happened to your parents?" Kalina asked.

Marsalis paused with his goblet in midair. "They were poisoned," he said after a while.

"But how can that be? You have food tasters," she pointed out.

"I have food tasters now because my parents were poisoned. We should talk about something else. This subject irritates me."

"It just doesn't make any sense. Why would Veagans kill your parents? They would have nothing to gain by their deaths for the next in line, you, would inherit the throne, and they would still be made to serve you," she explained.

"If you must know, I would have died that night as well had I not been sent away on an emergency errand by my father. My escort was delayed, causing me to miss the meal that led to my parent's death," he explained.

"Who would be king if you were killed?" she asked.

"My cousin is in line to inherit the throne if you fail to give me an heir. Why?" he asked, irritated by her question.

Kalina shrugged and looked down at her food.

"Answer me. Why do you ask?"

"It seems to me that you have wasted your life blaming my people for the death of your parents when it is obvious that this cousin of yours had the most to gain by wiping out your bloodline," she said, looking into his eyes.

"He is my father's sister's son. He has never been groomed to rule.

He knows the chances are unlikely that he will ever rule Lavitia," he explained.

"Perhaps, but if the assassin had succeeded in wiping out your family all those years ago, he would be king now. You have never thought about that?" she asked, looking over her goblet.

Marsalis rose from the large pillow he sat on and walked to her side. He stood over her, staring down at her. Kalina was frightened by the emotionless stare he gave her. Now he would strike her for not knowing when to bite her tongue. She raised her head slowly and met his eyes.

"You are right. It has always been the throne. Shalyndria and I were to be married. The night I announced it to court, he killed her." He dropped his head. "I knew then that he wanted my throne, but I never thought he was responsible for my parents, and now that I know he will die." He marched to the door and left. He returned moments later. Kalina was still seated on the floor, eating. He walked directly to her and extended his hand to her. He quickly raised the other and the servants turned and filed out of the room. Kalina took his hand and stood up from the pillow on the floor.

He unhooked the clasp that held the sheer silks to her body. It slowly caught the air currents and slid down her body into a soft pool at her feet. She was a golden sight with the white silk wrapped around her, but now, in her truest glory, she was like a goddess stepping out of a chrysalis shell. He moved slowly toward her and placed his hands on her well-rounded hips, then slid them slowly up her side, gripping her waist for a moment, then moving up and around to the shallow canyon in the middle of her back, across the slope of her shoulders, and quickly past her neck. He closed his fingers tightly around her long black locks and pulled her head back slightly, then kissed her with a drugging passion that left her holding on to him to keep her balance. He picked her up and carried her to the bed. He let her body slide slowly down the length of his as he placed her feet on the floor.

"You are a beautiful woman," he whispered softly into her ear. "The green and gold of your eyes is hypnotizing…your skin"—letting his gaze sweep across the length of hers—"must have been kissed by the sun, dipped in the sweetest honey, and molded by the Great Creator himself. I will make love to you as only a king can; with such perfection," he said, lifting her chin so he could see into her eyes. He sat down on the edge of the bed and pulled her down beside him. Then he pushed her back into the pillows. "Only a king should. Will you allow me to love, for just a moment?"

"You—I —" She breathed out of desperation. She couldn't concentrate on what he was saying and doing to her at the same time. His hands swept across her body slowly. He whispered against her skin, causing her to wiggle and squirm beneath his warm breath and airbrushed kisses.

"Have you ever been touched by a king?" he said softly against the soft column of her neck, slipping his fingers into her warm cove. "I can take your body to heights of ecstasy, the likes of which you would never dreamed possible. " Kalina never knew this much pleasure was possible. This man had the ability to make her forget that they were enemies. "But you must give yourself to me completely." Kalina simply nodded. He handled her as if she were made out of glass and would shatter into a million pieces at any given moment. His caresses tickled and soothed her all at the same time. He gently flipped her over onto her stomach and whispered against the nape of her neck, "My queen, take into you my seed and may it flourish in your womb." He wrapped one arm around her belly and pulled her into the curve of his body. He kissed a path across her shoulder, using his tongue to trickle wet trails down her spine. She wiggled and squirmed in his arms as the effects tickled and aroused her at the same time, and then pushed into her. Kalina let out a moan riddled with pain as well as pleasure. Her fists held the pillows tightly as he conquered her deepest desires with each powerful thrust. She matched his rhythmic movements as he pushed and pulled her into ecstasy. He flipped her over to complete his mission. She wrapped her arms around his neck as he kissed her. Warm tears trickled down her cheeks as Marsalis looked up at her face. He moved up toward her slowly and touched his forehead to hers. He used his thumbs to wipe her tears away and kissed her fiercely one last time as he spilled his seed into her body.

She lay sated next to him, her head on his shoulder, her arms draped across his hard stomach. He stroked her fingers playfully, then suddenly rose before her. He took her hands and pulled her up and out of the bed.

"Come. Stand before me," he said. He went to the trunk that had been brought in earlier by one of the servants and opened the lid. He took the gown out and took it to her. "I had this made for you. Put it on."

Kalina looked it over and turned it in her hands. It was just one long piece of silk.

"I don't know how," she admitted after her second attempt. Marsalis clapped twice and a servant girl entered the room. She stood near the door with her head bowed.

"Dress her," he said. The girl took the silk and put Kalina's arm through a slot at one end. She brought the material down over her breast and across her opposite hip, leaving an open triangle at her waist. It was then wrapped around her butt twice. The servant let the mass of the material fall to the floor. It was a lovely white toga gown but her mind was in another place.

"You do not like it?" he asked when he didn't get the response he was looking for.

"I do like it. It is very lovely, thank you," she said honestly. Marsalis was dressed by his attendants but he only adorned some pants. They fit him securely around the waist then billowed to the floor; the access material was placed over his left arm. He gave her a wicked smile then took her hand and led her from the room. He took her to Shalyndria's chambers and unlocked the door.

"These rooms use to belong to your sister. The pool has been drained, but it can be refilled. They are now yours to do with what you wish," he said, handing her the key. "Tell me about you," he said as she walked into the chamber.

"There is not much of interest I could say that you don't already know," she replied, picking up the silk wrap that had been thrown across one of the couches. Her sister had worn it.

"What is your favorite color? What is your favorite stone? Do you like sewing or music? These are things I need to know so I can keep you happy here. I know you are upset about the means in which you have come to me, but you are mine just the same. I want to see you happy, honestly, or at least content," he said, shrugging his shoulders.

Kalina turned and gave him a wary look. What was his game? Why was he being so nice to her? And why did she have the insane urge to believe he was truly being sincere?

"Well," she said after a while, "I don't really know. I like to work on tapestries when I'm bored and I like blue. Do you mean what you say about wanting me to be happy here?"

"Of course," he answered.

"Then please allow me to send word to my family," she said. Marsalis dropped his chin to his chest then looked up again and walked toward her. He took her face between his hands and kissed her gently.

"I cannot. Your heart will be lonely for a time, but you will forget your pass life as soon as my son is born. Come. Let us return to my chambers."

"How could one child replace another?" she asked, stepping away from his grasp.

"Lies will not sway me to your will, despite your beauty," he said, pulling her back toward him.

"I would not lie to you," she said, looking into his eyes.

"A woman that has never been touched by a man cannot possibly have a child," he countered.

"She is not of my womb, but she is my child nonetheless. I've raised her since she was days old. Please, she must be devastated not knowing what has happened to me."

"I'm sorry, but I must protect my kingdom, even from its queen."

Kalina dropped her head to her chest. Marsalis lifted it and looked into her eyes. He wrapped his arms around her waist and hugged for a moment, then led her back to his chamber where he left her in the care of her lady's maids.

He spent most of the next couple of weeks with her. He took her to his court a few times and had her seated on the throne beside him. She sat quietly as she watched him govern his people, and it surprised her because he was stern but he was always fair. Most of the time he was civil with her. He had gotten very angry when she asked him about his father's reign and the evils of slavery. After he had frightened her into a corner of the room then stormed out of the door, she had decided to stay away from that subject.

Kalina had expected that though; what had alarmed her was his gentleness. She was amazed by how quickly she had become accustomed to his touch, the security she found in his arms. The thought that she might actually be falling for him frightened her most of all, and she was glad he would be leaving soon. The things he did to her and the way he made her feel was starting to corrupt her rationality. One night, she had awakened to find him lying on her stomach with his hand caressing her abdomen. That morning he had left as usual. When he returned, he was dressed in full armor.

"I leave for the training grounds. These guards will protect you. They will also keep you from trying to escape. These ladies will serve you. You remember Salena and Miriam. If you need anything you may call on Lord Kail," he explained.

"Am I allowed to leave the room while you're away?" she asked as he reached the door. A part of her was glad he would be leaving, but a part of her was reluctant to see him go. After all, she would be all alone.

"Yes, but you are only allowed in the harem and the queen's wing of the palace without me," he said.

"Where is the queen's wing?" she asked.

"Your lady's maids will show you. Come, kiss your king good-bye," he said, standing in the doorway. She walked slowly to him and kissed him sweetly. Then Marsalis knelt before her and kissed her abdomen. "Grow, my child. I will return soon." He left Covax Castle and headed to the Theslian border to see about his army's progress.

CHAPTER 29

Reconstruction

United Rose Fortress, Theslia

After weeks of reading and practicing, Saroja finally finished the book. She had finally learned to separate her emotions from her powers. She rode out with Alexander and their six guards through the valley and into the woods. She pulled water from the ground, and practiced splitting the stones open. She did everything in her power to keep her mind off Kalina. She could still feel her, she had to be alive. *Where was she?*

Alexander picked up the stone and carried it to her, smiling. He dropped it when he noticed the blood trickling from her nose.

"Let's stop for the day," he said. His voice was laden with concern as he wiped her nose with a handkerchief. He lifted her chin and looked into her eyes. "Are you alright?" he asked. The wedding would have to be soon. The tiny bulge was starting to be noticeable. And despite what he told her to ease her mind, he didn't want anyone questioning the legitimacy of his child.

She nodded solemnly that she was okay. He looked up at the sky and noticed dark clouds moving in overhead. He took in their surroundings for a moment and breathed a sigh of relief. The small clearing was filled with birds, squirrels, and butterflies. He could see the sorrow on her face; in her eyes, the light that made her seem to glow shone slightly dimmer. He took her hand and led her to the horses. They mounted and walked them slowly back to the castle.

"Good day, Your Majesties," Cain called as he passed them by, heading toward the castle with three other men. Alexander nodded his head toward them, thinking it was strange to see him heading back to the castle when he was certain his father had ordered him to the frontlines. But he shrugged, thinking that perhaps he had been sent for.

That evening in his chamber, Saroja told Alexander she was ready to show the king the extent of her powers. They planned a demonstration for him in the gardens the next day. Saroja sat nervously by her favorite fountain waiting for Alexander and the king to arrive. The news of the demonstration must have spread through the castle because it seemed as if the entire court had come to see what she would show the king. The battlements were littered with soldiers. Courtiers came and walked around the gardens as if nothing were amiss when they were usually empty save for her, Sasha, and the gardeners. The servants even lingered in the doorways, watching her anxiously.

Kalina's coven arrived, and Saroja dropped her head. She had to find her center. She wished Kalina was here to give her support. The king had not received any word, but her necklace had been found at the campsite. Saroja knew that was not a good sign; she would not have willingly left it behind, but her body had not been among the others that had been brought back for proper burial She closed her eyes and took a deep breath and her spirits were immediately lifted. Soon Alexander arrived with the king. Several servants followed them and set the throne on a flat surface in the front of the garden. Saroja had wondered why they had such a large area of stone in the middle of the grass.

She bowed formally. "Your majesties, I am going to use my powers to reshape the garden. I hope you like it when I'm done. If not, I can always change it back."

"Proceed," the king said.

Saroja decided she would use her hands as a safeguard. She didn't know all these people would be here.

"First, I must ask that everyone is still, and if they could move to the center of the garden that would also help," she said.

Benjamin stood and looked around. "Be still or leave," was all he needed to say. People sat on the benches and the grass, on the edge of the fountains, and under the statues while the others stood still. The servants standing in the doorways backed out of sight.

Saroja turned her back on them and took a deep breath. Alexander sat back with an arrogant smirk on his face. She turned back around so she could see everyone, then raised her arms to the sky and closed her eyes. The ground started to shake and the people started to panic. Suddenly there was a great split in the earth just a few feet in front of the king. It grew deeper and wider, wrapping a block-shaped moat quickly around the garden. It grew wider and suddenly started to fill with water. Alexander watched Saroja; she seemed to be conducting a symphony. When the water ran completely around the moat surrounding the garden, she used the dirt had pulled out of the ground to conjured four stone bridges and placed them in the four directions as monuments to the winds. It was a beautiful addition to the garden. When she was done, she brought her hands down and curtsied low to the king.

Cain stood on the battlements, disgusted by what he had just witnessed. He thought he had rid the world of their kind years ago. His men still searched the land, destroying all those suspected of practicing the black arts. His people were the true rulers of this land. He had waited all this time to strike because his king had ordered them to wait. He thought they had finally put a king on the throne that had covered all the loose ends. Now this fool would put the evil back in control of the country again. It wouldn't be long before their kind littered the land as they once did, spreading evil like a plague through every village and city. They had been the ones who were responsible for leading the revolt all those years ago. He could no longer stand aside and watch. It was time for Lavitia to regain control.

"I will not allow that scheming, evil little witch to sit on the throne," he said, marching from the battlements. He would devise a plan and send word to the king. "We must move quickly."

"I think it was phenomenal," King Benjamin said, escorting her down the hall. "I will discuss the plan with my royal council and get their input before I make my decision." Alexander walked behind them. He couldn't wait until this ordeal was over so his father could sleep at night.

"Father, we should move to the border as soon as possible before words of our plans are able to reach Lavitia," Alexander said.

They ate dinner then enjoyed the entertainment. After the meal Alexander excused himself and followed his father into his private chambers where the council waited. The king nodded to start the meeting and Simo stood up first.

"Your Majesty, I think the princess was sent to us by the Great Creator. The things she will be able to do for the country. There would not even have to be a war," Simo said, sitting down. Thulamnul and James agreed. Cain stood up, shaking his head.

"Your Majesty, if we allow the people to think the use of witchcraft is allowed—" he started.

"She is not a witch," Alexander said sternly.

"We all know the prince's position on any matter concerning his future bride, but if we allow this, soon we will be overrun with crime and corruption. I think we should take the time to consider another alternative," he continued. If he got them to postpone their plans until he could get word to Marsalis, the king would be able to make his move and he would surely be rewarded.

"If there were another alternative," Prince Alexander said when Cain sat down, "we would have used it years ago. I think we should think of Theslia for a moment. Finally, she would be safe."

King Benjamin listened to all the arguments and thought them all over. Finally, he stood and said, "Princess Saroja has been given a gift, and as a member of the royal family she has seen fit to use that gift for the betterment of the country. She placed her own life in danger by letting it be known that she is Pheolatian. Such powers could never be used for evil. I think she has Theslia's best interest at heart. I will allow her to go forward with her plan to separate the land. Alexander, you will inform her to be ready to leave for the border on the morrow."

Saroja sat at the table watching everyone. Some of them avoided her gaze; others seemed a little too eager for her attention, smiling and bowing. Maja came and sat down next to her.

"I wanted to apologize for the things I said to you about Kalina," Maja said.

Saroja just looked at her then dropped her head.

"I was so proud of you today and it was absolutely beautiful. Claris could not believe you are able to do all that on your own. You made it look so easy. We were wondering if there was anything we could do to help you," she said.

"Yes, if the king decides to go through with it, I was going to ask you if there was a way that you could watch Gativa during the separation to make sure they aren't flooded, pushed into the ocean, or in danger of hitting any of the offshore islands," she said, glad she would not have to do both jobs at the same time. "I think I should go to bed. For some reason, I am little nervous about them knowing about my powers. Auntie Lina…" she said, tears started sliding from her eyes. She turned her head away so Maja couldn't see her face. Then she got up and walked quickly toward her chambers. Her guards hurried behind her.

"Maybe when this is over we won't have to hide our powers from the world," Kaemar said.

"We will have to take it slow. People are not so easily changed, but I believe when Saroja sits on the throne Pheolatians will finally be safe from tyranny," Claris said.

CHAPTER 30

Taken

Saroja walked with Sasha down the hall. Her guards followed behind them and took their post at the door as they entered. The servants arrived moments later with the tub and Saroja took a quick bath. Sasha dried her off and slipped the nightgown over her head. She sat down before the fire and gazed into the dancing flames. Sasha pulled the cord for the servants to return, then stood behind the chair and bushed Saroja's hair dry. Then she braided it into a long braid and secured the end with a ribbon.

The servants came and took the tub away as Saroja crawled into the bed. Sasha picked up the discarded clothes from the floor and placed them in the bundle for the laundry. She took Saroja's jewelry from the table where she had placed them before her bath and placed them in a small box that resembled a miniature treasure chest.

"Is there anything else you need, my lady?" she asked, walking to the door.

"In the great hall, I felt so tired. Now I'm not so sure. Will you pull the cord so someone could bring me a pitcher of wine?" she asked politely.

"I will bring it myself, Your Highness," Sasha said, bowing.

"Sasha, has there been any word on Auntie—I mean, Lady Kalina?"

"No, my lady, I'm sorry," Sasha replied, then left the chamber.

"Then she must be dead. She would have sent word by now," Saroja said, dropping her head to her chest. Despite all the things that had happened in the past few months, Kalina had been her mother, the only mother she'd ever known, and a part of her died inside at the thought of never being able to see or speak with Kalina again. She would never hold her child or give her advice. She had been hard on herwhile she was growing up, but now Saroja finally understood her reasons.

Saroja tossed and turned restlessly in the bed. She couldn't shake the feeling that something terrible was about to happen. She clutched at her swollen abdomen. She prayed to the Great Creator to give her strength to do what was needed so their country would be safe. A few minutes later she was asleep.

Cain and his men walked casually down the hall toward Saroja's room. They nodded to the guards as they passed by them. Moments later they walked by again. This time the three men rushed the two soldiers, quickly subduing them and lowering their bodies slowly to the floor. Cain pushed the door slowly open and found the princess asleep in the bed. They quietly dragged the bodies into the room.

"Wait here as if you were her guards. I will go in alone just in case she wakes. Where is the chloroform?" Cain asked in a whispered voice. "The witch must be bonded by the hands quickly so she will be unable to use her magic on us. They are powerless without their hands," he explained to the men confidently.

Saroja lay facing the door. Cain moved slowly toward her, stopping at the edge of the bed to fill the handkerchief with the chloroform. He quickly placed it over her mouth and nose, holding it firmly in place when she opened her eyes, struggling against his hold. Moments later the drug took hold and she fell into a deep sleep. Cain moved to the door and allowed the other two men to enter. They quickly tied Saroja's hands behind her back. Then they pulled a blanket over her body and carried her from the room. They hurried down the hall and slipped behind the tapestry and escaped from the castle.

"Make sure you keep an eye on her," Cain said from the front of the wagon. "If she stirs, use the chloroform."

Sasha stopped and looked over her shoulders. She had an eerie feeling that someone was following her. She continued down the hall then stopped to drop the clothes off to the laundry room. She took a torch off the wall then headed down to the cellar to get a new bottle of wine for the princess. Suddenly, she was engulfed from behind and pushed into the wall.

"Are you finished with your duties for today?" Evard asked, turning her in his arms.

"Evard, you scared me half to death."

"I was just trying to get your heartbeat racing. Are you finished with your duties?" he asked again, kissing the soft column of her neck.

"Almost, but first I must return this wine to the princess. I will meet you in the east solarium when I am done, I promise," she said.

"The princess can wait a moment or two. You have been neglecting me of late. Don't tell me you have changed your mind," he said as he pulled her into his arms.

"I'm sorry, Evard. You knew I would have more duties when I became the princess's lady-in-waiting. And I have not changed my mind. I want to be with you, but we must first be married. You are the one who's afraid to ask the king," she said, pulling out of his arms. She felt a little sorry for him as his face dropped at her mention of the king.

"I should not have to ask the king. You are not his daughter," he said, anxious to touch her in a more intimate setting.

"He has cared for Dora and me all these years. Who else would you think to ask? What are you so worried about anyway? Do you think he would deny you? Please let me pass."

"No, why would he? I think I am in the king's favor," he said, crossing his arms over his chest.

"Then what's the problem?" she asked. "You've changed your mind, haven't you?"

"I have not. I desire you above all others, I just—" he started.

"You just don't want to marry me," she finished.

"Of course, I want to marry you. I was going to say I want you now, why do we have to wait?" Sasha glared at him. "Very well, I will await you in the solar," he said, kissing her passionately before allowing her to walk away down the hall.

She had chosen a red wine. She carried it to the kitchens to retrieve a pitcher.

"Sasha, come see these necklaces my mother has made," Olivia said anxiously.

"I cannot, I must return this wine to Princess Saroja. I will see them later," she said. She walked quickly to Saroja's chambers. She slowed her step when she stepped on the hall and looked around nervously, wondering why the guards would leave their post. She would have to report their neglect to the king. The princess was also her responsibility. She opened the door and tripped over one of the soldiers on the floor, spilling the wine. She scrambled to her feet and pulled the emergency cord. Then went back to check the soldiers. Cash quietly whispered something and she moved over him and put her ear to his lips.

"Cain. It was…Cain," he said in a strained voice. Moments later King Benjamin, Prince Alexander, and a score of soldiers arrived at the chamber.

"Where is the princess?" the king asked, kneeling beside the wounded man.

"Taken," Cash whispered. "I'm sorry, Your Majesty."

"Rest easy, solider," Benjamin said over the fallen man. Isaiah was dead. Cash had been stabbed several times by a short blade.

"Sire, he said it was Lord Cain," Sasha said.

"He has been so loyal for so long. I would never have expected he would be the traitor," Benjamin said.

"Even after today's council…he couldn't stand the idea of using her magic to fix our problem. Maybe he is the one who told the assassin about the naming ceremony all those years ago. I've always wondered why he has a bald head. Perhaps he has been hiding golden locks all this time," Alexander said, pacing back and forth. "Father, we can track them, they can't be that far away. I have to find her."

"Go," Benjamin said.

Alexander left the room, followed by the soldiers. They were dressed and mounted in record time. They circled the castle, looking for horse tracks.

"I've found them," Simo said, pointing at the wagon tracks leading down into the valley.

"I saw him coming from that direction the other day," Alexander said.

Kalina's coven heard what had happened and immediately went to Saroja's room. As soon as they entered the chamber, the king said, "You and your friends will find her right now," he said. "Go now and get what you will need. Return here immediately."

"But, sire, we will need a fourth. Without Kalina, we can't use the magic," Claris explained.

Marsalis's Army Camp, Theslian Border

Cain and his men reached King Marsalis's camp after using the small passageway that led to the tunnel that had been dug through the mountains. They carried Saroja's limp body into one of the tents and threw her on the dirt floor. Cain removed the covers and looked her over. The sight of her golden flesh in the sheer nightgown made his loins ache. He grabbed her unconscious head and tilted it back toward the light.

"What a shame you had to be born one of those disgusting creatures," he whispered. "Inform King Marsalis that we have the girl," he said, stooping next to her body. The king arrived moments later in an angry rage.

"Who told you to bring that witch near me—and alive at that? Destroy her!" he said, then turned back to the exit. When she was dead he should have no problem taking the country back. "Inform the general. We are ready to move out." Avis immediately left to inform the troops that they would soon march on Theslia.

"Are you sure, sire? The Theslians would grant us anything for her and she is *very* beautiful. They would probably even surrender.

And she would be a fascinating addition to your collection of concubines," Cain said, nudging Masli and Elijah as he spoke. The three men looked at each other and smiled.

"It has been foretold that this girl would kill me, and you want me to take her back to my home? Perhaps living among these Theslians all these years has turned you into a weakling—or maybe there should be two fires pitched instead of one. I don't want them to surrender. I want them to die. I want the witch destroyed immediately! Is that clear, Cain?" King Marsalis said as he ducked out of the tent entrance.

"Well, for all our trouble, I think we should explore some of her more delightful qualities before we burn the rest. Besides, I don't think the witchcraft will help her now," Masli said, lifting Saroja's head from the floor, then letting it drop back helplessly.

"Yes. Afterwards we will kill her. The king is leading the army. We will have plenty of time to destroy her before he gets back," Elijah pleaded.

"Very well," Cain said. "But I will have her first. You make sure she does not wake up," he said, slapping Elijah on the shoulder. Cain pushed Saroja's nightgown up over her face while the two men secured her arms and legs with rope in a spread-eagle position.

United Rose Fortress, Theslia

"Sire, this girl says she is Pheolatian. She will help us find the princess," Maja said.

"What is your name, child?" the king asked.

"My name is Pita, Your Highness. I serve you in the kitchens," she said, bowing several times.

The four made a circle holding hands. They closed their eyes and tried to envision the princess.

"Oh, my Creator," Claris said, horrified.

"What is it?" King Benjamin asked.

No one answered. The women began to cry from the images they saw. Pita's eyes met with Benjamin's but she was unable to tell him what she had seen.

"I know where they are," Maja said. "It is not far from here. They have her tied up in an army camp near the border and they are…she looks dead. She does not move or try to fight them. Her eyes are closed."

"King Benjamin, I see soldiers, lots of soldiers. They march toward the border," Kaemar said.

Marsalis's Army Camp, Theslian Border

Saroja lifted her head slowly, trying to open her eyes. There was a man on top of her and the pain he caused was unbearable. She called for Alexander in a raspy voice, but he did not come to her. She tried to get up, but her hands and feet were tied.

Cain pushed himself into her warm body again, unaware that she was awake until her legs started pulling against the ropes. He looked up and pulled the clothing from her face, then hit her hard when she looked into his eyes. He put his hand around her throat and squeezed, cutting off her air as he continued his assault on her body. He squeezed and grabbed at her breast as she coughed and struggled to breathe. Thick roots suddenly burst free from the ground and pushed Cain off and away from her. He fell backwards onto the ground. The men pulled out their swords and started chopping at the roots. Masli kicked Saroja twice. A vine wrapped around his ankle and pulled him off balance.

"We should kill her now," Elijah exclaimed, frightened by what he was witnessing. The large vines moved up the ropes and pulled them out of his hands.

"Wait, man, what about my turn?" Masli said, cutting the vine free from his leg.

"She is awake. You must get the chloroform," Cain said, sure of himself.

"I would prefer she be awake anyway. I like to see the reaction on a maid's face when I take her," Masli said, falling down hard on top of her. He licked at her mouth and she tried with all her might to turn away. His breathe smelled of stale ale and rotting meat. When she still felt his wet tongue against her cheek, the urge to vomit was uncontrollable. She turned her head to the side and let it spill from her mouth onto the ground. She coughed several times then turned back and bit into Masli's face as hard as she could until she tasted blood in her mouth. Masli yelled and punched her twice across the face as he pushed hard into her. Her head dropped helplessly back to the floor and her eyes rolled back in her head.

"See," he said, looking back over his shoulder. "A strong fist beats chloroform any day."

"Yeah, it's probably cheaper too." Elijah laughed, pulling at the ropes that were tied to her legs. The roots and vines that snaked around the ropes trying to free her fell uselessly to the ground.

"Release her," a deep male voice called. The men looked around frightened, but didn't see anyone. "Release her. Now."

"Who's there?" Cain asked, drawing his sword, backing up against the tent walls.

Moments later, Saroja woke up screaming, "Please, please stop…I beg you!"

"Shut her up," Elijah said, looking out the tent flap. Cain walked over and kicked her in the side.

"Hey, man, you kicked me," Masli said, groaning like a pig.

"Just sit up for a moment," Cain said. He stumped his foot down into her midsection when Masli moved, knocking the wind out of her. "Now, you stay quiet, bitch, and maybe we'll let you live through the night. That would be much longer than I allowed that pretty mother of yours to live. She didn't even wake up, just choked on her own blood and died."

Suddenly a ghostly figure appeared before them. He had long, dark-brown hair that waved behind him. He moved toward Cain, then stopped when the man began slashing at him with the sword.

"He's not real. It's just her magic trying to frighten us," he said in a shaky voice. Then the tent was snatched away by millions of pixies that flew in, attacking the men with tiny arrows and sharp blades. The men swatted at them as if they were flies. The ghost slowly became a man of flesh and blood and Cain recognized him for what he was: an elf. He tried to stab him with the sword but he dodged the blow.

United Rose Fortress, Theslia

The women pushed their visions into a large cauldron in the middle of the floor so the king would be able to plan his defense. Pita's mind kept going to Saroja, so the girl's image kept floating in and out of the cauldron. Benjamin walked away. He could not stand to watch them assaulting that innocent girl. Only a Lavitian could be so cruel. When they were captured they would suffer long and hard for their crimes.

And Cain, all this time he had been working for the Lavitians. His son had warned him never to trust the courtiers. Now everything was finally beginning to make sense. The Lavitians always seemed to know just when to strike. There was a rumor that Marsalis had the ability to see things before they happened, but he had never believed that. He had always thought there was a traitor. He would be captured and skinned alive for his crimes.

Marsalis's Army Camp, Theslian Border

Saroja could take no more of this. The pain was excruciating. Her legs felt like they were being ripped apart. Her face hurt and she could barely open her left eye. Her idea of the world being a beautiful place open for her to explore turned to ashes with each revolting thrust. She closed her eyes and pushed her pain aside. "Desselb dniw llif em htiw ruoy srewop," she said. Suddenly her entire body started to glow.

"Quick, man, the chloroform," Masli said, with his eyes wide.

"No, Princess, do not do this," Stagg pleaded, but it was too late. She rose from the ground, breaking her restraints. Cain looked up at her, horrified. Masli got up and ran from the tent, fighting the pixies that surrounded him, stumbling several times over his trousers which were still around his ankles.

Saroja's eyes were almost red with rage and fury. Her deep black hair flew around her head. She picked Cain up and stared into his eyes. She remembered him from the castle, telling her how close he had been with her parents. She used the light beam that surrounded her to pull him closer. She could feel his hate and his fear. She saw the people he killed and the lives he had ruined. She saw him slaughter her father from behind and she watched him slit her mother's throat without an ounce of remorse. He taunted a young girl as he raped her, claiming he would release her after her father had poisoned an unknowing couple's meal.

Suddenly she pushed him away, leaving him suspended in midair. His body burst into flames but they did not consume him. He screamed as a blue flame crawled up his legs, wrapped around his chest, and engulfed his head. The heat slowly melted his skin. He tried to beat at it but the flames would not extinguish. Elijah screamed and ran out of the tent when she set him on fire. Stagg and the others disappeared as she ascended into the sky with Cain towed in her wake. The sky grew black as the clouds rolled in. The thunder crashed as a lightning bolt chased Masli down, killing him.

She swept through the sky like a dark demon enraged, on a quest for vengeance and death, heading back to Theslia and burning everything in her path. The slaves below her who were fortifying Marsalis's tunnel cheered and yelled as she passed. She looked down at the mountain, then sent a strong wind through its center pushing the remaining slaves from the interior. Then she closed her eyes and pushed the mountain back down to its base, then continued on her way.

Marsalis's army marched below, the size of ants, sparkling in their silver armor. She stopped and hovered above them and slowly lowered herself in front of them and floated just above the ground. Cain's screams continued as the fire burned all around him. She threw him to the ground in front of the marching soldiers. The green-and-blue flames that ripped at his face and his chest died away slowly, leaving him withering on the ground. The stale rank smell of charred meat filled the air.

"Return to your land. You are not welcome in Theslia," she said in a raspy voice.

"Those fools. I told them to destroy her!" Marsalis said, walking slowly toward her. "Kill the witch!" Marsalis ordered. The archers shot several volleys of arrows at her. Saroja held up her hand and watched as they fell uselessly to the ground.

"Leave now! You are not welcome in Theslia," she repeated. Her voice seemed meshed with the wind.

"This is my country and your kind is not welcome," Marsalis announced loudly. "If this be the moment of my death, I will stand before it with no fear and no regrets."

"No, you will kneel to death and pray to the Great Creator for his mercy on you for the evil you have spread across this land," she said as tears fell from her eyes.

Saroja held her hands up to the sky, then down toward them. The men screamed and ran in all directions as they were hit by giant balls of fire that shot out of the sky. Rain poured down and the ground started shaking beneath them. She descended slowly in front of Marsalis. She closed her palm into a tight fist, and then held it out to him. She sent all the images that had passed to her from Cain so he could see the destruction and grief his orders had caused.

"Father, Mother..." he said in a strangled voice, unable to believe what he was seeing. Then the realization that Cain had been responsible for the death of his parents hit him. "You bastard," he said, rushing him. He fell on the congealed man and hit him again and again in his face, unable to control the rage he felt.

Saroja lifted herself higher into the sky. The rain poured down all around her. The sky roared and screamed in rebellion to her assault. The land shook, then it split and spread apart like a page being ripped from a book. Marsalis struggled with his footing as he removed his sword from the scabbard. He plunged his sword into Cain's heart. Suddenly the land fell away beneath his feet. He lunged forward, holding on to the sword and a root protruding from the ground. The ground broke away beneath Cain's body and it fell into the earth. The sword slid free; Marsalis reluctantly let his father's sword go and grabbed onto the root with both hands. One more good pull and he would be free. The root suddenly tore from the ground and sent Marsalis plunging into the abyss.

Suddenly, the castle started to shake. Screams and panicked yells could be heard throughout the halls. Maja turned her focus to Gativa, remembering what Saroja had said to her at dinner. The waves were high and violent against the shore, but the water had not reached the village. She used the power of her coven to send the images to Saroja, who was now pulling Theslia up into the air, creating a high cliff. Big chunks of land and rock fell from the cliff into the water below. She pushed the two countries as far apart as she could, then fell hard to the ground, breaking both her legs.

When the ground started shaking the horses reared up into the air. They spun around, stamping and pawing nervously at the ground. As the land settled and the quaking stopped, the soldiers retraced their steps and continued their pursuit. The violent storm made him nervous, but it was proof that she was still alive. But what could possibly make her so angry? Alexander raced toward the border, desperate to find her. He jumped from JeNi's back. They finally found her lying on the ground, and he fell to his knees beside her. Her face was bruised badly across her cheeks. She had a black eye and her nose was bleeding. Her legs were turned in an awkward broken position. Her nightgown was soaked with blood. It was pushed up high to reveal the same streaks of blood on her inner thigh. Alexander couldn't control the tears that fell from his eyes.

"What have they done to you?" he whispered, wrapping his cloak around her body, trying to pick her up from the ground as gently as possible. She opened her eyes slowly and started screaming.

"It's me, my love. It's over now," he said, holding her tightly to his chest as she fought to be released. "I have you. It's alright."

"Alexander…I knew you would come," Saroja said in a hoarse whisper. He mounted his horse, securing his cloak around her when she started to shiver in his arms. Then her body went limp. He looked back at what use to be the border of Lavitia and saw nothing but thick black smoke rising from the land way off in the distance. He looked down over the edge of the cliff and watched as the ocean hit hard into the rocks below. It was as if the land had always been this way. Then he turned and rode hard back to the castle.

He took her directly to his room and laid her broken body on his bed. She opened her eyes and looked up at him.

"I'm sorry I let this happen. I think the babe is gone. I can't feel him anymore. I tried to use the magic to rewind time and fix this, but it wouldn't work," she said as tears streamed down her face. "I will understand if you don't want me anymore."

"Hush now, Saroja. Rest. Just rest," he said, hurt that he had been unable to protect her from such pain.

Soon Kalina's coven arrived. Alexander got up from the edge of the bed to let them see her. Claris fell to her knees with her hands over her mouth.

"Can you feel this?" Kaemar said.

"No," Saroja said in a raspy voice from the bed. Kaemar sat next to her and started administering her healing herbs. She worked for hours, fixing her broken bones. Then she was finally made to give birth to her deceased child. She cried the entire time and turned away when they wanted her to look upon his face.

Maja looked over Kaemar's shoulder, looking down at the princess. If they could only have a chance to be alone with the princess, she would be able to test out her theory concerning the sorceress's star and finally have powers of her own.

"Rest now, Your Highness. We will come to see you later," Kaemar said as they left the room when the servants arrived with the tub. She would see to the burial of the child.

Sasha tried to perform her duties without any feelings, but she had become attached to the princess over the last months and her heart ached to see her in this state. Alexander lifted her from the bed and lowered her gently into the water. He paced back and forth as the servants washed the blood and dirt from her body.

"Ow!" she cried when they tried to move her leg.

"Get out, all of you!" Alexander yelled. Sasha jumped at his sudden bellow. "Sasha, you clean her. Gently."

Sasha took her time and gently rinsed the dirt and blood from the princess's body. She tried not to rub so she wouldn't irritate her bruises. There was a red-and-purple bruise in the shape of a boot from her chest to her stomach. She pushed her tears aside and tried to do her job.

"I'm done, sire," she said.

He picked her up and put her in a chair. Sasha dried her off and braided her hair. Alexander placed her back in the bed. She turned her back to them and stared blankly at the wall and cried.

CHAPTER 31

Consequences

Raging flames started to surround her one after the other as she stood suspended in midair. There was a cloudy silhouette of a man sitting on a golden throne before her. He was made up of light and mist. To his left and right sat other misty creatures, all light sources within themselves and all of which stared at her as she looked around. She dropped her head and used her hand to shield her eyes from light.

She immediately thought she was dead. She had been placed before the Great Creator to be judged before her final place was chosen. Everything had happened so fast. She never remembered being so angry before and Alexander; she'd never see him again. Grief and a deep longing filled her chest and then being dead didn't even matter anymore. She stood up straight and raised her head.

"Fall to your knees," he said in a commanding voice. Without thought or hesitation she dropped to her knees before him and placed her nose to the ground, even though it didn't actually touch the ground. "You would dare defy my laws after I have seen fit to bless your people."

"I'm sorry, Father. Please have mercy. I don't know what came over me," she said. The least she could do was gain a proper place to spend the rest of eternity.

"Destroy her, Great One. I warned you she would be unable to handle such a power. Now she has broken your greatest law," Nasci declared from her throne.

"No, Mighty One, it was the humans that failed to teach her how to control such a power. Give her to me and she will never cause you trouble again," Aquius declared.

The room erupted with suggestions about what should be done with Saroja.

"Have you no excuse for your crimes?" he asked.

"No, I can only say that the pain was unbearable. It took over my thoughts and gained control of my emotions. Please forgive me, most merciful father," she explained, truly sorry for what she had done.

"She did endure great suffering before finally retaliating, even the death of her unborn child. Perhaps you could give her a place among us, Lord of Lords," said Caltrium, Lord of Wisdom.

"An interesting idea," the misty light said. "But that must be her choice. You have been offered a great gift, my child. Instead of taking your powers and your life, I will grant you immortality by offering you a place on my counsel. What be your answer?"

Saroja kept her head bowed as she moved to her knees. "But I thought…I thank you for the honor, o merciful father, but I am not worthy of your council. I have broken the law, so I should be punished. But if there were a choice, send me back to my world and I would happily die in the arms of my love," she said sincerely.

"You have been offered immortality, but instead you chose a man. You are right. You are truly unworthy of the mercy my father offers you," Nasci said.

"Any life without Alexander would be incomplete, begging your pardon, Lord."

"So," the Great Creator said, "If the choice be death and love for as long as that life lasts or immortality and power, what would you chose?"

"I chose Alexander," she said.

"Then you are a fool," Nasci piped in.

"You are just jealous because you will never know what it is like to love someone more than you love yourself," Timerius said, glaring at his wife.

"Very well," he said frankly and faded away, dispersing the flames that had caged her.

The sun was coming up when the king arrived at the prince's door. Sasha opened it and bowed as she left shaking her head.

"How is she?" Benjamin asked, standing over her sleeping body.

Alexander sat in a chair on the other side of his bed and said, "She is fine, considering what she's been through. Her nose keeps bleeding, but Claris says it is from having to concentrate so hard when she moved the land. She's been crying because of the loss of the child and she's in terrible pain. She just fell asleep. Maybe now is not a good time for you to visit her," he said, leaning forward in the chair, putting his elbows on his knees, looking down at his hands. He slid them slowly down his face and let out an irritated sigh. "I fear they have stolen her soul. The light has left her eyes, Father."

"You must give her time to heal. Come, I have come to talk to you," he said, walking into Alexander's inner room and closing the door behind them. "The council just met. They are concerned about the destruction she caused after…"

"Anyone of them would have reacted the same way if they had gone through that," Alexander exclaimed.

"They think that perhaps she is too dangerous. What if she became angry with us? Some say she should be destroyed. No one else would have been able to destroy the enemies' entire countryside in a matter of minutes. What if such power was used against us?" Benjamin said.

"Father, are you serious?" Alexander asked, crossing his arms.

"I am only telling you what was said in the meeting," Benjamin said, putting his hand on his son's shoulder to reassure him.

"Let me see if I understand you fully. She was ravished, beaten, managed to escape, destroyed the enemy, and separated the country so it would never be attacked again, and now the wise council wants to kill her because she's too dangerous! And you are actually considering their idea?" Alexander shouted. He had never been so frustrated and angry before in his life.

"We must think about the safety of the country," Benjamin said, raising his voice at his son's response. "And I suggest you remember who you're talking to."

"The country is safe because of her, can you not see that?" he said in a lower tone, trying to get through to his father.

"I agree," Benjamin said, nodding his head at that statement. "She should be praised, not imprisoned."

"What prison could hold her? Father, you go back to the council. Tell them that I said if anyone ever tries to hurt her ever again, her magic will be the least of their problems," he said, walking from the room when he heard her call his name.

"Alexander, please…Alexander," Saroja called.

The prince walked to her side. She was still asleep, but she tossed and turned frantically in the bed. Her brow was wet with sweat, but she shivered as if she were cold. Her skin was pale and washed out. He woke her up and he sat next to her on the bed and gently pulled her into his arms. Her skin was hot and clammy when he touched her.

Saroja buried her head against his chest and cried. She wrapped her arms around him and held on. She would hold on to him until the end. The Great Creator would take her soon.

"Every time I close my eyes…it happens all over again. Will they torment me for the rest of my life?" she whimpered.

"It will get better with time, my love. I promise," he said, gently rubbing her brow with a cool cloth. He looked down at her and gave her a smile. Her face was still very bruised, but she was opening her eyes now. He'd never seen her look so weak, not even when she was told Kalina might never be found. He prayed this experience had not ruined who she was inside and wished for the girl he fell in love with to return soon.

Time was the one thing she didn't have. The king walked to the foot of the bed. He looked her over and she closed up within herself.

She felt dirty. The look he gave her was one of sheer pity, and it cast a shadow over her. She squeezed Alexander tighter and willed him to go away.

"Theslia will forever be in your debt, Princess Saroja. I am so sorry for all you have endured. May the Great Creator grant you a speedy recovery," Benjamin said, walking to the door.

"Alexander," she said in a faint whisper. She wanted him to know so they could cherish the time she had left together. "I'm going to die," she said in a faint whisper.

"Don't say that. You're going to be fine. Just lay back and rest," he said, placing her back against the pillows.

"I killed those men. The Great Creator is very angry with me. He will take my powers and I will die," she explained weakly.

"That is nonsense, Saroja. Nothing is going to happen to you. I'll take care of you," he said quietly, watching her close her eyes. Tears slid from beneath her lids. Alexander grabbed her by the shoulders and hugged her tightly. He wiped them away with his thumbs and kissed her gently.

For the next couple of days Alexander remained at Saroja's side. He read to pass the time. After a week passed he acknowledged the fact that she wasn't getting any better. She burned with fever. And her nose bled ever so often, too often for him. Claris had said it would stop, but it had not. He got up and went to the door.

Sasha sat in a chair opposite the door with her arms folded neatly in her lap. She felt somewhat responsible for what had happened to the princess. If she had not stopped to fraternize with Evard she would have returned sooner and perhaps Princess Saroja would not have been taken.

"Sasha, go get the healer and send word to Claris that she's not getting any better," Alexander said.

By the time Lio arrived with an old woman following close behind, Saroja's bed was surrounded. The little old woman entered with her black bag in one hand and a tall wooden staff in the other. She had a gray scarf covering most of her hair while several white strands hung out around her wrinkled face. She had a small round head that didn't seem to go with her much larger body. She leaned forward slightly and waddled to the bed to look the girl over.

Lio went to the Prince. "You seemed uncomfortable the last time I examined Her Majesty. I thought a woman would be more to your liking. Have there been complications concerning the child?" he asked.

This proved that the rumors surrounding Lio were indeed true. He thought for sure everyone in the kingdom knew about the princess's abduction. As he opened his mouth to explain, the woman spoke.

"Who is responsible for this child?" the woman asked in a deep, raspy voice.

"I am," Alexander said, stepping forward.

"What has happened to her?" she whispered.

Alexander took a deep breath and told the woman what had happened to Saroja. The old woman looked up at Alexander; she gave him a sympathetic pat on the back and then turned to the people.

"Back up, everyone. She needs air," she said, placing her bag on the table. Everyone was directed by a servant out of the room and into the hall. The woman placed her hand on Saroja's brow. She used her hand to open her mouth then stared down her throat. She checked the bruises on her face and pulled the covers back to check the bruises on her body. After she had examined her she went to the king who sat in a corner with his son.

"I can find nothing wrong with her. The wounds have been cleaned. There is no sign of infection. She should be on the way to recovery, but her heartbeat is very weak. I cannot explain why her nose continues to bleed. There is nothing else I can do for her; perhaps she has lost her will to live. This happens when a woman is defiled in such a way. She is unable to live with the shame; let her die with her dignity," the old woman said, walking toward the door.

Alexander rose from his chair and went to the bed where Saroja laid, tossing and turning. He stared down at her shaking his head.

"I forbid you to die!" he yelled, bending over her. He grabbed her shoulders and shook her twice. "I forbid you to die, do you hear me? Say something, yell at me, tell me not to give you orders, but please, don't die." When he got no response he turned and stormed from the room. He ran down the halls, heading to the stables. He felt so helpless. He was angry with his father, Saroja, and even the Great Creator. Why would he send him an angel then take her away? Most of all he was angry with himself. The enemy was right under their noses all this time and he didn't even know it.

"Prepare my horse," he ordered. The stable hand brought the horse forward when it was saddled and bowed to Alexander as he took the reins from his hands. Alexander climbed aboard and raced down through the valley.

The king sat back on his throne with his hand on his head. He had a terrible headache. He pressed his hands against his temples, willing the throbbing pain to go away.

"Excuse me, Your Majesty," Sasha said. "Claris wishes to speak to you." The king acknowledged her and the others came and stood before him.

"We know why she is dying. She broke one of the three rules of magic. She used her powers to destroy life, so they will be taken away from her. She is a natural sorceress, so she will die. There is only one thing that might save her, but it must be done before all her power is gone. After that, there would be nothing anyone could do. The spell is very old and will require a lot of power. More than we can provide," she said.

"Then where would all this power come from?" Benjamin asked, tired with the whole situation, but that child had freed them finally from the Lavitians. He couldn't let her die if there was something he could do to save her.

"With your permission, I will need to send out a message, an urgent message to all the villages and provinces. We must dispatch the fastest riders with a letter. At the bottom it must bear this seal," Claris said, taking the symbol of her people from around her neck. "The letter should read: By order of the king, any and every person that recognizes this symbol should report to the United Rose Fortress. What do you think, Kaemar? Will she make it until the new moon?" Claris asked.

"Yes, I think so. We could try to fuel her to give them more time," Kaemar said.

"They should report to the castle before the new moon," she said, giving the symbol to a servant who in turn gave it to the king. Benjamin looked the shiny star over and said, "I've seen this symbol before. What does it mean?" he asked.

"It is the symbol of our people," Claris said proudly.

"It is carved into the doors leading into the great oak," he said, after giving orders that Claris's letter be sent out immediately. Alexander walked into the hall and the king called him to his side. He explained what was happening to Saroja and the woman's plans to save her.

"It would seem their magic has been protecting our people for years," Alexander said.

Alexander left and walked slowly to his chamber. He opened the door quietly and walked into the room. Saroja was asleep. She looked so pale and weak. He walked into his study and started reading over a parchment on his desk. He tossed it aside, stood, and then went to the window. He looked down on the gardens below and remembered her face when he had first shown it to her.

"Oh, Great Creator, hear my prayer. They say she will not live without help. Well, I feel it is your help that she needs or perhaps your forgiveness. Please, take away this cloud you have placed over us. Find another source of amusement. Do not punish her because you are angry with me. I likened her to an angel, now you will make her one. Can you not see that she is sorry? Those men were hurting her. She didn't mean to kill them. She is normally a gentle creature. Please, Mighty One, set her free," he said with tears forming in his eyes.

He walked to the bed and sat down in the chair. Sasha placed a cool towel on Saroja's forehead. There was a light tap on the door and she went to open it. Four holy men in white robes entered the room. They started setting up candles, and spreading smelling herbs around the room. They shook water and oil over her bed then started a low rumbling chant.

"Your holinesses, I am sorry, but I will have to ask you to leave," Alexander said. He would not allow them to prepare her soul for death because she wasn't going to die.

"Your Highness, the village healer informed us that nothing could be done to save the princess. We must perform the death chant or her soul will be trapped forever in her body," the tall, skinny man said. He turned back to the bed and continued.

"Sir, you don't understand, that was not a request. I need you to leave so she can rest. She's not going to die," Alexander explained.

The four men stopped at once. They gathered their candles and slowly walked from the room not saying a word. Sasha closed the door and walked back to the bed.

"You can retire for the evening, Sasha, thank you," Alexander said.

Sasha bowed and quietly left the room. Alexander crawled quietly into the bed next to her, but he dared not touch her. She was sleeping peacefully and he didn't want to disturb her.

"Alexander," she said in a faint whisper.

He turned to her and kissed her gently on her forehead.

"I have missed those eyes, little one," he said.

"Alexander…I am going to die. I broke the rule. Now the Great Creator will take my powers," she said, closing her eyes, then opening them slowly again.

"No, my love, there is a way to save you. Sleep. You will be fine," he said. Saroja looked deeply into his dark eyes with a look of confusion. Alexander nodded his head as she settled back into the pillows.

CHAPTER 32

No More Hiding

enjamin's soldiers rode through every town and village. They hung the proclamations on trees, temples, and buildings. They explained the importance of the message and that it came directly from the hands of the king. Everyone in the villages gathered around the postings to see if they had seen the symbol before.

Over the next week people started to arrive at the United Rose Fortress. They all carried the emblem in some form or another. Most of the people wore it around their necks. Some of the older people had it carved into the bottom of their walking sticks. They arrived day and night. The king was starting to get nervous about the number. He was running out of places to put them.

"How many people do you think we will need?" Benjamin asked Maja.

"As many as possible," she said, pouring herself a goblet of wine.

Alexander sat on the dais next to his father. He had never met a Pheolatian until he had met Saroja. Now he figured that maybe he had and was just unaware of it. There were so many people. It was the strangest party he had ever attended. Goblets and food floated through the air and everyone continued with their conversations as if that were a normal thing. He had just gotten used to Saroja's magic, but this was a different situation entirely. She would have enjoyed this dinner.

Claris, Maja, Pita, and Kaemar sat at a table near the king's dais.

"Do you think this is everyone? No one has arrived at all today," Maja said.

"We gave them until the new moon. We will have to wait until then to make sure. If we can't make the circle bright enough, it won't work, and all of this will have been in vain," Claris said.

"We will have to find out what class of magic each person has," Kaemar said.

"And teach the chant to those who don't know it," Claris said, praying everything would work out. She left the hall and went to visit Saroja, who slept quietly in Prince Alexander's bed. She pushed the loose strands of hair from her forehead and wiped the sweat from her brow. She was happy that her face was finally starting to clear up from all the bruises. Kalina was gone and Saroja was her child, even if she didn't give birth to her. Usually the daughter took the mother's place in a coven. What she wouldn't give to know what it was like to possess such powers. Saroja barely ever opened her eyes. Her skin seemed to grow paler as more and more of her powers slipped away. They had to do something soon before she was gone altogether.

The night of the new moon, everyone assembled in the great hall. Most of the guests still had no idea why they had been summoned to the castle. The proclamation was only answered because the star was on it. This could be a strategic trick to rid the land of their people once and for all. Finally, the king stood and addressed the audience.

"Thank you all for coming so soon. I know you have placed yourselves in great peril by doing so, but I would like to assure you that the days of your people's persecution are over. The Lavitians have been defeated and are no longer a threat to our country," he said in a loud voice for all to hear.

Claris and Kaemar looked at each other at that announcement. The people started cheering and hugging each other, but went quiet again when the king continued to speak.

"This brings me to the reason you were all summoned. Our princess was responsible for our liberation, but it would seem that one of your sacred laws was broken. Now she is dying because her powers are being taken away," he said, motioning for Kalina's coven to come forward.

"We have decided to save her despite the law. After we've done all we can, the Great Creator may decide to take her anyway, but we must try," Maja said as the king moved back to his throne.

"Most of you know the only way she can be saved is by using the Circle of Light Chant. The first thing that we must do is to sort everyone according to their class of magic," Kaemar said. "So, listen closely."

"If you were taught magic by another and are already a part of a coven, please gather with them on the far left of the hall. Since we are working against time, I must ask those who already know the chant to teach it to the others in your group that do not," Claris said.

"If you were born of one magical parent and have the ability to control your magic on your own, move to the right, but if you've joined a coven go with them," she continued.

"If you were born with two magical parents, come to the front of the room," she said, moving to her section of the room. Claris took Pita's hand and walked toward Maja and Kaemar. No one moved forward, which meant that Saroja was truly the strongest sorceress alive.

When everyone knew the chant well enough, Kaemar sent Alexander to get Saroja. He picked her up gently from the bed. Her skin was pale and she took long, exaggerated breaths. He held her close to his chest as he carried her outside. The whole way he begged the Great Creator to forgive her. Claris said they would need room to make the circles. So, the king decided the bailey would be the best place. When he reached the bailey, the Pheolatians were already set up into three rings of people. He walked through them and placed Saroja on the ground in the center then moved away to stand near his father.

They took each other's hands and raised them to the sky. They closed their eyes and began the chant, "With this magical circle of light, grant us the power to restore her life. Draw from the sun, the moon, and the stars. Draw from every celestial being to reignite her powers." They repeated this litany over and over again. It started off soft and slow but grew louder and louder. Suddenly, light started to emanate from the circles.

A buzzing sound seemed to rise in the distance and it grew louder as it got closer. The fairies created a circle of gold light and it wrapped around the outer circle and grew brighter as the Pheolatians continued their chanting. Then sparks of colors could be seen blended into the gold as the pixies joined the fairies circle. The elves appeared suddenly, in the center-most ring, raising their arms to the sky.

Moments later the wind filled the bailey and Saroja started to lift from the ground. Tiny white lights circled around her body, making her rise higher into the sky. The light grew brighter and brighter. Alexander had to use his hand to shield his eyes. Saroja's legs and arms folded to her body in a fetal position. Her body glowed as it turned over and over slowly in the sky. The bright white light started to pulsate as it emanated from the circles of power and was pushed into her body.

Alexander watched Saroja closely, trying to see some reaction to all this, but she was too high for him to see if her eyes were open. He looked to his father and noticed his tired expression. His brow was wrinkled, and his eyes squinted as he watched. He sat back on the throne with his head pressed back against the pillow.

"Father, are you well?" he asked quietly.

"I am fine, my son, this ordeal has truly taken something from me. I will be fine after a good night's rest," Benjamin explained.

Alexander stood when Saroja started to descend back to the ground. He ran to her side and turned her over in his arms. He pushed the hair from her face as she slowly opened her eyes.

"Saroja, are you awake?" he asked.

"I…my head hurts," she said weakly, looking around like she was confused.

He looked into her eyes and smiled. She was going to be alright. He picked her up from the ground and pulled her to his chest then turned to his father.

"It worked!" he said, feeling as if a great weight had been lifted from his shoulders. The entire bailey erupted in cheers and applause.

The fairies and pixies zipped across the sky in a magical dance of celebration. Alexander walked through the crowd and stopped next to Stagg, who was holding the red headed elf's hand. Stagg bowed his head to the prince. Alexander returned his greeting with a slight nod of the head, and then he carried Saroja back to his chambers. He placed her in the bed, and held the cup of water to her lips and allowed her a couple of sips.

"The Great Creator has forgiven me?" she asked in a hoarse voice.

"You have done nothing to warrant forgiveness," he said, walking to the door and pulling the cord for the kitchens. "Are you hungry?"

She nodded her head and tried to get up from the bed. She slowly swung her legs over the side and pushed up from the bed, but ended up crumbling to the floor. Alexander picked her up and put her back under the covers. Saroja's hips and her legs felt numb. When she tried to move them, there was a dull pain at the junction between her hips and thighs. And all at once the memories of that terrible night filled her mind. She closed her eyes, trying to block the horrible invasion to her brain, but it didn't work. She could feel them on top of her, smell their breath, and hear their groans as they ravished her body. And she remembered their screams as they died.

"Alexander," she called, suddenly feeling dirty. "Is it too late for a bath?"

"It's never too late, but I will have to send for Sasha to assist you. Your legs were broken in several different places, especially at your hips. That's why you're having trouble moving them. Don't worry, they will heal and you'll be perfect again before you know it," he said when she dropped her head to her chest.

"You could assist me. I would hate to wake her at this hour," she said, really not concerned with waking Sasha. She just didn't want to face anyone right now. She was embarrassed because she was supposed to be this powerful sorceress, but her magic hadn't been able to protect the child she carried or herself from their assault on her body.

"I would be happy to assist you, but Sasha was just in the bailey," he said, pulling the cord for the servants. Just as he turned to walk away someone tapped on the door. He opened it.

"Kaemar sends these herbs for the princess, Your Highness," Pita said.

"Thank you. Bring some stew, bread, and wine. And inform the servants that the princess wishes to take a bath," he said. The girl bowed and left to do his bidding.

Moments later the servants arrived with the tub and the food. Alexander picked Saroja up and carried her to the table. He wanted her to eat so she would be strong again.

She ate slowly as the servants filled up the tub. When she was done, Alexander picked her up and set her down slowly into the hot water. He washed her hair gently, massaging her scalp. He used slow circular motions to wash her back. He cupped the water in his hands and used it to rinse the soap from her skin. He moved around the tub and kneeledon the floor in front of her. He lifted her leg slowly from the water and set it on the side of the tub. Saroja lifted her head and gave him a faint smile. He could tell she was troubled. He finished washing her, then picked her up out of the water and put her in a chair. She wiped the water from the front of her body with a towel as Alexander dried her back. She picked up the brush and started to work the tangles from her hair. He took it from her hands and brushed her hair. When he was done, she pulled it over on her shoulder and braided the damp hair up into one.

Alexander put her back in the bed and pulled the covers up over her shoulders. By then she had tears in her eyes. He kissed her and wiped them away, wishing he could wipe away her hurt just as easily. He took off his wet clothes and crawled into the bed beside her. She curled up into a ball and turned to her side. Alexander pulled her into his embrace and slowly stroked her hair. Moments later she was asleep.

Covax Castle

Kalina walked the halls of the enormous palace. She had to admit it was beautiful. The rooms were very spacious and most had marble floors and high ceilings. There were no chairs like she was used to, only plush couches and lots of pillows. Most of the people sat on the floor, even when they ate. The tables were built low to the floor to accommodate that practice.

The servants were kind to her and it surprised her because they were Lavitians. They bowed and smiled, but the nobles and the other courtiers called her names and taunted her. When she reached Marsalis's chamber she poured herself a goblet of wine and sat down in front of the tapestry she had started. Suddenly the door was pushed opened and two men rushed in. They grabbed her by the arms, knocking over her chair, and dragged her from the room.

"Where are you taking me? Stop it, you're hurting me," she said in a panicked voice as they continued down the hall. She was taken to the great hall, where they threw her to the floor.

"Marsalis is dead," Kail said sitting on a long couch looking down at her. "In Lavitia, a queen cannot rule without a king. The council has decided to follow our laws of protocol in this situation, which states," he snapped his fingers and the servant handed him a scroll. He looked down at her, pulling the scroll open. "That upon the death of an heirless king his queen is given a full moon's cycle. If within that time she begins to bleed, she should be discarded into the sea. My wish is that you crash into the new cliffs of your precious Theslia. If there is a child you will remain here at the palace until the child is born. If it be a male child, he will be groomed to rule and will take the throne after his twelfth year. If the child be a girl, she will be trained as a queen and will be betrothed to the Calitric prince upon her birth. They will be married when the child reaches her fifteenth year. This alliance will restore our country."

"And what will happen to me if I give birth to a child?" she asked.

"You will remain here as the royal mother, of course, and since you will be unable to escape to Theslia, you have been given the rights of a free woman. These guards will accompany you when you wish to leave the palace, but do not leave their sides because it is still forbidden for Veagans to walk the streets of Lavitia without an escort," he said, waving two men forward.

Suddenly one of the servants arrived in the doorway. Lord Kail nodded toward the man, and he hurried forward.

"Lord Kail, Lord Laven has arrived. He is trying to claim the throne," the servant explained.

"Just as Marsalis predicted. Take her to the middle chambers and place guards around her doors. The law states that the queen must be given one moon's cycle to show proof of an heir before the crown is passed. Our country will not be led by that boy lover. Marsalis assured me there would be an heir. He is probably unaware that Marsalis even took a wife," Kail explained.

"Perhaps that is for the best," another council member added.

"No, he must be told Marsalis has a queen or he will declare himself king now. At least we have the law on our side. He would not dare go against royal protocol," Kail said, leading the group to the throne room. "Lord Laven, we apologize for the wait. It seems you are unaware of Queen Kalina."

"Queen? Explain yourselves. My cousin had no queen," Laven said, disgusted by the possibility. He had waited all his life for this moment, and no woman was going to keep him from his throne. "Besides, a queen cannot rule without a king."

"Yes, sire, the king took a queen, nearly a fortnight has passed. According to the law we must wait to see if she will produce an heir before the crown can be passed to you," Kail explained. "It is merely protocol, my lord."

"Where is this woman? I wish to speak with her," Laven said. He had no desire to wait for another Covax to be born.

"I'm sorry, sire, the law also states that she cannot be seen until the allotted time has passed to give no question about the legitimacy of the child. We are obligated to protect her at all cost. You may see her in a month's time," Kail said. He bowed and walked from the room, leaving Laven steaming where he stood.

CHAPTER 33

A Smile Will Bring Back the Sun

The United Rose Fortress

Alexander reluctantly walked to his father's chamber. He knew why he had been summoned. Saroja's depression had placed a black cloud over the castle. The rain continuously fell from the sky, but who could blame her. She would not even speak of the child anymore; it was like it never existed to her and he knew it did. He had tried reading to her, having the musicians play to her. He had bought her a beautiful necklace to which he had received a faint smile and a thank you, but nothing had worked. The guards opened the door for him and he went in.

"You have to do something. This cannot go on the valley is already flooded. I haven't seen the sun in weeks. Something must be done," Benjamin ordered.

"Father, what can I do?" Alexander said in a defeated voice. He had already tried everything he could think of to cheer her up. When she wasn't crying, she just sat quietly, buried within her own gloom. She rarely spoke except to say a few words in response to a question asked.

"She's getting better, though. The violent storms have turned to quiet showers and dark forecast. I just have to think of something that unconsciously makes her happy." And it came to him. "I'll fix this, Father, you have my word." He bowed then turned and marched quickly to his chamber.

Saroja was in the bed, facing the wall. He knew not whether she was asleep or awake, but he didn't care. He'd been going about this all wrong. He scooped her up in his arms and carried her from the room.

"Where are you taking me?" she asked, wrapping her arms around his neck as he moved quickly down the hall. He ignored her and continued. She buried her head in his chest and started to cry. "Alexander, I don't want to see anyone. Please take me back."

When they reached the stable he had his horse saddled. He put her on JeNi's back and climbed up behind her.

He rode around the castle toward the forest.

"Look what you're doing to the valley," he said, nudging her arm when she wouldn't look up. "Look!" She turned in the saddle. The valley looked more like a lake.

"Dry it up," he said to her sternly. "I know you can."

"I can't," she said in a whisper.

"Try, my love," he said pleading now.

"I can't, please take me back. I don't want to be out here," she said.

"Hmm, out here," he whispered to himself. He kicked the horse forward into the water. He stayed to the edges and worked his way around to the forest. Saroja lifted her head as soon as they entered the trees. He rode on then pulled the horse to a stop. He got down and then grabbed her around her waist. The ground was wet and muddy and his feet immediately sunk into its depths when he added Saroja weight to his own, but he had a theory. He placed her gently on the ground then got back on his horse and moved as far away as he could without losing sight of her.

"Alexander, this is ridiculous. Please, take me back," she said in a weak voice that was harboring tears in its wake. She still couldn't walk, and now sat on the ground looking up at him, those big golden pools slowly filling with water as he watched her, but couldn't let this go on, and he had a feeling the forest would heal her inside and out.

After about an hour, Alexander watched as a doe moved in slowly toward her. It sniffed at the air, pausing for a moment. Saroja stared down at the ground but lifted her head when it got close enough and stroked its forehead. Soon he could see small plants sprouting from the ground.

He'd never watched a plant grow before and was sure no one really understood the splendor of such a phenomenon. First tiny green sprouts fought their way through the land, curling toward the sky for nourishment—pulling toward Saroja for nourishment. They grew bigger and tiny buds extended from them. The sprouts themselves unfolded into long leaves. The stem continued to pull toward her as a shiny green bud swells as it is pushed higher and higher. Slowly, the bud cracked and opened to reveal lavender petals turned in on themselves. The tips of the petals pulled apart and opened into a deep red hibiscus flower, which turned a brilliant yellow before his eyes.

In just a few minutes a dozen of these magnificent flowers had opened around her. There were different kinds as well but these were the most beautiful to him, maybe because he had seen it from its start and now felt he had some sort of familiarity with the plant. The vines in the trees seemed to hang lower. A butterfly landed on her head and she started laughing. He couldn't help but smile. And then the glorious brilliance of the sun shone down on the clearing where she sat. He let it shine down on her for a while, hoping the rays were healing her as they riveted across her skin.

He kicked his horse forward and slowly walked toward her. The animals reacted immediately to his presence, disappearing from sight. She looked up at him and smiled, but he could still see how hurt she was. He climbed down from his horse and picked her up from the ground. He kissed her gently and placed her on the back of his horse.

Over the next week he took her to the forest every day for a few hours. She still refused to use her powers, but at least she was controlling them again.

"Come on," Alexander said as Saroja tried to stand on her own from the side of the bed for the first time since her abduction. She could still feel a slight twinge of pain at the junction between her legs and her hips, but at least she could feel her legs again. She stood up straight, praying her knees didn't give out. She took small steps at first, testing the strength of her legs, then looked up and walked slowly to Alexander.

"Sasha, get her dressed, I will return in a moment," Alexander said, walking toward the door.

"Where are you taking me? To the forest?" Saroja asked, sitting down slowly in a chair.

"Not today. Now you need to reconnect with people. A walk around the castle will help you to regain your strength," he answered, looking back at her.

"I don't want to go," she said, looking out of the window.

"You can't stay cooped up in this room forever, my love, and I think it will be good for you to talk to someone other than me and Sasha," he said, coming to kneel before her.

"I can't. I don't want to see anyone yet," she said, looking down at her hands.

"I will take you to the gardens. I'll make sure no one is there but us. Maybe you could call the corners. You told me that ritual gives you strength, and you don't use your powers anymore. It took a lot of effort and a lot of people to give them back to you. I think you should try," he said, taking her hand.

"No, magic is the reason this happened," she said, pulling her hand free.

"Listen to me! Those bad things happened to you because some evil men took you away. If anyone should be blamed for that, it should be me for not providing a safe home for you to live in. They could have killed you, but instead they chose to torture and defile you. It had nothing to do with your magic. It happened because sometimes life is hard and bad things happen. The same thing happened to my mother and your parents. Now they are dead, but you are alive. You cannot stop living. I won't allow it.

"Sasha, get her dressed. When I return you are going with me to the gardens. You don't have to use your powers ever again, but it would be a shame that you would stop using them now that you don't have to hide," he declared, then walked out of the chamber and slammed the door closed behind him.

Saroja and Sasha looked at each other at the same time.

"Well, what color gown would you like to wear today, Your Highness?" Sasha asked.

"Just pick something simple," Saroja said, folding her arms across her chest.

"Your Highness, may I speak?" she asked.

"Yes, of course," she said.

"I think you look wonderful, considering the way you looked when Prince Alexander brought you home that night. The servants are all very worried. Every soldier volunteered for the position when the king announced that you would need new guards. Now you will have six. Prince Alexander is in charge of making the final choices, though. He has become a different person since all this happened. He barely left this room when you were ill. Everyone wonders when you will return to court, and Cash has also been asking about you," she said, holding a hand mirror in front of her face. "And your face has healed nicely."

"Yes, my face has healed, but I can barely walk and everyone knows what those men did to me. How can I face them? I don't want their pity," Saroja explained.

"I don't think anyone could ever feel pity for the woman who saved us from tyranny. You will see for yourself when you look into their faces. It is not pity, it's more like…admiration," Sasha said, pushing the gold band down over her head. She took the comb and made a part in the center of her forehead, then combed the hair to two sides. She twisted the hair on each side from the center to the back and braided it all together, then secured the end.

"Are you ready?" Alexander said, opening the door. She rose from the chair and walked slowly toward him.

"You look beautiful," he said, taking her arm.

"I feel terrible," she said, stepping out into the hall. The guards on the outside of the door fell to their knees before her, touching their noses to the ground.

Saroja didn't know what to say. She took their hands and tried lifting them to their feet. She looked at Alexander with a furrowed brow. He winked at her.

"Have you put them up to this?" she whispered.

"No, I promise," he said when she gave him an accusing look.

"Will you take me to see Cash?" she asked. Alexander nodded and led her toward the chamber wear the soldier was recuperating. He had been stabbed several times and had it not been for his girth he probably would not have survived.

When they reached the soldier's barracks, Saroja walked to the bed. Sasha pulled a chair up so she could sit down. Cash opened his eyes when the princess touched his face and struggled to sit up straight.

"No, you should relax. I have come to see how you fair. When you get better, your job will be waiting. That is, if you still want it," she said.

"I would be honored to serve you, Your Majesty," Cash said, touched by the offer. He thought he had failed the princess and would be punished upon his recovery. He should have been ready for a rush attack, but they had come so fast. He had been wounded several times and pushed off his feet. Was he even worthy of the position? He had failed her once and the fact that she would put her life in his hand again unmanned him. He couldn't even think of what to say.

"We will leave now so you can rest," she said, rising from the chair.

Alexander led her out of the room and down the hall. The servants bowed low as they passed, then turned and followed them down the hall.

"Return to your duties," Alexander said over his shoulders as they walked through the entrance way to the gardens.

"Do you want to call the corners?" he asked as they walked across the bridge.

"Maybe tomorrow. Every time I think of my powers, I remember how I lost control of them. I let my anger control my actions and almost died because of it. Alexander, I could have destroyed us all," she said, looking up at him.

"But you didn't. Come, I want to show you something," he said, leading her through the side door. When they reached the stables, Alexander had his horse saddled.

"I can't go riding," she said, holding her head down.

He used his hand to lift her chin slowly. He wiped the tears from her eyes and picked her up from the ground. He set her on JeNi's back and climbed up behind her then led the horse from the stables. She wrapped her arms around his waist and thanked the Great Creator for sending him to her. He took her to the border and climbed down from the horse. He grabbed her gently around the waist and helped her to the ground. Then he walked her to the edge of the cliff and pointed at Lavitia.

Saroja stared at the land in the distance. She looked up at Alexander, then put her hands over her mouth.

"I did that all by myself?" she asked. Saroja couldn't believe that the land way off in the distance used to touch the land she was stand-ing on. She could barely see the coast because it was covered by a thick layer of fog. The mountains seemed farther away than they had ever been. The land near the coast was barren. There was just sand as far as the eyes could see.

"Do you still think you had no control?" Alexander asked, speaking softly, close to her ear.

"I can't believe I am responsible for this," she said, turning toward him.

"That is because you are unaware of how amazing you are. I've never known anyone as humble as you. You deny your beauty, your talents…your powers?" he asked, waving his hand to display the view behind him.

"I think that I am a fair singer, and the credit for my talents with instruments has to go to Kalina; as for being beautiful, I think I am no prettier than any other girls I have known or seen since I've been here. Perhaps my skin is lighter than most, but the value of a person is found within," she said, walking across the land.

"Your Highness, you are far from average, and what would you say of your dancing?" he asked.

"Well, I like dancing and I've heard from a reliable source that that skill runs in my family," she said, smiling up at him.

It was the first time he'd seen her smile with that twinkle of care-free happiness in her eyes since he carried her home that night. He walked slowly toward her, coming to stand just inches from her face.

"I know that you are not yet able, but I want you to know how much I desire you at this very moment," he whispered against her lips, pressing his body against hers so she could feel the firmness between his legs, looking deep into her eyes. After what seemed like an eternity of silence, he finally took her hand.

"You would still have me as your wife, even though I have been ruined?" she asked, looking up at him.

"I know you would never willingly give yourself to another. Let's just forget it ever happened," he said, putting her on the horse.

She turned in the saddle when he climbed up behind her. "But I can't forget. And as much as I wish it didn't, it happened and now it is a part of me. The world doesn't even seem like the same place any-more. There is a fear inside me that wasn't there before. I had never known that people could be so mean and brutal toward one another for no reason at all,"

"Now, my love, you are ready to be a queen," he said as they rode back down the dusty road that led to the castle.

CHAPTER 34

The Stone Pond

Saroja stared up at the ceiling from Alexander's bed. For the last few nights Alexander had kissed her good night, then turned his back to her and went to sleep. She missed his touch. She was so confused. He had told her that he still desired her. Perhaps he had changed his mind. Maybe he was just marrying her now because he felt he had to. She got up from the bed quietly and poured herself a glass of wine, and then she sat down on the floor before the fire.

Alexander watched her as she walked to the table. He had tried to stay as far away from her in the bed as he could. She was so close and he wanted her so bad, but he knew she wasn't ready and he had no desire to hurt her any more than she had already been hurt. Moving away from her was all he could do to keep his hands off her, besides sleeping on the floor. When she was near, he had to guard against so many different things to keep himself from being aroused; the smell of her hair, the softness of her skin, the gentle way she touched him. He would lay awake all night, thinking of her; his body aroused, so much so it was almost painful.

Saroja sat at the foot of the bed staring at the flames. She had always been fascinated by fire. There was something about it. Sometimes she found herself a little jealous. Fire had so much strength and free will. The flames were hypnotizing. They danced around, changing colors freely to tease her. She raised her hand to the flames and watched them rise in the fireplace. She made a fist and opened it to a single flame moving around in her palm. It surprised her that the fire didn't burn her hand as it moved around her palm.

"Well, hello, little one," she said softly, smiling. Then she closed her fist and put the flame out. Alexander got up from the bed and sat behind her on the floor.

"Did I wake you?" she asked when he wrapped his arms around her.

"I could not sleep," he said, taking a deep breath and having his nostrils filled with lavender and jasmine. He kissed her gently on her neck and along her shoulder. Saroja smiled to herself and put the goblet down on the floor. She turned in his arms and kissed him passionately in return.

"I have missed you," she said, holding his face close to hers.

"I thought this would make you think of…that night," he said, holding her tightly in his embrace.

"There is nothing in your touch that could ever remind me of that terrible night," she whispered around his lips.

He laid her down on the thick rugs and used his hands and mouth to make love to her. He kissed her from her head to her toes, then picked her up and carried her to the bed.

"We should try and get some sleep. Father has planned a celebration in your honor tomorrow night. It is supposed to be a surprise, so don't forget to be surprised," Alexander explained, placing her gently on the bed.

"Does that mean we have to stay the whole time?" she asked, wary of the idea.

"Yes, my love, you have to stay until it's over. How would it look if the guest of honor were to leave the celebration before the party was over?" he asked, lying on his side, facing her.

"And what is it that we're celebrating?" she asked.

"Theslia's liberation of course," he said.

"If only my father were alive to see it," she said, turning over on her stomach.

"Your father sees what you have done for this country." He took her in his arms. He stroked her hair and caressed her scalp as he held her securely in his arms until they fell asleep.

The next day when she woke up he was already sitting at his desk in the next room. She got up from the bed and went to him.

"Good morning, sweetness. How are you feeling today?" he asked when he saw her standing in the doorway.

"I am fine. What is all this?" she said, noticing the stacks of parchment.

"These are the proclamations that will be sent out declaring that the persecution of Pheolatians now to be considered murder on the grandest scale. All magical people have been given noble titles for their services to the crown. I just have to sign them. Father was supposed to do this, but he needed some rest. All I have to do is finish signing these so they can be sent out…along with another announcement," he said, looking up at her.

"What announcement? Can I do the calligraphy?" she asked, sitting down in the chair across from his desk.

"Sure," he said. "But we do have scribes for that. You make one and I'll have them make copies," Alexander said, handing her the ink and pen.

Saroja rolled out the blank parchment and set the weight on the bottom and top. She adjusted the ink so she could reach it better and grabbed hold of her sleeve. She took the pen in her hand then looked up at Alexander.

"What is the message?" she asked.

Alexander leaned back in his chair. "It should read, after the normal formalities: All of Theslia is granted a day of jubilee to mark the wedding of the first son of the kingdom, Prince Alexander, son of King Benjamin Casesar sovereign of Theslia, to her royal highness Princess Saroja Minunette of the house of Shakur on the eve of the full moon," he said, smiling when she paused and looked up at him.

"Truly, Alexander?" she said, pushing out of the seat. She moved around the table and jumped in his lap, wrapping her arms eagerly around his neck.

"Yes, Father told me last night. He will also announce it tonight at the celebration. You will begin lessons tomorrow to learn the rituals. Father wants us to have a traditional ceremony," he said, sounding disappointed.

"What is wrong with a traditional wedding, Alexander?" she asked, confused by his response.

"Nothing, it is just that you will have to perform the *flusha* before the entire court, and I am not looking forward to having other men watch you dance in such a way," he said, watching her hips sway from side to side as she walked back around the table.

"You need not worry, Your Highness. To me, you will be the only man in the hall," she said.

They worked on their documents all morning until Sasha arrived to help Saroja dress for the day.

"What color dress would you like to wear today?" Sasha asked.

Saroja looked over the selections and pulled two dresses from the rack. She looked them over and held them up so Alexander could see them from the next room.

"I like the white one," he said.

Saroja handed Sasha the white gown and sat down in the chair. After she was dressed, she helped Alexander finish the proclamations.

"I must train with the soldiers today. Will you be alright on your own for a while?" he asked, realizing this would be first time she would be away from him since her abduction. "I will see you again before dinner."

"Alexander, where are the instruments in the castle?" she asked, deciding to spend her day practicing her music.

"They are displayed around the stone pond. Sasha will show you the way. Have a good day, my lady," he said, kissing her sweetly before he left the room.

"If we are going to the stone pond, I think you should choose another outfit, Your Highness. The stone pond is where the women of the court spend their days relaxing," Sasha said while digging through one of the trunks, looking for a more suitable outfit. Finally, after going through two trunks she realized all the clothes belonged to Prince Alexander.

"Your Majesty, I will have to return to your chamber to get the *chari*," Sasha said. She bowed and left the room. Saroja poured herself a goblet of wine and peered out of the window. Alexander's chambers had a beautiful view of the entire garden. She walked to the study and read the parchment again. Soon she would be a married woman, truly a married woman. It seemed only yesterday she was hunting eggs and sneaking away to play in the woods.

She only regretted not having her family there. Auntie Lina wouldn't be there to help her dress, and she couldn't ask Grandma Tilda for advice about how to be a good wife. She had a different kind of love now than the kind they had given her; Alexander's love, she would let it consume her.

"Your Majesty," Sasha called from the other room.

Saroja walked out and took the dainty outfit from Sasha's hand and looked it over, then placed it on the bed. Sasha helped her out of the dress, then slipped the top of the outfit over her head. It was comprised of three pieces. The entire outfit was turquoise blue with white and emerald green colored jewels on it. The top fit her very tightly and came down just enough to cover her breast. The next part was a short under garment that cut off just above her thighs. Then there was a long sheer wrap that went around her waist several times before Sasha secured it with a large gold brooch that had a large crystal in the middle. The end of the skirt was pulled up high on her hip, leaving a slit open on the side.

Saroja looked at herself in the mirror and smiled. She liked the outfit, but she didn't think Alexander would. She thought it would make a great costume to dance in. She shrugged her shoulder and sat down in the chair. Sasha braided several small braids with white ribbons in each one all around the front of her head then placed the gold band down over her forehead. She used pins to secure them around her head. Then she separated the remaining hair into two sections, creating a part that ran from ear to ear and braided the top into two ponytails. She used the two braids to make two loops in the back and allowed them to hang down over the hair she left loose in the back.

"You are ready, Your Majesty," Sasha sai,d handing her the mirror.

"It is beautiful," Saroja said, turning her head to see the side of her hair. Then she got up from the chair and followed Sasha to the stone pond.

When they entered the room, the tranquility of the place took her breath away. Soft music played in the back ground, but stopped instantly when she stepped into the room. There was a large round pool in the middle of the floor. The water was so clear you could see straight through to the bottom where roses could be seen on the floor. Golden instruments surrounded the pond. The air smelled of flowers and spices. The women who were playing instruments and the ones lying on the long chairs stood up and bowed.

Everyone wore the *chari* and it created a rainbow of colors as she looked around the room. The walls were white while all the furniture and fixtures were gold. White and gray pillows of all sizes, along with plush rugs covered the floor, which explained why no one wore shoes, so she stepped out of hers. Sasha picked them up and put them on the shelf near the door. Saroja had never dreamed of such a place.

"Why didn't Alexander show me this room before?" Saroja asked quietly as she walked down the steps toward the pool.

"Men are not allowed in this room, except the prince and the king, I mean, they enter where they wish, but they never come here," Sasha explained. She motioned Saroja toward a large chair set up against the far wall. Saroja shook her head and pointed to the harp in the corner. She sat down and started to play a slow delightful melody. All at once the chatter in the room started again. The women in the pool threw a light weighted silver ball around. Some of them walked together, talking, while others laid across the long chairs as servants rubbed oils on their backs.

After playing the instrument for a while, Saroja got up and sat on the edge of the pool. A servant came to her with a tray of fruit. Saroja took a few grapes from the tray, then stood up and walked down the steps into the water. She submerged her head then came up again, pushing the cool water from her face. The water was cool, sweet, and soft against her skin. She played with the lilies that floated on the top and giggled when the ball hit her on the head.

"My apologies, Your Highness," a girl said, coming to her side.

"It is fine," Saroja said, picking up the ball and tossing it to another woman. "What is your name?" she asked.

"My name is Lady Desmonia of Mesmona," she said, bowing her head to the princess. "Let me introduce you to the others. Come, ladies, the princess wishes to meet everyone."

Desmonia was a small girl. Her hair was a dark brown. Saroja had never seen hair be any other color except black. It was gathered into one long pony tail by several gold bands. She had a sweet delicate face and beautiful eyes. They were light brown with a hint of green.

"Where is Mesmona?" she asked curious about her features.

"It is on the far side of Lavitia. Father says we will have to journey by boat if we wish to return, but I told him that I would much rather live in Theslia," she said with a smile. They walked slowly to the edge of the pool where Sasha waited with the princess's towel. She blotted at the water and escorted Saroja to her seat. The women formed a line and introduced themselves.

Saroja gave each woman a polite nod as they introduced themselves, kissing her hand.

"It will take some time for me to remember everyone's name, but my wish is that we will all become good friends. Please, let us continue with the game," she said, rising from the seat. They entered the pool and threw the ball around. When she got tired, she got out and laid down on the softest chair she'd ever felt. Sasha waved her hand and a servant brought Saroja a goblet of wine. Then Sasha gave her an oil massage and informed her that it was time for midday meal.

"Will you join us in the solar for midday meal, Your Highness?" Lady Athena of Grecian asked. "Conversations in the great hall are always overrun by men."

"They talk loud and rarely have anything of importance to say," Lady Andesa of Tribeca added, getting a laugh from the other women.

"I would be delighted to join you," Saroja said.

When she finally returned to Alexander's chamber, she fell against the bed. She had had such a wonderful day, and to think she thought the women at court didn't like her. Alexander entered and she turned to him with a big smile on her face.

"Oh, Alexander, I have had the most wonderful day. I made new friends and we have decided to form a quintet. I will play the harp, Desmonia will play the lute, Andesa will play the mandolin, Athena will play lyre, and Penelope will play the aulos. Isn't that wonderful? Do you think those instruments will sound good together?" she rambled on excitedly.

"I'm glad you are happy again, my love," he said, opening the door, allowing the servants to enter with the tub. He was sweaty and very dusty. He stepped into the water and submerged his head. He pushed the extra water from his face and laid his head back against the tub, exhausted from today's exercises on the training ground.

Saroja kneeled beside the tub on the floor.

"Andesa's father is returning from Tribeca tomorrow with a new style of gown. If I like one, may I buy it?" she asked. He touched her face and looked her over. She looked absolutely breathtaking in the revealing *chari*. It was wet and it clung to her body as she moved.

"You have scores of gowns you haven't even tried on yet, but if you want one from Tribeca you may have it," he said, unable to deny her anything. "The style of Tribeca is very different from what you're used to. Remember the man in that inn who offered to buy you? He was from Tribeca," he said.

She tried hard not to think of that unfortunate man, but she did remember thinking he had looked very funny to her when he approached their table. "Well, I like the dresses Andesa showed me today, and did you know there were Lavations living here?" she said, working the soap gently into his hair.

"Yes, during the rebellion years ago some Lavation families were exiled for giving aid to your father. You should start getting dressed now. The celebration will begin soon. Where is Sasha?" he asked after rinsing the soap from his hair.

"She is outside," Saroja said, walking to the door. "Do you need her?"

"No, you need her. It is time for you to get dressed. You should not be walking around like that anyway," Sasha entered and stood with her head down awaiting her orders.

"It is time for Her Majesty to get dressed," he said from the water. The muscles in his arms tightened as he grabbed hold of the side of the tub. The water rolled slowly down his wet skin. He wrapped the towel around his waist and walked to the table for a goblet of ale. Saroja stood near him, admiring his body. It had been a while since he had joined with her. The sight of his wet body glistening from the light of the fireplace made her heartbeat speed up in her chest.

"Go to your chambers and get dressed. I will come soon to escort you to the great hall," he said, watching her. She chewed on her bottom lip as her eyes looked him over. When her eyes met with his again, they were filled with desire. He ran his finger slowly along the curve of her breast as she looked up at him. Sasha came forward and placed her hand under her forearm escorting her toward the door. He watched her as she walked to the door and felt a great amount of pride when she looked back at him over her shoulder, as if it pained her to leave him.

Sasha led her to her chamber and opened the door. There was a beautiful pink gown on the bed with matching jewelry and slippers.

Sasha helped her take off the wet chari, the knots ha tightened and had Sasha mumbling under her breath by the time she got them loose. Sasha patted the princess down with a towel then rubbed her down with jasmine oil before she helped her dress.. She thought for a while about a hairstyle, then decided to leave it down this evening. When she was finally dressed, Sasha removed a beautiful crown from a small box that was placed on her table. The crown was covered with rubies, sapphires, emeralds, diamond, and amethyst and came to a chevron point in the middle. Sasha handled it very carefully. She placed it on Saroja's head and secured it on the inside by putting pins through the tiny loops attached to the crown on the inside of the band.

Saroja stood and walked to the mirror. Then she turned to the portrait of her parents and looked up at them.

"I did it, Father," she said. "Theslia is safe. Now you can have peace."

At that moment Alexander opened the door. She turned and walked toward him. He thought she looked absolutely heavenly. He took her arm and led her from the room. He held his head up high, feeling on top of the world. His kingdom was safe and he was about to marry the most beautiful woman in the land because he loved her. They stopped just before the door. Saroja took a deep breath when the doors were pulled open.

"Announcing their royal highnesses, Prince Alexander and Princess Saroja," the man near the door said in a loud voice.

Everyone in the hall stood and bowed. Alexander escorted Saroja to her seat on the dais near the king, and then took the seat next to her. The king stood and walked forward.

"Tonight, we celebrate our beloved princess. Thanks to her, our kingdom is safe from invaders. I would also like to take this time to thank the Pheolatian people among us; without their help, the first daughter of our kingdom would have been lost," he said.

The crowd applauded and went silent again when he held his hand up.

"This night will also be used to celebrate another happy occasion. On the eve of the full moon Prince Alexander will finally be wed to Princess Saroja." Alexander grabbed Saroja's hand and squeezed. She looked over at him and smiled. "So, I ask you all to join me in a toast. To my son and his bride to be, may your union bring our kingdom happiness and prosperity," Benjamin said, holding up his goblet. He took a sip of the wine and placed it back on the tray the servant held. "Let the celebration begin!" he said.

The musicians started to play and the servants entered with the food. Acrobats and jugglers performed all around them. A man made flames shoot out of his mouth while another pulled a long sword from his throat. When the musicians started playing a popular folk dance, the servant opened the door to the grand ballroom. The couples lined up around the room and danced about. Saroja danced with the king and found him to be a very different man in an individual conversation than she had expected of the stern ruler. Soon Alexander came and took her hand when a slower song started. The crowds formed their lines and moved about the room.

Saroja didn't see any of her new friends when Alexander left her to talk with some men. Moments later the musicians stopped and moved to the center of the room. They started playing the music for the *flusha* as fifteen girls entered, wearing beautiful customs. They carried tambourines and long, flowing scarves. Saroja found their performance delightful. She smiled and clapped her hands.

Alexander watched her from across the room. She was a beautiful woman and he was glad that she was smiling. She was small and fragile but he would never deny how strong she was. She had endured so much in so little time, and now she was able to smile. He had no doubt that she would make a good queen.

"Claris, you go and speak with her now while she is alone. She likes you," Maja said, watching Saroja as well.

"She has already made her decision. Leave her be," Kaemar said.

"She could pass us natural power. That cross will act as a vessel. Don't you see? This is our chance to have *natural powers*. Claris, go and speak with her," Maja said. She had always made the decisions in their coven. She use to butt heads with Kalina, but after she had left, Kaemar and Claris simply towed in her wake. They were easily manipulated with a proper explanation.

Claris sat down next to Saroja at one of the tables.

"Are you having a good time?" Saroja asked.

"I'm having a wonderful time. I'm so proud of you. You have saved our people from persecution," Claris said.

"I will admit that I moved Theslia from Lavitia, but the king saved our people because they saved me. They liberated themselves," Saroja corrected.

"I will be leaving soon," Claris said suddenly.

"Why?" Saroja asked, upset about the very idea.

"I must return to my family. I would ask that you take Kalina's place and come with us. I know I am asking for you to sacrifice a lot, but we need you," she explained.

"You want me to leave and miss my wedding," Saroja said.

"No, I only ask that you consider joining us after the ceremony. I realize that it is selfish for me to ask you, but we will have no powers without you. Pita has decided to stay in the castle with her mother and brother," she explained.

"I still don't understand why all of you can't live here," Saroja said.

"We have families. The others have to leave and so do I," she said.

"So, you will have me deny myself a family in order for you to be able to practice magic. Well, I will miss you, and I am sorry you will be unable to use your powers, but my answer must be no," Saroja said, giving her a big hug.

"Princess Saroja," Claris said, taking her hands. "If you will not join our coven, will you not consider passing us some of your power?"

"I did not know such a thing could be done," she said, pulling her hands free.

"There is such a spell," Claris said, looking hopeful.

"Excuse me, Your Majesty, may I have the honor?" Alexander said, bowing before her. Saroja nodded and took his arm. Claris went back to the others.

Later that night, Saroja stood by the door to the great hall with Alexander, bidding the guests good night. She looked up at him and smiled. She had had a good time. The girls had returned to the party after their performance, giving her friends to talk with while Alexander mingled with the guests. She thought for a moment about Claris then decided she would look for the answer in Matilda's spell book. Surely if there was such a thing as passing powers, she would have remembered reading it there.

King Benjamin had retired early, but Alexander said that was normal. He didn't seem normal to her, but Alexander would know him better than she did.

"Are you ready to go?" Alexander asked, pulling her from her thoughts.

"Yes, of course," she said looking back over her shoulder. "Sasha, I want a small bowl of that soup we had with dinner, please."

"Yes, Your Highness," she said, bowing.

Alexander escorted her to her chamber.

"You will sleep in your chambers until we are married. I also want you to know that this is Father's doing," he explained. He bent and kissed her good night, feeling a little nervous as he pulled the door closed. Twenty soldiers lined the hall, putting his mind at ease. He knew the Lavitians were no threat, but just as Cain had been a spy for years, so could there be others that wished to harm her. He wasn't taking any chances.

Saroja had her soup and then a quick bath. She shared a goblet of wine with Sasha as she brushed her hair until it was dry, then braided it. Saroja crawled into her bed and placed the wine on the night table. She couldn't sleep. She was frightened by the shadows. The last time she was in this bed, the men had come for her.

"Sasha, will you stay with me until I fall asleep?"

"Of course I will, Your Majesty. I will not leave you."

She snuggled under the covers. Her thoughts kept going to the king and how her grandmother had died. She prayed she was wrong for Alexander's sake. Finally, after tossing and turning to find a comfortable position, she drifted off into a fitful sleep.

CHAPTER 35

High Priest Langir

The next morning when she woke up, Sasha was standing at the foot of her bed with her hands folded. Her breakfast was on the table and the clamps and pins for her hair were set up on another table next to her chair.

"Good morning, Your Highness," Sasha said.

"Good morning," Saroja replied, walking to the table.

She ate her breakfast and got dressed. Sasha did her hair and escorted her to the great hall. A holy man in a white robe stood in front of the king's throne. He bowed to Saroja as she closed the distance between them.

"Greetings, Your Highness," he said in a pleasing voice. "I am High Priest Langir."

"I am honored to meet you," she said with a smile.

"From across the room I could see Queen Tess in you, but now that you stand before me, it is Alosis I look upon," he said, looking into her eyes. "The eyes are a bit too light, but they suit you."

"Did you know my parents well?" she asked, walking with him back to the doors of the great hall.

"Actually, I was engaged to be married to your widowed grandmother when the trouble started, but when it was over, of course you know, she was gone. Alosis was like a son to me," he said, his voice fading off. "I brought your parents together, I married them, and I am responsible for the royal seal on your ankle," he explained.

"What did you mean when you said she was gone? What happened to her, my grandmother, I mean?"

Langir paused. "How could you not know?" he asked, looking at her with a horrified look on his face.

"Your Holiness, last year I didn't even know I was a princess. I know nothing of my grandmother aside from the fact that she was a great sorceress and her name."

"Well, someone should have told you of your family, what they did for us, how much they sacrificed, at least. They are a part of you. Where do you think you got all that power from?" he trailed off, shaking his head at the injustice.

"I've heard stories since I've been here of the invasion, the war with Lavatia, but the details about my parents are still pretty bleak."

'Well, I will tell you. Would you walk with me?" The rituals can wait." Saroja laced her arm through his when he offered it.

"When I met your grandmother, she was scared and alone. Her husband had just died. Alosis was maybe sixteen. He was having a hard time. It is a terrible thing to lose your father especially at such a crucial age. He was becoming a man, and his powers were also developing, extreme powers, in a time when being different was against the law. Lynea hid him for two years in a cave in the woods while she taught him to control them. Nature responded to him, you see, especially water."

"He was a wise person even at his age. He told me before his mother and I were to be married that he was glad he would have a father again because that would make his mother happy. I never realized I needed his approval until he spoke those words. They made me feel good inside. Everyone was gathered at the temple for the wedding, even Alosis, against his mother's wishes. She knew that public parties and celebrations were high risk for Lavatian soldiers, and she was right.

"Before the ceremony even began, the soldiers arrived and surrounded us. They asked for all Pheolatians to step forward to be arrested. Lynea had spoken to me about standing up to the soldiers one day, but I never imagined she meant this day. I should have known she would not let them near Alosis. I tried to stop her, but she said it was time they learned who they were dealing with.

"She sacrificed herself to save him then?" Saroja asked.

"Not quite, she stepped out of the crowd and told them that she was Pheolatian, but she would not allow them to arrest her. They dismounted, in an attempt to try, but she was able to repel them using burst of light from her hands. Soon the villagers lined up behind her and a battle began. We had a small village and little weapons to defend ourselves against an army."

His shoulders slumped as he thought back. By now they had reached the gardens. The priest gestured to a bench, and they sat together. He took a deep breath and continued.

"Lynea realized we could not stand against them. She encased herself in glass so the soldiers couldn't touch her and started chanting. Suddenly, we were all in the forest. We stayed hidden for months, Lynea had the power to make things grow; she made us amazing dwellings in the trees. We lived there quietly until your father suggested that we start preparing ourselves for the soldiers return. Lynea agreed, but she thought our best defense would be the very magic they were trying to get rid of.

"Your father and a handful of men left to recruit men to become soldiers to fight for our cause." He looked at her with a serious expression on his face. "You do understand the hardships and dangers of such a task?"

Saroja nodded. "I guess it would be hard to convince men to stand and fight."

"You must remember that Veagans were still slaves then. Alosis and his men could only travel under the cover of darkness. They would have to visit villas and plantations owned by powerful Lavatians, convince the Veagans to leave their families and shelter to venture off into the woods, and risk everything for something they never believed was possible." Langir continued.

"Lynea and I stayed behind. She started a school for the gifted while I scouted for potential students for her to teach. I found your mother and her father soon after. She had a connection with the animals that I thought could be very useful with the right training. After convincing her father, I sent them to Lynea. Alosis had just returned when they arrived. He was ensnared by little Tess when he first laid eyes on her. Her father joined Alosis's army. His name was Edmond.

"The army was an impressive sight by now, and Alosis felt it was time to move. They set out across Theslia, taking the villages back from the Lavatians. Of course, by now, word had reached Marsalis of our hidden encampment. It seemed like as soon as the army left, the Lavatians came. There was no one left but women children. They hit the trees with catapulted balls of fire. Lynea tried to protect us, but there were too many. She was hurt badly," he said, the pain in his voce obvious before she looked over at his grievous face.

"She told me to take her to the river and leave her there, but I couldn't. I laid her on the ground. She got up on her knees near a small oak sapling and spoke to it. I'll never forget what she said. If I'd believed it was even possible for her to do what she did, I would have stopped her. She said, "Tonight we tried, but again we must hide, or all will be lost. I choose you as our sanctuary. Little oak tree, become one with me and serve as a shelter on the darkest nights where my people can turn to for warmth and light."

"That tree grew and grew and with it the mountains and the river. I was so engrossed by what was going on around me that I wasn't paying attention to what was happening to her. When the ground stopped shaking and the river calmed, it had nearly tripled in width, and the tiny sapling towered above me. Lynea was gone, completely vanished. I thought I had let her be swept up by the river until the water started to move away at the base and the steps appeared to me. I knew then what she had done."

"When Alosis returned with the army, I explained what had happened. He agreed with me. She had given her soul to that tree.

The Lavatians couldn't destroy it or even cross the river, which is why the castle was built here."

"My grandmother gave her soul to the Great Oak tree to protect our people," Saroja said in a stunned whisper.

"Oh my, where has the time gone? Let's return to the hall. I'll show you a few things today and finish up tomorrow," Langir suggested, but Saroja's mind was in the past.

"Would you mind if we start fresh tomorrow, Your Holiness? I am a bit tired," she said.

"Are you alright, my dear? I didn't mean to upset you. I only wanted you to know that because of her sacrifice, your father's army was able to win. The army was safe in the Great Oak at night, and armed with their magic, they were unstoppable. We thank you for your sacrifice as well. I felt you needed to know what runs through your veins."

"Thank you so much for telling me. I will see you tomorrow. Sasha," she called over her shoulder then walked away from the priest.

Once they reached her chambers, Saroja started pacing back and forth. "Where is Alexander?" she asked.

"I believe he took some soldiers to the village, Your Highness," Sasha said, busy mending the hem of a dress.

"Do you know when he is to return?" Saroja asked subtly.

"I believe around nightfall."

Could she journey to the Great Oak and be back by nightfall? What would Alexander say if she wasn't here when he returned? She worried at her bottom lip as she thought things over. She didn't want him to worry for her, but she had to go to the Great Oak. No one would let her out of this room without an escort, perhaps if she left him a note and explained where she would be if he got back before she could return. She entered her study and wrote a quick explanation.

"Sasha, I need you to help me with something," she explained.

"Yes, of course, what is it, Your Majesty?" Sasha answered, laying the dress aside.

"I need you to stay in this room until I return."

"But, Your Majesty, I'm supposed to stay at your side…"

"Listen to me," Saroja explained, coming over to her. "I need to journey to the Great Oak, but I need to go alone. The guards will follow if you come with me, but if you stay here they will think I am here.'

"Won't they see you leaving, Your Highness?"

"Yes, but they won't stop me…if I'm you," she said quietly. Sasha's eyes widened, and she started shaking her head.

"If something should befall you, the king, the prince, they will have my head. What if Prince Alexander returns before you come back? Perhaps I should come with you, Your Majesty, and some guards to see you safe," Sasha pleaded.

"No, I must go alone, and Alexander would never allow that. If he returns before I do there is a note in my study for him. Don't worry, Sasha, I will be fine. Just promise me that you will stay here until I return, please." Sasha gave her a weak nod and sat back down in the chair.

Saroja whispered the enchantment and changed herself into Sasha.

The girl gasped from chair. "I promise I will return before nightfall."

She walked slowly down the hallway and took the direct route to the stable. Then she stopped at the door. She would never make it there and back in time on Midnight. She closed her eyes and thought of the Great Oak. When she opened her eyes, she was inside the base of the huge tree.

"I know this is silly but, Grandmother, if you're there, our country is safe now. I wanted you to know that it's finally over. You can rest." She walked to the wall and grabbed hold of a vine. The vine grew warmer in her hand and started to pulsate. There was a great flash of light, and Saroja spun around.

A tall slender woman stood before her in all white. She had long black hair and brown eyes. "Thank you," she said. She walked slowly toward Saroja and embraced her. Saroja wrapped her arms around her and started to cry. No one had to tell her who this was.

"I'm glad you came back. You look so much like him." She looked Saroja over and smiled. "I wanted to do that the first time you came, but you were not ready. What is your name, granddaughter?"

"Oh, I'm sorry. My name is Saroja. I had to come after the High Priest Langir told me of your spell on this tree. I never expected you would be here like this. Now that everything is safe, you can come back with me."

"Tennyson Langir…I would love to come with you, but I cannot leave here," Lynea said sadly. "I am just glad that I've been able to meet you at last." Lynea said, caressing her face.

"I will come to talk with you often, but I promised my maid I would return before nightfall." Saroja explained.

"I would love for you to return, but you are in grave danger. The gods are in an upheaval. Most did not want you to live. They are uncomfortable about a mortal having such powers, and for that reason, you will never see me again. My spirit exists now only through this tree. I want you to remember that you are never alone. Now go home and be safe, my child, my love…" She said as she faded away.

Saroja closed her eyes and returned to the stable, the sun was just going down changing the sky to a warm orange. She changed back to Sasha and made her way back to her chambers. Sasha breathed a sigh of relief when the door opened, and she stared at her own image. Saroja smiled and changed back, then she dismissed Sasha to think over the day's events.

The next day, she met the priest again. "I have no sad words for you today. Let us get started."

"When you enter the hall on your wedding day, you will stop here at this holy altar. One of the priests will give you a candle. You will use that candle to light these candles, creating the lane. Then place the candle in the last stand. It will be empty. After that, you will walk to the throne. Bow low to the king. Be sure to keep your head bowed until the king asks you to rise. He will say: Rise, my child. Then you will rise and he will remove your veil. Do you have all of that so far?" he asked, turning slowly to look at her. Like all priests he was bald. He had kind eyes that lit up when he smiled.

"Yes, your holiness, but do I have to use a candle? Alexander would prefer I use my powers," she said.

"Very well, I guess that will be alright. Come, let's try it once before we go on," he said, escorting her out of the hall. "The door will be opened then you enter. Yes, walk very slowly."

"Do I stop here before the fire pit or do I walk around to the altar?" she asked.

"You will go all the way around. The priest will be standing here," he said, moving to the position. Saroja moved to the spot, then went back to the top of the hall and started over. She walked slowly down the aisle, then around the fire pit to the altar. She pretended to light the candles on the lane leading to the throne, then bowed and waited.

"Rise, my child," the priest said. She stood up straight then waited.

"Was that right?" she asked, turning to him when she was done.

"Yes, very good, but we're not done yet. After the king removes your veil, he will escort you to the prince. You will take his hand and bow to him then I will start the ceremony. Your hands will be wrapped together. There will be a priest standing here and here," he explained by standing in the positions. "When I say: Your separate flames must now be extinguished. You will walk around to this side because your hands will still be tied together. As you walk together down the aisle of candles, you each will extinguish them. Then you will light the fire pit.

Then you will be married. You will kiss and offer the Great Creator a burnt offering of your choosing."

"I can choose anything?" she asked.

"Yes, you may choose anything. When the offering is given, you will both kneel before the altar. The priest will untie your hands. You will then walk around the fire pit back to the king. Make sure you go this way. Prince Alexander will go to the right. Bow before the king and he will crown you both. You kiss the king, then the servants will come and take you to a chamber to change your clothing so you can perform the *flusha*. Do you know the steps of the dance?" he asked, escorting her back to the throne and allowing her to sit in the king's seat.

"Yes, your holiness," she replied.

"Are you sure? A lot of women claim to know the steps. I have arranged for an instructor to come and teach you," he said.

"Sir, I have had *flusha* lessons every week since I was ten, but I will take your instructions if it will make you feel better. I enjoy performing the dance. At the ceremony, may I add my own ideas to the dance?" she asked.

"What sort of changes will you make?" he asked, turning to her.

"I will change nothing, only the way I enter," she said.

"Very well, we are done with practice today. We will do it again before the ceremony and your dance instructor will meet you near the stone pond tomorrow," he said as he walked from the room.

Saroja went back to her room and changed into a light green *chari*, then went to the stone pond. The girls stood and bowed when she entered. She went to her seat on the far wall and ate the food Sasha had brought her for midday meal. When she was done she walked slowly into the pool and swam to the others. They talked and played games, and then out of nowhere the room fell silent. Saroja looked around, wondering what was going on. When the girls bowed she looked to the door and noticed Alexander standing on the top of the stair.

"May I speak with you for a moment?" he asked.

"Yes, of course, Your Highness," she said as she moved toward the end of the pool. She stepped out of the water and Sasha wrapped a towel around her. She followed Alexander from the room and down the hall. "Is something wrong?"

"No, but Father said it is time that you to start your duties as our queen. These are the castle grounds. These are the new supplies. You must tell the chatelaine where you want them to go. Those two tapestries were made by two of your new friends. They have asked that they be hung in the castle," he explained.

"I understand. You want me to start handling the household affairs. I know how to do that. Where is the inventory list?" she asked, taking charge of the situation. Alexander handed her the parchment and watched as she delegated the servants with the separating of the items. She sent a servant for the chatelaine and explained to her where she wanted the materials to be sent. She decided since the tapestries were made by her friends that they should be hung on the hall leading to the stone pond. She didn't want to mess with the interior because she found the room perfect the way it was.

"Are you going back to the stone pond now?" Alexander asked.

"No, I would like to spend some time with you, if I may," she said, handing the chatelaine the list. She got up from the chair and took the arm he offered her.

"There will be a schedule of things for you to do each day. Now you are truly my queen," he said, looking down at her. Kalina had taught her well.

"Alexander, I don't want to alarm you, but is your father well?" she asked.

"I spoke with him just before I came for you. He is fine. Why do you ask?" he said, opening the door to his chamber.

"He just looked tired to me after the celebration, it reminded me of the night my grandmother died," she said, sitting down on his bed.

He handed her a goblet of wine and sat down next to her.

"Don't worry about Father. He's fine. He may look old, but he's as strong as an ox. All you need to worry about is the preparations for our wedding. The merchants will arrive tomorrow with new silks for you to choose from," he said when she leaned back against him.

"The priest says I have to take lessons to learn the *flusha*. I told him I already knew how to do the dance, but he advised me that I should take the lessons to make sure," she explained.

"Well, Father wants the ceremony to be traditional, so just humor him," he said, sifting through her hair.

"It will be traditional, but I have some plans for the ceremony. Do you think your father will be angry?" she asked.

"Probably, but by then it will be too late. You add whatever changes you want. It's our wedding," he said with his eyes closed.

Saroja curled up in his lap and fell asleep to the lulling steady rhythm of his heartbeat.

CHAPTER 36

With the Dawn

oments later they were disturbed by a light tap on the door. Sasha bowed after she walked into the room.

"Your majesties, the king has requested your presence in the great hall for dinner," she said.

"Very well," Alexander said, lying back against the pillows. Sasha bowed her head and pulled the door close as she left.

"Meals in the great hall are so long. Can we just see what your father wants and then leave?" she asked.

"Maybe, but you should still get dressed. You can't wear a *chari* to the great hall," he said. "Go…get dressed. I will come for you."

She rose reluctantly from the bed and walked to the door. Alexander watched her hips sway from side to side as she turned the handle and left the room.

They reached the great hall and took their places next to the king. As the meal progressed Alexander noticed a change in his father. He was much quieter than usual.

He leaned over and whispered, "Father, is everything alright?"

"Yes, my son, everything is fine. I was just thinking of the night you were born. I was so nervous. That is how I feel right now," Benjamin said.

"Why?" Alexander asked.

"Because I have decided to pass the crown to you," he said, looking at Alexander. He saw his beloved wife in his son's face—he missed her so much—but he also saw the man that he had become. He had been shaped and molded into his idea of what he thought a good king should be; he just prayed that he was right.

"Father, I don't understand—" he started.

"It is done, Alexander. The ceremony will take place tomorrow morning at dawn," Benjamin said.

"Maybe we should talk about this, Father, the country still needs you," Alexander tried to explain.

"I will still be here to counsel you. Don't worry, you're ready," he explained.

"Father, this makes no sense. I'm to be married in five days' time. Why this decision, now? I just don't understand this…Father, are you ill?" Alexander asked, lowering his voice.

"No, but I am old, and I feel it more and more every day," Benjamin explained to his child. "It is your turn."

"Father, you have centuries ahead of you. How old are you now? Sixty?" he asked.

"I will be forty-three next spring. I am twenty years older than you, my son."

"Then why must we make such a decision now, Father? Simo told me he's one hundred." Alexander said, gesturing toward the soldier.

"One hundred and three," Benjamin corrected. "My body feels fine, but my mind is weary. Sometimes I find myself confused, lost in the moment. I tell my guards where I'm going so I can just follow them. These are not good qualities for a king. It is time to step down."

Saroja couldn't hear the hushed conversation between Alexander and the king, so she concentrated on the meal, but she was a little nervous about Alexander's body language.

After dinner, he took her out on the veranda. The sky was full of stars and the air was crisp and cool. Winter would be upon them soon. She leaned against the balcony looking down over the edge and said, "What happened with your father?"

"I am to be named king of Theslia at dawn," he said, slowly taking in a lungful of air and letting it out again.

"This is all happening so fast. I was just getting used to being a princess. Now I'll be a queen tomorrow morning," Saroja said.

"No, you'll still be a princess until we are married," Alexander explained, walking up behind her. She turned in his arms and gave him a reassuring hug.

"You will be a great king, my love," she said.

Early the next morning before the sun came up Alexander sat in his study dressed in his ceremonial robes. His palms were wet and his legs were shaking. All his life he knew this day would come. Why he was so afraid? He got up from the chair and walked slowly to the door. As he opened it, he was surprised to see Saroja seated in the chair across from his door. Sasha stood to her right.

"I thought I would have to wait forever before you came out of that room," she said. "I have come to escort you to the great hall, my lord."

"I'm glad you are here," he said, taking her arm.

She walked him to the great hall and kissed him gently on his lips before he turned to walk through the doors.

"The next time I kiss you, you will be my king," she said softly.

Benjamin stood before the throne near several priests. The members of the council and several other important men were also present. The priest started the ceremony and Alexander kneeled before his father on the floor. The priest spoke about the responsibilities of a king.

He took the crown from Benjamin's head and placed it on a pillow held by another priest who in turn walked it slowly toward Alexander. Another priest picked it up and placed it on his head. Alexander rose slowly from the floor and walked up the steps to the throne. He turned in front of it and was handed the royal scepter. He sat down slowly and was declared the new king of Theslia.

When the ceremony was over he gave his father a big hug.

"I will not fail you, Father," he declared.

He placed the royal scepter back on its stand and took the large crown from his head and placed it back on the pillow.

Saroja paced back and forth in the hall just outside the great hall waiting for Alexander to return. When he opened the doors, she dropped into a low formal curtsy.

"Rise, my love, come riding with me," he said, smiling at her.

"How was the ceremony?" she asked, taking his hand. He led her down the hall and toward the passage that led to the stables.

"Long and boring…The winter winds are coming. Are you cold?" he asked as their horses were brought to them.

"No, I'm fine. Come, I haven't ridden my horse since I got here," Saroja said, greeting the massive stallion. Midnight lowered his head in front of the princess as she reached up to stroke his forehead. "How have you been, baby? I've missed you."

They rode down through the valley and over the grassy hills into a wooded area with their guards following close behind. They rode through the streams and around the trees laughing like carefree children. Saroja's looked back over her shoulder smiling. Alexander watched her as she kicked her horse in full gear and raced through the woods. He leaned in, kicked JeNi's flanks, and raced after her. When he caught up to her she was kneeling near a stream. It reminded him of the first day they had met. She still looked like an angel and soon she would be his in the eyes of the law and the Great Creator.

"We should head back now, I have some matters to attend to when we get back to the castle. When I'm done I will meet you for breakfast in my new chambers. Sasha will—"

"I will meet you when I return, I am meeting with the village healer in the solar to discuss a way to make her job easier," she explained.

"Very well, then come to the great hall for midday meal," he said.

"I'm not sure if I can. I have to choose silks for the wedding ceremony," she said.

When they reached the stables, Alexander helped her down and gave her a passionate kiss.

"Follow your schedule today and I will follow mine, but tomorrow be sure to tell Sasha to plan some time for us to be together," he said. He led her back through the doors and watched her walk away.

Over the next few days Alexander only saw Saroja during midday meal. His duties kept him busy throughout the day and when he did find time to seek her out she would be busy with some task or another. She had started a class in which the village healer taught twenty young girls where to find certain herbs for medicines and how to administer them. That way she was not burdened by so many people needing her attention during the coming winter months when sickness tended to flourish. He missed spending his days with her, but soon she would be his wife and her nights would belong to him.

After her class with the village healer Saroja went to Alexander's study. She changed the desk into a circular dining table. Then she conjured some candles and set them up around the room. She created a strawberry tart dessert and a bottle of champagne, and then changed her plain yellow day dress into a sleek black evening gown. Then she sat down in the chair across from the door and waited. Alexander arrived moments later with three other men.

"I'm so sorry...I wanted to surprise you," Saroja said stumbling to her feet.

"Sire, we can have the meeting at another time if we are interrupting," one of the men said.

"No, I will leave. I'm sorry, Your Highness," she said, bowing to him several times. Alexander was a young king. She didn't want these men to lose respect for him because of her. Such an act could cause them to doubt his ability to lead. One of them might even try to challenge him for the throne. That act would ultimately lead to a war, and they had just brought peace to their country. She waved her hands back and forth through the air and changed the room back the way it was when she entered and left the room.

"Gentlemen, would you mind if we continue this meeting tomorrow morning?" he asked. The men agreed and left the room. Alexander followed them out of the room and headed straight to Saroja's chamber to find her, but she wasn't there. He checked the stone pond, the gardens, and even the stables, but she was nowhere in sight. He went back to the great hall, thinking she might have gone there, but found the room empty except for a few soldiers. Finally, he decided to wait in her chambers knowing she would return sooner or later.

"Your Majesty, I was wondering if you had a chance to think about what we had discussed at the banquet," Claris said as she, Kaemar, and Maja met Saroja along the hall.

"I have given the matter great thought and from what I've read there is no way for me to safely pass you powers without putting my life in danger. The only spell I found was a litany created by a mother to pass her adopted son her powers on her death bed. That being said, my answer must be no. Will you excuse me?" she asked, taking the northern tower, leaving them standing at the base.

"Well, I guess that's it. She said no," Kaemar remarked. "Now, can we start for home?"

"Kaemar is right. Let's just go back to our lives," Claris said.

"Yes, the two of you will return to your loving families and I will wait to see you once every few months. Well, I won't have it. That girl has enough power for ten men. She's just being selfish. All she has to do is change the words," Maja said, following Saroja and watching her as she climbed the stairs followed by six guards and six lady's maids. "You two leave," she said, really to herself. "I would like to spend a little more time at court."

Alexander had drunk nearly an entire pitcher of ale before Sasha quietly opened Saroja's door.

"Where is the princess?" he asked, startling her.

"Sire, she awaits you in your chambers. It was getting late so she sent me for her nightshift," she answered, bending to retrieve the garment from one of her trunks.

"I will take it to her," he said, getting up from the chair.

When he opened the door Saroja was sitting in the middle of his bed with her legs crossed.

"I'm sorry for interrupting your meeting. I just missed you," she said, getting up from the bed.

"I cancelled the meeting. I looked everywhere for you. If Sasha hadn't come to your chambers to get this," he explained, handing her the garment, "I'd still be there waiting for you."

"I was delayed for a moment. Then I went to the chapel to speak with Father Langir, then I went to the gardens, and then I came here hoping you would be finished with your meeting."

"What did you speak with the Father about?" he asked.

"I had some personal questions to ask him," she said, avoiding his eyes. "May I stay here with you tonight?" she asked. Standing up on the bed towering over him.

"I wouldn't have it any other way, but you will not be in need of this," he said. Pulling the garment up and over her head. Then he pulled her into his arms. She wrapped her legs around him and lowered her head to his.

"Tell me," he whispered against the smooth column of her neck.

"Tell you what?" she asked as he let her body slide down the length of his.

"Tell me what is troubling you so much that you had need of counsel from our priest," he said, looking down at her.

"It was nothing. I just wanted his advice on...on how to rid myself of the shame that I walk around with every day. I wanted to know if I would bring this shame to you by becoming your wife, but the priest assured me that the sin is not mine to bear. He said I did nothing wrong," she explained against his chest.

"He is right, my love."

"Then why do I feel this way?" she asked, gazing into his eyes, searching for an answer she knew he could not give her.

"Only time can heal your wounds, and even then, you will never forget," he said. "Let me love you. I can't wipe your pain away as easily as I can wipe away your tears, but I can love you; take you to ecstasy if only for a time."

CHAPTER 37

A Beginning and an End

Saroja stood still as four women wrapped her in layers of white silk. She could hardly breathe. She felt like she had been standing there for hours. She moved slowly to the chair they offered her and sat in it. One of the attendants arranged her dress around her feet as Sasha placed her formal crown on her head then wrapped her hair into several small buns and pinned them together into an elegant style. Then they used paint and powder to decorate her face. She stood before the long mirror one of her maids held up and didn't recognize the image that stared back at her. Finally, a translucent veil was thrown over her face and arranged so the lace decorations hung just right.

"It's time, Your Majesty," Sasha said smiling.

She stood before the ceremonial hall door and took a deep breath when the doors were pulled open. The people stood and bowed slightly as she walked by. Beautiful white and pink roses littered the hall. The candles placed around the room cast a dim glow along the walls. Soft music played in the background.

Her gaze swept by each person as she searched for one face. When she found it, a giddy feeling swept through her body and she couldn't help but smile. He was gorgeous. He wore all white with the red-andgreen banner over his shoulder. Red rose petals were thrown at her feet as she started down the lane lighting the candles without even touching them. She bowed low to Alexander and his father and waited for him to tell her to rise. The priest looked at him when he hesitated a moment too long.

"You may rise," he said. She shimmered as she stood before him. He couldn't remember her ever being so beautiful. He stepped down from the dais, pushed the veil back over her head, and took her hand. One of the priests wrapped a cloth around their hands while another started to speak, but Saroja wasn't really listening to what he was saying. She had heard it all before. She just wanted this all to be over with so they could be alone.

She had only seen him a few times since that night they had spent together, and for some reason he had decided to wait until this night to make love to her. Saroja thought he was still nervous about hurting her. She had assured him that she was completely healed, but he would not be moved. Instead he had carried her to his bed and placed her naked body in the center. He rubbed her down with silky oils and kissed her everywhere she could imagine. His touch was warm and inviting, and before she knew it, she was so relaxed she had fallen to sleep. When she woke up the next morning, he was kissing her good bye. Now he stood before her and she wanted him so bad she could taste it.

Alexander couldn't take his eyes off her. The last time they had been together he had to use all his willpower to obey his father's orders. She was the most gorgeous woman he'd ever seen. She smelled like flowers and his body ached to have her.

He led her back down the aisle, extinguishing the candles that she had lit. When they reached the fire pit, he looked at her and winked. The fire erupted in the pit. He stepped closer and kissed her sweetly, gaining a awed hush from the crowd. It lasted only a brief moment, but it was tenderly sweet, and she knew that this simple kiss meant that he was hers and she was his and that idea suit her just fine.

Saroja threw the dried lavender braid she had made into the flames to honor Kalina; it had been the scent she used to use in her soap. The priest untied the couple's hands and the hall erupted in applause.

Moments later Saroja was whisked away by her attending ladies. She changed into the custom that she would wear to perform the *flusha*. It was white with sheer strips of material hanging from the legs and the arms. There was a shiny gold elastic band around her waist and at her wrist. She sat in the chair while the women took her hair down and placed the thin band of gold over her head. She followed them to the door and told Cash, Silus, and the other guards to wait for her in the great hall. After a lengthy explanation, they finally obeyed her orders.

When they entered the hall without her, Alexander rose to his feet, panicked. Cash hurried to the throne to explain, but before he could reach it the music began to play. A strong wind swept through the hall and the room went dark. The fire in the fire pit came back as a single blue flame that grew larger and larger. It started to flicker orange, then green blue, red, then yellow orange. There was flash of white light and Saroja appeared encased in the flame. The flames unfolded like the flower he had watched bloom with her encased in the middle. She stepped out holding a long stemmed red rose. She walked through the air as if there were steps that led toward Alexander. He sat back down slowly on the throne, not being able to take his eyes off her. Saroja stepped onto the floor and bowed low before him. Then she started the dance, swaying slowly back and forth.

She used spirals of smoke as sashes, flipping them through the air, allowing them to surround her body. Erotically, she moved to the music twirling and spinning. The crowd started to clap as the music got faster and faster. He had never seen anyone move the way she did. He forgot all about their audience and rose from his seat. He had an overwhelming desire to touch her. His father grabbed his arm as he started down the dais.

"Alexander, you must wait until the dance is over," Benjamin whispered.

"I cannot," he said, moving toward her.

She gazed into his eyes as he walked toward her. She gave him a seductive smile while backing slowly away from him as he got closer. Then she turned and walked away from him. She turned back around after a while and offered him the rose, but before he could reach it she let it go, leaving it suspended in midair. He grabbed it and continued to follow her toward the fire pit. When he finally grabbed her hand, she wrapped her arms around his neck. Suddenly a strong wind swept through the room, dousing all the light in the hall. The room was filled with hushed whispers as the crowd waited for something else to happen.

Finally, one of the servants began relighting the candles in the hall. Saroja and Alexander were nowhere to be found. Benjamin stood and clapped his hands together twice. The servants entered bearing trays with the food, ale, and wine and the celebration began. He stood after a while and walked slowly to his chambers.

When Alexander released Saroja from his embrace he was surprised to find they were in his chamber.

"I'm sorry," she said. "I just couldn't wait any longer."

"Well, I'm glad to see you using your powers again, but this is no longer my—I mean, our room," he said, lifting her from the floor. He hugged her and took a deep breath filling his senses with her smell. He opened the door and carried her down the hall. Then they turned suddenly and took the stairwell. He brought her to two beautiful doors. Golden roses had been carved into the panels. "Open it. Use your powers." The doors swung open. It was like something from one of her dreams. The furniture was white. There were red rose petals all over the floor. A huge bed sat in the middle. It had sheer white curtains wrapped all around it. There was a pool with flowers and candles floating across the top.

"It's beautiful, *husband*," she said as he walked in to the room. He gave her a kiss and swept the curtains back to put her on the bed. "I had forgotten how good it felt."

Suddenly there was a loud knock on the door.

"We are not to be disturbed," he said loudly to whomever was on the other side.

"It's your father, sire," the voice called back. "He has collapsed."

Alexander and Saroja immediately got up from the bed and followed the soldier quickly to Benjamin's chamber.

"Father, are you alright?" Alexander asked.

"I'm fine," Benjamin coughed. "I just got a little dizzy, that's all. Just leave me. Go, enjoy your wedding night."

"Alexander, I think we should send for the royal healer," Saroja said after feeling Benjamin's forehead. He didn't have a fever, but his skin was clammy and he had a confused look in his eyes.

"That's not necessary," Benjamin explained, sitting up in the bed.

"Father, we will send for him just to be on the safe side," Alexander said, giving the order to Cash.

"Well, I'm going to sleep. Wake me when he arrives," Benjamin said, closing his eyes.

"I'll stay with him. You should probably get changed," he suggested to Saroja, who was still wearing the provocative outfit.

"Very well, I will return soon," she said, leaving the room.

White fog and mist floated through the air. Moments later Benjamin found himself lost in the forest. Wet mist covered the ground as he weaved in and out of the trees. He heard his name being called faintly in the distance, and he followed the sound trying to see through the haze.

"Benjamin," the soft voice called again. He finally caught up with the image that kept trying to elude him.

"Benjamin," she said sweetly, coming to stand before him.

"Rosaly," he said stunned by how real she appeared in this dream. "Is that you?"

"Yes, my love. I have missed you so much," she said, wrapping her arms around his neck. Her face was as young and as beautiful as he remembered it. She wore a simple white gown that seemed molded to her frame.

"I have longed for your touch," he said, squeezing her tightly. He kissed her passionately and hugged her with all her might. Her scent drifted by his nostrils and he closed eyes, trying to lock in the memory.

"It is time for you to come with me, my love, it has been too long," she said, gazing up at him with the most beautiful almond-shaped eyes.

"But Alexander, he needs me," Benjamin explained. He hugged and kissed her, trying to take in as much as he could before this dream was over.

"You have done an outstanding job raising our child, but now he is a man. He will find his own way," she said, taking his hand. "I need you now."

Benjamin thought about what she was saying for a moment, then decided she was right. Alexander would be fine without him and he didn't think he could leave her again. He had lost her once; now that she was in his arms, he had no intention of ever letting her go again. So, he held her hand tightly and followed her into the mist. He looked back for a moment, thinking how much he would miss his son.

"Goodbye, Alexander."

When the healer arrived Saroja met him as he reached Benjamin's door. She turned the knob and allowed Lio to enter first.

"How is he?" Saroja asked, walking to the bed.

"He sleeps soundly," Alexander said. "Maybe he was right. Father, the healer has arrived."

"Maybe we should just let him rest," Saroja said.

"Father," Alexander repeated. "Father," he said, shaking him gently. The healer moved forward and placed her head on Benjamin's chest.

"King Benjamin has left this world," Lio said, placing his hand gently on Alexander's shoulder.

"No, no, no—Father, please, wake up," he pleaded, kneeling on the floor.

"Alexander," Saroja said, kneeling beside him. She wrapped her arms around his shoulders, wiping the tears away as they started sliding slowly down her cheeks.

"How will I do this without him?" he asked, looking into her eyes. Saroja just hugged him tighter.

"I'll be here for you," she said, trying to be strong for him. After a moment, he rose from the floor and gave orders to the servants to prepare his father's body.

Benjamin was carried by six royal guards to the valley below the castle where Alexander had his tower built. Hundreds of people came to pay their respects. He was placed on the top platform as the royal priests circled the bottom chanting and spreading their herbs. When the death chant was finished, Alexander rose from his seat on the dais dressed in formal black robes and took the torch the priest offered him. He climbed the steps and placed a kiss on his father's forehead then lit the dried bush that surrounded his body then climbed back down. He took his seat next to Saroja and watched as the tower went up in flames. Saroja took his hand and squeezed it. Then she stood up from her seat and raised her hands above her head then rose into the air. Suddenly fully bloomed red roses started sprouting out of the frozen ground. They blanketed the snow and covered the valley floor, then she descended slowly back to the dais. The sun was going down in the distance. She pulled her cloak around the front of her gown finding the air extremely cold.

The kingdom mourned Benjamin's death for eighteen days, one day for every year of his reign. On the final night, Alexander threw a party to celebrate his reign. He stood next to his bride on the veranda of his castle and watched the fireworks explode in the sky. When the guests finally left he escorted Saroja to their chambers.

"Are you going to be alright, my love?" she asked, knowing the pain he must be feeling.

"I will be after a while, I guess," he said, watching her as Sasha untied her corset.

Finally, she crawled into the bed and sat down beside him.

"Do you want some wine?" she asked, using her powers to retrieve the goblets from the table. Alexander took the goblet and had several small sips before placing it on the table by his bed. He pulled Saroja suddenly to his side, causing her to spill all over them.

"I'm sorry," he said, getting up to retrieve a towel.

"That won't be necessary," she said, causing the wine to evaporate from the covers and her night gown with a simple thought.

"We have unfinished business to attend to," he said, smiling at her seductively.

She returned his kisses and used her hands to hold him close.

"Tonight, we will create our heir," he said.

"My king, I think that is a wonderful idea," she said.

*** The End ***

EPILOGUE

aroja tossed and turned in her bed. She flipped to her back then turned back to her side. After repeatedly flipping over in the bed, Alexander gently grabbed her and pulled her into the curve of his body. She nestled into his embrace, then drifted back into a fitful sleep.

She found herself walking down a beautiful hall of an enormous palace. The marble floor was cold beneath her bare feet. She walked until she came to a large door where two guards stood holding long Kwan Do blades.

"May I pass?" she asked, but they did not respond.

She walked passed them expecting them to cross their blades, blocking her path, but they did not. She looked at the guard on the right as he continued to stare forward down the hall. She pushed the door open and slowly walked into the room. As she turned the corner her face lit up.

"Auntie Lina," she exclaimed, running to the bedside. She tried to wrap her arms around her but they passed through her like the wind through trees. A woman came to the bed, walking straight through her. Saroja stumbled backwards and watched the woman place a small babe in Kalina's arms.

"You have given birth to a healthy son, Your Majesty," the maid said, handing her the child. Kalina smiled at the small bundle in her arms, glad that she finally had a reason to go on living. She was a prisoner in this land with no way to get home "I will inform the council."

Kalina turned the child in her arms and gazed into his face. He looked like his father. She would have to be reminded of him every time she looked at her child, and then she smiled, remembering how he had known from the start that he was there, even before she did. She remembered his last days with her and how much he had wanted this child.

"He would have loved you. That I am sure of. You will be a better king than your father ever was. You will be just and fair, and when the time is right we will take this country from these evil people and free the Veagans in this land. And in eight days I will declare your name to be Darius Degar," she said to the sleeping newborn. Moments later the councilmen arrived. They took the baby and looked him over.

"What will you call him?" one of the men asked.

"I will tell you in eight days at his naming ceremony," she explained.

"You keep forgetting that this is not your pagan Theslia. We name our children when they are born. In eight days, the child will have a ceremony, but he will then be circumcised," he explained.

"Very well. His name is Darius Degar," she said.

"Send word out over the land. Darius Degar Covax, heir to the throne of Lavitia has been born to the royal mother Kalina Covax, wife to our lost king. Declare this day to be an annual celebration. Our country has been saved. Someone inform Lord Kail that the child has been born.

Saroja sat up in the bed, wiping her eyes. She was in her own chamber again with Alexander sleeping soundly at her side. It was just a dream, she told herself while laying back down, but it had felt so real. She tried to go back to sleep, but couldn't shake the feeling that she had seen actual events. She sat up in the bed and moved slowly to the edge. She had to try twice before she was able to stand; her swollen abdomen was starting to make rising from a seated position a task. She walked to the fireplace and stared into the dancing flames. Kalina was alive and she had a son.

"My queen, are you alright?" Alexander asked in a groggy voice, leaning up on one elbow.

"Kalina… I saw her in my dreams," she said quietly, focused on the fire.

"It was just a dream, my love. Come back to bed," he said.

"No, she is alive. I know it," she said, sitting down slowly on the edge of the bed then laying down next to him. Alexander flipped the covers over her and pulled her into his arms.

"She is in Lavitia. She is alive and we must get to her," she said.

Alexander caressed her face and kissed her on the tip of her nose. She closed her eyes as he looked down on her, wondering how they would succeed in reaching Lavitia to save her, but she knew they must.

Covax Castle, Lavitia

Kail walked down the hall with a smile on his face.

"Ah! Lord Laven, I am happy to inform you that the queen has delivered a healthy baby boy. Marsalis would have been happy; the child already favors him. So, we will no longer be in need of your services. I will set up an escort for your trip back to the eastern provinces," Kail said, calling a servant forward to deliver his orders.

Suddenly Laven moved forward with a dagger in hand, intent on killing the only man that stood in his way. He would kill him and this heir and finally the throne would be his. Kail sidestepped the blow and knocked him to the floor with the walking staff he always carried.

"Take him to the dungeons!" he exclaimed.

"Lavitia will be mine, old fool. It will be mine!" he screamed as he was dragged away down the hall.

The nursemaid gave Kalina back her baby and left the room. She hugged the child to her chest and vowed that she would do everything within her power not to allow them to rob him of his soul, but deep down inside she wondered what Saroja was doing and if she'd ever see her again. She remembered when she was born and how small and delicate she was. Then her child started to cry and she realized that she had to stop living in the past. Darius needed her now. Now he would be her new source of power.